LILY MILLER

DEAL BREAKER

DEEP COVE MILLIONAIRES SERIES

BOOK 1

LILY MILLER

PLAYLIST

Ashes - Dipole, Bailey Zimmerman
6 Months Later - Megan Moroney
Daisies - Justin Bieber
Love In Letting Go - Warren Zeiders, Lanie Gardner
Missing - Morgan Wallen
Brunette - Tucker Wetmore
The Giver - Chappell Roan
Bar None - Jordan Davis
Sally, When The Wine Runs Out - ROLE MODEL
All Backroads - Just Jayne
I Ain't Coming' Back - Morgan Wallen, Post Malone
Just In Case - Morgan Wallen
Happen To Me - Russell Dickerson
girl you're taking home - Ella Langley
3,2,1 - Tucker Wetmore
Wish I Never Felt - Nate Smith
Never You - Dierks Bentley, Miranda Lambert

ONE

F ord

My gut knew it before my head did—this wasn't going to be just another day at the office.

The morning started the same way they all do. Coffee at six. Run by six-thirty. Cold shower. Get dressed for the office: black joggers, black T-shirt, runners. I checked my inbox before I left the house, answered two emails, flagged one for the marketing team. On the road by 7:25 a.m. Organized, efficient, in control. Just like always.

I drove to work in silence, forest giving way to traffic as I entered the city center. The office rose ahead in the distance, all wood beams and glass, solid against the skyline.

Cove. The company I built from nothing. Every decision, every product line, every polished square inch of this company has my fingerprints on it. Built from the ground up with my brothers. Brick by meticulous brick. And now, it runs like a machine—efficient, effective, predictable.

Which is exactly how I like it.

But today, something felt different. Not bad, just...off. I

pulled into my usual parking spot and cut the engine, unable to shake the heavy feeling in my chest, a weight I couldn't shift no matter how hard I gripped the wheel.

I'd felt this way once before. That sense that the ground had inexplicably tilted beneath my feet, that something was shifting even if I couldn't see it yet. Back then, what came next hollowed me out, left me raw and reeling.

I forced my mind to stay in the present. This is a crucial time for the company, and Cove doesn't run on pointless, sentimental walks down memory lane. It doesn't work with me sitting paralyzed in the parking lot mulling over my feelings.

Cove runs on control.

I'm standing at the floor-to-ceiling window in my corner office, second cup of coffee in one hand, tablet in the other, watching as the town of Deep Cove is just beginning to wake up. Morning fog curls over the tree line, softening the jagged peaks that surround us. The storefronts along Front Street glow warm and golden, old brick buildings housing artisan bakeries, unique boutiques, and a brewery that's been here longer than I have. There's money here, thanks in part to me and my brothers. But just beneath the surface, past the crowded patios and craft cocktails, it's still the same small town where we grew up. Same stubborn people. Same clifftop that cuts through the place like a scar.

It's quiet here. Tucked into the mountains two hours north of Vancouver, there's enough beauty to lure in the developers and millionaires who want a piece of it. They come for the views, the adventure, the lifestyle. They stay because once you've been to Deep Cove, it's very hard to leave.

I could see the changes starting to happen here—an uptick in tourists and the amenities that started popping up to cater to them—before they really took hold, and that's when the idea for Cove was born. Cove is more than a brand—it's a way of life.

A way to move through the world. Rugged but refined. Wild but curated. It's adventure for the person who doesn't mind spending a grand on a weekender bag so long as it's made from ethically sourced leather and comes with the prestige of the label.

I built this company with sweat and grit. It was years of long nights, lost sleep, an impossible workload and no backup plan, but now we're on every top 10 list in every single Canadian lifestyle magazine that used to pretend not to see us. We design upscale gear: apparel, boots, gear that works in the wild but looks good enough to wear in the boardroom.

It wasn't supposed to work, but my brothers and I made it happen.

I turn back to the conference table in the center of our wide-open workspace, where images of our new Sierra line are spread across the polished oak surface. Technical outerwear with a luxe finish. Alpine-grade jackets with water-resistant seams designed with clean lines, heritage tones, and materials that'll survive a decade of abuse.

Beyond the worktable, desks stretch toward the glass walls, Cove employees moving between them with tablets in hand, the low hum of conversation mixing with the distant hiss of the espresso machine. Anyone can walk in off the reception area and find us here—no doors, no walls—just an open space buzzing with work. Near the entrance, our receptionist sits behind a sleek, minimal desk, close enough to greet visitors, but far enough that anyone walking in from the lobby has a clear view straight to where we're meeting.

I run a hand down my jaw, already scanning the supply chain breakdown on my younger brother Noah's tablet.

"We're still greenlit for international distribution?" I ask.

"On track," Noah says from his seat, tapping his screen. "Inventory's ahead of schedule."

"Good." I nod once before turning to my other brother Jesse. "Performance first in every campaign. I don't want to see a single marketing push that uses the word 'cozy.'"

Jesse groans dramatically. "You really know how to kill a vibe."

"I'm not here to sell a vibe," I say, still focused. "I'm here to sell products that work."

"Spoken like a true CEO who hates joy," he mutters.

I glance up, and Jesse throws me a lazy grin. He doesn't rattle easily, which is probably why I keep him around as our Chief Marketing Officer. He's all charm and swagger and flash, but beneath it, he gets the job done. He's one year younger than me, two years older than Noah and three years older than our youngest brother Wes. His campaigns are smart. They're bold and risky and sometimes I let him push the line because I trust him not to cross it. Most of the time.

"We need to address the headlines," Noah says, shifting gears. "This isn't going away, it's all over socials."

"I'm figuring it out," Jesse nods, clicking into something on his laptop. "I'll have a spin on it soon."

I nod. "The accusations are bullshit. Just make it go away."

Footsteps cross the polished floor behind me, the sharp click of heels cutting through the low hum of the meeting. Nobody wears heels in Cove offices—boots, sneakers, maybe the odd pair of loafers, but never heels. The sound is off, out of place.

"Meeting's already started," I say without looking up from the table.

Silence. The kind that shifts the air in a room. The kind that makes the hairs on the back of your neck stand up.

I glance towards the sound.

And everything stops. My entire body fucking locks up. My chest clamps down so tight I swear it might crack. It hits before my brain catches up—an electric full-body jolt, like taking a punch straight to the gut.

Everything else vanishes. The low hum of voices, the phones ringing, the shuffle of feet across the floor—it all disappears.

Fuck.

She's standing next to Chloe at reception. Her hair is swept up in that soft, effortless way she always wore it. A loose blouse tucked into a pair of dress pants. Heels that give her petite frame three extra inches. She looks like the first day of June. Like the kind of memory that hits you out of nowhere and wrecks your whole damn day.

Landyn.

I tighten my grip on the edge of the table. Christ.

She hasn't changed. Not really. Still the same coffee-brown eyes and long dark-blonde hair, still that mouth that used to smile against mine at midnight, still the only woman who ever made me feel like I could have something more than the chaos I came from. Somehow, she still feels like the beginning of everything. And the end of it, too.

"Ford," she says softly as she approaches us. My name on her lips after seven years.

The walls press in on me, this whole damn building suddenly feels too small.

"We're done here," I say, eyes still on her. "Everyone can go."

Chairs scrape back. Pages shuffle. The team disperses fast, no one daring to question my tone. Jesse is the last to leave, his eyes flicking between us like he's catching on, but he knows better than to ask. I barely register him.

His footsteps fade to nothing, and then it's just her and me.

And seven years of silence bearing down on us in like a goddamn freight train.

She's fidgeting. Shifting from foot to foot like she's waiting for someone to tell her where she belongs. Her gaze flicks around the lobby, never landing anywhere for long, like she already regrets stepping inside.

And I see it all over her face—that pinched, uncomfortable look that says she's bracing herself for impact.

It shouldn't matter. But fuck, it does.

Heat spikes in my chest, sharp and bitter. Why the hell is she here? Why now?

The ghost standing a few yards away is the same one who gutted me once, ripped my heart straight out and walked away with it like it was nothing. And yet here she is, looking like heaven and hell in the same breath, as if showing up in my world again won't split me wide open.

"You've got 10 seconds," I say, my voice low and cold, "to explain what the hell you're doing here."

"I didn't know this was your company," she says. Her voice is calm, even. "I didn't even know you were still in Deep Cove."

I laugh once, dry and sharp. She flinches—just barely—but I see it.

"I took the job through a consulting agency," she continues. "I didn't know I'd be walking into this."

"This?" I echo. "You mean my company? My life?"

"Ford, I didn't come here to—"

"To what? To wreck my life again?" I take a step toward her. "Did you figure it's been long enough, that maybe I've forgotten about how you left? Or vanished, to be specific. No warning, no goodbye. Just gone. Maybe you thought after all this time I'd let it slide?"

Her jaw tightens. "I didn't come to dredge up the past. I came to do my job."

"And what is that, exactly?" I snap.

Her eyes flash, but she holds her ground. "I'm here to lead a campaign to revamp Cove's brand image. I signed a contract. I moved my life here. I didn't know I'd be reporting to you."

"That makes two of us."

We stare at each other, the silence between us louder than shouting could ever be. My pulse is a kick drum in my ears. She's so close I can see the little freckle just above her jaw. The one I used to kiss every morning.

I thought I buried this.

I thought I buried her.

Landyn crosses her arms, eyes narrowing slightly. "I get that you're pissed," she says, voice low. "I get that you're not happy to see me, but I'm here, so we should try and find a way to work together."

The steel in her voice surprises me.

I stare at her. *Work together?* She actually thinks we can work together? Everything about this is a mistake. Her being in this room. In this building. In Deep Cove. It's a bad idea. How can we work together when just looking at her knocks the ground out from under me? When the sight of her makes my pulse do something I don't fucking understand? When I've spent the last seven years trying to forget the sound of her voice?

"This isn't going to work," I say flatly. "You and me working together. It won't work."

Her eyes flick away for half a second before she pulls them back to mine. "I'm not asking you to like it, Ford," she says cooly. "I'm just asking for you to try."

My jaw locks. A big part of me wants to tell Landyn that there's no way in hell she's working for my company. But she signed a contract. Jesse obviously thought she was qualified for the position and right now, Cove needs her.

"Fine," I spit out, the word like gravel on my tongue. "You'll work under Jesse. Not me. This isn't going to be easy."

"It never was," she says quietly.

I grit my teeth and step back. "I want weekly reports. Every detail."

"Done." With that, she turns to leave the room.
"And Landyn?"
She pauses near reception. Doesn't look back.
"Stay in your own lane."
She leaves without a word.
And I don't breathe until she's gone.

TWO

F ord
I don't slam the door behind me.

I close it. Calm and controlled. But the soft click as it shuts does nothing to quiet the storm brewing under my skin.

She's here.

Landyn Sinclair was just standing in my conference room, asking me to be professional like she didn't vanish off the face of the earth seven years ago.

I make it halfway down the hall before I hear Jesse's voice.

"Man, that went well."

He's leaning against the wall with a smug grin on his face like he's waiting for me to blow a gasket.

"You knew," I say, rage slowly simmering just beneath the surface.

He shrugs. "Not until two days ago. My assistant pulled her résumé when we were vetting consultants. Honestly, I didn't think she'd actually take the job."

I stare at him. "She's Landyn, Jesse. You think she'd back down from a challenge?"

Jesse raises both brows, but he doesn't push. He never does.

He's the only person who's ever understood exactly how far he can poke before I start swinging.

"We need her," he says simply. "She knows what she's doing."

"I don't care."

"Well, I do. And so does Noah."

I turn away, gripping the railing of the mezzanine that overlooks the floor below. Designers, marketers, logistics teams—they're all moving, building, believing in this thing I created from the ground up. Every spare cent, every sleepless night, every piece of myself. I bled for Cove. And now she's in the middle of it.

"I'm not over it," I say, not looking at him.

"I didn't think you were," Jesse replies. "But she's not here for you. She's here for the brand."

The brand.

That's what matters, but all I can see is Landyn's face. That chin tilt. That fire in her eyes. "I'm here," she had said, like it didn't cost her anything to walk back into my life after seven years and act like we're strangers.

"She'll work under you," I say.

Jesse's quiet for a beat. "You sure you can handle that?"

"I'm not handling it," I say flatly. "I'm avoiding it."

I push off the railing and leave Jesse in the hallway. I avoid my office, instead heading down the stairs and circling the floor like I'm checking in on things, like there's a fire somewhere only I can put out. But all I'm doing is trying to outrun the image of her standing in that room with her head high, her voice steady, completely unbothered.

Eventually, I give up the fight and head back upstairs to my office. I shut the door behind me, lean against it, and let the silence swallow me whole.

My office is spotless, as always. Floor-to-ceiling windows pour late afternoon sunlight into the room, illuminating the polished walnut desk. I designed every inch of this place, from the recessed lighting to the pair of deep brown leather wing-back chairs to the gold fixtures on the built-in shelving that runs the length of the room. Every single detail of this office, this building, this company is exactly how I want it.

Except her.

I cross the room, sit down, and open the small box I keep in my desk drawer I haven't touched in years. A thin leather cord with a silver clasp. It was looped around her wrist every day of our first year of college, until she gave it to me, telling me it was lucky. We were only 21 at the time.

"Don't lose it," she'd whispered, brushing a kiss to my jaw. "You're going to do something big one day."

I didn't lose it.

But I lost her.

I pick it up, roll it between my fingers. It's ridiculous that I kept it. But I did. Along with everything I never said to her. Like how she was the only thing in my life that made sense to me. How I thought we had time. How I would've followed her anywhere.

Now she's back. In Deep Cove. In my company. And I'm expected to pretend we're strangers, just two people who happen to share a past we've both outgrown.

Except I haven't.

Not even close.

The day drags. I stay at the office longer than I need to, answering emails and pretending the pain behind my eyes is from staring at a screen for too long. By six thirty, most of the team has cleared out, the office quieting into that after-hours hush I usually like.

Not tonight.

Tonight, it feels like the calm before a storm.

I head out with my keys clenched in my fist and make the familiar drive home. Past the highway. Past the pine-studded hills that hide the winding trails we used to hike in the fall. The ones she said made her feel like she could breathe.

I grip the steering wheel tighter.

Deep Cove has always been beautiful. Rugged, a bit isolated. People live here for the views, the ocean, the high-end hiking and world-class skiing. But underneath it all, it's still a small town. You can't hide here... especially not from a girl who you've never been able to forget.

My place is just outside town. A sharp-lined cedar and stone home tucked into the hills with a view of the ocean. I built it three years ago, right after Cove really took off. Everyone said I should've moved to Vancouver, but I didn't want noise. I wanted quiet. Solitude. Control.

I pour a drink. Neat. Two fingers of the whiskey I save for nights when everything feels like it might snap. This feels like one of those nights.

I take the glass outside, lean against the railing of the deck, and inhale the cool, crisp night.

From here, I can see the lights of town starting to glow against the night sky. It's peaceful. It should be enough to settle my nerves. But there's a hollowness in my chest that hasn't eased since Landyn walked into that conference room like no time had passed. Like we didn't fall apart without warning.

When she left, it almost destroyed me. She had a reason. She must have. For years, the not knowing has haunted me. But now that she's back, all I can think about is how much I've missed her.

I drain the glass and don't let myself recall the way she looked at me today—like I was both a stranger and something so much more.

THREE

L andyn
There's a fine line between brave and stupid. I'm pretty sure I sprinted across it.

I stepped out of the conference room yesterday, chest tight, stomach twisting in the same anxious way it used to before finals. There wasn't a door to shut in that big open space, but it felt like one had slammed between us anyway — solid and final —locking me out with Ford Winters on the other side, all unreadable silence and razor-sharp control.

God. He looked exactly the same.

No, it's worse than that. He looked better. Sharper. Broader. Thick dark hair, perfectly styled, ruggedly handsome with a Roman nose and chiseled jaw that looks like it's been carved out of stone. And those eyes... steel gray and unflinching. Everything about him said he'd built himself into a man who could walk into any room and own it. He wasn't just the boy I fell in love with anymore. He was a man now. One who'd built an empire, and I just walked straight into it.

My phone buzzes in my hand. I don't have to look to know who it is.

> Mom: Checking in. It's no rush. Want me to
> feed P lunch?

I exhale, guilt prickling at the back of my neck before I type out a reply. I hadn't meant to be away so long. My mom would never say it, but I worry it's too much for her considering everything that's been happening with her health. Until we get answers from doctors, I need to limit how much she's babysitting and make sure she's getting lots of rest.

> Landyn: Yes, please. There is a sandwich in the
> fridge for her. I'll be home soon.

I slide my phone into my bag and check the counter for my second oat milk latte. I've spent the day holed up in a coffee shop in downtown Deep Cove, doing a deep dive on everything to do with Cove so I'm ready for my first day in the office.

Yesterday's meeting with Ford replays through my mind. The Cove headquarters is stunning, with raw cedar, black steel, and floor-to-ceiling windows that frame the trees outside like a postcard. It feels like nature and power fused together to form something unique and beautiful. Everything about it screams Ford—deliberate, precise, expensive.

It's everything he said he wanted to accomplish back in college, when we used to sit on the floor of the tiny off-campus apartment he shared with his brothers eating out of boxes of take-out from the Chinese food place down the street as we talked forever about the future. Our future.

And it hurts like hell, because I left. And he built it anyway.

I look up towards the entrance of the coffee shop as a cool, crisp April breeze floats through the door. Deep Cove smells like fir trees and ocean mist, like cedar and soil. It's cooler here than I remembered for spring or maybe it just feels that way because of the way Ford looked at me yesterday.

God, what were the odds?

I hadn't known Cove was his. I swear I hadn't. The consulting agency listed the client as a private outdoor lifestyle brand looking to expand their marketing team. The assignment sounded perfect—creative control, big budget, flexible hours. The kind of job that would keep my daughter in her dance classes and my resume in motion.

I knew there was a chance I could run into Ford if I came back to Deep Cove, but I never dreamed we would be working together. I didn't come here looking for a reunion. I came home because my mom hasn't been feeling well, and it's been going on far too long. She's brushed it off, the way she always does—she's just tired, it's just a cold, nothing to worry about.

She's dragged her feet on getting checked out, putting off doctor's appointments like if she ignores it long enough, whatever it is will just go away. But it's not going away. If anything, it's only getting worse. Over the phone she's seemed exhausted and forgetful. She has prolonged dizzy spells, even though she tries to play it down. When I've talked to my dad about it, I can tell that he has become worried too. I've been trying to help, but I can't do much when I'm living in another province. So, I finally made the decision to move Poppy and I to Deep Cove so I can be closer to my parents. It's a bonus that it will give Poppy a chance to really get to know them too.

But of course, the man I left behind also happens to own the company that just hired me. Of course, the father of my child is the CEO who just looked at me like I burned his life to ashes and smiled while doing it. I press my fingertips to my eyes, shaking my head at the universe's twisted sense of humor.

When my order is called, I walk to the counter, pick up my drink then slide back into the corner booth where I've been working all morning. Brew House is my favorite coffee shop in Deep Cove so far. It's usually fairly quiet, tucked behind the bookstore and the florist. As soon as you open the door, you're hit with the comforting smell of cinnamon and roasted espresso beans.

My fingers shake a little as I peel off the lid and set it aside, steam rising from the freshly brewed latte.

Ford doesn't know about Poppy. All he knows is that one day I was there and the next I was gone. No explanation. No goodbye. He just never saw me again. Until yesterday, when he looked at me like he hates me. Like I took something from him that he couldn't name.

I did.

I took everything.

And I've had to live with that every single day for the past seven years.

I cradle the coffee cup between my hands, letting the warmth chase away the chill in my bones. My brain won't stop spinning. Ford's voice, sharp and low. The flicker in his eyes when he saw me. I wasn't expecting him to look so... angry. Hurt, maybe. Closed off, sure. But that fire—that simmering fury under all that control? That caught me off guard.

I'd forgotten how Ford Winters could silence a room with just a look. Even back in college, when he barely had two dollars to his name, he carried himself like he owned the world. He didn't talk much, but when he did? People listened. I used to think it was hot—okay, incredibly hot—how he could command a space without raising his voice.

Now?

Now it just terrifies me.

Because if he knew, really knew, why I left, or what I've been hiding...

The bell above the café door chimes, and when I glance up and see a tall, broad-shouldered man in the entrance, my breath suddenly catches in my throat. But it's not him. Of course it's not him. Ford wouldn't come here. This place has too much charm, not enough sharp edges. The Ford I saw in the conference room yesterday is all straight lines and efficiency. He probably drinks double espressos. He has no time for frothy oat milk or still-gooey cinnamon rolls. No room for nostalgia or the past or messy things like old girlfriends who left without a trace.

I press my hand to my chest, trying to slow the pounding behind my ribs.

Breathe.

Just breathe.

He doesn't know.

And that's the only reason I'm still sitting upright instead of curled into a ball on the floor.

I fish my phone back out and pull up the last photo I took of Poppy yesterday. She's sitting cross-legged in a field of grass at the edge of the beach. Her tiny hands are stuffed full of pebbles, her smile lopsided. Dark blonde curls, almost brown, wild around her face, sand on her jeans. The eyes that stare back at me are the same eyes as the man I faced in that conference room.

Storm-gray. Too knowing. So much like him.

I drag my thumb across the screen, heart aching with something fierce and maternal and guilt-soaked.

She's six. And she's everything.

I didn't leave Ford because I stopped loving him. I left because I didn't know how to tell him we were having a baby. Because I was scared. Because he wasn't ready.

I thought I could outrun the truth. I was wrong.

And now we're here.

In the same town.

In the same building.

Back in each other's lives.

I blow on my coffee and take a sip, my mind already turning to what comes next. I need to finish my research, then meet with Jesse, since apparently, he's my new supervisor. Most of all, I need to keep my head down and stay focused. No drama. No distractions. And definitely no falling back into the arms of the man I never really stopped loving.

Even if his daughter has his eyes.

BY THE TIME I GET BACK TO THE LITTLE RENTAL COTTAGE AT THE edge of town, the late afternoon sun is spilling gold across the mountains. Poppy's laughter echoes off the porch as I walk up the path to the house. She's chasing a bubble. One perfect, translucent orb, drifting just out of reach.

My mom sits on the steps, smiling as she watches Poppy with her mug of chamomile tea balanced on her knee. She lifts a hand in greeting when she sees me.

"Mommy!" Poppy squeals, abandoning her chase as she flies off the porch and into my arms.

She's all sunshine and wild curls and I drop to my knees and press my face into her hair. "You smell like dirt and strawberry jam," I whisper.

She giggles. "Grandma made cookies. And we picked flowers. I found one with a bee inside and I didn't scream at all."

"Brave girl," I murmur, brushing her hair off her forehead. "You're so brave, Poppyseed."

She beams. "How was your new office, Mommy?"

"Oh, baby, no office for me today. Today, I just got ready for when I start in a few days."

"Did you talk to the new people yesterday? Are they nice?"

I swallow hard. "They're... intense."

She tilts her head. "Is intense like mean?"

"No, baby. Just big. Like, they think big. Talk big. Create big things."

She squints. "Like castles?"

I smile. "Kind of."

She nods at that and then pats my cheek. My mom stands and brushes off her pants, walking toward us with a gentle smile. "She was an angel. Didn't even ask for her iPad."

"Because Grandma brought chalk," Poppy says excitedly. "And we drew a dragon that eats ice cream!"

She grabs my hand and pulls me to the patch of concrete beside the house, where there is a chalk art drawing of a rainbow-colored dragon with curly eyelashes and neon yellow toenails standing beside a pink ice cream cone that's just as big.

"Amazing!" I tell Poppy, brushing the curls back from her forehead.

My mom raises her brows, like *you're welcome*. I mouth a thank you.

Inside, our house smells like baked apples and sugar. Like comfort wrapped up in four small rooms and a porch with peeling paint. It's not much, but it'll do. And it's temporary. Just until I get settled into the new job. Until I can get to the bottom of what's going on with my mom. Just until I figure out how to breathe again with Ford living in the same postal code.

Dinner is grilled cheese and tomato soup, and we eat together around the small kitchen island. Poppy insists on dipping everything. Even the apple slices.

After bath time and stories and exactly three minutes of her very dramatic rendition of *Twinkle, Twinkle, Little Star* on a plastic xylophone, I tuck her into bed.

She holds out her pinky. "Promise you'll be here when I wake up?"

"Always," I whisper, wrapping my finger around hers.

And I mean it. With every bone in my body.

FOUR

F ord

I drive into town, stopping at Brew House, the coffee shop off Front Street where everyone knows your name whether you want them to or not. I don't come here often, not anymore. Too many familiar faces, too much small talk, but it's on the way to the office and I need the caffeine since my assistant double-booked my first two meetings.

The bell over the door chimes as I walk in. Low chatter, the grind of the espresso machine, the warm scent of cinnamon and something freshly baked. I nod at the owner, a woman named Rosie who talks a mile-a-minute. She gives me a grin like she knows something I don't.

I step in line behind a man ordering half the pastry case. Tap my fingers against my phone. As I wait—I hear her.

Laughing. It's the softest sound. Light-filled.

She's tucked into a corner booth by the window. I don't even have to look to know.

I look to my left and see her. Landyn Sinclair. Hair in a low twist, sunglasses perched on top of her head. Laughing with her mother. There's a half-eaten muffin in front of her and a bright pink notebook open beside it. Like she's settled in. Like this is home again.

I'm supposed to walk away.

Instead, I stare. Just for a second. But it's long enough to feel what it was like to know her all over again. To love her.

She looks up.

Our eyes lock.

And the smile slips right off her face.

I should turn around. Forget about my coffee, go directly to the office and pretend I didn't just make eye contact with the woman who blew my world apart. But I don't because I'm a goddamn masochist or because part of me still wants answers I'm not ready to hear. Either way, my feet move before my brain does. One step, then another, until I'm standing at the edge of her table. Too close.

She straightens in her seat. Her mom, Carolyn, goes quiet, glancing between us with a slow, knowing look. "I'll see you outside," she says to her daughter, sliding out of the booth before Landyn has a chance to respond. "Ford, it's good to see you," she says as she moves past me and out the door.

Landyn doesn't speak, just watches me with those wide, dark eyes I used to know better than my own.

"So, you're back for good," I say finally, voice low.

She nods. "Just moved into the cottage by the beach."

Of course she did. She always said she wanted to live near the water, near the ocean. And now she's doing it, settling into her life in Deep Cove like she never left.

"Deep Cove's a small town." My gaze locks on hers, sharp and unflinching. "You must've known you'd run into me eventually."

Her chin tips up a fraction. "I did."

"Well," I say, leaning back slightly, the wood of the booth creaking under the shift of my weight, "here we are. And just so we're clear, I'm not really a let-it-go kind of guy."

Her throat works, and for the smallest second, I see something flicker across her face—guilt, maybe. Or regret.

Good.

Because she deserves to feel every ounce of the storm she left me with and I don't owe her anything. Not after the way she left. Not after seven years of silence. Not after the worst goddamn heartbreak of my life.

Except when I look at her now—flushed cheeks, the faintest tremble in her jaw—I wonder for the first time if maybe she was broken too. I wonder if maybe she still is.

"I'll stay out of your way," she says quietly. "I'm here for the job. That's it."

I nod once. Sharp. Controlled. "Good," I lie, and then I walk away because if I don't, I might ask the question I swore I never would.

Why did you leave?

And I'm not ready to hear the answer.

By the time I get to the office, I've just about convinced myself I imagined that conversation. The tightness in her voice. The flush in her cheeks. The way her eyes didn't let go of mine.

It's nothing. It's in the past. She's just a girl I used to know.

Jesse's already in the lounge when I walk in—feet kicked up on the coffee table, sleeves rolled to the elbows, like he owns the place. Which, to be fair, he does. One-third of it, anyway.

He looks up from his phone, and a slow, wolfish grin spreads across his face. "Well, well," he drawls. "If it isn't our fearless leader, fresh from a run-in with the ghost of heartbreak past."

I ignore him and head for the espresso machine.

"She still as hot as you remember?" he asks casually, like

he's asking about the weather. "Hotter? Don't answer that, I saw her yesterday. Ten out of ten. Would self-destruct over."

I shoot him a look over my shoulder. "You done?"

"Not even close." He leans forward, elbows on his knees. "Come on, man. You show up here all broody, look like you haven't slept, and you expect me not to bring up the fact that Landyn freaking Sinclair is working down the hall?"

"She's here for the job. That's it."

"And yet your jaw's been clenched since you walked in."

I slam the lid of the espresso machine into place harder than necessary and don't say a word.

Jesse lets out a low whistle. "Yikes. Okay, noted. We're repressing." He stands, crosses the room, and claps a hand on my shoulder. "I'm just saying, if you need to talk about your feelings, I can book you a therapy session. Or supply the tequila. Your call."

"I need neither."

"You need something, man. Because you're acting like a guy who just saw a ghost."

I meet his gaze. "She left, Jess."

"Yeah," he says softly, sobering for half a second. "But she came back."

I exhale through my nose and take the shot of espresso in one go. Jesse watches me, the teasing gone now. "You know," he says after a beat, "you never talked about it."

"There was nothing to say."

"Bullshit. You were wrecked. You just buried it under 12-hour workdays."

I turn away, but Jesse keeps going. "You loved her."

"I don't anymore."

"You sure about that?"

Silence.

I set the empty espresso cup in the sink, fingers braced

against the counter. My jaw ticks. My pulse hammers. And still, I don't look at him.

"For the last few years, I was damn sure," I finally say.

Jesse leans against the counter beside me, arms crossed loosely, his tone softer now. "You don't have to forgive her. Hell, you don't even have to talk to her. But maybe you should stop pretending like seeing her didn't mess you up all over again."

I stare straight ahead. She left without a word. Without a note. Without a goddamn goodbye. And now she's back—cool and composed and untouchable—and I'm the one who feels like the ground just gave out beneath me.

"I don't know what she wants," I say finally. "Is she really back for a job? That's all?"

"Maybe, or maybe she doesn't know either." Jesse shrugs. "But whatever it is? You've got backup. Always."

That's the thing about Jesse. He'll push, tease, crawl under your skin just to watch you squirm, but when it counts, he shows up. Every time.

"Thanks," I mutter.

He grins. "Don't mention it. Just do me a favor and try not to fire her in the next 24 hours, yeah?"

"No promises."

FIVE

Landyn

The office really is beautiful.

Glass and wood beams. High ceilings. Natural light spilling through the windows and reflecting off the reclaimed wood floors. It's simple, but it feels expensive. If I didn't know better, I'd think I was walking into a luxury retreat instead of Cove headquarters. But then again, that's the point. Luxury mixed with nature. Boardroom meets backcountry.

I swallow the lump rising in my throat and step through the front doors like I belong here. Like I didn't spend the night tossing and turning in the cottage, wondering if coming back here was the biggest mistake I've ever made.

People look up as I pass. A few polite smiles. Some curious stares. One woman gives me the kind of once-over that feels more like a warning shot than a welcome. It feels like everyone knows who I am.

That's Landyn Sinclair.

The one who broke Ford Winters's heart.

The one who left and never looked back.

But it's obviously all in my head. After all, how could they know? I left Ford years before he built this empire.

My heels click against the polished floors as I make my way to the main reception desk. Behind the mahogany is a young assistant with bright eyes and a high ponytail who greets me with a tight smile.

"You're Landyn, right? Mr. Winters said you'd be starting today."

I nod. "That's right."

She checks something off on her tablet. "You'll be reporting to Jesse. His office is down the hall, second left, last door. He'll be expecting you."

Of course I'll be working under Jesse. Ford made that crystal clear.

I thank her and head down the hall, pulse pounding harder with every step. I haven't seen Jesse since college. Back then, he was all swagger and wicked smiles—Ford's opposite in every way. I have no idea what to expect now.

When I knock on the door, it swings open before I can lower my hand.

And there he is.

Same tousled brown hair, same cocky grin, only now it's paired with a dangerously expensive watch and a Cove long-sleeve rolled to the elbows.

"Landyn Sinclair," he says, like my name tastes good in his mouth. "Well, shit. You grew up even better than I remember."

I arch a brow. "Still a flirt, eh?"

"Only with people who make it worth my time." He steps back and waves me in. "Come on, PR princess. Let's get you settled. We've got work to do and a reputation to repair."

I follow Jesse as he moves through the building like he's giving a TED talk, pointing out the coffee station, the lounge corner with a leather couch that probably costs more than my car, and a massive corkboard plastered with magazine covers, campaign shots, and photos of the brothers standing in front of towering pines or snow-covered peaks.

"This is our wall of ego," he says with a grin. "Or, as Ford likes to call it, our legacy."

I smile despite myself. "It's impressive."

"Yeah, well, Ford built most of it with blood, sweat, and sheer determination. I'm convinced the guy doesn't actually sleep. Like, ever."

I raise an eyebrow. "And you?"

"Oh, I've been sleeping like a baby. But I'm also the reason this brand is in the press at least once a week." He flashes a roguish grin. "For better or worse."

He walks over to a framed photo from a *GQ* spread. Ford in a dark coat, jaw set like stone, standing on a cliff edge. The headline reads: "The Rugged Rise of Cove: From Small Town to Global Obsession."

"We started out selling boots," Jesse says, eyes still on the photo. "One pair. One design. Built for hikers and anyone else who gave a damn about quality."

"And now?" I ask, even though I already know the answer.

"Now we've got three flagship stores, a waitlist for our limited seasonal lines, and partnerships with Olympic athletes."

"Your brother Noah is behind that last one?"

He shoots me a look. "You did your research."

"I always do." There was a time a few years ago when you couldn't turn on a sports channel without seeing Noah Winters's face on your screen. He went to the Olympics for downhill skiing and came home with a gold medal.

Jesse's smile fades slightly. "Which brings us to the reason you're here."

I follow Jesse to his desk, where he takes a seat. I sit across from him as he opens the cover on his tablet and taps the device a few times before spinning it toward me.

The headline is brutal: "Tarnished Lifestyle Brand: Is Beloved Cove's Clean-Cut Image Just Marketing?"

Underneath is the sub text: "New allegations suggest Deep Cove's beloved lifestyle brand has abandoned its commitment to eco-conscious factories. I scan the article, heart sinking."

"Ford has spent years building trust," Jesse says, voice tight now. "And I've spent years making sure the world knows it. But a single accusation like this? It's enough to crack the whole damn thing."

"Is it true?"

Jesse shakes his head. "Not the way the media is making it sound. It's a supplier issue that slipped through the cracks. We caught it and cut ties fast, but we didn't get in front of it in time."

"And you think I can fix it."

"I know you can."

I look up at him, surprised by the certainty in his voice.

"I know you're good, Landyn," he says. "I read about how you singlehandedly turned that flailing fashion brand into one of the fastest-growing companies in the country. I remember the campaign." He leans in slightly. "I've looked at your work. I'm the reason you're sitting in that chair. I told Ford we need you."

"Ford doesn't want me here," I say quietly.

Jesse shrugs. "He needs you and he knows it."

I sit back, fingers curling around the arm of the chair. I would be lying to myself if I said I'm just here to fix a PR problem. I'm here to face the past. To look Ford in the eye. To act like we're nothing more than colleagues when every inch of me remembers exactly how he kissed.

"Okay," I say finally. "Let's fix it."

Jesse grins. "Atta girl.

"You do realize the Cove brand has been marketed very seriously," I say, squinting at one of the old campaign slogans Jesse's pulled up. "Earn the wild." I snort. "Did someone write that in a tent after six days without coffee?"

Jesse grins like he finds me amusing. "Don't knock it. That campaign sold 30,000 units in a weekend."

"Broody, rugged marketing. Got it."

He taps the screen. "Axes and flannel, baby. It's a lifestyle."

I laugh as I adjust the font on the mock-up. Jesse leans a little closer, peering at my screen. "Okay, now that is hot. Subtle, but bold. Just like me."

I raise a brow. "I don't know about subtle, but you're definitely bold."

"Close enough."

We've spent the last few hours hunched over an oversized table in a shared workspace on the main floor. Our laptops are open, mock-ups pulled up on a screen in front of us. It feels good, the buzz of collaboration. Familiar.

I've always had a passion for my work. My career had barely begun when I found out I was pregnant. After Poppy was born, I took time off to be with her, to learn how to be someone's everything. I wouldn't trade that year for anything, but there were moments I forgot what it felt like to be good at something other than being her mom.

Eventually, I got a job at a tiny marketing firm—nothing major, barely even a blip on a map, but they were flexible, allowing me to work shorter days and juggle freelance work at night. Over time, the clients got a little bigger, the campaign I oversaw got some recognition. It wasn't easy. A lot of the time, I felt stretched way too thin struggling to build my resume and also raise my daughter.

Fortunately, I wasn't totally on my own. When I left Deep Cove, I moved to Alberta where my aunt, my mom's sister, opened her door to me. What was only supposed to be a year or two of Poppy and I living in her spare bedroom, somehow turned to almost seven. It wasn't glamorous, but it worked.

Taking this fulltime job with Cove isn't just about the paycheck. I want the challenge. I want to take the next step. I want to prove to myself that I can excel in my career and be a good mom. But being away from Poppy so much? That part is the hard part. Dropping her off at a new school in a new town, her big, gray eyes glossy, her little voice whispering, *You'll come back, right?* It makes my chest ache in a way I've never known.

Jesse leans closer, pointing at a sample caption. His shoulder brushes mine, and I don't move away.

"Change 'wilderness' here to 'wild within,'" he says. "It's got more edge."

I nod, making the change. "Got it."

And then I feel it.

That shift in the room that makes the hairs on the back of your neck rise before your brain has a change to catch up.

Jesse notices it too. His smirk pulls a little wider. "Well, well," he drawls quietly so that only I can hear him. "If it isn't our brooding leader."

I glance up and there he is.

Ford.

He's standing in the doorway, his eyes locked on us. More specifically, he's glaring at Jesse, who is sitting only inches from me despite there being plenty of space at the table. The workspace in front of us is cluttered with things Ford hasn't been included in. His expression is unreadable, but the tension in his jaw gives him away. Barely.

"Not like you to work through lunch, Jesse," he says, voice clipped.

Jesse leans back in his chair, unbothered. "Nice of you to notice," he replies with a grin. "Just trying to save the brand from total combustion."

Ford doesn't look at him. His eyes are on me now. Cool and unreadable. "We agreed she reports to you. That doesn't mean you do the work with her."

I lift my chin, keeping my voice calm. "Jesse's been very helpful. We're getting a lot done."

Ford crosses his arms. "Funny. Looks like flirting."

Jesse snorts. "That's just my face."

Ford's gaze sharpens, but Jesse keeps going like it's all a game.

"Relax, brother. We're just trying to fix the mess we've found ourselves in. You want in, or are you just here to glower?"

For a long second, Ford doesn't answer. He just watches me, like he's trying to decide what exactly I am now—an asset or a mistake. Maybe both.

"I'll pass," he says finally. "I'm needed elsewhere."

But before he turns, I catch it—that flicker in his eyes. A crack in the facade. He doesn't like seeing me here. Doesn't like seeing me with Jesse. But why does he care after all this time?

The question lingers like smoke, curling through my chest. I thought walking away would be enough. Leaving town and not looking back, giving him the space he needed to make his dreams come true. But now that I am back, I can feel it again. That current. That impossible pull.

And the worst part?

I'm not sure I hate it.

I turn back to my laptop, hands on the keys, mind nowhere near the work in front of me. This job was supposed to be a fresh start, but the past has a way of finding you. Especially when it has the same gray eyes that have haunted me for years.

"Well," Jesse says, stretching his arms behind his head with a dramatic sigh. "On a scale from one to nuclear, I'd say that was about a six-point-five. Maybe a soft seven."

I give him a look. "What are you talking about?"

"That whole 'I'm Ford Winters and I hate feelings' routine he just did? Yeah, I've seen that look before. Usually right before he goes full blast on someone."

I sigh and close my laptop. "He doesn't want me here."

"He doesn't want anyone here. That man would run this company on his own from a cave in the Yukon if we let him."

Jesse stands and leans a hip against the edge of the table next to me, voice a little gentler now. "Look, he's going to come around. He has to. You're too damn good at this. Even he won't be able to ignore it for long."

I nod, even if I don't believe it.

"I just…" I hesitate, then meet Jesse's eyes. "I didn't expect it to hit this hard."

"Still some feelings in there?" he asks, his tone kind.

I smile tightly. "It's not that simple."

"Yeah," he says, pushing off the table. "It never is."

SIX

F ord

I should've walked away.

Instead, I stood there like a damn idiot, watching her and Jesse huddled over their work. Hearing her laughter, her head tilted just far enough back for the familiar curve of her smile to punch the breath straight out of me. She looks different—older, or maybe just a little less wide-eyed and innocent. But still her. Still Landyn.

And that is the problem.

I don't want her here. I don't want the memories she carries with her like static electricity latching onto me, clinging to places I sealed off a long time ago.

Jesse caught my eye and smirked like he was reading my mind. Of course he was. My brother has always been too good at that. I muttered something about being needed elsewhere and turned on my heel, ignoring whatever clever remark he tossed out after me. I didn't care. I just needed space. Distance from the scent of her perfume lingering in the room.

Back in my own office, I shut the door harder than necessary and braced my hands against the edge of the desk, head bowed, pulse still pounding, deep and steady under my skin.

She's here. After all these years, all that silence, suddenly she just shows up. In my town. At my company. And the worst part? The absolute, soul-punching worst part?

I can't decide if what I really want is to fire her or fall back into her.

I close my eyes and let my head fall back against the chair behind me. It's been years since I've thought about the first time we met. Not because I'd forgotten it but because remembering her has always hurt like hell.

Landyn was standing at the back of a packed lecture hall, arms crossed, eyes narrowed like she was already bored before the class had even started. Long, dark-blonde hair and chocolate-brown eyes, wearing a denim jacket. Not even pretending to hide the fact that she didn't want to be there. And I was gone. Just like that.

I didn't believe in that kind of thing—love at first sight. That was my brother Wes's territory. But with her, it wasn't love. It was like the universe had dropped her into my world and whispered, *pay attention, this one is different.*

She caught me staring and raised one eyebrow, unimpressed.

I grinned.

She rolled her eyes.

Ten minutes later, she was sitting one row in front of me. A week later, she was drinking coffee from my mug and stealing the covers like she owned them. Three months after that, I was falling in love.

I shift in my chair and stare at the window, watching my own reflection in the glass. CEO. Powerhouse. Leader. That's what the world sees now. They don't see the kid who used to hide a box of granola bars under the floorboard because he didn't trust someone would cook for him the next day. Or the teenager who learned how to cope with his mom's death by himself because his dad was too busy getting drunk.

My parents were ghosts long before they were gone. My father had a short temper and wasn't around. The only time he seemed to notice us was when he was yelling about something. My mother was ill for as long as I can remember. Her headaches were so bad she'd spend days in her bed.

I was 12 when she died of a stroke and my father started to drink. When he wasn't drinking, he was working. I figured out pretty quickly that no one was going to take care of us. Four boys under one roof, and no roof that could hold us for long. So, I stepped up. I stopped being a kid and started being everything else.

Protector. Provider. Planner.

The leader.

Wes found his charm and eventually found the sky, training to become a pilot, and Noah—the kid was pure fire, always chasing the next win on the slopes. Jesse was out every night, living it up with women and mischief. But me? I got a job. I learned how to cook. I got into college and studied in whatever spare minutes I could find. I kept us together, even when I was breaking.

And Landyn... she understood me.

One night, she asked me about my parents, and I told her everything. I told her about my dad who I was no longer in contact with, who drowned himself in alcohol and buried himself in work after my mom died. I told her about all the nights I made Kraft Dinner for my three younger brothers. About driving Noah to the mountain when he had a ski lesson. About sitting at the kitchen table night after night with Jesse, forcing him to get his homework done. She never flinched. Never pitied me. She just curled into me, laid her head on my chest and whispered, "No one should have to grow up that fast." She made me feel like I wasn't something that needed to be fixed. Like I wasn't broken.

Which is probably why it gutted me so bad when she left.

Because if someone sees all of you—every messy, sharp-edged part—and walks away anyway? That kind of wound doesn't just cut deep. It stays open. Sometimes I think maybe it's still bleeding. Even now.

I close my eyes for a second, just one, and try to force the memories back down when my phone buzzes on the desk.

> Jesse: Heads up, Sinclair is coming to the
> gala. Try not to scowl through the whole thing.

I stare at the text, jaw clenched.

Of course she's coming.

The Deep Cove Founder's Gala is this Saturday. It's a night honoring the town's history and an opportunity to raise money for its future. Local business owners and community leaders come together for dinner, speeches, and a silent auction. Cove is the founding sponsor, which means I have to show face. It's an important night for us. I have a company to represent and a brand to protect, and I have to do it with a room full of people watching me, waiting for any signs of cracks in the Cove facade. If there was ever a time to showcase Cove in a positive light, this is it.

And now, thanks to Jesse, Landyn will be watching too. I'm sure he thinks it's funny, a way to get under my skin.

But he doesn't know what it's like to come face to face with someone who had vanished. He doesn't know what it feels like to still be haunted by something that doesn't even exist anymore.

By Thursday, the tension in the office is so thick it is practically visible. It's not just Landyn and me, the entire Cove team is trying to get everything ready for Saturday night. The gala isn't just a community event, it is a chance to reintroduce ourselves to the city. To do some damage control. This year has been a shitstorm, and Deep Cove is watching to see how we're handling it. So are a few out-of-town investors that we invited.

I'm supposed to be laser-focused, but every time I turn the corner, there she is. Chatting with the marketing team around the worktable. Laughing with Jesse on the patio. Catching my gaze in the mirror as she passes me in the main hallway.

Part of me wishes she didn't fit in here so easily, but I've noticed how quickly the team has warmed up to her. How natural it feels to see her moving through the halls like she's always been here. I'm the only one who's been giving her the cold shoulder.

We're only two days out from the gala, but all I can think about is the questions I can't seem to silence, no matter how hard I try.

Why did she leave and what would it take to make her stay this time?

SEVEN

Landyn

By the time I pack up my things, the office is a ghost town. The overhead lights have been dimmed to half-power, casting scattered shadows across the polished floors. Somewhere, a vacuum hums softly but otherwise Cove is silent. The building has been buzzing with energy all day, but this late at night it's calm in a way I've never seen it.

I hike my bag higher onto my shoulder, balancing a thick stack of gala notes against my chest as I make my way to the elevator.

And that's when I hear it.

Footsteps behind me. Steady. Heavy. I don't have to turn around to know it's him. Ford Winters moves like he owns the ground he steps on, authority in every stride. He has a confidence that doesn't exist in most people.

I keep walking, pretending not to notice the way my pulse stutters. Pretending the energy around me doesn't change the second he's near.

"Long night?" he asks from behind me, his voice low and rough around the edges.

I pause at the elevator door as a shiver erupts over my skin, jabbing the button with more force than necessary. "You could say that. I've taken on the gala too."

He stops a few feet away, hands shoved into his pockets. The sleeves of his Cove crew neck are pushed to his elbows, the dark gray fabric clinging to the broad lines of his forearms. He looks unfairly good for someone who probably hasn't slept more than a few hours all week. Ford was always a terrible sleeper.

"You don't have to kill yourself over this gala," he says. "It's not life or death."

I laugh under my breath. "You could've fooled me. Jesse acts like the fate of the world rests on how many string lights we hang."

Ford ignores me, keeping his eyes on the elevator display as it counts down the floors. Silence stretches between us, thick and charged.

I shift the papers against my chest, trying to find something, anything, to say. "I'm just trying to pull my weight," I offer, softer now. "I know... this isn't easy. Me being here." His jaw ticks, just slightly, but I catch it. "You didn't have to give me the job," I add, my voice barely above a whisper. "I would've understood if—"

He huffs a laugh, low and humorless. "This isn't about you. It's about the company."

A flash of anger and embarrassment rushes up my spine.

I lift my chin. "Right. Strictly business."

"Exactly."

And that is the thing about Ford Winters—he doesn't waste words. He doesn't fill silence with empty thoughts the way most people do. Every word he gives, he means. Every word he chooses not to say, I feel just as much.

The elevator dings. The doors slide open behind me. I swallow hard, the length of my throat burning, but I can't move.

Not yet. Not when Ford is standing here, looking at me the way he is. Like there is something on the tip of his tongue that he doesn't trust himself enough to say.

For a moment, we just stand here, the distance between us measured in heartbeats. Fast, frantic ones that no amount of us pretending can slow.

"You were hired to do a job, and I expect you to finish it," Ford says roughly. "You walked away once. Don't think for a second I forgot."

The words hit harder than I expect. Not because they are cruel but because they are true.

I swallow against the lump forming in my throat. "I never asked you to forget."

For a long, tense moment, we stand perfectly still, staring at each other, the clock above the elevator door ticking into the silence as the seconds pass by until it dings.

He steps closer, closing the space between us by a fraction. Just enough that I can breathe him in—pine and salt air, the same scent that has always clung to him. The same one that can undo me in an instant.

The elevator dings again.

"You think you can just walk back into my life, into this, and we just pretend like none of it happened?" His voice is rougher now.

"I'm not pretending anything."

He stares at me so intensely that my skin starts to prickle. "You should go, Landyn," he says, his voice gravel and grit.

Without another word, I turn and step inside the elevator, my heart crashing against my ribs.

The door slides shut, but I can still feel him. His anger. His hurt. His pain.

I lean back against the cold, metal wall, squeezing my eyes shut for a second, trying to catch my breath. Ford is angry and he has every right to be. I *did* walk away. But that doesn't quiet the part of me that still burns at the memory of him. It doesn't stop the ache that has never really gone away.

By the time I pull into my driveway, the cottage is dark except for the porch light my dad always leaves on for me. I slip inside quietly, toe off my shoes in the entryway and walk towards the small living room at the back of the house. The scent of sugar and chocolate wafts through the air and I follow it to the kitchen where my dad is removing cookies from a cooling rack.

"They smell good, Dad."

He looks up when I walk in, his face soft and full of that steady love that always manages to make my throat tighten.

"Poppy wanted to bake. Your mom thought you could also use a little sugar after a long day at the office. She's resting with Poppy but she's fine."

I smile back even though I still feel a little shaky after my run-in with Ford. "You both know me so well," I say, my voice quiet. "Thanks for watching Poppy. I know it's...a lot."

Dad shrugs like it was no trouble at all. "She's easy. Besides, it's good to have you both home."

Home. The word tugs at something deep inside of me.

He wipes his hands on a dish towel, then looks at me with an expression that carries the questions he doesn't ask. He knows Ford is my new boss. They both do. He pulls me into a hug and presses a kiss to my forehead. "Get some rest, honey. Tomorrow's a new day. I'm going to get Mom and take her home."

I watch them from the small porch as they pull out of the driveway, then head back into the house. I exhale into the silence, the weight of the day settling on me. The gala prep, my run-in with Ford, the look in his eyes when he told me I should leave. The way my mom leaned on my dad as they walked to the car, his arm around her waist to support her. I am suddenly so tired that I feel like I could collapse on the spot, fall to the floor and stay there until the morning light seeps through the blinds. Instead, I turn and make my way upstairs to Poppy's room, the old floorboards creaking softly under my feet.

Pushing open the door to her room, I find her curled up in bed under a mountain of pink blankets. She has her thumb tucked against her cheek, just like she used to do when she was a baby.

My heart cracks open at the sight. She's still so small and he's missed so much.

I cross the room and kneel beside her bed, brushing a few strands of her curls off her forehead. She stirs but doesn't wake. "I'm here, baby girl," I whisper, pressing a kiss to her temple.

I stay for a long moment just watching her breathe, memorizing the tiny rise and fall of her chest and the way her eyelashes brush her cheeks.

My throat burns.

No matter how hard this gets, no matter how much the past claws at me, I'm not going to run this time.

Not from Ford.

Not from the life I owe her. The life she deserves.

I know I need to figure out a way to tell Ford about Poppy, and I need to do it soon, before the truth comes out in a way neither of us is ready for.

I smooth the blanket higher over her tiny shoulders then stand and back out of the room, leaving the door cracked just enough so that I'll hear her if she wakes.

Resting my forehead against the door frame, I realize something terrifying. Coming back to Deep Cove hasn't quieted the ache inside my heart. It's only made it impossible to ignore.

EIGHT

Landyn

Late afternoon sunlight spills through the windows of my bedroom as I stare at my reflection in the mirror, hair half-pinned up, a curling iron clutched in one hand like a sword. It's Saturday, the day of the gala. I've been up since 7 a.m. after tossing and turning for much of the night.

"This is ridiculous," I mutter, fighting the urge to throw my hair into a messy bun and call it a day.

From across the room, mom laughs softly as she buttons up P's jacket. "You look beautiful, sweetheart," she says, smoothing a hand over Poppy's hair, which she'd somehow managed to tame into two neat braids. A feat I've never quite mastered.

"I look like someone who's trying too hard," I say, twisting a loose curl around my finger and frowning.

"Trying isn't a bad thing," Mom says, a knowing look flashing in her eyes. "Especially when the right person notices."

I roll my eyes, but my stomach tightens all the same. Part of me wants Ford to notice me. The other part is scared he'll notice too much.

"I'm not getting ready for anyone," I say, a little too quickly. "It's just work."

"Of course," she says, smiling in that way only moms can, like she already knows all the things I haven't said out loud.

Poppy skips over to me, her pink sneakers squeaking on the hardwood. "Mommy, you look like a princess!" she says, wide-eyed.

I kneel down to her level, feeling something tender break open in my chest. "Not even close, baby," I say, tucking a strand of hair behind her ear. "Just trying to look like I belong."

"You always belong," Poppy says with the confidence of a 6-year-old.

I press a kiss to her forehead, breathing her in. She is my entire life. The reason I have to believe that coming home won't turn out to be the biggest mistake of my life. The reason I'll fight to make this work, no matter how complicated it gets.

"You're going to be late. Don't worry about us, we'll be just fine." My mom hands me my black clutch from the dresser. "You go knock 'em dead."

"And if I don't?" I ask, smoothing the skirt of my simple black dress.

"Then at least you'll look good," she says with a wink.

I laugh, feeling a little lighter as I grab my jacket and keys. Poppy hugs my legs fiercely, and I promise I'll be back before she wakes up the next morning.

But as I head for the door, that gnawing knot in my stomach twists tighter. Because it isn't just the gala or the town or the company that scares me.

It is the man waiting inside all of it. The man who still has the power to undo me without even trying.

The drive into Deep Cove feels different, like the town knows tonight is something special.

I turn onto Front Street and have to ease off the gas. The entire street is glowing under strings of lights, crisscrossing over the road like a net made of stars. Shops that just two days ago were a little dusty and dim are now gleaming, their windows polished and full of carefully crafted displays. It is beautiful. And it reminds me that Cove's influence is everywhere.

People in floor-length dresses and pressed suits wander the sidewalks, their laughter spilling into the air, mingling with the muted sound of a string quartet playing somewhere up ahead. This isn't the town I'd left. It has matured in the years I've been away, and somehow, I still feel like I don't belong.

I find the designated parking lot tucked behind the event hall and pull in, my palms a little sweaty on the steering wheel. For a second, I just sit here, staring out at the glowing lights ahead, my heart thundering behind my ribcage. I could turn the car around. Head back to my little house, climb into bed next to Poppy, and pretend none of this ever happened.

No one would blame me.

Except maybe Ford.

My stomach twists.

I press my forehead lightly against the steering wheel and close my eyes, breathing deeply. As much as I would like to turn and run, I know I need to stand on my own two feet, no matter how hard it is.

Squaring my shoulders, I grab my clutch from the passenger seat, check my reflection in the rearview mirror—yep, still visibly terrified—and climb out of the car.

The night air is cool against my skin, lifting the hem of my dress as I cross the parking lot. Ahead, the event hall glows like something out of a dream, the front steps lined with lights, a red carpet rolled out like a movie release party. Cameras flash at the entrance, catching the shimmer of dresses, the easy smiles of people who know they belong.

Ford's name is everywhere tonight. The Winters brothers have turned Cove into something bigger than this town could ever have imagined.

And here I am, walking into the world he's built, like I have any right to be part of it.

I clutch my bag tighter and repeat the same lie I've been telling myself for days: I am here to do my job, to smile, and represent Cove, and most importantly, begin to repair the company's tarnished name. That's all I have to do. That and pretend Ford Winters doesn't still have the power to crack me wide open with a single look.

Easy.

The lie is almost convincing...until I take my first step onto the red carpet and feel the ground shift beneath me.

Like somehow, he already knows I am here.

NINE

F ord
There she is, like a punch to the gut I didn't see coming.

Landyn steps through the entrance to the gala and the entire room narrows down to her. The noise, the chatter, the cameras all fade away next to the sharp ache of seeing her. She's wearing a long black dress, her hair swept off her face, highlighting her deep, coffee-colored eyes and light olive skin.

She's so fucking pretty, but Landyn is so much more.

Our eyes lock the second she walks in. One breath, then another, and the utter sense of control I had when I got here unravels. God, she is beautiful. Same fire in her eyes. Same quiet defiance in her posture. She freezes when she sees me... like maybe she feels it too. The weight of everything we'd been. Every word we left unsaid.

My chest constricts and the grip on the glass in my hand tightens until my knuckles turn white. I can't look away. Neither can she.

Then Jesse appears at her side with that damn effortless charm and easy grin, sliding an arm around her shoulder like they are already old friends. She blinks, finally breaking our stare as Jesse leans in and says something that makes her laugh.

And just like that she's gone.

Still here in the room with me.

But not mine.

Not anymore.

I watch them for a moment longer than I should, stomach twisting, heart hammering inside my chest. Then I turn and walk away.

I move towards the bar, nodding at a few familiar faces along the way, cutting a slow path through the sea of handshakes and compliments.

When I finally make it to the bar, I find Noah is already there, which doesn't surprise me. He's leaned back like he doesn't have a care in the world, glass of Scotch in hand, watching the room unfold in front of him with that trademark stillness of his. Always the observer. Always 10 steps ahead of everyone.

He doesn't look over, just pushes a second glass toward me. "Figured you might show up here when you saw her. How are you doing?"

I take the glass without thanking him and drink. "Doesn't matter," I say when the glass is empty, setting it on the bar in front of me.

"Clearly, it does."

I exhale hard through my nose. "She left, Noah. No explanation. No goodbye. Just gone."

"And you never moved on," he says.

"You don't know that," I reply sharply.

"I know you," he says. "I know the way you haven't let anyone in since her. Not really."

There's an ache forming behind my eyes. I hate how right he is. I've dated, sure. Nothing worth remembering. Just enough to remind myself that I was still wanted. But none of them lasted more than a few months. I was too tired, too busy, too focused on building Cove. At least that's what I told myself. The truth is much simpler: none of them were her.

"You gonna talk to her?" he asks.

"I already did," I mutter. "Told her she works under Jesse. There's nothing more to say."

He raises a brow. "You think keeping your distance is going to help?"

"I think it's the only way I survive this without losing my mind."

He's quiet again. Then, "You ever think maybe this is your shot to finally get answers?"

My chest goes tight. "Not sure I want them anymore."

Noah leans his elbows on the bar. "Liar."

I don't argue. Just look out at the crowd, scanning for a glimpse of her like some damn addict. "It still hurts," I admit.

"Then it's not over."

After Landyn left, when it became clear to me that she wasn't coming back, I refused to allow myself the luxury of wandering down memory lane. I forced myself to close the door on that chapter of my life, to close the door on her the same way she slammed it shut on me. But there's one night I've never been able to stop thinking about, no matter how many years stack on top of the memories. A storm had rolled in knocking out power and Landyn and I were curled up on the couch in my apartment waiting for the worst to pass. I lit every candle I could find just so I could keep looking at her. Her head was propped in her hand as she watched the lightning flash across the sky, and I remember thinking... *this is it*. This is what everything's supposed to feel like. "You know we're going to be one of those annoying couples, right?" I said. "The ones everyone hates because they're too happy."

She snorted and rolled her eyes. "You're already annoying, so we're halfway there."

I kissed her just to shut her up. Slow, Certain. Like I knew exactly what I had in my hands.

And I did. I knew it then. I just didn't know how fast I could lose it.

I clap Noah on the shoulder and leave the bar, joining the crowd of Deep Cove's most notable faces. I can't hide out forever, as much as I might want to.

THE BALLROOM IS GLOWING, WITH STRINGS OF LIGHTS DRAPED across exposed beams and clusters of candles on the tabletops. This gala is supposed to be the crown jewel of Cove's year. A celebration of the community and the values our company is rooted in.

It's a big night for us, and I should be proud. Instead, all I can think about is the way she looks in that dress. How she doesn't belong here and yet somehow fits in effortlessly.

After dinner, I don't let myself search the room for her again. I've done that too many times tonight already.

"Still brooding?" The voice comes from beside me, low and dry.

I turn to find my brother, Wes, standing beside me, drink in hand, expression unreadable. Typical. Always quiet until the moment he chooses not to be. Wes was the golden boy once—valedictorian, star athlete, the one everyone thought would leave, blow the dust off this town and never look back. He did end up leaving, just not the way anyone expected. After the scandal, the moment his life changed forever, he took off to go to flight school and resurfaced a few years later. He flew commercial for a while but walked away from that too. Now he takes on charter jobs when he's not off the grid and when he's in town, he does some consulting work for Cove.

"Not brooding," I mutter. "Observing."

He huffs a short laugh. "You only call it that when you're trying not to punch a hole through a wall."

I give him a look. "Do you need something?"

He shrugs. "Just making sure you haven't combusted. You look like you're one forced smile away from setting the place on fire."

I don't answer. My silence is answer enough. Wes doesn't press. He never does. But he steps closer, his voice dropping slightly. "So. She's back. And she's at Cove."

I don't look at him. "You heard."

"You know Jesse, he couldn't keep it to himself if he tried."

I tip my head in a nod, gaze drifting back toward the center of the room where Jesse is now talking animatedly to the mayor. No Landyn in sight.

"She working out so far?" Wes asks.

"She's smart. She knows the brand." I pause, wondering where Landyn is. "She's good. She should be able to help get us out of the mess we're in."

"But?"

"But nothing."

Wes arches a brow. "Ford."

I exhale. "I don't know what the hell she's doing here. Or why now. But I can't let her distract me from everything we've built."

Wes is quiet a long beat. Then he says, "You ever think maybe this—her being here—is part of what we built?"

That lands like a punch I'm not ready for.

"She's not part of Cove," I answer tightly.

"No, not now. But she once was and she might still be part of you."

The words hang there, between us, until someone calls Wes's name from across the room.

He gives me one last look. "Try not to ruin the night. Or

light Jesse on fire." Then he walks away, disappearing into the crowd, leaving me standing here with nothing but old memories and a heartbeat that still hasn't settled.

I need air.

Too many faces. Too much noise.

I slip away from it all, through a quiet, dimly lit hallway, and for a minute, I let myself breathe until I see her.

Landyn stands near the window, silhouetted by silver moonlight, her arms wrapped around her waist like a shield. She doesn't see me at first, and I don't move. I just watch her like a man who has never stopped wanting what he couldn't have. She turns before I can pretend that I'm not staring at her, and the second our eyes meet, everything inside me pulls tight.

"I just needed a minute," she says, voice soft and hesitant around the edges. "I'll get back to the gala."

"I didn't come out here to scold you."

Her jaw tightens. "Right."

I'm not surprised to find her here. Landyn always liked quiet. It's one of the reasons she used to love the ocean. She said the noise in her head got quieter when she was close to the water.

"I didn't come out here to check on you either," I add. "I came out for air. Same as you."

"I'm sorry, Ford."

The words fall out of her like they've been weighing her down for years, but they don't land anywhere close to enough. Nothing she could say ever would.

My fingers shove through my hair, yanking hard at the roots, trying to dull the sharp edge of pain lashing through me. It's useless. It's impossible to control.

When she left, I didn't handle it well. That is putting it mildly—I came apart at the seams. For weeks, there was nothing outside my grief. Nothing but the hole she'd left behind.

"I'm sorry," she whispers again, bowing her head as if she can hide from it. Her hands tremble before she forces them to still. "I'm not proud of what I did, Ford. I feel horrible."

I let out a rough, bitter laugh, shaking my head. "By the time I started thinking straight, I tried to find you. But you'd blocked me." My voice cracks, anger mixing with years of hurt. "Even if you hadn't, I don't know what I would've said. Not then. I was so goddamn mad... but I would've liked to at least get an answer from you. Something."

Her nose scrunches, like my words physically hit her. She swallows hard. "I... I didn't know what else to do," she admits quietly. "I had to—" Her voice breaks, and she shakes her head. "To survive it, I guess."

The confession slices through me, sharp and merciless. *What was she trying to survive?*

She squeezes her eyes shut and inhales, but I can feel her pulling away. Not just physically, emotionally too. I guess it shouldn't come as a surprise. I've been keeping her at arm's length since she walked into my company and back into my life. Every meeting, every passing interaction, I've made sure to keep my tone clipped, my words measured, my attention on anything but her. I've been building this wall, making her pay for walking out on me, making her pay for breaking my heart. The funny thing is, it's not making me feel any better. It's only making me feel worse.

She gives me a mock salute then she walks towards me, stopping before she walks back inside. "It's amazing what you've built, Ford," she says, sincerity in her voice. "This night, and all of those people in there, it's all because of you."

I feel her words land in my chest, not my ego. My wounded heart has been begging for a fight, but right now—just for a moment—I need to tell it to call a truce. "Thanks. You always looked at me like you saw something worth keeping," I say, unable to stop myself now. "Even when I didn't have anything."

"I did see something," she whispers. "Still do. Even if you hate me being here."

I dig my teeth into my bottom lip. I should walk away. Instead, my feet stay rooted to the floor beneath me.

"I've hated you for a long time," I admit. "For leaving. For letting me believe we meant something and then disappearing. For never telling me why."

"I hated myself, too."

Her words hang between us, thin and frayed, and they do nothing to loosen the knot in my chest. I'm still so damn mad at her. The kind of mad that's been simmering for years, low and steady, burning everything it touches.

Looking at her now makes my skin feel too tight, like it's trying to hold in something too big to contain. Every inch of me is wound up, strung between wanting to walk away and wanting to grab her just to make her feel this too.

I shouldn't be here. I shouldn't be talking to her. Every instinct I have says to turn around, walk out, put a wall back between us that's so high she can never scale it. But my feet don't move, and I don't know why. Maybe because some part of me still wants answers. Maybe because I hate that she still makes me feel anything at all.

"Ford—"

"I shouldn't be saying any of this," I mutter, talking over her, scraping my hands through my hair.

"Then don't," she says, eyes lifting to mine. "But don't pretend it doesn't matter."

I stare at her, at the way the moonlight dances across her skin, and I know from the charge in the air, this thing between us isn't dead. It's buried. Waiting.

"I'm not sure what we're doing here," she finally says, her gaze shifting to her feet. When she looks at me again, something flickers in her eyes. Not anger. Not sadness. Something deeper.

"We aren't doing anything," I snap.

"Then stop looking at me like that," she says softly.

I freeze because she's right. I'm looking at her like I haven't stopped wanting her since the day she left.

"I should go," she says, voice trembling slightly. "But Ford, I want you to know that I didn't come back to hurt you."

I nod once, but it feels like a lie in my chest. "Doesn't make it hurt any less."

For a long moment, we just stand there in the hush of the hallway, the only sound the muted swell of music spilling out from the ballroom.

"I should get back," she says finally, straightening her shoulders, like she's putting her armor back on. "Jesse's probably wondering where I am."

Of course he is.

She brushes past me, and I catch the scent of her perfume, same as it used to be. That scent used to cling to my sheets for days. She doesn't look back as I watch her walk away, every part of me aching with the weight of what we'd been. Of what we are now, beneath all the years and damage.

One thing I know for sure...

This isn't over.

Not even close.

TEN

Landyn

By Monday morning, I'd mostly convinced myself that the gala had been a strange, glittery dream. A wildly unexpected, emotionally loaded, candlelit fever dream. And then I walked into Cove, and it was all right there—proof that it really had existed. Crates of glassware waiting to be picked up by the caterer, the slightly slower pace of still-tired employees. And the ache in my chest like I'd left something unfinished. Which, of course, I had.

Ford hadn't said another word after our hallway run-in. Just stared at me from across the room like I'd set something on fire. Again.

I step inside my office, leaving the door ajar a few inches, and immediately spot the small, gift-wrapped box sitting on my desk. Brown craft paper, tied with a navy-blue string. No note. No name.

I pull the string to undo the bow and peel the paper back to reveal a hardcover book, one I immediately recognize as the collection of Annie Leibovitz photographs I used to keep on my coffee table in college. The one I'd lost during my rushed move to Alberta. I hadn't seen it in years.

Tucked between the pages is a card.

June—
We've got history. That doesn't just disappear. This doesn't fix anything. But maybe it opens a door.
—F.

My throat tightens. He used my old nickname. Just one word, but it's enough to trigger a rush of emotions. No one else has ever called me that.

"Morning, Landyn!" Becca calls as she pops her head in, followed closely by Marco, both of them clutching their cups like their lives depend on the coffee inside. Quickly, I slip the book and the card into my bag before they ask any questions. "You in the mood to be productive, or should we just pretend today doesn't exist?"

"Pretending sounds good," I say, forcing a grin. "But I already answered three emails on the walk from the parking lot, so I think I'm officially past the point of no return."

Marco groans and drops into the chair across from me. "Ugh, you're one of those high-functioning morning people."

"Well, when you have a —," I clear my throat, catching myself before I tell them about Poppy. "Um, when you have a spare minute, there always seems to be something to fill it. Besides, my mom never let me sleep past seven, so I'm just wired that way."

Becca chuckles and nudges Marco. Becca is a Black woman in her mid-forties with a trendy bob and thick, tortoise-rimmed glasses. Marco is her closest friend here, and also her complete opposite. Beneath her buttoned-up disposition, Becca is a firecracker who never backs down when she knows she's right—

which she usually is. Marco is in his twenties, he's an open book with a great sense of humor and a drive to make a difference. They've both welcomed me to Cove with open arms. I already consider them to be friends.

"Speaking of duress, did you see Ford this morning?" Becca asks.

Marco sits up straighter, eyes wide. "Okay but seriously, what is up with him lately? He's walking around like someone canceled Christmas."

"Cancelled it, lit the tree on fire, and threw the turkey out the window," Becca adds. "The man is broody but he's never *this* miserable."

I shrug, keeping my face neutral. "He's probably just stressed. Running a company tends to do that."

"Sure," Marco says, clearly unconvinced. "But this feels different. It's like...personal. Like someone messed with his color coordinated sock drawer."

Becca snorts. "I'd pay money to see that sock drawer."

I bite back a laugh and reach for my coffee, grateful to have friends here. But they don't know my history with Ford and I'm not about to clue them in. Not yet.

"Or maybe someone stole his protein powder," Marco mutters, peering dramatically at us over the rim of his coffee cup.

We all laugh, and for a second, the tension lifts. But I can still feel the weight of the gift in my bag beside me, the unspoken history humming like static in the background.

There's a creak as the door to my office is pushed all the way open and Becca and Marco immediately go silent. I don't even have to look to know who has just walked in.

"Landyn," Ford's voice is calm, clipped.

His hands are shoved into the pockets of his black Cove quarter-zip which seems to be the standard office uniform. His gaze flicks from me to the others and back again. "Can I see you in my office?"

Marco's mouth actually drops open.

"Sure," I say quickly, standing and grabbing a notepad I know I don't need.

Ford gives a short nod before turning and walking away.

"He didn't even growl once," Becca whispers once the coast is clear.

Marco leans over the desk, eyes wide. "What the hell was that?"

I shrug, tight-lipped, then take one more sip of my coffee. "I guess I'm about to find out."

"Text us if you're kidnapped," Marco says as I pass them.

I walk down the hall towards Ford's office, my heart already racing. The door is ajar, so I tentatively push it open and step inside, shutting it gently behind me.

Ford stands at the window, posture perfect, shoulders broad. The sunlight slants through the glass, catching on the sharp line of his jaw, the slight furrow between his brows. He looks steady from the outside, but I know him well enough to see the current roiling just beneath.

He must know I'm there, but for a long moment, he doesn't turn around. When he finally does, his eyes meet mine, and just like that, everything feels too quiet. Too close. Like the room has closed in on us.

"Hi," he says, his voice softer than I expect.

"Hey," I reply, the word catching slightly in my throat.

He gestures toward the chair across from his desk. "Have a seat."

I nod, crossing the office slowly and lowering myself into the seat. My fingers find the hem of my shirt, smoothing the fabric with a kind of nervous energy I haven't felt in years. Not with anyone else.

The silence that stretches between us is thick with memory. His pristine, polished office makes me think back to the makeshift workspaces and late-night, coffee-stained plans we used to piece together when Cove was still just an idea.

"I hope it's okay," he begins, before trailing off, leaving the sentence unfinished.

I meet his gaze. "The gift?"

His expression shifts, but not enough to read. He nods. "Did you open it?"

"I did," I say softly. "I remember. The handwriting. The name."

His jaw flexes, just barely. "You always hated nicknames."

"I didn't hate that one," I answer. "You gave it to me when we met. It was June."

His eyes soften for a split second like he's somewhere other than here in his office with me. "You saw me staring at you, and you looked at me like you already knew I was gone for you."

The words hang between us, painful in their precision. I look away, the memory so vivid, threading itself through my ribs like a breath I hadn't realized I was holding.

He shifts, leaning back against his desk, arms crossed but not closed off. "I'm not trying to make things harder. I just..." He exhales, gaze dropping briefly to the floor before finding mine again. "I didn't leave that gift to mess with your head. I just hung onto it. I thought maybe...maybe you'd want it back."

"I...," I whisper. "I do."

He nods. "I meant what I wrote. The gift doesn't fix anything. But it's a peace offering. We're going to be in the same place five days a week, and I'm not interested in wasting time pretending we don't exist to each other." He pauses, holding my gaze just a beat longer. "And I didn't forget about us."

Neither have I.

And that is the hardest part.

"I'm not expecting this to be easy," I offer after a beat. "But I want to be here. For Cove. For you."

His eyes search mine, something unspoken swimming in the gray. "Cove was supposed to be ours," he says.

My breath catches and I blink back the tears that suddenly sting my eyes. "I know," I whisper. "I really do hate that I wasn't strong enough to stay."

His eyes narrow, but he doesn't move. Doesn't speak. Another beat. Another stretch of silence. "You're here now," he says, his voice low.

I smile faintly, thankful that he didn't ask the question that must be running through his head: Why?

"I am."

He smiles too, the barest twitch of his mouth. "Welcome back, June."

The sound of it cracks something open in me.

I *am* here and I won't run this time.

"Landyn?" My mom's voice calls from the hallway, followed by the familiar sound of the faint jingling of her keychain. She pokes her head into the kitchen, a glass mason jar in her hand. "Just dropping off soup I made today. Thought I'd check in and see how your first real week's going."

I flip the card shut from Ford closed too fast, shoving it under the stack of mail on the kitchen table.

Her eyes land on the package. "What's that?"

"Just...something from an old friend," I say, hating how my voice wobbles.

She gives me a knowing look. "Friend, huh?"

I don't respond because what am I supposed to say? That the man whose heart I broke had somehow found the exact crack in the armor I'd been building for the past seven years? That he remembers me better than I remember myself? And that I hate how good it feels to be remembered?

"Mom, it's nothing. It's no big deal," I mutter, bringing P's dinner dish to the sink to distract myself.

She doesn't let it go. "I don't know, Landyn. You've been awfully tight-lipped about things lately. Since when do you hide things from me?"

"Fine, it's from Ford, but I really don't want to talk about it right now. I want to talk about you and what you're doing here this late when you should be on the couch with your feet up."

"I'm fine, Landyn. You don't need to worry about me. Besides, your dad drove me here, he's waiting outside," she says, putting the soup in my fridge. "Make sure P knows it's here—it's chicken noodle, her favorite."

"Thanks, Mom. I love you," I say wrapping her in a tight hug. "I should get Poppy ready for bed."

"Okay, go on. But just remember, I'm here when you're ready to talk. I'll see you tomorrow." She smiles, tossing one last look at the package on the table before heading to the door.

I sit on the edge of Poppy's twin bed, running a brush gently through her damp, honey-brown curls. She's in her favorite pajamas, the ones covered in tiny golden retrievers wearing tiaras. She yawns dramatically every few seconds like she deserves a medal for surviving a day of grade one.

"You're going to pull my hair out," she mumbles, her voice heavy with sleep.

I smile, brushing slower. "You have about four strands tangled. You'll live."

She tilts her head to look up at me, those wide gray eyes blinking. "Mommy?"

"Yeah, bug?"

"Can we get a dog? Like, a real one? One that sleeps in my bed and eats pancakes?"

I laugh softly, pulling the brush through the last section of her hair. "Why would it eat pancakes?"

"Because its name is gonna be Pancake." She sounds exasperated that I even have to ask. "Duh."

I press a kiss to the top of her head, heart tugging hard. "We'll see, okay? Maybe after we get settled."

She frowns. "We already are."

I pause. "I know. I just mean... more settled."

She scrunches her nose at me but seems too tired for any more questions. Instead, she wriggles under the blankets, pulling her stuffed bunny tight against her chest, and I smooth my hand over her curls again.

"You know," I whisper, more to myself than to her, "when you were born, you had this little wrinkle between your eyebrows. Just like now, when you're tired. You looked so serious for such a tiny baby."

She grins sleepily. "I was thinking about important things."

I laugh, blinking back the burn behind my eyes. "I bet you were."

My mind drifts, uninvited, to when I lived in Alberta at my aunt's. Poppy was a newborn, and we shared a bedroom with barely enough room for her crib. I was terrified. But then I would look at her little face and everything else just fell away. She looked just like him. Still does. Same sharp jaw, same fierce eyes. The same stubbornness that lives in her bones.

She's breathing heavier now, almost asleep, one arm still looped around Cinnamon the stuffed bunny.

"Night, Poppyseed," I whisper, brushing one last kiss to her cheek.

Downstairs, I flick off the lights and head to the kitchen. The gift from Ford is still on the table. I pick it up now, fingertips grazing the sleek, familiar cover. My thumb brushes over the edge of the note tucked underneath.

June.

Just that. A word. A memory. A version of me I'm not sure I can be again.

I don't open it. I don't throw it away either. Instead, I carry it upstairs and tuck it into the drawer of my nightstand.

Out of sight.

But not out of mind.

ELEVEN

Ford

"We still good for the site meeting this afternoon?" I ask, stepping into Jesse's office, already half-scrolling through the floor plan on my tablet. After the factory backlash, we're building a state-of-the-art, sustainable manufacturing facility 45 minutes from town.

He spins in his chair and winces. "Yeah, about that... I can't go."

"Why not?"

He holds up his phone. "Last-minute pitch call with the PR firm. It's the only time they could squeeze us in. You know... saving Cove's ass and all that."

I stare at him. "And Noah?"

"Supplier issue. He's already halfway to the coast."

"Wes?"

Jesse shrugs. "Wes is allergic to people."

I rub my temples. "So, what, I go alone?"

A beat. Then Jesse's grin turns calculated. "Take Landyn."

"No."

"Why not?"

"She doesn't know the facility."

"She's in marketing. It's literally her job to understand it."

"She—" I pause, jaw tight. "It's not a good idea."

Jesse leans back, lacing his fingers behind his head. "She's free. And interested. Aren't you, Landyn?"

I turn toward the doorway just in time to see her walk in, a folder tucked under her arm, lips slightly parted like she'd only caught half the conversation.

"Interested in what?" she asks slowly, looking between us.

Jesse grins. "Interested in joining Ford at the site tour today. Right?"

She glances at me—quick, unreadable—then back to Jesse. "If that's what you need."

I exhale sharply through my nose. "Fine. Let's go. I'll meet you at the elevator in ten."

She doesn't flinch at my tone, which is harsher than I meant it to be. She just nods and then steps aside to let me by her, like this isn't a bad idea for everyone involved.

She's waiting by the elevator ten minutes later, a tablet in one hand. Her hair is swept up, a few blonde pieces framing her face, and when our eyes meet, something shifts. Less ice. Less steel. Just...her.

We nod at each other—my peace offering from earlier in the week still holding. The silence between us in the truck isn't uncomfortable this time. It's filled with something unspoken but not unkind. The drive is one I've made countless times, but today it feels different. I notice the way Landyn turns to watch the trees blur past, how she tucks her lip between her teeth when she's thinking. I'd forgotten that about her.

I decide instead of sitting here, next to her, locked up in my own head, I should suck it up and say something—anything— to make this drive less unbearable.

"You're gonna like the site," I say, eyes still on the road. "It's on a beautiful piece of property in the country. Makes the build headaches feel worth it."

She turns to me, maybe surprised that I'm speaking to her. "I've seen photos, but yeah, I'm looking forward to seeing it in person."

"And you're getting out of the office," I tell her. "A reward for surviving a full week with Jesse."

She laughs, and it's warm. It's real. "God love him, he's a lot."

"He's the kind of 'a lot' that sells product. But yeah…I've considered shoving him in a storage closet more than once."

She's still smiling when we pull into the site, and I kill the engine. It's quiet for now—lunch break for the crew—which gives us some time.

She steps out of the truck, the gravel crunching under her heels, and she stumbles slightly, catching herself with a hand on the truck door.

"You good?" I ask, rounding to her side.

"Fine. Just my incredibly professional entrance," she says with a grimace. "I'm probably not dressed for the occasion."

I reach out, steadying her elbow. "I mean, you were always a little clumsy. Some things don't change."

Her gaze flicks up to mine. There's something there. Familiar. Unspoken.

We walk the site side by side. I point out the glass-walled design center, the production wall where the solar arrays are going to be installed along the roofline. Landyn listens, asking smart questions and nodding like she's mentally redesigning our whole strategy. It shouldn't affect me, but it does. Her being here, being part of this legacy. When it's done, Landyn will have played a part in making it happen.

We stop at the overlook, the green valley laid out before us eventually erupting into layers of towering, deep blue mountains. But I find myself watching her more than the view. The wind pulls at a loose piece of her hair, and before I can think twice, I reach over and gently tuck it behind her ear.

She looks at me, startled.

"Thanks," she says quietly.

And for once, I don't look away. We don't say much as we walk the rest of the site, but the silence feels different now—charged, somehow. Like we're standing on the edge of something neither of us know what to do with.

By the time we make it back to the truck, the sun has shifted overhead and a few of the crew have returned, nodding as we pass. Landyn's quiet, and I get the sense she's lost in her own thoughts.

We drive back with the windows down. She kicks off her shoes, tucking one leg under her on the seat like she's been doing this forever. I catch her glancing my way once or twice, and when we hit a stretch of road lined by pines, she finally speaks.

"It really is impressive," she says. "What you've built. What you're continuing to build."

I glance at her for a moment before turning my eyes back to the road. "We've still got a ways to go."

"Still," she continues, looking out the window. "You did it. Even when no one thought you could." She turns to me, and for a moment, the air between us feels heavy again. "I didn't mean me. I never doubted you, Ford. Not once. You know, it wasn't just the dream of the company that meant something to me back then."

I stare straight ahead, but my pulse kicks up.

"Don't," I say, quietly.

But she keeps looking at me, like she's trying to find the version of me she left behind.

"Ford…"

I shake my head. "Let's not do this. It's been a good day, and this is about Cove. Let's leave it at that."

She sighs. "Fine. But I'm not running this time."

"Good," I say, voice rough. "Because if you do, I'm not chasing you."

She nods, swallowing hard, as I flick on the turn signal and change the subject to anything other than us. "Should we grab lunch on the way back? You must be starved."

Landyn looks surprised, but she quickly overcomes it. "Sure," she says with a grin. "But I'm choosing the place."

"As long as it's not that vegan stuff you tried to get me to like. Dress it up however you want, cauliflower will never be a steak."

She laughs. "No vegan. Promise."

We end up at a small sandwich shop that Landyn spots just off the highway. Nothing fancy. The bell above the door jingles as we step inside. The place smells like toasted bread and dill pickles, and there's a guy behind the counter with a stained apron and a name tag that says Buzz. The place looks like it hasn't seen a coat of paint in decades, but it's charming in a comfortable, grease-splattered kind of way.

We each grab a faded menu from the counter, and I look around, the place feeling eerily familiar. "We've been here before, right? In college."

Landyn grins, brushing a strand of hair behind her ear. "We came here a few times. You swore this place had the best meatball sub in the county."

I laugh, remembering. "That's right. And it did."

She looks skeptical. "It gave you food poisoning."

"One time," I say, pointing at her. "And you still made out with me after."

She snorts, shaking her head, eyes closed for a beat. "Mistakes were made."

I don't reply, just let the smile pull at my mouth as I step up to the counter. "Two meatball subs," I tell Buzz. "One with extra cheese. And a small fries."

"Ordering for me?" she says, one eyebrow raised.

"Habit," I say with a shrug. "Old ones are hard to break."

She studies me for a split-second, lips parting like she wants to argue but doesn't.

"Guess it's muscle memory," I add, shrugging my shoulder. "Like knowing you'll steal the last fry or fall asleep in the car on long drives."

Her cheeks flush and her mouth curves like she might smile. Her eyes flick to mine, something unreadable behind them, and she looks away quickly. I feel it too—that moment where it could get heavy, where it could drift back into everything we left unsaid. But I don't want that right now. Not when she's standing beside me like this, flushed from the drive with the window down, looking exactly like the version of her that used to feel like home.

We find a booth by the window, the vinyl seats cracked and slightly sticky. She slides in across from me and leans on her elbows, her smile returning. The meatball subs are delivered in minutes, and we both dig in, famished after a long day.

"I forgot how weirdly perfect diner food tastes when you've been on the highway."

I glance up at her, chewing. "That's because you don't give a crap what you eat when you're starving."

She smirks and takes a bite out of her sandwich. "You used to eat two of these in one sitting. Don't tell me you've outgrown diner meatballs, Mr. CEO. Is it strictly caviar now?" she teases.

I point a fry at her. "That's a baseless accusation."

"Still stubborn." Landyn grins.

We eat in comfortable silence for a few minutes, and I watch her across the table. She's picking at her sandwich, eyebrows drawn slightly. Not sad. Just...thoughtful.

"You like being back?" I ask, keeping my voice casual.

She shrugs. "It's familiar. Which is both comforting and suffocating, if that makes sense."

"It does."

She glances at me. "What about you? You ever think about leaving?"

"No." I sip my drink. "Cove was never just a business to me. It was the one thing I could build and keep. The one thing I could control."

Landyn nods slowly. "That's how I felt about leaving."

We look at each other again, something deeper tugging beneath the surface. This time, neither of us looks away.

"Did you mean what you said earlier?" she asks finally. "That you're not chasing me?"

I study her, the way her mouth tightens at the corners. Like she's bracing for something.

"I meant," I say carefully, "that I don't want to chase someone who's already running."

She leans back, crossing her arms. "Maybe I'm not running."

My chest tightens. "I hope not, June."

Her breath hitches. Just slightly. But enough.

Before either of us can respond, Buzz shouts, "Hey, lovebirds, you done hogging the best table in the house?"

Landyn grins, flicking her napkin at me. "Let's get back on the road before he charges us rent."

I stand, grabbing our wrappers. "Still can't eat a full sandwich, huh?"

She lifts her chin. "Guess I still need someone to finish it for me."

The words were nothing, tossed out with a shrug and a half-smile but they remind me that I used to do that. I would finish her sandwiches, steal her fries, kiss the corner of her mouth after she wiped it with a napkin and missed a spot.

A litany of things I didn't realize I'd memorized.

We don't speak again until we're 15 minutes into our drive home. But the silence isn't awkward. It's something else entirely. Something almost like understanding.

Landyn next to me, in the passenger seat of my truck feels so familiar, it aches, like a memory I'm still not sure I'm ready to feel. She shifts slightly in her seat, her voice softer now, her gaze fixed on the blur of towering evergreens rushing past the window.

"You've been awfully quiet. That's suspicious."

She smirks, keeping her gaze on the blur of trees racing past the window. "Maybe I'm just enjoying the peace."

"Peace," I scoff. "You? You've never been quiet a day in your life."

She cuts me a look, amused. "That's rich, coming from you. You used to lecture me for talking too much on road trips."

"That was different," I say, shifting gears smoothly. "Back then, you were distracting me while I was trying to look cool driving."

"You? Cool?" she laughs, the sound bright and warm. "Ford Winters, you once missed an exit because you couldn't stop staring at my legs on the dashboard."

My jaw ticks as the memory slams into me—sunlight on her skin, her laughter echoing in the cab, me gripping the wheel so hard my knuckles turned white because I couldn't look away.

"Pretty sure that was a strategic choice," I say, keeping my tone even.

"Strategic?" She arches a brow, leaning back like she's got me cornered.

I glance at her, just long enough to catch the spark in her eyes. "Yeah. Gave me an extra half hour with you in the truck. Worth every mile."

Her lips part, caught somewhere between a laugh and a

sharp inhale, and for a second the only sound is the hum of the tires on the road. The air shifts, charged and a little dangerous, and I have to drag my focus back to the yellow line ahead.

"Careful, June," I tease gently. "Keep laughing like that, and I might start thinking we're friends again."

She turns her head, surprised. "Maybe we are."

She looks out the window, a small furrow between her brows giving her away as she drifts deeper in thought. "I didn't expect any of this. I didn't come back to stir up the past."

"Then what *did* you come back for?"

Her voice catches slightly. "To build something new."

I glance at her again. "What are you running away from, Lan?"

She meets my gaze, and there's that flicker of hurt, the quiet kind that comes from too much time spent carrying things alone possibly. "I'm not running, Ford. I just needed to be back closer to my parents."

"How are they doing?"

She fills me in, telling me her dad still works the same government job, her mom slowing down in her retirement years.

I nod, remembering them clearly. "Your mom always made the best shepherd's pie."

Landyn smiles. "She still does. She actually brought me some the other night."

I look back at the road. "I always envied that. Your house, your family."

She doesn't say anything right away, but I know she remembers. The house I grew up in never felt like a home.

"You used to say my family felt like too much sometimes," she murmurs.

"It was," I say. "Too busy, too much structure. Too... perfect."

She's quiet for a beat. "But you liked it anyway."

I nod once. "Yeah. I liked it because it was yours."

I can feel her watching me, like she's trying to piece together who I am now, to find the parts she used to know, the parts that are new. I don't look at her. If I do, I might not be able to stop the past from sinking its claws into me, drowning me in memories I swore I'd buried for good.

TWELVE

L andyn
Ford's elbow rests casually on the door, his hand at the wheel, his gaze focused but relaxed. I keep sneaking glances at him, trying to remember if this is how it used to feel...before everything between us fell apart.

The road winds in long, slow stretches, the fading sun bleeding through the windshield in soft pinks and purples. He takes the bends quickly, his foot barely touching the brake. Ford drives like he does everything else—confident, in control. It's so hot. His right hand is wrapped loosely around the wheel, fingers long and tan and dusted with faint calluses. There's a small scar at the base of his thumb that I don't remember, a faint reminder that he's lived a whole life I wasn't part of.

His profile is sharp—strong jaw, faint scruff, his mouth set in that familiar but unreadable line. His nose is straight, a little too perfect, like the universe gave him one lucky break after dropping him into a childhood that would have none. His dark hair is longer than I remember, curling just a little where it brushes the collar of his shirt, messy in a way that still looks flawless.

He sits with this quiet, commanding confidence, like nothing in the world could rattle him.

Except maybe me.

I shift in my seat and look out the window, not wanting to stare too long, but eventually my eyes drift to the radio. "Since when do you listen to country music?"

Ford's mouth curves, barely there, his eyes still on the road. "I know it's what you like."

My chest squeezes. "I can't believe you remember that."

He flicks me a quick glance, something unreadable in his expression. "I haven't forgotten a thing."

His admission wraps around me, soft and sharp all at once. I turn back towards the window, hoping he doesn't notice the way my throat tightens. Trees blur by outside my open window. The sky's washed with pale purples. "Thanks for not making today weird," I say finally.

Ford glances at me, brow raised. "Weird?"

"I don't know." I shrug. "Awkward. Tense. You could've made the entire trip miserable, and you didn't."

He doesn't answer for a second. Then, quietly: "You think I want it to be miserable?"

"No," I say, just as quiet. "I don't."

The conversation stops there—unspoken things suspended between us—until the Cove building comes into view and we're back to reality.

By the time we step into the office, I've built my walls back up just high enough. I head to my desk and drop my bag. Before I can even take off my jacket, Becca's up from her chair and walking towards me, eyes wide.

"Did you just walk in with Ford?"

I nod. "We were at the site."

Marco's leaning against my desk three seconds later, coffee in hand. "I thought I saw you leaving with him earlier, but I figured I hallucinated it."

"He took her to the site," Becca stage-whispers. "Like the actual site."

"Yes. I was there. And look—I survived!" I laugh, shaking my head.

"He only takes his brothers to the site. Like, *ever*," Marco says, eyes narrowing like he's trying to solve a crime. "Seriously. Even then, Jesse had to talk him into taking Wes."

"I didn't realize it was a big deal," I say, feigning nonchalance. "We had to look at some layout stuff. It was fine."

"Fine?" Becca nearly chokes. "This is Ford Winters we're talking about, right?"

"Yeah, 'fine' doesn't track, Landyn. The guy is intense as fuck," Marco adds.

I think back to the way he gently held my elbow as I teetered on the loose gravel. His easy smile when I teased him at the diner. The way he looked at me like I mattered. "It's not a big deal," I say, pulling off my coat and draping it over my chair.

Becca and Marco exchange a look but don't push. Instead, Becca tips her head. "So, Landyn. Tell us more about you."

I smile, carefully. "Which version do you want? The one that sounds good on my resume or the one that's half-coffee, half-chaos?"

Marco grins. "Chaos. Always chaos."

I laugh softly. "Well, I've been in marketing for about eight years. I was living in Alberta for a while but moved back to Deep Cove recently. Fortunately, this opportunity at Cove came up so it was good timing."

"Alberta?" Becca asks. "What brought you back here?"

I hesitate, searching for the right words. I've never been someone who shares much about my private life. We're still not sure what's happening with my mom's health. If it turns out it's something serious, I'm not sure I'll be able to handle it. "I moved back to be closer to my family. The job posting seemed perfect for me too, and I just felt like it was the right time to return home."

Becca nods, like she understands that pull too. "Your parents live here?"

I glance down at my water bottle, twisting the cap. "Yeah. My mom and dad live here. And now my daughter and I do too."

Marco blinks. "You have a kid?"

"Her name's Poppy. She just turned six. That's part of why I moved back—it's been just the two of us for a long time, and I wanted her to have more family around. She loves her grandparents. I want them to have a relationship. I know it sounds cheesy, but that kid is my whole world."

Becca smiles. "Not cheesy at all. I feel the same way about my own kids. Is she in school here?"

"Grade one. She goes to Bayview. I was a bit worried about uprooting her, but she's already made so many new friends. It's amazing how resilient kids can be."

Marco leans against the edge of my desk. "So, you're doing this job, raising a kid, and still managing to look like you've slept in the last decade?"

I shake my head, grinning. "It's all smoke and mirrors. And caffeine. So much caffeine."

"And is there a partner in the picture?" Marco asks, eyebrows raised. "Husband? Boyfriend?"

"Nope," I answer honestly. "I'm too busy for that, if I'm not working, I'm with Poppy."

"Yeah, good call," he nods, letting out a loud sigh. "It's slim pickings out there anyways. I went out last weekend with a guy my cousin set me up with and it was a disaster. He said he'd pick the place, and we ended up at Arby's. In the drive-thru. I love crinkle fries as much as anyone, but not on a first date, and not in the front seat of your mom's Honda Civic."

Becca coughs out a laugh, and I'm grateful for the opening

to gently steer the conversation back to work, to the marketing push that's coming up. I'm relieved they don't ask more—about who Poppy's dad is or why I really came back.

I'm not ready to answer those questions.

Not yet.

Eventually, the workday winds down. People start trickling out. I gather my things slowly, giving my brain a second to catch up to everything that happened today. When I sling my bag over my shoulder and head for the exit, I catch a glimpse of him through the glass—Ford, in his office, talking to Noah.

He glances up. His eyes find mine. A beat. A breath.

I raise my hand in a small wave. He nods once.

It's nothing. It's everything.

I walk out before it can turn into more.

But I only get as far as the pavement outside of Cove when I hear his voice behind me. "Landyn."

It stops me mid-step.

The tone of it, the hesitation laced beneath all the usual Ford Winters certainty makes me turn. Slowly. Too slowly. Like if I look at him too fast, everything I've been holding back might break loose.

He's already coming down the steps toward me. He stands in front of me, close enough that I swear I can feel the heat radiating off him in the early evening air.

"I just...I want a little more time with you, to talk," he says. "Not about work. About us."

Us. That word slices through the quiet and I feel it settle in my chest. My heart thuds once. Hard.

I grip the strap of my bag more tightly, already inching back towards my car with my keys tangled in my fingers. I can't do this right now. Not without completely unraveling. Not when I need to get home for dinner with Poppy. Not with the weight of the secret that exists between us.

"I really should get going," I murmur.

"Dinner," he says. "Tonight. Just you and me."

It's not a question. But it's not a demand either.

My mouth opens. Closes. Panic spikes low in my stomach because I wasn't expecting this. Not now.

"I—I can't," I say, too quickly.

His head tilts, and his eyes narrow just slightly. "Why not?"

"Plans," I say, wincing. It's not exactly a lie, but I know it's far from the truth.

Ford pauses, studying me for a long beat. I know he sees through my excuse, but he doesn't call me on it. Doesn't push. Instead, he nods once, slowly, like he's giving me the out I clearly want but don't entirely deserve.

"Tomorrow then," he says.

His words land heavily like a dare I'm not sure I'm brave enough to take. "Maybe."

We stand there for a moment, the silence stretching between us full of unsaid things and every version of us we never got to be. I turn before I can do something stupid. Like tell him the truth.

"Just think about it," he says quietly to my back, the rough edge of his voice pulling at my heart like a tether. "One night. One dinner where we stop pretending like there isn't something still there between us."

I stop walking, but I can't turn around. I can feel the weight of his presence behind me and the weight of what he just said. What we could still be if I wasn't hiding the one thing he has the right to know.

"Ford—"

He lets out a frustrated breath. "Just tell me, June. Tell me why you can't stop running."

My guilt burns a hole through my chest, but not here, not now. I can't tell him about his 6-year-old daughter on the sidewalk in front of Cove.

"I'll think about it."

"Eight o'clock tomorrow at Breakwater. I'll be waiting."

I nod. "Okay."

I squeeze my eyes closed, unable to breathe for a beat. Then I walk away before I change my mind.

THIRTEEN

Ford

The sun's going down, a chill settling in the air as I step onto my back deck, glass of whiskey in hand. I'm already dressed—black button-down, jeans, boots. Casual, but not careless. I have to keep reminding myself this isn't a date.

I sip the whiskey slowly, leaning against the railing, trying to let the cool air break through the heat crawling under my skin. I've checked my watch four times in the last ten minutes, and I hate myself for it.

Even the dogs are restless. Wes's rescue mutt, Scout, who I somehow got roped into watching for the week, is pacing by the back door. Stella, my Boston Terrier, is anxiously watching him. I let them out of the house and toss a stick half-heartedly across the yard. Neither of them chase it. They just look up at me like they know I've got too much on my mind.

I scrub a hand down my face. This was a bad idea.

One afternoon with Landyn, and I'm making reckless decisions. I shouldn't have asked her to come for dinner. I shouldn't care whether she shows up. But I do.

I walk inside, dump the glass in the sink without finishing it, and grab my keys. If she doesn't show, I'll order a beer. Eat a burger. Pretend this was never about her.

If she does...

I lock the door behind me before I can finish the thought.

Breakwater Bistro sits tucked against the coast, low lights glowing from the wraparound windows, the sound of the ocean just behind it providing a constant soundtrack. It's upscale enough to pass for a date spot, but laid back enough that I won't feel like a jackass if I end up eating alone.

I push through the front doors and nod at the hostess, a girl who looks fresh out of college and slightly startled to see me. Cove has roots in this town. People know who I am, and they know I don't go out much.

"Mr. Winters," she says, glancing down at her reservation list. "Do you have a preference for where you'd like to sit?"

"Corner table," I say. "If it's open."

It is. Of course it is.

She leads me through the busy dining room, past the clinking glasses and murmured conversation, to a quiet table, half-tucked beneath the curve of a wide bay window. From here, I can see the water. I can also see the entrance.

I sit with my back to the wall and thank the hostess when she sets the menu down.

I don't touch it. I check my watch. It's 7:58. Not that I'm paying attention to the time.

The server comes over and I order a whiskey, neat. I barely take a sip before I'm glancing toward the door again. Every time it opens, my chest gets tight. Every time it's not her, it gets tighter. I wonder what she's doing. If she's still standing in front of her closet, trying to talk herself out of this. Or if she made up her mind hours ago and is letting her absence tell me all I need to know.

8:04.

I look down at the drink in my hand, swirl it, and try not to care.

The door opens again.

And this time, it's her.

Landyn is wearing a black dress that hugs her body and falls just above the knee, simple but devastating. The neckline dips just enough to make me forget how to breathe. Her hair is pulled half up, soft waves brushing her shoulders, catching the light when she moves. It's not overdone—nothing about her ever is. But somehow, she still looks like the most dangerous thing in the room.

Her eyes sweep the restaurant until they land on me. I don't move. Don't blink. Don't breathe. And for a second, I think she might turn around and walk out. But she doesn't. She crosses the room with purpose, every step pulling a string tighter in my chest.

When she reaches the table, I stand automatically, dragging a hand over my jaw like it'll help me keep it together.

"Hey," she says softly.

"Hey," I echo, my voice low, rougher than I mean it to be.

I pull out her chair and she gives me a look—surprised, a little wary—but she takes a seat without saying anything. I sit down across from her and for a heartbeat, it's just the two of us and the sound of the ocean outside the open windows.

"I didn't think you'd come," I say quietly, sitting back down.

"I almost didn't," she answers, placing her purse on the chair next to her.

"But you did."

She lifts one shoulder, her lips pressing together. "Yeah. I did."

And just like that, something shifts. Not forgiven. Not forgotten. But something.

The waitress appears, breaking the moment. We both glance away like we've been caught doing something we shouldn't. Landyn orders a glass of wine. I ask for another whiskey, neat. Once she's gone, silence settles over the table again. Not the uneasy kind. This one feels like… waiting.

"You look beautiful," I say, trying to keep it casual, but the words land heavier than I intended them to.

Her mouth tips into a cautious smile. "You clean up okay yourself, Mr. CEO."

"I'm in a black button-down shirt, Landyn. That's me trying."

She huffs a laugh, and the sound untangles something tight in my chest. "Well, you wear it like you don't care, so it works."

"That's the goal."

She traces the rim of her water glass with one fingertip, her gaze moving to the view of the ocean outside the window.

"You always liked this place," I say.

"I did. You used to bring me here when you wanted to bribe me after an argument."

My brow lifts. "Not this time."

She glances sideways at me. "No?"

"No," I say, quieter now. "This is just me wanting to see you."

She doesn't answer. Doesn't look away either.

"You're different now," she says finally. "You're…steadier."

I shrug. "Maybe. Cove taught me how to stay still. And how not to blow things up when they get hard."

She nods slowly. "That's a good thing to learn."

Her wine arrives. She lifts the glass, takes a slow sip, then sets it down carefully. There's so much I want to ask her. Why she really came back. Why she left. What happened in the years between. But I know better. Instead, I lean back in my chair and say, "Thank you for coming with me to the site."

Her gaze flicks to mine. "You really only take your brothers there?"

"You've been talking to Marco and Becca."

Her lips twitch like she's trying not to smile. "You've been watching me."

I nod, slow and deliberate. There's no point in denying it. "Guilty, and to answer your question... yeah. Or investors. But mostly my brothers."

"Then why me?"

I hold her stare. "Besides Jesse setting it up, you mean? We spent so many hours dreaming about something like Cove. You had such a vision for it. I wanted to see if you still have that fire in you."

Her eyes narrow slightly. "And?"

I smirk. "Nothing's changed."

She looks down at her glass. A small smile curves her lips, but there's a flicker of emotion there.

I lean in slightly, keeping my voice low. "Why'd you come back here, June? There are plenty of jobs you could have gotten that aren't in Deep Cove."

Her gaze shoots up to mine. The nickname hits its mark, just like I knew it would.

"I told you, "she says, voice lighter now. "To build something new, And my parents are here so this seemed like a good place to do it."

I nod, but I'm not ready to let it go. "So that's what you came back to do. Why did you leave in the first place?"

Her lips part, and for a moment, I think she might actually tell me. That she might finally give me the piece of the puzzle I've always been missing. But she only shakes her head gently. "Some things hurt too much to look at."

I sit with that. Let it sink in. Because I know exactly what she means.

Our food arrives, and the moment breaks but it lingers like smoke between us.

Landyn shifts in her seat, giving a small, appreciative sound at the sight of her food. "Okay," she says, picking up her fork. "Truce over roasted chicken?"

I nod, lips twitching. "If that's what you want, June."

FOURTEEN

Landyn

The door to Breakwater Bistro clicks shut behind us, and the night air cuts sharp against my skin. The warmth of the restaurant lingers, but the nerves are starting to build again, curling low in my stomach.

Ford's already a step ahead, hands tucked into the pockets of his dark blue denim, head tilted like he's considering something.

"Walk with me?" he asks.

His voice is low, unreadable, but something in the way he says it makes it impossible to say no.

We fall into an easy pace, side by side down Front Street. Most of the shops are closed, quiet and darkened behind frosted windows. The quiet feels like a bubble, soft and private, like the world forgot we were still here.

We pass a familiar storefront, and I pause. "Didn't this used to be a record shop? That one we loved?"

He glances over his shoulder at the sleek candle boutique it's become. "Yeah. Don't you remember, you tried to convince the cashier to let you DJ from behind the counter."

I roll my eyes. "I played one Stevie Nicks song."

"You played three. And danced in the aisle."

I laugh, and it comes out breathless and real. It feels good. Dangerous, but good.

We keep walking, the sidewalk gleaming faintly from a recent drizzle. Our hands brush. Once. Twice. The third time, his pinky curls ever so slightly around mine, but it doesn't stay long. Just enough to make my pulse stutter and my skin erupt in a shiver.

At the far end of the street, the town opens to a lookout point above the water. He and I stand at the railing overlooking the ocean below, the sound of the tide rolling in slow and steady. Wind lifts my hair, and I hug my arms around myself. Ford stands beside me, close enough that I can feel the heat of him. His eyes are on the dark, moonlit horizon.

"I used to think," he says quietly, "that if I ever got you back here, I'd know what to say."

His words hit like an echo of something I've tried hard to bury.

"And now?" I ask.

He drags a hand down his jaw, like the words are caught in his throat. "Now I'm just trying not to ruin it."

My heart plummets to my feet, a free fall I can't stop. I press my palm to my chest, enthralled by the wild, frantic pounding beneath my hand.

"You still do that thing with your hand when you're nervous."

"What thing?"

"You flatten your palm over your heart."

I freeze, caught in the middle of doing exactly that.

His mouth lifts in the faintest smile. "You did it the first time I kissed you."

My breath catches. His gaze drops to my lips, and my whole body goes still. Ford steps in closer, slowly, like he's afraid I'll run. At the same time, his hand lifts, fingers brushing a strand of hair from my face. The back of his knuckles skim across my cheek. "I've wanted to kiss you all night," he says. "I feel like I'm drowning in you."

My heart is thudding so loudly I'm afraid he can hear it. I lean in without meaning to, pulled by gravity or history or maybe just the ache in his voice. Our faces are inches apart. So close I can feel his breath, but I stop, then I pull back. The moment snaps like a rubber band stretched too far.

"I can't," I whisper. "Not tonight."

His hand falls to his side. The air between us cools instantly, but the heat of what almost happened clings to me. Ford doesn't look away. He doesn't push. "Okay," he says, voice low and even. "But I mean it when I say it, June. I'm not walking away."

I nod, but I can't speak.

Not with the weight of the secret between us.

Not when I have to be home to kiss Poppy goodnight.

Not when he doesn't know that I'm not just a ghost from the past, but the mother of his daughter.

I take a shaky breath and turn back toward the street, the sound of the waves behind us echoing through my chest.

"Landyn," he says softly.

I stop.

"I want to see you again."

I don't turn around.

"I want to see you again," he repeats, slower this time. Like he means it more than he's meant anything in a long time.

Still, I say nothing. Because if I open my mouth, I'm not sure the truth won't come spilling out.

"Saturday night. My house, I'll text you the address. Eight o'clock. I'll be waiting."

Exhaling a long breath, I keep walking. I don't look back, because if I do, I know I might run to him and tell him everything, shattering the fragile space I've tried so hard to keep between what was and what is.

By the time I reach my car, my hands are shaking. I sit for a full minute with the door closed and the engine off, forehead resting against the steering wheel.

Poppy.

Our daughter.

The secret curls inside me like a live wire, buzzing and dangerous, impossible to contain. It's not just guilt that eats at me—it's grief. For what could've been. For what I never gave Ford the chance to know. And the worst part? He was kind tonight. Still rough-edged, still infuriatingly controlled, still very much Ford Winters—but also open. Vulnerable, in the quiet looks and the way he said my name. The way he said June.

I press a fist to my chest, trying to settle the ache there.

He deserves to know.

But telling him changes everything. It risks Poppy's world. It risks mine. And selfishly, I don't know if I can stand to watch him look at me with betrayal in his eyes. I made a choice—right or wrong—to raise her on my own and now she's six and he's sitting across from me at dinner asking me to try again, not knowing he already has something that means so much more than a date or a kiss or a second chance.

He has a daughter.

He just doesn't know it yet.

THE FRONT DOOR CLICKS SHUT BEHIND ME AS I STEP ONTO THE porch, the night air cool against my flushed skin.

"Thanks again, Tessa," I say, walking the babysitter out to

her car. I wait until her headlights disappear down the street before I go back inside, locking the door behind me.

Tessa is a sweet 17-year-old-who lives two blocks over. She's always polite and responsible, and was recommended by a couple of teachers at Poppy's school who promised she was the babysitter that every parent trusted. It helps that Poppy adores her.

The house is quiet now. I toe off my shoes, shrug off my coat, and let the silence settle as I pad down the hallway. Poppy's door is cracked open the way it always is when she goes to bed, a slice of warm yellow light spilling into the hall.

She's curled up in bed, her princess gown twisted around her knees, her stuffed bunny tucked tight beneath her chin. One sock half-off. One arm flung to the side. I crouch beside her and smooth the hair from her forehead. For a moment all I do is stare. Memorize the curve of her cheek, the flutter of her lashes. The tiny sigh that escapes as she slips deeper into sleep.

She looks so much like him. She always has. And tonight, with his voice still in my ears and the scent of his cologne lingering, it's harder to pretend I can keep them apart forever.

"I saw your dad tonight," I whisper, my voice barely a breath.

My throat tightens. I blink hard, swallowing the emotion that's been clawing at me since dinner.

"You'd like him, Pop. He's stubborn and bossy, and he thinks he's always right—but he's good. He's so good. And he used to make me laugh so hard my stomach hurt."

She stirs but doesn't wake.

"I want to tell him," I add. "I just don't know how."

My fingers trail across her forehead one last time, then I press a kiss there before backing out of the room.

I leave the door cracked.

And this time, I close mine all the way—like that'll somehow keep the ghosts at bay.

FIFTEEN

Ford

I wake up too early. Again.

The house is still as I sit on the edge of the bed for a few moments, elbows on my knees, trying to shake off the constant reel of images in my mind.

I saw her last night.

Not just saw her—was with her. Walked beside her. Nearly kissed her under the stars like no time had passed. And then she pulled away, a sharp reminder that it had.

I drag a hand through my hair, scrub it over my jaw. I haven't trimmed the scruff on my face in two days. I'm sure I look as rough as I feel.

The coffee maker percolates in the kitchen. I don't even remember pressing the damn button. I pour a cup, black and scalding, and stand at the wall of windows, staring out over the expanse of trees. I've always felt like this is the most peaceful place in the world, but right now all I feel is lost, like everything I want is just out of reach. Landyn being back in Deep Cove changes everything.

Last night, after dinner, I hadn't planned on asking her if I could see her again. I don't know how I thought the evening would go, or what would come after, but when it came time to go our separate ways, all I knew is that I didn't want to say goodbye. The thought of Landyn and I going back to exchanging awkward, forced greetings in the office sat like a stone in my stomach. It's not enough. It's nowhere near enough. I still have unanswered questions, and I know that she isn't telling me the whole truth about why she's back in town. But when I am with her, I feel more like myself than I have in years. I feel understood in a way I don't with anyone else. It's familiar, comfortable, like returning to a place that used to feel like home. And the intense pull I feel towards her every time she walks into a room—I've only ever felt that with her, and it hasn't weakened in the time we've been apart. So last night, when she turned to leave, I couldn't let that be the end.

When I told her I wanted to see her again, I had expected her to be hesitant, maybe to offer up some excuse about it being a bad idea. Instead, she'd said nothing, but when I looked in her eyes it was like watching someone holding their breath underwater... and now, I can't stop thinking about her. About the reason she left. About the things she's still not telling me. About how much I want her anyway. But last night wasn't the right time to push her. I know Landyn, and she'll open up when she's ready.

My phone buzzes on the counter.

> Jesse: Meeting at 9. Bring coffee. Or donuts.
> Or both. You owe me.

By the time I arrive at Cove, the office is already in motion. I drop my jacket in my office and then head down the hall to pour myself a cup of coffee but stop dead in my tracks when I spot Jesse and Landyn in the shared workroom.

Jesse is standing too close again. He's leaned over the table, one hand braced on the back of her chair, an easy smile on his face. She's looking at something on her laptop, looking up at him every few seconds and gesturing enthusiastically with her hands the way she always does when she's trying to make a point.

It's too familiar between them. Too damn comfortable. I don't realize my jaw is locked until Becca walks past with a stack of papers and shoots me a look. "Good morning, Mr. Winters."

Jesse glances up just in time to catch my eye. He smiles at me, clearly amused, and then lifts his chin in my direction as if he's waiting for me to say something.

I don't.

I turn and walk straight back to my office.

Later in the day, I find Jesse in the break room sipping on one of those green juices that look like swamp water.

"You need something?" he asks.

I stare at him a beat too long. "Yeah. I need you to cut it out."

He blinks. "Cut what out?"

"The flirting."

Jesses chokes on his smoothie. "With who?"

I give him another look.

"*Oh,*" he says. "You're talking about Landyn." He grins like it's hilarious.

"It's not funny."

"Dude, you're acting like I'm hitting on your—"

"I'm not acting like anything," I snap. "Just keep it professional."

Jesse studies me for a second, more serious now. "Noted."

Just then Becca pops her head in. "Hey, Landyn left without the campaign files she was working on. Do you want me to call her? She'll need these tonight to prep for her presentation tomorrow at noon."

"It's fine," Jesse says. "I'll drop them by her place, so she doesn't have to come back in."

"I'll do it," I tell him, a little too quickly. "You have to get ready for tomorrow too, and I'm heading in that direction anyway."

A lie, but he thankfully doesn't call me on it. He just smirks. "Sure. Whatever you say, Ford."

Becca looks from me to Jesse and back again, before holding the folder out to me. I take the file and head back to my office to get my things, telling myself it's not a big deal. It's just a delivery. A favor. It's not an excuse to see her.

It's just a file. That's all.

I ignore the tiny voice that scratches at me, the one that whispers that the thought of Jesse in Landyn's home, being let into a part of her world that I haven't seen, was enough to make my blood go hot.

She's renting one of the old cottages on the edge of the cove —one of the Ashcroft properties. We used to come out here on weekends, back when we were in college and time felt endless and easy. We'd rent kayaks, pick up a couple of cheap sandwiches from the deli, and paddle until our arms gave out. Then we'd float in the sun along the water's edge, salt drying on our skin and the ocean breeze in our hair and play that dumb game she made up—Pick Your Dream House.

She'd always choose something small. Some place with wildflowers in the yard, a crooked porch strung with twinkle lights. A place that looked like it had a story.

I, of course, picked the opposite—big, sharp-lined, modern mansions. Imposing all-glass structures surrounded by perfect landscaping.

Half an hour later, I'm in my car, the asphalt giving way to gravel, the trees thickening on either side of the narrow lane. Eventually, I pull into the clearing, where the last cottage sits. In my memory, it was painted a washed-out baby blue, faded and battered by years of sun and ocean air. It had a small front porch that was missing a beam or two, an overgrown thicket of reeds obscuring its view of the water. The home I'm looking at now barely resembles that long-ago place. It has new cedar siding, white-framed windows, potted herbs on the steps. A porch swing sways gently in the breeze like it's been waiting for someone to take rest there. There's a pair of rain boots tucked neatly beside the door and a kid's bike leaning against the steps—probably a neighbor's, this area is full of young families. Everything about the cottage is soft, warm, and so unmistakably her.

I take a deep breath and swing open the truck door, file in hand. I should've texted her first. Actually, I should've just let someone else bring the damn file, but it's too late to turn and run now.

The porch creaks under my weight as I climb the steps, and I pause at the top. A child's sketchbook lies open on the bench beside the door, a rock holding a page in place. Crayon streaks of yellow, blue, and pink create something vaguely resembling a sun.

Something twists deep in my chest, but I ignore it, knocking on the door firmly and then taking a step back. It's just a moment, maybe two, but it stretches on for what feels like forever.

Then the door opens.

Hair pulled back, sweater falling off one shoulder. Her expression is caught somewhere between surprise and something heavier. Guilt, maybe. Or nerves. Or both.

"Ford," she says, her voice quiet, cautious. "What are you doing here?"

I hold up the file. "You left this. Becca said you'd need it tonight."

Her eyes drop to the folder. "Oh. Thank you. I...I didn't even realize I left it."

I nod, but I don't hand it over right away. My eyes flick past her shoulder into the warm, lived-in space behind her. Soft lighting, a blanket tossed over the arm of the couch, a mug on the entry table. Cozy. Safe. Hers.

Before I can say anything else, Landyn steps forward, quickly closing the door behind her and joining me on the porch. Her posture is careful. Guarded. Like she's nervous that I'm in her space.

"I haven't been out here in a while," I say, watching the tension settle in her shoulders. "Place looks different."

"It's been fixed up a bit."

"It's nice," I say after a beat. "It suits you."

Her fingers close around the file, but instead of lingering like last night, she pulls back quickly. Her movements are sharper now, like standing this close to me is a risk she doesn't want to take.

"Thanks again for bringing it by," she says, her voice tight. She shifts, already angling her body toward the door. "I should—"

"I didn't want you scrambling before the call," I interrupt, trying to keep my tone steady, trying to keep her here with me.

"Well, I've got it now, so I'm good."

She smiles, but it doesn't reach her eyes. I glance at the closed door behind her. "Everything okay?"

She nods, too quickly. "Yeah. Totally fine. I just have a lot to do before tomorrow."

She looks to the yard, then her eyes slide back to the door. Her stare is anywhere but on me. She's trying to shut the moment down, and I can feel it slipping away.

I don't know what I expected, but it wasn't this. Last night had felt intimate, vulnerable. Now it's like she's scrambling to rebuild the wall between us.

I try again. "I'm happy they cleaned the place up. It's a lot better than it used to be."

"Yeah, I guess," she says. "They did a nice job with the renovations. Anyway, I should—"

She takes a step backward and her heel bumps against the door. She nearly drops the file but catches it and clutches it against her chest like it's a shield.

I take a slow breath. "You always liked it out here."

"Ford," she whispers. "I... I really need to go." She fumbles with the doorknob behind her. "Thanks again."

I nod slowly. "Sure."

She opens the door, stepping quickly inside. Before she disappears, she hesitates—just for a second—and looks at me. There's something in her eyes. Like she wants to say more. Like she's just about to tell me something.

But she doesn't.

And then the door closes between us.

Again.

SIXTEEN

Landyn

I press my back against the door like that might somehow keep everything out. The guilt. The nerves. Him.

My fingers are still tight around the file, which feels like a brick in my hands. My heart is hammering in my chest, loud and wild.

Ford looked at me like he knew something. Like he was about to ask a question I'm not ready to answer. I squeeze my eyes shut, thinking of how I practically pushed him off the porch.

He was at my house—*our* house—and the swing was swaying, and Poppy's sketchbook was still sitting out, and her painted rocks sat in a line at the side of the porch, and there was so much he could've seen. So many clues scattered around like little breadcrumbs leading to the one truth I'm not ready to tell him.

That he has a daughter. That she sleeps in the room down the hall. That her favorite kind of pie is peach, and she wrinkles her nose when she's concentrating... just like him.

I drop the file on the living room table, walk into the kitchen and grip the counter with both hands until my knuckles turn white. When I saw the look in his eyes—soft, searching, maybe even forgiving—the truth was on the tip of my tongue so fast I almost let it slip.

Almost.

But if I tell him now, everything changes. Not just for me. Not just for Ford.

For Poppy.

And that feels too dangerous. I take a deep breath and let it out slowly. Then I turn toward the hallway to get Poppy ready for her bath. I need to get her into bed, clean up the kitchen, put the laundry in the dryer, and then get to work.

For now, the truth stays locked inside me.

But the weight of it? It's getting harder to carry.

THE HOUSE IS QUIET.

Poppy's been asleep for a few hours, and I'm curled up in bed with the lamp low and my phone in my hand, scrolling through absolutely nothing. I'm not even pretending to read anymore. I'm just waiting for the sleep that won't come.

My phone buzzes.

> Ford: You still stay up too late?

A smile tugs at my lips before I can stop it.

> Me: Bold of you to assume I'm not already
> asleep like a responsible adult.

Ford: It's 10:58. You never made it to bed before midnight when I knew you.

Me: Fair enough. I guess some things never change.

The dots appear, flicker, disappear.

Ford: Some do. But not everything needs to.

There's a pause. The kind that feels loaded.

Ford: Can I ask you something?

Me: I think so.

Ford: Where were you living before you came back?

Me: Alberta. I lived with my aunt in her tiny, split-level house. It needed some work…the dishwasher or the washing machine was always breaking, and no AC so the place was an oven in the summer. But there was a little park across the street, and I could hear the birds singing in the morning. There was something nice about that.

Ford: You always liked being surrounded by nature. I remember you once said quiet made you feel safe.

Me: It still does. You still hate the city?

Ford: Too many people and not enough trees.

Me: You sound like you're 80 years old.

Ford: You sound like the girl who once made
me pull over in the pouring rain just to watch
the fog roll across the lake.

Me: It was beautiful.

Ford: It was freezing, and you had no jacket. I
gave you mine and then got sick for a week.

Me: Worth it. You always did have a hero
complex.

Ford: Just for you.

My hearts skips. Once. Maybe Twice.
I don't respond right away. I just stare at the screen.

Ford: See you Saturday, Lan.

Another text follows with his address. For just a moment, I picture myself alone with Ford, in his home, but I immediately abandon the mental image. There is no way I can let that happen. I'll make up an excuse on Saturday morning.

Me: Goodnight, Ford.

Ford: Night, June.

I'm barely three steps into the office when I see it—a small box, wrapped in the same brown paper, sitting neatly in the center of my desk.

Again.

My stomach does a little flip.

I drop my bag in my chair and then quickly glance out the door, half-expecting to find him watching, waiting, but Ford's nowhere to be seen. Just Becca typing rapidly at her computer and Marco stirring a heaping spoonful of sugar into his morning coffee at the counter across the room.

I sit behind my desk and unwrap the package as quietly as I can, trying not to draw attention. Inside is a simple and elegant matte black, hardcover journal, heavy in my hands. The kind you want to fill with things that matter.

There's no note this time. Just a folded scrap of paper tucked inside the cover with one word written in his familiar, slanted handwriting:

June.

I suck in a breath and quickly tuck it into my bag, but I'm too late. Becca's already peering at me over a laptop she has clutched to her chest where she stands in my doorway. "Ooh. What's that?"

"Nothing," I say, a little too quickly.

Marco walks over, eyebrows raised. "That is not nothing. That's a gift. At work. On a Friday."

Becca grins. "Very mysterious. Do you have a secret admirer?"

"Don't be ridiculous," I stammer, shoving the journal deeper into my bag.

"Okay, Bec. Looks like we'll have to guess," Marco says, eyes gleaming.

"I know! Is it from the hot contractor guy who was in here on Monday?" Becca asks. "Because I would be totally rooting for that."

"No," I say, shaking my head.

Marco is tapping a finger against his lower lip, clearly enjoying this a little too much.

"I'm going to guess... Seth."

Becca coughs out a laugh.

"Isn't that the guy in shipping with the bad combover?" I ask as they crack up.

"Hey, don't sleep on Seth," Marco objects, composing himself. "Did you know he once toured with Guns N' Roses? He was a sound engineer or something. The guy's a legend."

"I'm sure he is," I say, laughing now.

"Wait," Marco says suddenly, narrowing his eyes. "Is it from Ford?"

Becca gasps. "*Ford* Ford?"

I hesitate for half a second too long.

Becca practically squeals. "Oh my God! It is from him."

I groan. "Can we not make this a thing?"

Marco smirks. "Too late. This is absolutely a thing."

Becca leans across the desk, all faux-casual. "How do you know him? Please say you had a torrid summer fling with the CEO."

I inhale a breath and look up at the ceiling while I try to figure out what to say. Their jaws drop in unison when my gaze lands back on theirs.

"You're kidding," Marco says.

"Don't turn this into more than it is," I plead.

"Whatever it is, just know that we are all the way in," Becca says, grinning. "Tell us more."

I shake my head, trying not to smile. "There's nothing going on. We're just...old friends."

Marco snorts. "Old friends who used to get it on. He's giving you gifts, Landyn. That's gotta mean something."

I glance at my bag again, the journal tucked out of sight but still pulsing in my mind like it's a timebomb. I don't know what makes me say it; maybe it's the way the three of us have become fast friends or maybe I'm just tired of keeping everything so tightly wound.

I sigh and lean against the edge of my desk. "I've known Ford for a long time."

Marco arches a brow. "Define long."

Becca leans in like she's about to miss the plot twist of a soap opera. "Like... met-him-at-a-party-a-year-ago long? Or I-had-a-crush-on-him-in-high-school long?"

I pause. "We were... together... for a while."

Becca's jaw drops. "You dated Ford Winters?"

"Years ago. Back in college. Before he launched Cove. Before all of this," I say, waving a hand at the office around us.

Becca points at me. "So, you're the one he built character over."

"I'm sorry? What does that mean?"

"There's this office hunch," she says, her voice lowering even though there's no one within earshot, "that something happened a long time ago that made him swear off anything resembling fun. Or dating. Or joy."

Marco nods in agreement. "He's always so serious and no one has ever seen or heard of him being with a woman. Even though the man is clearly very dateable."

Becca nods. "So, you're the one who made him swear off fun."

"I didn't do any of that," I protest, laughing despite myself. "We were young. It ended. That's it."

Marco looks pointedly at my bag and then back at me. "Does it look like it ended to you?"

My heart twists a little. "I don't know what it looks like."

"I can tell you what it looks like to me," Becca says, arms crossed as she leans against my desk with a satisfied grin on her face. "Ford Winters left a gift on your desk, and now you're blushing."

"I'm not blushing."

"You are absolutely blushing."

I shake my head and grab a pen just to give my hands something to do. "You two are impossible."

Marco smirks. "We prefer deeply invested."

"And on that note... how does this play out?" Becca muses. "Secret office romance? A second chance at love?

"None of the above," I say, though my voice comes out a little softer than I mean it to. Because the truth is that I have no idea how it plays out.

Becca and Marco reluctantly return to their work, leaving me at my desk, alone with my thoughts of the gift and the way Ford had written *June*. No note. Just that one word. That name that only he ever called me, and before I can talk myself out of it, I'm standing in front of his office door, lifting my hand to knock.

Two soft taps.

"Yes," he calls from inside.

I step in, and he looks up from his desk, surprised but controlled. His gaze holds steady on mine, and he sits up in his chair. "Hey."

"I just..." I hesitate in the doorway, fingers still curled around the door handle. "I wanted to say thank you. For the journal."

His brow softens, just a little. "You like it?"

"I do." I smile. "You were always good at that, picking out gifts that I would actually use and love."

A moment stretches between us. There are things I could say. That I read his text messages last night three times before going to sleep. That I almost replied again just to keep the thread going.

But instead, I nod. "Well, that's all," I say, backing up a step. "Just... thanks."

He watches me for a beat before standing up and rounding his desk. "Landyn."

I pause in the doorway.

"You don't have to thank me for remembering what you like."

My chest tightens. I don't have a good answer for that, so I just meet his eyes for a second too long, nod once, and step out of his office before I unravel.

SEVENTEEN

L andyn
The text is still open on my screen.

Short and direct. No pressure. But somehow, that message on my phone feels like a grenade in my hand that I've been staring at it for the past 20 minutes. I told myself I'd make the call when the time came.

Well, it's here.

I'm sitting cross-legged on my bed, still wearing leggings and a T-shirt, hair half-dry from the quick shower I took after Poppy left with my dad.

It was a great day. Poppy had her dance class this morning. She wore her sparkly pink leotard and twirled through the studio; her little face lit up like the sun breaking through on the first warm day of spring.

After class, we got ice cream—chocolate for her, vanilla for me. We sat on the curb outside the café, our knees bumping, and she told me about a kid in her class who can do a cartwheel and how she thinks she might try it tomorrow in the living room, but only when Grandma isn't looking.

My mom texted not long after, asking if Poppy wanted to stay over at their house for the night. Her response? A very enthusiastic, jumping-on-the-couch "yes!" My mom assured me she was feeling good today, that she actually slept through the night for once, and Dad would be home to help keep Poppy entertained.

So now I'm home, alone, trying to ignore the voice that keeps whispering that maybe it's a sign that my mom offered to take Poppy tonight without me even needing to ask. I pull my knees up, rest my chin on them, and read Ford's text again.

Dinner. His place.

Eight years ago, I wouldn't have hesitated. Eight years ago, I would've run to him. But tonight, I keep asking myself the question I've been avoiding all week.

If I go to his place… how much of me is going to come back different?

Thirty minutes later I'm behind the wheel, not quite sure how I ended up here, trying to think of nothing other than the directions coming from my GPS.

The road winds away from the center of town, each turn pulling me deeper into the quiet stretch of mountains and trees. I pass the shops, the school, the old gas station, and then I'm on the highway before turning up the mountain, the town eventually fading away behind me.

The drive steepens as pine trees press in on both sides, tall and dark and swaying in the evening breeze. Homes occasionally dot the rugged landscape, long, paved driveways leading to sprawling properties. I grip the steering wheel a little tighter.

It's a far cry from where Ford grew up, but I'm not surprised he ended up here. Even when we were young, he always had his eyes on the finer things. This part of town isn't really town anymore. It's vaster, quiter, harder to reach. And the privacy that lends owners doesn't come cheap.

I know Cove does well, but this?

This is another world.

My little car feels out of place as I follow the final turn, climbing into a neighborhood of sleek, modern estates, all glass and cedar, the ocean glittering below them like a million scattered diamonds.

When I spot his driveway—long, sloped, carved into the mountainside—I have to double check the address before turning in slowly.

His house sits at the top, tucked behind a row of towering spruce trees. The sun's just starting to set, painting the sky in soft lavender and gold. The home itself isn't flashy but it's still stunning, with clean lines and big windows, and a dark wood exterior that blends into the landscape. A place built for someone who's done running. Someone who's rooted now.

I park, cut the engine, and take a deep breath to calm my nerves. I'm still not sure I should be alone with Ford, but there's no backing out now. I grab my purse and step out into the cool evening air, tinged with salt and the faint scent of pine. I tug my sweater more tightly around me, suddenly aware of how quiet it is up here. No traffic. No chatter. Just the wind through the trees and the distant, steady crash of the ocean below.

I glance down at myself as I make my way up the stone path. I didn't overthink it—at least, not too much. My favorite jeans, ankle boots, a soft cream sweater that falls off one shoulder without meaning to. Casual but not careless. Comfortable but not lazy.

My hair's down in loose waves. At first, I had pulled it back into a loose bun, but when I looked at my reflection it felt too... controlled. Tonight, I don't want to wear armor. I want to see what happens when I don't.

I pause at the front door, heart thudding, then I lift my hand

and knock before I have a chance to second guess what I'm doing here. A breath later, I hear movement inside, and then the door opens to Ford.

He's standing barefoot in faded jeans and a fitted charcoal Henley that clings to his chest and arms like it was made for him. His hair's a little messy, like he ran a hand through it one too many times, and he holds a half-full whiskey glass in one hand. At his feet sits a black and white dog with the sweetest face and curious eyes.

"Well, hey there," I say, crouching instinctively. "Who are you?"

"Stella," Ford says. "She's friendly."

Stella's whole body leans into my touch when I scratch her behind her ears and she gives me a soft little huff of approval. With a final pat, I straighten to find Ford watching me.

He looks like he's been pacing. Or brooding. Or both. He's breathtakingly handsome. His eyes land on me, and for a second, neither of us says anything. Then he speaks, voice low, soft around the edges. "I'm glad you came."

"I can't believe this is where you live." My gaze drifts to the view of the ocean behind me, the perfectly manicured lawn.

"Shocking, I know," he deadpans. "Half the time, I still feel like a kid who shouldn't be parking in this neighborhood, let alone living here."

My heart tugs. "Ford...it's beautiful. You deserve it."

Something flickers behind his eyes. Not quite relief. Not quite surprise. Something that says this moment means more than either of us wants to admit. He steps back and gestures for me to come in.

I cross the threshold slowly, my boots echoing softly off the wide-plank hardwood before I toe them off. The house smells like cedar and whatever cologne he always wears. It's woodsy and warm and familiar enough to make my chest ache.

The entryway opens up into a large, open concept living

space. It has high ceilings and huge windows that look out over the water. A sleek kitchen with black cabinets and gold hardware that somehow feels both modern and lived in. There's a fire lit in the fireplace, low and crackling.

The house is stunning, and I can feel him in every detail.

"This is incredible, Ford," I say, not sure where to put my hands or my nerves.

He closes the door behind me. "Thanks. Built it a few years ago."

I turn to face him again, heart thudding. He studies me for a moment, like he's trying to remember something and hold onto it all at once.

"You look beautiful," he says finally.

"So do you," I say. "I mean... not... you look good."

He nods, smiling, then gestures toward the living room. "Can I get you something to drink?"

"A glass of wine if you have it, that would be great."

He disappears into the kitchen, and I take a deep breath. I touch the soft leather of the couch, grounding myself.

I'm here.

He's here.

And the space between us feels like something waiting to catch fire.

I wander slowly toward the windows, letting my fingers trail along the smooth edge of the console table beneath them. The view is unreal—open water stretching out for miles under a darkening sky, the last traces of sun flickering along the horizon.

Behind me, I hear the quiet clink of glass and the hum of the fridge door opening.

"You still like an ice cube in the glass?" he calls, not looking up.

The question startles me. For a moment, it's like no time has passed.

"Yeah," I say. "I do."

He comes to stand beside me at the window, his fingers brushing mine as he hands me the glass of wine. "Thanks."

He nods once, then turns back toward the stove. I follow. There's a pan already resting on the burners, and I catch the scent of garlic and herbs, something roasting in the oven. It's the kind of smell that makes you feel at home, cared for.

"You cook now?" I tease gently, moving to lean against the kitchen island.

He glances at me, mouth twitching. "I actually cook pretty well, thank you very much."

I lift a brow. "That's new."

He tosses a towel over his shoulder. "A man can learn."

I take a sip from my wine glass, watching him as he stirs the pan, then adds something from a small bowl on the counter. He moves with a quiet confidence, just like he does at the office and, I imagine, everywhere else.

"What are you making?" I ask.

"Miso-glazed seared halibut with roast vegetables."

I blink. "Okay, Gordon Ramsay."

He shrugs one shoulder. "You're not the only one who evolved."

I smile despite myself. "You really didn't have to go to this much trouble."

"I wanted to," he says simply.

I watch him in the low kitchen light, sleeves pushed up, brow slightly furrowed in concentration. There's something intimate about it—standing here while he cooks for me, the air thick with memory and the ache of wishing things could be simple again.

But they're not. And maybe they never will be.

Still, we're here.

And that has to mean something.

Ten minutes later, dinner is ready and plated. Ford sets the plates on the dining table then pulls out a chair and gestures for me to sit. I try not to stare at the way his forearms flex as he reaches beside me to adjust the silverware.

I take a bite first of the halibut that turns out to be perfectly cooked and let out a quiet hum of surprise. "Okay...this is actually amazing."

"Actually?" he asks, raising an eyebrow. "You sound shocked."

"I just didn't expect—" I stop, laughing. "You used to survive on ramen and black coffee."

"And now look at me." He lifts his glass slightly. "Practically domesticated."

I smile, but something in my chest tightens. This version of him is new to me, but still so familiar. Like the man I loved never really left. It's disarming how easy it feels to sit here with him, how quickly my guard wants to drop. My mind keeps flashing to the way his hand brushed mine when he passed the bread, the way his eyes softened when I laughed at something small. It's dangerous, letting myself enjoy this. Because underneath it all, I don't know what this means. I don't know what he wants from me, from us. And before I can talk myself out of it, the question slips out.

"Why am I here? Why did you invite me to dinner?"

He doesn't blink. "Because I wanted to spend time with you."

I glance down at my plate, my appetite fading as the weight of that answer settles. "It's just that simple?"

"It could be." His voice is low and steady, but there's heat beneath it. Controlled, but barely.

I look up. He's watching me intensely. The air between us feels heavy now. "I don't know what you're hoping for," I say quietly.

He leans forward, elbows on the table, his gaze locked on mine. "I'm not hoping. I'm wanting."

I swallow. Hard. Now is the time to look away. To shut it down. To laugh it off, get through dinner, and then get out of here.

But I don't because I can't. I've always been powerless to Ford Winters.

"I'm remembering," Ford tells me, eyes still on me.

I stare back. "And what exactly are you remembering?"

The corner of his mouth lifts, just slightly. "How you used to eat the tomatoes off my plate. How you would hum a little when you were concentrating on something. How you always wore socks to bed, even in the summer." He pauses, eyes locked on mine. "I'm remembering what it's like to want something and not know if I get to have it again."

I'm pretty sure I gasp. The table between us feels too small. The air feels too hot. There's a hum under everything. Desire. His eyes flick to my mouth and back, and I feel it like a jolt.

I reach for my wine just to do something with my hands. I push a roasted carrot around my plate, pretending I'm still hungry. I'm not. The food is perfect, but I couldn't taste a single bite after what he just confessed. He watches every movement. The tension in the room crackles and it feels like we're hurtling towards a cliff edge at full speed.

And the worst part is...I want it. I want him even though I know better. There's no way this ends well. Not when he finds out the secret I've been keeping.

We finish dinner in silence. Ford watching me, quiet, eyes dark like he's trying to decide what to do next.

"I'll help clean up," I say, voice too tight, my chair scraping against the floor as I rise abruptly from my chair before I can unravel.

"You don't have to." His voice is measured, steady.

"I want to."

We move around the kitchen in sync. I wash the plates, he

dries them. He hands me a towel. I pass him the silverware. It's too easy. Too familiar. Too *us*.

I pass him the last plate, our fingers brushing briefly. He takes it, towel in hand, and starts to dry. When I glance up, his gaze is already on me. Steady. A little unguarded. Something in my chest pulls tight.

"I used to picture this," he says, voice like gravel, quiet but heavy enough to land deep. "You in this kitchen with me. Not just for a night. For longer."

The words steal the air from my lungs.

"I know I shouldn't admit that," he adds. "But it's true."

I turn slowly to face him as if any sudden movement will shatter the fragile thread between us. His eyes catch mine— steady, searching—and then he lifts a hand. The pad of his finger grazes my temple as he tucks a strand of hair behind my ear. It's a soft, almost meaningless gesture. Except it isn't. His touch lingers, the heat of his skin searing in the space between us.

"Tell me not to kiss you," he murmurs.

The words hang there, dangerous and impossible.

I should say it.

I should stop him.

But my breath catches, and before I realize I'm moving, I step forward.

He meets me halfway, fingers sliding along my jaw, feather-light, testing, like he's bracing for me to pull away. I don't. I tip closer, pulled by something older than our hurt.

When our lips meet, it's not tentative—it's urgent.

Like no time has passed.

His lips fuse to mine, warm and firm, and the second he deepens the kiss, tilting his head, parting his mouth, I let out the softest breath against him. His tongue grazes mine, slow and unhurried, but full of intent.

My fingers curl into the front of his shirt before I can stop them, gripping the soft fabric like it might anchor me, like if I don't hold onto something, I might fall apart right here in his kitchen.

He tastes like whiskey and heat and something that aches down my spine. His hand slides down to my waist, large and steady, drawing me in until my chest presses against his. He kisses me deeper then, longer, and my knees nearly go weak from the weight of it. From the way he groans low in his throat when I kiss him back just as hard.

It's not frantic. It's not careful. It's slow and devastating and full of everything we've tried not to say. Everything we lost. Everything we still want.

When we finally pull apart, it's not because we want to, it's because we have to.

His forehead rests against mine, our breath tangled in the small space between us. I feel the rise and fall of his chest against mine, the faint tremble in his fingers, still gripping my waist. Then his hand slides slowly—deliberately—from my waist to my hip, then lower, fingers brushing along the curve of my thigh through my jeans.

"Lan," he utters raggedly into my mouth. "Oh god."

"I know—,"

His eyes lift to mine. Something sharp flickers there—desire, frustration, a kind of hunger I remember too well.

Then he leans in and kisses me again, this time with no hesitation.

His mouth claims mine—slow, deep, like he's trying to relearn every inch of me. His tongue sweeps across my lower lip, coaxing it open, and I melt into it, gasping softly as he kisses me harder, like he's been waiting years to taste me again.

I don't move away. I can't.

His hands slide up, over my ribs, under my sweater, fingertips grazing my skin, and I shiver at the contact. His touch is careful but possessive.

He pulls back just long enough to look at me. His voice is rough. "Tell me to stop."

I don't. I can't.

He searches my face for hesitation, and when he doesn't find it, he nods once and then he lifts me in one fluid motion and sets me gently on the kitchen counter, stepping between my legs like he belongs there.

Because he does and always has.

His hands slide under my thighs, pulling me flush against him. I gasp when I feel how hard he is through his jeans, and he growls softly at the sound.

"You drive me fucking crazy," he mutters, dragging his mouth down my neck, kissing and tasting until my head tips back and my hands grip the edge of the counter like it's the only thing keeping me from falling apart.

His fingers slip beneath the hem of my sweater, slowly, reverently, dragging the fabric up my stomach. I raise my arms, and he peels it off me, tossing it somewhere behind him. His eyes move over me, hot and sharp, like he doesn't know where to touch first.

But he does.

His hands slide up my sides, fingers grazing the edge of my bra. His thumbs sweep lightly over the swell of my breasts, and I whimper at the contact.

He kisses me again, deeper this time, tongue sliding against mine, hips pressing forward until there's nothing left between us but heat and memory and the ache of how much we still want this.

"God, Landyn," he murmurs, breath ragged. "You feel the same. You taste the same. You still ruin me."

I pull in a shaky breath, my fingers gripping his shoulders, nails digging slightly into his skin.

And all I can think—through the fog of want and heat and

everything we've been holding back—is that I've never been kissed like this. Not before him. Not after.

Not like this.

He groans against my mouth, and the sound of it nearly undoes me. The way his hands move like he knows me. Like he still remembers what I like, where to touch, how to make me melt with just his thumbs brushing under the curve of my breasts.

"Jesus, June," he murmurs against my neck, voice wrecked. "It's so easy to get lost in you."

I gasp when his hips press forward, grinding his erection slow against me. The friction shoots through me, and my fingers dig into the back of his shirt.

Every move, every sound, every breath feels like we're falling deeper into something we may not be able to undo.

I want him. God, I want him.

But then—I see her.

Poppy. In the back of my mind, like a whisper. And it slams through me, like ice in my veins.

I freeze.

Ford feels it instantly. His mouth stills. His hands pause at my ribs. His forehead drops against mine, his breath still ragged.

"What is it?" he asks, voice low. "Where did you just go?"

I shake my head, chest tight. "I can't."

He doesn't move. Doesn't step away. Just breathes with me, forehead still pressed to mine.

"Hey," he says softly. "It's okay. I'm not going anywhere. We don't have to rush."

I nod, even though I'm not sure it is okay.

His hands slowly fall away from my body, dragging longing and regret with them.

I slide off the counter and land on shaky legs, my bra strap slipping slightly down one shoulder. He reaches for my sweater

—quietly, without a word—and hands it to me. I pull it on, swallowing hard.

"I'm sorry," I say, avoiding his eyes.

"Don't be." His voice is calm, but there's an ache underneath. "You don't owe me anything."

I grab my bag, fingers trembling slightly, and when I turn back, he's just standing there—jaw tight, eyes unreadable.

But he doesn't try to stop me.

And that almost hurts more than if he had.

EIGHTEEN

Ford

Her sweater is back on, and her purse is in her hand, and I know that she's leaving. I stay where I am, every part of me wanting to reach for her again, but also knowing that I can't. I don't want her to feel cornered. Still, I can't let her walk out of here without saying something.

"Landyn."

She looks up, slowly. I know there are things she could say too, but her expression, still guarded, tells me she's still not ready.

"You don't have to explain," I tell her gently. "I just want you to know it's okay. We're good."

She nods, but I see the way her throat works when she swallows. "I didn't come here planning for that to happen," she says.

"I didn't either."

She lets out the smallest breath of a laugh. "Yeah, well... you didn't have your sweater on the floor."

A smile tugs at my mouth and I'm grateful to her for easing the heaviness that has settled around us.

"I didn't stop because I didn't want you," she adds, voice softer now.

My heart bottoms out to my feet. I feel every word. "I know," I say, and I mean it, and still, it nearly kills me to say it without pulling her back into me. But I don't. Instead, I move toward her slowly, reaching up to tuck a strand of hair behind her ear. My fingers brush her cheek, and she lets her eyes flutter closed for just a second.

"You don't owe me anything," I say, and she nods again. This time when her gaze meets mine there is something close to sadness in it. "Come on," I murmur. "Let me walk you out."

We step into the night together, the cold brushing over both of us pulling us back into reality. We walk slowly, like neither of us is ready for the evening to end. I walk beside her, close enough to touch her but fighting the urge to do just that. When we reach her car, Landyn turns to face me.

"Thanks for dinner," she says quietly.

"Thanks for showing up."

I step closer and wrap my arms around her. She leans into it and that's all I need. With a sigh, she sinks into me without hesitation, arms sliding around my waist, face against my chest, and when she takes a deep breath, it feels like maybe whatever is weighing on her lightens just a little. I press a slow, lingering kiss to her forehead without saying anything else then I hold her until she pulls away.

I open her car door, and she slides into the driver's seat. And then she's gone, leaving me standing here with my hands in my pockets, watching her taillights disappear into the dark.

I already miss her.

I wait until the sound of her tires on the pavement fades and the silence settles back in like it never left, then I head inside. The feel of her mouth on mine, the whisper of my name on her lips, still lingers. I look at the counter where she sat. Her glass is still there, half-full. The kitchen still smells like the faintest scent of her shampoo. It's soft. Familiar. And it makes my chest ache. I run a hand through my hair and let out a breath I didn't realize I was holding.

We were close. Closer than we've been to anything real in a long damn time. And then she pulled back. And I let her because whatever's holding her in place—it's bigger than me. But I felt the way her body arched into mine like it was second nature. The way she looked at me later—like she hated leaving and couldn't stay all at once.

She wanted me, but I felt it the second it changed—when something else slammed into her hard enough to shatter that moment between us.

I walk to the window and rest my hand on the frame, staring out into the dark. *What is she hiding?* I know guilt. I know uncertainty. That's not what pulled her from my arms and sent her running. It was heavier, like she's guarding something.

Tonight left me with even more questions about the woman I used to know better than I knew myself. One thing is for certain, though: whatever secret she's keeping, it can't stay hidden forever. It's bubbling closer to the surface, whether she's ready or not.

"She's not just here for work," I say out loud. "She didn't just come back to Deep Cove for a job."

I'm at Cove early the next morning, buried in reports. Bad press keeps snowballing faster than we can contain it. The kind of press that can make people forget about all the things we've done right. I shove my hands through my hair and close the window on my computer, moving to this week's schedule. It's packed.

Board updates, supplier negotiations, a feature piece with *Pacific Lifestyle Magazine* that Landyn is spearheading, plus a meeting with the bank to secure the last distribution of funds for the factory. Every minute is accounted for. And next week's no better.

The Greenstream partnership we've been working on still isn't finalized, and this morning I learned that there's a three-day summit in Whistler starting Friday—a chance to meet with investors and sustainability leaders, and hopefully generate the kind of PR that could go a long way towards salvaging Cove's reputation.

This is important. It's our chance to prove to our clients and shareholders that the company's values are more than just words on paper. That we have the vision and the drive to position ourselves as a global leader in this sphere. It's critical, and it's something that Landyn needs to be a part of.

I reach for my phone and type out the message without overthinking it.

> Me: Block off next Friday through Sunday. We're going to Whistler for the Sustainability Summit. I want you there for the panels and meetings. Clear your schedule if you need to.

I return to the consumer reports that Jesse sent me this morning, but I'm distracted, checking my phone every few minutes to see if she's replied. Twenty minutes later, I give up my weak attempts to get any work done. I leave my office, glancing at Landyn's empty desk as I pass it. I head to the workspace where she and Jesse usually meet in the morning. When I don't find her there, I scan the floor, hoping to catch sight of her. Nothing.

I drag a hand through my hair in frustration, all too aware of the fact that instead of dealing with the dozens of emails needing responses from me, I'm wandering around the place like a lovesick teenager.

Until I see her.

She's in the lunchroom, her back to me, pouring coffee into a branded Cove mug. She's dressed more casually than she usually is at the office—jeans, a fitted black sweater, ankle boots—but it's a gut punch. Effortless. Beautiful. The sun shining through the window catches the natural highlights in her hair, which is pulled back off her face. When she turns and sees me standing just outside the doorway, her eyes widen just a fraction, and she smiles.

"You following me, Winters?"

"Maybe." I smirk.

The air shifts between us. Thickens.

I close the distance slowly, not crowding her, but enough that she feels it. The space narrows. My pulse kicks harder.

"You got my message?" I ask, keeping my tone casual even though I feel anything but when I'm around her.

Her fingers curl around the mug. "Whistler. Three days."

Every nerve in my body fires up being this close to her again. I keep telling myself to take it slow, play it cool, but she makes it impossible. She's magnetic, every glance or smile pulling me in, daring me to forget all the reasons I should hold back. My heart's hammering in my chest, and I'm not sure if it's from the memory of kissing her yesterday or from how badly I want to do it now.

"Two nights," I add, watching her carefully. "You'll be there?"

She gives a small shrug. "You're not really giving me a choice."

"You're the only one who can handle it. This—" I gesture loosely, meaning Cove, the scandal, all of it, "—this needs you."

It's true, and she knows it. For a moment, she looks away, out the window, like she's weighing what this really means.

Three days away with me. When her gaze returns, it's sharp. Unflinching.

"Will anyone else be joining us?" she asks cooly.

"Jesse is trying to be there for some of it." She nods as if she's appraising me. "And what do you think about it, Lan? About us being away for the weekend?"

"I think you need me there," she says, meeting my gaze. "For Cove."

My mouth curves, but the look in my eyes is serious. I exhale slowly, stepping in closer, bracing my hands on either side of the counter she's leaning against. I'm close enough to feel the warmth of her but not touching. Not quite. Not yet.

"What are you *really* thinking, Ford?"

"I'm thinking," I say, voice low, "that I want to kiss you right now, but I don't know what the rules are anymore."

Her breath catches. Just barely. But I see it. "You've never cared much for rules," she says, trying for coy, but her voice betrays her.

"I haven't," I admit. "But I've never been this worried about messing things up, either."

She's quiet for a moment. Eyes searching mine. "What are you afraid of ruining?" she asks, softer now.

I don't hesitate. "Us."

Maybe I shouldn't have said it. But it's the truth. It's how I feel.

For a breathless moment, she just stands there, staring up at me, but she doesn't walk away.

I reach out, slow but sure, and brush my fingers along her forearm. It's feather light, barely there, but I feel her shiver under my touch. Her eyes close for a heartbeat and when they open, they're softer. Warmer. I don't kiss her. Not here.

"See you in the boardroom, Sinclair," I say, voice low, pushing off the counter.

That's enough for now.

NINETEEN

Landyn

The kettle whistles, sharp and shrill, but it barely registers through the thud of my heartbeat. It's too early for this kind of adrenaline. But here I am—pacing my tiny kitchen, double-checking my bag, glancing at the clock for the fifth time in as many minutes.

Ford said he'd pick me up at 8 a.m. and drive us to Whistler. It's 7:42.

"Landyn, sweetheart, you're going to wear a groove in the floor," my mom calls from the living room, her tone warm but amused.

I glance over to see her perched on the couch, coffee in hand, like this is just any other morning. Poppy's curled up beside her, half-watching cartoons, half-singing to herself, blissfully unaware of the storm brewing in my chest.

"I'm fine," I lie, shoving my charger into my tote.

"You're nervous."

"I'm not nervous."

"Of course you are," she says, smiling into her cup. "It's Ford."

I freeze. "It's work."

"Mm hm," she hums, unconvinced.

Two nights ago, I'd asked my mom if she and my dad would mind taking Poppy for a few days so I could attend the conference in Whistler. I didn't want it to be too much for them, especially my mom, so I arranged to have Tessa take Poppy both afternoons to give them a break. I sat at her kitchen table when I asked, twisting my hands together like an anxious teenager asking for permission to stay out past curfew.

"Will Ford be there too?" she asked. I wasn't surprised; my mom has always been direct. She also doesn't shy away from sharing her opinion—whether it's asked for or not.

"Yes, he'll be there. It's an important conference."

She nodded, looking at me thoughtfully. "Seems like your paths have been crossing quite a bit since you came back to town."

"He owns the company I work for, Mom. It would be hard for us not to see each other."

"Landyn, I'm not going to tell you what to do. But I do think you need to be honest with yourself. You've kept Poppy from him even now that the two of you are living in Deep Cove. Is that still about protecting her? Or is that about fear?"

Her words landed like an anchor in the pit of my stomach. When I made the decision to leave here, I did it to protect my child. I was protecting Ford too. I found out I was pregnant and panicked. Not just about the baby, but about Ford, about what it would mean for him. He had dreams. Big ones. He was working like hell to build something out of nothing; to prove he wasn't his father. To give him and his brothers the life they all deserved. And kids? He wasn't even sure he wanted them. Not yet. Maybe not ever.

So, I left. At first, it was just for space. To think, to breathe, to figure out what I was going to do.

But one day turned into two, and two turned into weeks,

and then... it was too late. I'd gone too far to turn around without shattering everything.

"It wasn't easy, and maybe it wasn't even right, but I made the best choice I could," I reminded my mom, tears pricking my eyes.

She reached across the table, her hand warm over mine. "I know, honey, but you're not that scared girl anymore, and he's not the boy he was when you left."

She agreed to watch P but not before giving me one more bit of advice: "You don't have to have all the answers right now but if he's going to be part of your life again in any way, you owe him the truth."

I couldn't meet her eyes after that, but I knew she was right. I need to tell Ford about his daughter.

But how? It's all I've thought about for the past two days, my stomach in knots. I still don't have an answer. I check my phone, hoping for some last-minute reprieve. Maybe Ford can't make it after all. Maybe the entire thing has been cancelled.

No new messages. No escape.

"Hey, Pops?" Mom tickles her tiny foot. "If we want to make those pancakes we talked about, we need to get moving."

Poppy's head snaps up, eyes wide. "Let's go!"

My mom chuckles softly. "Then Tessa wants to take you to the pool."

I shoot her a grateful look. She catches it, says nothing.

"Shoes, go," I say, motioning toward the door. Poppy bounces off the couch and hurries to grab her sneakers. She's still humming as she wriggles into them, blissfully unaware of why I'm herding them out the door like it's a fire drill.

Ford can't see her.

Not today.

This conference is important to Ford and to Cove. He can't afford to be distracted.

"Landyn, it's not a bad thing to be nervous," my mom says quietly as she shrugs on her coat. "It just means it matters."

I nod. She's right and that's exactly the problem. It matters. It's everything.

I open the door, my heart hammering.

"Alright, girls," I say, forcing a smile. "Have fun. Text me later, okay?"

Poppy lunges in for a quick hug. "Love you, Mama."

My throat tightens. "Love you too. I'm going to miss you, my Poppyseed."

I watch them walk down the path, Poppy's backpack bouncing with each step. My mom throws me a last look over her shoulder—half-encouragement, half-warning. I close the door before it can settle.

Not five minute later, the sound of tires crunching on gravel has my pulse spiking. Ford is here.

There's a knock on the door. Solid. Sure. Just like him. I take a deep breath, placing a hand over my stomach to calm my nerves. Then I open it.

Ford stands there in faded jeans, a Cove jacket over a fitted black Henley, sunglasses hooked in the collar. His hair still has that just-showered look, like he ran his hands through it and every strand fell exactly where it's meant to. It suits him.

"Morning," he says, voice low, eyes scanning mine. He has this way of looking at me like he's cataloguing every thought I'm trying to hide.

"Morning." My fingers tighten around the strap of my bag. "You have a Porsche."

He reaches for my duffle. "I do." Of course he does. "But I prefer my truck."

He glances past me into the entryway, like he's checking for signs of life. My heart stutters. But there's nothing to see. Just me.

"Ready?" he asks.

As ready as I'll ever be. "Yeah. Let me lock up."

When we reach his car, he opens the passenger door for me. Chivalry, or maybe habit. Either way, it makes my breath catch. Once we're both inside, he starts the sports car and the engine rumbles to life. The car is quiet—not awkward, not tense—as the ocean flashes in and out of view, the forest around us growing closer and denser.

"Thanks for agreeing to drive up with me," he says, glancing at me. "I know you'd been planning on taking your own car."

"You're the boss," I reply with a teasing smile. "Is there a reason you wanted to travel together? What's your plan?"

"I just figured two hours in a vehicle with you would get me further than three months of board meetings," Ford says, eyes steady on the road, mouth curving in that infuriatingly subtle way.

"Is that so?" I glance sideways at him, already suspicious.

"Yeah." He taps his thumb against the wheel. "I think we should get to know each other again. You can ask me whatever you want. I'm an open book."

That makes me snort. "Since when?"

"Since you walked back into my life." His tone is casual, but there's a thread of truth under it. "Go ahead, Sinclair. Hit me with your best shot."

I can't help but smile. "Alright. What's your guilty pleasure TV show?"

He groans. "You're gonna use this against me."

"Probably."

A beat of silence, then, "The Great British Bake Off."

My jaw drops. "You're kidding."

"Dead serious. The show is stressful, but in a cozy way."

I burst out laughing. "That's...unexpected."

"See? You're learning things already," he says, shifting in his seat. "Alright, my turn."

"Should I be nervous?"

"Probably," he grins. Then, casually—but not really—he asks, "What's your biggest weakness"

I frown, confused. "My what?"

"Your biggest weakness. The thing you can't seem to resist, no matter how hard you try."

I raise a brow. "Trying to psychoanalyze me now?"

"Absolutely." His grin is quick, dangerous. "It's for professional purposes, obviously."

"Obviously," I echo, fighting a smile. "Not answering that one."

"Why not?"

"Because then you'd know how to use it against me."

He grins, eyes still on the road. "Come on, tell me."

"Fine, coffee. I'm useless without it."

He huffs out a laugh. "That's not a weakness. That's a requirement for survival."

"I guess you're not wrong," I say, shifting in my seat. "Okay my turn. What's your tell?"

His hands flex on the wheel, but his voice stays smooth. "My tell?"

"Yeah," I shoot back. "The thing you do that gives you away.

His jaw tightens, and I can see he's in his head, turning something over before he decides whether or not to say it out loud.

"I go quiet. Withdraw." He cuts me a look. "But you already know that."

Rather than risk looking at him, I turn my gaze out the window, pulled back into memories from what feels like a lifetime ago. At first it frustrated me, the way Ford would retreat when he was stressed or anxious, but eventually I came to understand that it was just his coping mechanism. Over time, we learned to navigate each other's habits and idiosyncrasies. A lot changed in seven years, but the more I get to know this version of Ford—the CEO, the entrepreneur, Deep Cove's success story—the more I realize that at his core, he's still the same boy I fell in love with.

"Okay, serious question," he says, snapping my attention back to the present. "What did you miss most about home?"

The softness of it catches me off guard. I think for a moment, watching the pines blur past outside my window. "The quiet. The space to breathe. Bigger cities always felt like they were swallowing me whole."

When I look back at him, he's watching me.

"And you?" I ask, shifting the question. "What's kept you here? With everything you could've built somewhere else...why stay?"

His expression changes. It's not a smile, exactly. More like the ghost of one. "Because here...people remember where you came from. They remember when you had nothing. Makes it harder to pretend you're someone you're not." He takes a breath, swallows hard. "Leaving just never felt like the right answer," he adds. "Not when we built Cove here. Not when this place made me who I am."

I nod, feeling that. More than I want to admit. Before I can stop myself, I ask quietly, "So who are you now, Ford?"

His jaw flexes, but when he looks at me, there's nothing guarded about it. "Trying to figure that out, June."

The nickname lands soft but sharp, hitting right where it hurts. I swallow hard, my throat tight.

"I missed this," I admit, barely above a whisper.

"What?"

"This. Us. Talking like this."

His knuckles brush mine where our hands rest between the seats. Not quite touching. Almost. "Me too."

TWENTY

F ord

The resort sprawls out in front of us, all timber beams and glass, tucked into the mountains. Whistler's ski hills loom large above the hotel, snow glistening under the spring sun. The village is packed with tourists and locals alike, everyone eager to get a few last runs in before the season comes to a close.

I kill the engine in front of valet and glance over at Landyn. She's staring out the windshield, absentmindedly twisting the rings on her fingers, probably not even realizing she's doing it.

The drive up together was good. Better than good.

She was soft and open, letting me see pieces of her she's had guarded since she came back to town. It's the closest I've felt to her in a very long time. But now that we're here, I can sense the walls being rebuilt, protecting the careful space that exists between who we were then and who we are now.

"You ready?" I ask, hoping to draw her back to me.

"Always." She flashes me a quick smile that doesn't quite reach her eyes.

We get out of the car, and I hand the keys to the bellman,

then we grab our bags from the backseat. Hers is small. Practical. That was always her—efficient, never trying to impress anyone.

The lobby is sleek but warm, all wood tones and floor-to-ceiling windows. The hum of quiet conversations reverberates off the stone floors as people move around us. We navigate through the room full of tourists—some still in robes from their spa treatments—conference guests, families, people with less intense schedules and less complicated backstories. At the front desk, the concierge smiles broadly and welcomes us to the hotel.

"We're here for the Sustainability Summit. Winters, Cove Group," I say, handing over my ID.

"Of course, Mr. Winters. We have two rooms reserved under your name. Side by side, as requested."

I glance at Landyn. Her mouth twitches, but she doesn't look at me. The concierge slides two key cards across the counter and Landyn takes both, handing one to me. When I take it, my fingers brush hers by accident—or maybe not. Either way, the jolt it sends through me is very real.

"This resort is beautiful," she says as we head toward the elevators.

"Not just the resort," I say, before I can stop myself. My eyes meet hers. She looks away, but she doesn't call me on it.

We step into the elevator, alone now. The doors close with a soft thud. The tension? Not so soft.

"Let me guess," she says, glancing up at me. "You're thinking about schedules and panels and investor meetings."

I smirk. "I'm thinking you're trying very hard to keep this professional."

"That's because it is professional."

"Right," I say, leaning back against the wall. "That's why you've been twisting your rings since we pulled into the hotel driveway."

She glares at me, but she doesn't deny it. When the doors open, we step into the hallway.

Room 312. Room 314.

It's probably not a good idea. It's probably far too close, considering the attraction I'm feeling towards her, but at the same time, it's nowhere near close enough. We stop at her door.

"Dinner's with the panel hosts tonight. Will that be enough time to do what you need to do?"

"It will be fine," she says, sliding the key into the lock. But before she goes inside, she looks up at me.

"Ford."

"Yeah?"

"I can help you. Help Cove. I want to. Don't go easy on me just because we have history."

"I never planned to," I tell her, meaning every damn word.

For a second, she just watches me. Then the corner of her mouth curves, a flash of that familiar fire sparking behind her eyes. She turns, her door clicking shut behind her, and I'm left standing here wondering how the hell I'm supposed to keep this professional when all I want to do is follow her into her hotel room.

With a sigh, I walk the few steps to my door. Inside my own room, I drop my bag on the chair in the corner and then sit on the bed, hyper-aware of the fact that Landyn is just feet away. The wall between us doesn't do a damn thing to shut her out of my head.

The room's nice. High-end finishing, impressive view, the kind of understated luxury I usually appreciate. Tonight, it barely registers because all I can think about is the way she said it. *Don't go easy on me just because we have history.*

I tug my jacket off and run a hand through my hair. The mirror above the dresser catches my reflection. Same face. Same sharp edges. But something in my expression feels...

unsettled. It's been a long time since someone's thrown me this far off balance

I spend the afternoon working, stopping only to order a late lunch from room service. Before I know it, it's 5 p.m., time to get ready for this evening's dinner. I take off my shirt, trading it for a clean black one, rolling the sleeves up to my forearms. In the bathroom, I splash some cool water on my face and take a few calming breaths. Something about seeing her tonight—out of the office, away from Deep Cove—feels like crossing a line we've been dancing around since she came back.

I teased her earlier about keeping this trip professional, but the truth is I'm the one who needs that reminder. Because I know what I want. I want more.

My phone buzzes on the counter beside me with a meeting reminder, but it barely cuts through the noise in my head. If Landyn keeps looking at me like she did in the elevator—like part of her still remembers what it felt like to be mine—then these next three days are going to be hell.

A slow, torturous, tempting kind of hell.

My phone buzzes again and this time I pick it up, noticing that there's a message from my brother waiting for me.

Jesse: So… how's the romantic retreat going?

Me: It's not a retreat. It's business.

Jesse: Right. Funny how that business required you and Landyn to disappear into the mountains together for two nights.

I stare at the screen for a bit, thumbs hovering.

Me: You're enjoying this too much.

> Jesse: I'm guessing not half as much as you
> are. Tell her I say hi.

Jaw tight, I lock my phone and then check the time. Dinner is in 15 minutes, which gives me plenty of time to pull myself together. Or at least to try.

Tucked into the Whistler resort, the restaurant is sleek, modern and expensive—a perfect setting for the kind of people Cove needs to impress tonight. The warmth of the gleaming hardwood floors is offset by deep, dark blue walls. Velvet chairs line the marble-topped bar, its collection of amber-filled bottles catching the light of the scattered candles that cast a soft, golden glow throughout the space. It's a stunning room.

And it all fades to nothing when I see her.

Landyn is standing a few feet from the bar, flipping through the menu. Her knee-length fitted, emerald-green dress is simple, elegant, devastating. Her hair's pulled back off her face into a slick bun at the nape of her neck. She doesn't see me yet, and that might be a good thing. It gives me a second to get my head on straight.

I approach slowly, stopping just beside her, close enough to inhale the scent of her perfume. "You're early," I say.

She glances up, a small smile tugging at her lips. "So are you."

"I like to be prepared."

"I like to eat," she replies, holding up the menu. "Priorities."

God, I missed this. The way she could throw a jab with a smile. The way she never let me get too comfortable.

"Stunning, June." My eyes move over her. A faint blush creeps up her cheeks.

"Come on," I say, nodding toward the table where our hosts are gathering. "Let's go charm the hell out of them."

We settle into the table—six of us in total. Investors, panel organizers, and Cove's newest PR lead. Landyn slides effortlessly into the conversation. Sharp, poised, asking the right questions, listening to every word that's said. She makes it look easy, but I knew she would. What surprises me is the way she glances at me sometimes, quick flicks of her eyes, like she's checking to see if I'm paying attention.

I am. I always am.

"So," one of the panel hosts, an energetic woman named Natasha, leans forward, wine glass in hand. "Cove's making big moves with this new sustainability initiative. Do you think it will help mitigate the negative stories in the press?"

Before I can answer, Landyn speaks up. "Responsibility," she says smoothly. "It's not just about innovation—it's about integrity. The backlash in the press is baseless, and we fully intend to prove just how wrong they are. Cove was built on function and quality, but most importantly we evolve with our community's values."

I could kiss her for that.

"Exactly," I add, giving a nod. "We're not interested in empty gestures. This isn't a pivot. It's a course correction."

The conversation flows easily after that. They're buying it. No—believing it. Because Landyn knows how to tell a story people want to be part of.

Beneath the surface, though, there's still that current pulling at both of us.

Her foot brushes mine under the table. Maybe it's accidental. Maybe not. I look at her. She doesn't flinch. I feel my mouth twitch.

By the time dessert comes, I've answered half a dozen questions, secured two follow-up meetings, and just barely managed to keep my focus on business.

When we stand to leave, Landyn thanks the others, her smile professional but warm, then we step out into the cool night air, away from the crowd. We walk slowly through the darkened village, the muffled sounds of laughter and music escaping from the restaurants that line the central square.

"Well?" she asks, stopping to look at me. "How'd I do?"

"You know exactly how you did."

She grins, and damn if it doesn't hit me square in the chest.

"I told you not to go easy on me," she says, eyes narrowing.

"I'm not," I promise. "Not even close."

The air between us shifts again. Tightens. The space feels smaller, even out here. But before I can say—or do—anything else, she tucks her hair behind her ear and takes a step back.

"Come on, Winters. It's been a long day." She turns back in the direction of our hotel, and I follow reluctantly, not ready for the night to end.

We pass a narrow alleyway strung with soft bistro lights and the faint sound of an acoustic guitar drifting out of a small, tucked away café. Without thinking, I catch her wrist. "Come on," I say.

"I thought we were calling it a night."

"Plans just changed."

She could say no. She could remind me that we're here for work, that there are lines that cannot be crossed. But instead, she lets me guide her down the brick path, toward the glow emanating from the café's windows.

It's a nice night, so we grab a small table on the patio, in the corner, away from the few other groups. We each order a drink, and the server deposits them at our table without much fanfare. The place feels like a hideaway, a forgotten spot, tucked away from everything and everyone. For a minute, we just sit here. No Cove talk. No press strategy. Just the faint sound of her fingers tracing the rim of her glass.

"This was always your move," she says after a moment, glancing at me. "Detours. Distractions."

"Maybe I just wanted to keep you in my orbit a little longer."

That same old spark flickers in her eyes. "You're impossible," she mutters, but there's no bite in it.

"You didn't seem to mind, back then."

"I didn't. That's the problem."

Her eyes glisten as she pulls in a breath and I feel it in my core. For a while, we just sit there, letting the quiet do what words can't. The tension's still there, but it's gentler now. Less like a wound, more like a magnet.

"Ford," she says, voice low, serious now. "What are we doing?"

I meet her gaze. Steady. Unflinching. "Having a drink. Taking a detour."

"I know you, and you've always got a plan," she says, and there's a spark there now. One I haven't seen in a while. She taps her fingers in time to the music, a habit I remember.

"You want to dance?" I ask, already knowing the answer.

Her eyes flick to mine, defiant. "No."

"Liar."

Her lips curve, betraying her. "There's no dance floor."

I stand, hold out my hand. "We'll improvise."

She stares at me, weighing the offer. With a dramatic sigh, she sets down her drink and takes my hand, letting me pull her from her chair. Her fingers slip into mine, warm and certain, like they never forgot the shape of this.

"Always reckless, Winters," she says as I pull her gently toward the open space near the edge of the patio.

"Only when it's worth it."

The guitarist shifts to a slower, bluesy rhythm. Just enough to move to. I rest a hand on her waist, feel her tense—just for a breath—before she melts into it. Her other hand finds my shoulder. Familiar. Natural.

We move slowly. Just the rhythm, the press of her body against mine, the faint sounds of conversation from nearby tables fading into the background.

"You're surprisingly good at this," she says, tilting her head back to look at me.

"I wouldn't go that far," I reply, spinning her slowly. "You're just good at making me look like I know what I'm doing."

She shakes her head, smiling up at me. "You don't give yourself enough credit."

She's laughing now, breathless as we move, and it knocks something loose in my chest. For a few perfect moments, it's like we're 21 again. No walls. No wounds. Just this.

We keep dancing. It feels good, effortless. Like breathing. When the song winds down, I spin her one last time, pulling her back in, closer now. She doesn't step away and neither do I.

"See?" I say softly. "Detours aren't so bad."

Her smile could bring me to my knees.

"You might be right, Winters."

"I missed you, June." Her fingers tighten against my chest, right over my heart, like the words hit her physically. "I missed you so much it still pisses me off sometimes," I add, my voice dropping lower, meant only for her.

She doesn't look away. For once, she lets me see it. The way her walls start to crack. The way her chin tips up like she's fighting to stay steady.

"Ford..." she whispers. My thumb brushes her side, slow and reverent, as if reminding both of us that we're still here. Still breathing.

"I'm not asking for anything from you tonight," I tell her quietly. "I'm not expecting you to fix what broke. I just needed you to know... losing you never stopped hurting."

The words settle heavily between us, bringing an end to the lightness of the last few minutes. But I had to say them.

Her hand drifts up, fingertips brushing my jaw, light as air. That small, familiar touch wrecks me more than a kiss ever could.

"I never wanted to hurt you," she says, her voice barely audible.

"I know."

It's not forgiveness. It's not closure. But it's honest and right now, that's enough. For a long, breathless moment, we just stand there—swaying slightly, holding onto each other like maybe, just maybe, the world can pause for us tonight. When she rests her forehead against my chest, I let my hand slide up to the back of her neck, cradling her gently. Not pushing. Just holding onto her because after everything, I think that's what we both need most.

We walk back to the hotel in silence. Her hand brushes mine once by accident. When it happens a second time, I grab it. She doesn't pull away. And I don't let go. I intertwine her fingers with mine, grounding myself in the fact that after all this time, she's here, beside me. It's stupid how good it feels. It's like slipping back into something so comfortable and familiar. Something I almost stopped believing I ever had.

It feels like the whole world has collapsed into this small point of contact—her hand in mine. In this moment, there is nothing else that matters.

For a man who's built walls around everything he touches, holding her feels dangerous, but for the first time in a long time, it feels like the kind of risk I'm willing to take.

The lobby's quieter now. We ride the elevator in silence, but the air between us crackles. When we reach our floor, my pulse hammers louder than our footsteps.

Room 312.

She stops in front of her door, keycard in hand, but she

doesn't move. Her throat works as she swallows, and I see the exact second her resolve starts to crack.

And then I don't think.

I move.

I back her into the door, one hand braced beside her head, the other curling around her waist, pulling her flush against me. Her breath shudders and for a beat, we just stare at each other.

And then she's on me, or maybe I'm on her. Doesn't matter. Her hands fist in my shirt as my mouth crashes into hers—frantic, hungry, like all that pent-up tension has nowhere else to go but this. Her back thuds softly against the door, and she moans. I devour her gasp, my fingers sliding up into her hair as her body arches into mine.

She tastes the same. She feels the same. But this isn't the past. This is now and right now, I need her more than I need to breathe.

Her hands tug at my jacket, pulling me closer. I break the kiss just long enough to murmur. "Tell me you want this too."

Her eyes, dark and wild, meet mine.

She doesn't say it. Instead, she pulls me back in. Hard.

And that's all the answer I need.

Landyn

His mouth crashes into mine before I can even get the key in the door.

There's no hesitation, just heat. The kind that's been building between us since the second I walked back into Cove, and maybe long before that. It's years of silence and of want, it's everything we didn't say back then crashing into now. He backs me into the wall beside the door, one of his hands sliding around the back of my neck while the other tugs at the hem of my dress, like he needs me undressed, now.

I gasp when his hips press into mine. God, he's already hard, thick and solid through his jeans, and it sends a jolt of pure desire through me. The ridge of his erection presses against my stomach as our mouths open to each other, tongues tasting, searching. His scent—clean skin and man— floods my senses, grounding me in something that's always felt like home.

The keycard slips from my hand and hits the floor but neither of us moves to grab it. Ford keeps kissing me—deep, rough kisses that steal every breath I try to take. His mouth moves with intention, like he's trying to remember every inch of me, trying to memorize the way I taste.

"Get us inside," he murmurs between kisses, lips brushing mine.

I bend for the key, grab it blindly, and manage to swipe us into the room. The second the door clicks shut behind us, he's back on me.

"God, I've thought about this," he groans between kisses. "Too many fucking times."

His hands are everywhere— in my hair, on my hips, drifting over my hips to my ass before they find the zipper at the back of my dress.

He growls low in his throat as he pushes the straps of my dress over my shoulders with both hands. The fabric slides slowly over my hips and down my thighs, his knuckles brushing bare skin, igniting a trail of heat as he goes. His eyes drag over me slowly, like he's seeing me for the first time and remembering everything all at once.

I'm left in nothing but a thin, black matching set. His gaze darkens.

"Black lace," he says under his breath, voice hoarse. "Of course you'd still kill me with this. Fuck, Landyn..."

He stands here for a heartbeat with his chest rising and falling, then grabs the back of his neck like he's trying to restrain himself.

Needing him badly, my hands move to his chest, tugging at the buttons of his shirt. My fingers tremble as I undo each one, then drag the fabric down his shoulders until it hits the ground, revealing the hard ridges of his chest and abs. Three columns of defined abs, pecs that have been sculpted in the gym, a light dusting of dark hair. He's all firm muscle and strength, and when I run my hands down his torso, he sucks in a breath like I just punched the air out of him.

"I used to dream about you like this," he says, low and

rough, his hand sliding around to cup my ass as he walks me backward toward the bed. "Wearing this. Looking at me like you needed me."

"I do need you," I whisper, and I mean it in ways I can't even say out loud.

The back of my knees hit the bed, and I sink onto the mattress, heart racing so fast it's almost dizzying. He nudges me, gentle but certain, and I fall back with a breathless laugh, one that dies the second he follows, crawling over me with that look that's always undone me. His hands brace the mattress on either side of my shoulders, caging me in like he's not giving me a chance to run.

I suck in a sharp breath when his knee presses between mine, spreading me open, making room for him until he's right there, settled deep between my thighs, all heat and solid muscle. His bare chest brushes mine, warm and sure, like it belongs here. Like he belongs here.

When he grinds his cock into me, through the rough denim of his jeans and the flimsy scrap of my thong, I can't hold back the moan that rips from me. It's hard, hungry pressure against the aching center of me, the friction hitting all the right places until I can't think past it. Past him. It's perfect and blinding and a little bit dangerous because if I let myself feel all of it, I might never want to stop.

"Oh my god—" I gasp, arching up into him.

"Feel that?" he rasps against my neck, rocking his hips. "That's what you do to me. Always have."

His cock rubs right against me, thick and hard, dragging across the spot that makes me dizzy. The friction is too much and not enough. My hands claw at his back, pulling him down so I can feel more—taste more—of the man I never stopped wanting. I arch beneath him, rolling my hips up to find his arousal, greedy for more.

"Please..."

His mouth moves over my collarbone, between my breasts, down to the curve of lace. "I want to tear this off you," he growls. "I want my mouth everywhere. I want to see how wet you are for me."

I moan, head falling back into the pillows. "Yes. Ford, yes."

"God, June," he groans, kissing me again, deeper this time like he wants to consume me. When his fingers slip beneath the band of my underwear, dipping between my folds, I can't hold back the desperate sound that escapes me.

"You're so wet, baby," he murmurs as his fingers trail back up my body, just barely brushing over the waistband of my underwear. "You want me this bad?"

I can only nod, eyes glazed, lips parted as he leans in to kiss me again, deeper this time, hungrier.

We're tangled, frantic, the room echoing with gasps and whispers and the soft rustle of sheets. I reach for the button of his jeans and—

My phone rings.

Loud, sharp, coming from my purse across the room. It cuts through the moment like a blade. A chill skates down my spine when I hear the ringtone. The one I assigned to my mom, who is taking care of my daughter right now.

Ford groans, forehead dropping to my shoulder. "Let it go to voicemail."

"I can't," I whisper, suddenly cold even though my skin's burning.

He leans back, confused, breath still ragged. "Why?"

"I just—" I sit up fast, heart in my throat. "I have to get it."

Without looking at him, I climb off the bed in my bra and underwear. My legs are unsteady, shaking from the intensity of everything we were just wrapped up in. I find my purse near the door, dig through it, and grab the phone as guilt slams into me like a fist.

I shoot Ford a look I can't explain and turn away, walking

into the bathroom where I swipe to answer the call, trying to steady my breath.

"Hi," I say, as calmly as I can manage.

In the other room, I can feel Ford's presence. Quiet and waiting for an explanation that I don't know if I can give to him. Without looking back, I shut the bathroom door behind me as gently as I can.

My heart is pounding—wild and erratic—as I press the phone to my ear and sink down onto the closed lid of the toilet, my pulse still buzzing with everything I just walked away from.

"Hi, Mom," I say again, forcing air into my lungs. "Is everything okay?"

There's a beat of silence on her end, and then, "Everything's fine, honey. Poppy just wanted to say goodnight. She got a little upset when she didn't get to talk to you before bed."

My eyes sting. Guilt coils tighter in my chest. "Oh. Yeah. No—I'm glad you called." I lower my voice, like that'll help contain everything I'm not ready to spill. "Put her on?"

There's some shuffling, the muffled sound of footsteps, and then that tiny, sleepy voice comes through the speaker.

"Hi, Mama."

My throat catches. "Hi, baby."

"I made a card for you," she tells me. "It has a bunny on it. Grandma said we'll put it on the fridge tomorrow."

I close my eyes, resting my forehead in my hand. "I can't wait to see it. Did you have a good day?"

She tells me about pancakes and the swimming pool and how Grandma let her stay up 15 extra minutes. Her voice is soft and sleepy and full of love and here I am, hiding half-naked in a hotel bathroom, caught between the man I once loved and the daughter he doesn't know exists.

"Are you coming home tomorrow?" she asks.

I blink back the burn in my eyes. "Not yet. Just a couple more sleeps, okay?"

"Okay," she says. "I love you."

"I love you more."

The line goes quiet. My mom comes back on. "She's okay now. Just missed you."

I nod, even though she can't see me. "Thanks for calling."

There's a pause on her end. "Landyn?"

"Yeah?"

"You have to tell him."

I close my eyes. "I know," I whisper, and for the first time, I mean it.

We hang up. I set the phone down on the counter and stare at myself in the mirror. My cheeks are flushed, my hair a mess, my eyes still lit with the leftover sparks of something I almost let happen. Something I still want so badly it aches.

I exhale, steadying myself, then I open the bathroom door.

Ford is sitting on the edge of the bed, shirtless, jeans half-undone, elbows braced on his knees. His head lifts when he hears the door. His eyes meet mine, and I know.

He doesn't understand what just happened, but he knows something's off, and he knows it's big. He's going to start asking questions and he won't let me dodge them for long. I tell myself I can't do it this weekend. Ford needs to focus on Cove and putting out the fire from bad publicity. Once I get through this weekend, I'll tell him about Poppy.

His eyes scan me—slowly, carefully, like he's reading every line of my face, every inch of skin that's still flushed from what almost happened.

"You okay?" he asks, voice low.

I nod. "Yeah. Just... my mom." Not a lie, not the whole truth either.

He doesn't say anything right away.

"She just wanted to check in. All good." I force a soft smile, something light, like everything between us didn't just shift on its axis.

Ford leans back slightly, studying me like he's trying to decide what to believe. "Everything's good," he echoes. It doesn't sound like a question.

I bend down and grab my dress from the floor, straightening it out as casually as I can. "Yes, she's fine. Sorry about... that. The call."

He stands slowly, running a hand through his hair, jaw tight. "Yeah. No problem."

But it is.

It's a problem.

Because now everything's off.

He doesn't push. Doesn't press.

"I think I'm gonna call it," I say, suddenly very aware that I'm still in nothing but my bra and underwear. He just watches me quietly as I slide the dress back on, tug the straps into place, avoid his eyes.

He nods once, slowly. "Yeah. Sure."

He picks up his shirt from the floor and tugs it back on. I open the door, and he follows me, stepping into the hallway and then turning to face me.

"Goodnight, June," he says, and his voice is so soft, so careful, it nearly undoes me.

I glance at him, heart aching. "Goodnight, Ford."

He holds my gaze a second longer—eyes searching, but lips pressed shut—then turns and walks down the hall. I step back into the room, close the door behind me, and rest my back against it.

TWENTY-TWO

F ord
    I lie in bed, staring at the ceiling after waking up from a restless sleep. Even hours later, my head is still full of everything that didn't happen last night. My body is still humming from everything that did.

Landyn had brushed off the phone call, but everything changed after that. The way she slipped back into her dress and into silence like there was nothing to explain. Like it didn't even matter.

But it did.

It does.

I can't shake the way she looked when she came out of that bathroom. She tried to act calm and steady, but it didn't take much effort to see past all of that. It looked like something inside her was cracking wide open.

Eventually, I throw off the covers and get dressed, then head downstairs. The hotel gym is empty, the only sound coming from the dull thud of my sneakers on the treadmill as I try to outrun my cycling thoughts.

I push harder. Faster.

Landyn's laugh last night.

Her dress pooled at her feet.

The soft gasp when I pressed into her.

Then her phone rang and everything just…stopped.

I don't know what that call was, but I know now without a doubt that she's hiding something. And as much as I want to understand what it is, I can't force her to open up to me.

After 40 minutes and a shower that doesn't do a damn thing to cool me off, I head down to the café in the lobby, and I text her one word:

Me: Ready?

She replies a minute later.

Landyn: Meet you in five.

I'm already standing near the elevators when the doors slide open, and I see her. Black trousers with a Cove tee and a blazer rolled to her sleeves. Her hair is pulled back into the bun she always wears to work. She looks polished, efficient, controlled. And so beautiful that I'm not 100 percent sure I'm still breathing.

She's in work mode now, her armor back on, but when her eyes flicker to mine I can see she knows I haven't forgotten last night. Neither has she.

"Morning," she says lightly, falling into step beside me.

"Morning," I return, and it comes out rougher than I mean for it to.

She's holding a paper coffee cup, her fingers wrapped tightly around it.

"We've got back-to-back panels today," she says. "Lunch with the tech consultant, then that pitch meeting with the outdoor gear group."

I nod. "And we'll want to loop in the sustainability team before the cocktail hour."

She glances up at me. "Already sent a note to Becca. She's lining up the notes we need."

Of course she did. She's three steps ahead, and it doesn't surprise me. That's the Landyn I've always known, only now I can't stop wondering who else she is, what parts of her I'm still not seeing.

The day passes in a blur of panels, meetings, networking, and pitch sessions. Landyn handles every conversation like she was born for this. Polished. Poised. Smart enough to answer every question, charming enough to make people forget why they were skeptical in the first place. She's good and Cove looks even better with her out front. We sit beside each other all day, nodding through presentations, fielding questions, leaning in close to whisper the occasional strategy call. Her scent makes it hard for me to think straight, and every time her arm brushes mine it becomes more difficult to remember this is supposed to be professional. And even though her voice is steady, even though she laughs in all the right places, I know something's off. I can't shake the feeling that whatever it is she's holding back has something to do with me. With us.

By the time we get back to the resort, the sun is low, casting a warm, golden haze over the mountains. The cocktail hour is already set up on the terrace—string lights glowing above linen-draped tables, small fires crackling in sleek stone pits. The vibe is relaxed. Glasses clink. Laughter floats. Everyone's loosened their ties and dropped their inhibitions.

Everyone except us.

Landyn's across the terrace, talking to one of the event coordinators, her fingers twisting the stem of the glass of white wine in her hand. She's smiling, but it doesn't quite reach her eyes.

She must feel me looking at her, because her eyes suddenly meet mine and it hits me square in the chest. Tonight might be my last shot at getting through to her. I'm not walking away without at least trying.

I pick up my drink and cross the patio, pulled to her like a magnet. The expression on her face is unreadable, but she's antsy, fingernail absentmindedly tapping the rim of her wine glass.

"You look like you're considering an escape," I say, nodding toward the doors behind her.

Her mouth curves. "How far do you think I could get in these heels before one of the presenters tackles me to talk about supply chain management?"

"You'd make it 10 feet. Maybe less."

"I'm scrappy," she replies, lifting her glass and taking a sip. "You forget that."

"I already told you, Lan. I don't forget anything."

That slows her. She tries to cover it with a sip of wine, but I catch the breath she pulls in first. The light out here is soft, casting a hazy, golden glow, and for a second, it's easy to forget the people around us, the clinking glasses, the quiet hum of conversations. It's just her. Just us.

"Today went well," she says, filling the silence. "You didn't glare at the analytics guy even once."

"Barely gave me a reason to," I say, stepping in just a little closer. "I had a good buffer."

Her lips press together like she's fighting a smile, but I don't want to talk about work. Not tonight. I gesture toward an unoccupied fire pit. "Walk with me?"

She hesitates, eyes narrowing just slightly, but then she nods. We move toward the edge of the terrace and for a moment just stand together, looking out at the mountains, silhouetted against the colors of the dusk sky. The firelight casts a warm glow across her skin, moving through the waves of her hair. We sit on an outdoor couch, so close that our knees touch.

"So, how are you really?" I ask.

She glances at me, surprised.

"After everything," I add. "Coming back. Walking into Cove. Working next to me."

She's quiet for a beat. Then, "It's been...a lot."

I nod. "For me too."

She looks at me again—longer this time. The fire crackles between us, low and slow. "You said last night that you missed me," she says softly. "After all these years...do you still feel that way?"

I move closer, slowly, carefully, until there's only a breath between us. "I don't miss you, Landyn," I say. "I ache for you. Every time you walk into a room. Every time you laugh at someone else's joke. Every time you look at me like I'm a stranger...when we both know I'm not."

Her breath catches, and I can see it—the crack in the mask she's been wearing all day.

"I know there's something you're not telling me," I add, voice lower now. "And I'm not asking you to spill it. Not yet. But I'm not backing off either."

She opens her mouth. Closes it. Swallows hard like the words are there, perched on the edge, but she can't bring herself to let them fall.

"There you two are!"

We both turn at the same time, instinctively moving a few inches apart as we do.

It's Claire, one of the panel coordinators, striding toward us with a flute of champagne in one hand and a schedule in the other. She's relentlessly energetic, the human equivalent of a can of Red Bull, and she's been trying to corner me since this morning. Her eyes flick between Landyn and me with piqued interest she doesn't even bother hiding. "You've been impossible to pin down tonight, Ford," she admonishes, lowering her chin so she can look at me over the rims of her thick, black glasses. She turns to Landyn next. "And *you* were brilliant on the panel earlier. Literally spellbinding!"

Landyn laughs. "Thank you, Claire. Spellbinding. I'll have to add that to my CV."

"You absolutely should," Claire gushes, squeezing Landyn's arm enthusiastically.

"I agree," I say to Landyn, trying to suppress a grin.

"Now, don't run off just yet," Claire says, stepping in closer. "There's someone from the VanEdge group I'd love for you both to meet. I told them they do not want to leave this summit without talking to the folks from Cove. They're very interested in your upcoming fall line."

"Sounds good, we'll make sure to find them before we leave," I tell her.

"No time like the present!" Claire enthuses, not taking the hint. "That's them at the bar."

Landyn glances at me briefly, like she's not sure whether to be relieved or resentful that we've been interrupted yet again. And me? I'm pissed that the opportunity to connect with Landyn is gone. Snatched away before it could become something more.

I give Claire a polite nod. "Sure. We'll be over in a minute."

She hesitates—clearly wanting to drag us there by the wrists, but eventually flashes that polished event-host smile and retreats back toward the crowd.

I glance at Landyn. Her gaze is down, focused on her wine glass. One finger traces the rim slowly, and for the first time tonight, she looks tired. "We don't have to go," I murmur. She looks at me then, and our eyes lock.

She shakes her head. "We should. I'm sure Claire has a couple of Bloodhounds on standby if we try to get out of it."

She's probably right. Even so, she doesn't move to leave and neither do I, until a burst of laughter around the fire pit next to us fractures the moment.

THE HOTEL ROOM IS TOO QUIET. I'VE CHECKED MY EMAILS THREE times, flipped mindlessly through a report that Jesse had asked me to go over, watched 20 minutes of a remarkably unfunny sitcom, and took a long shower. I thought maybe the day would catch up with me by now. Exhaust me enough to sleep.

It hasn't.

It's just after eleven, and I'm still wound tight. Thoughts spinning, body still buzzing from the way she looked at me out on the terrace tonight. The way she almost told me something. The way she didn't. I run a hand through my hair, sit on the edge of the bed, and stare at my phone like I can will it to light up.

It doesn't.

She's in the room next door, probably doing the same thing—pretending today was just another day. Pretending last night didn't nearly break us wide open.

I lie back, arm slung over my eyes. Five seconds pass. Then ten.

Then I'm up again, walking toward the window, trying to resist the urge to do the one thing I've been telling myself not to do all night. Don't reach out. Don't push her. Don't knock on her door.

I grab my phone anyway.

One message. Simple.

Me: Still up?

I hit send before I have a chance to overthink it. And then I wait.

One minute.

Two.

And then—

Landyn: Yeah.

I stare at the screen, thumb hovering, when another message comes through.

Landyn: Can't sleep. You too?

I don't reply. I'm already grabbing my keycard off the dresser. Already stepping out into the hallway. Already heading toward her door.

I knock once and wait in the empty hallway, adrenaline rushing through me. The ice machine across the hall hums. A door thuds shut somewhere nearby. My heart kicks like it's trying to escape my ribcage.

And then her door opens.

Her hair has been pulled from its bun and she's barefoot wearing a loose T-shirt and a pair of soft cotton shorts that make it really fucking hard to remember why I shouldn't be standing here right now. She looks jittery, like maybe she's spent the last hour pacing her room too.

She blinks up at me but doesn't say anything right away. Neither do I, because seeing her like this—unguarded, vulnerable —is almost too much.

"I couldn't sleep," I say finally.

She nods. "I know."

We stand there, a breath apart. Closer than we should be. Still not close enough.

Her fingers tighten slightly around the edge of the door and for a second, I think she's going to close it, to make some excuse not to let me in.

Instead, she takes a step backwards.

And just like that, I'm inside.

TWENTY-THREE

Landyn

Ford steps into the room, and then we just stand there looking at each other—me barefoot and in my pajamas, him still fully dressed. I try to still my hammering heart. Everything is fine, I tell it. This is totally normal.

Except it's not.

There's nothing normal about the way Ford looks at me. Like he wants to touch me, but he's afraid I'll disappear if he does.

"I'm not here to start anything," he says quietly, his hands in his pockets like he's trying to keep them from reaching for me. "I just...wanted to be with you."

The simple honesty of it makes my chest ache. I nod, because God, I get that too. "Me too."

The air is thick with silence. I walk to the bed and sit down on the far side, curling my legs beneath me. He follows, slower, lowering himself to sit beside me. The mattress shifts, our shoulders just barely brushing.

"Do you remember the first time we went camping?" I ask.

He looks over at me. "Silver Lake."

I smile faintly. "You thought I'd be okay sleeping in a tent."

"I got you an air mattress and I brought my duvet from home for us because you were worried you'd be too cold in your sleeping bag."

"And I was right. I stole the whole duvet in the middle of the night. Along with your hoodie."

He chuckles softly, shaking his head. "I froze for three hours."

We sit in that memory for a minute, warmed by it, then I lie back against the pillows, and without asking, he does too.

We don't touch. We just stare up at the ceiling, like maybe we'll find the answers up there.

After a while, his fingers find mine. At first, just a small brush of his pinky against mine, but then I lace my fingers through his. I shiver when his thumb sweeps gently across the back of my hand.

"I'm glad you're here," I whisper.

"Me too," he says. "I'm not ready to let you go again."

I close my eyes, afraid that if I speak, I'll say too much, and even though I want this—him—more than I can explain, I'm still terrified of what happens when the secret I'm keeping finally finds the light. But right now, in this bed, in this small, quiet space carved out of a mountain town far from everything real—he's here. With me. And for tonight, maybe that's enough.

"Can I stay here tonight?" he asks.

I nod once. "Yeah. You can."

His shoulders ease, just barely. Like even though he knew the answer, part of him still needed to hear it.

We move slowly. He stands beside the bed and draws back the covers, and I slip beneath them as he turns off the overhead light, the room dark now with just a sliver of moonlight slicing through the midnight sky through the sheer curtains.

He kicks off his shoes and then pulls his shirt over his head and sets it neatly on the chair in the corner before unbuttoning his jeans. He undresses quietly, his movements slow and controlled. Like we've done this a hundred times before, and I guess we have, in another lifetime.

My breath catches. The sight of him—half-dressed and standing in the soft light in only his boxer briefs—is incredible. His body is all sharp planes and defined muscle, broad across the shoulders, cut down his stomach. There's a fine dusting of hair covering his pecs and leading into his navy boxer briefs. He runs a hand through his thick hair, his jaw flexing just slightly as he glances at the bed, and at me.

I don't look away. Not this time.

There is meaning in this moment, like something sacred is passing between us. Not just lust. Not even longing. Just the aching, quiet awe of seeing someone you never stopped loving in their most unguarded form.

Ford climbs into bed beside me without a word, the mattress shifting under his weight, and I draw the covers up over both of us, my heart pounding in my chest like I've been holding my breath since the day I left him.

And then we're here...side by side with only inches between us.

I lie on my side, facing the window, and then, softly, hesitantly, he says, "I think about it sometimes."

"Think about what?"

"If we'd done it differently." His voice is rough, like he doesn't trust it. "If I'd found you. If you'd stayed."

The air tightens. But I don't look at him.

"Me too," I whisper.

There's a pause. "Do you regret it? Leaving?"

Yes. No.

Every single day.

"I think...I did what I thought I had to do," I say instead.

He doesn't press. He never does.

After a beat, his arm slides around my waist, warm and

firm, pulling me gently back into his chest. I let my body settle into his—spooned perfectly, like we've always belonged here, just like this. His hand rests just below my ribs, his breath brushing against the back of my neck, slow and steady.

We say nothing more, but I feel everything.

Then I close my eyes and fall asleep in the arms of the only man who's ever made me feel safe.

I WAKE SLOWLY.

The morning light slips through the curtains, barely touching the edges of the bed. Ford's arm is heavy around my waist, his chest pressed warm to my back, our legs tangled beneath the sheets.

I don't want to move. I don't want to ruin the rare peace of this moment, but then his arm tightens around me, his nose brushes the back of my neck, and his voice is soft in my ear.

"You always made me sleep like this," he murmurs.

I smile against the pillow. "I don't remember you complaining."

"I liked it." He pauses. "Still do."

I shift just enough to turn toward him, our faces only inches apart. His hair's a mess, his eyes still heavy from sleep. He looks like something I dreamed up.

"I missed this," I whisper, my fingers lightly brushing his chest.

His eyes search mine. "Me too."

His hand slides down my thigh, slow and sure, and then dips beneath the sheet, grazing over the top of my underwear. "I always loved waking up to you," he says quietly, and I inhale sharply. "And I never forgot how you'd wake up to me."

I let out a shaky breath. "You're dangerous, Ford Winters."

He kisses me once, soft and slow, then he pulls back.

"Shower?" he murmurs.

I nod, heart already racing.

He rises from the bed and crosses the room to the bathroom, pausing at the door to glance back. "Come on, June."

The nickname, that voice. I'm already sliding out of bed, following him. He flicks the bathroom light on and turns the water to hot. Steam begins to build instantly, fogging the mirror. He turns back to me and starts to undress me slowly. First my T-shirt, peeling it off inch by inch. Then my underwear, which he slides down my legs, hands warm as they trace along my thighs.

"You're gorgeous," he murmurs, voice low. "You always were."

I dip my fingers inside the waistband of his boxers brushing through the soft hair at his groin before sliding them lower and pushing the fabric down over his erection. He steps out of his boxers, and my breath catches.

He's already hard.

His cock is thick and full, flushed at the tip, curving up toward his stomach and nearly touching his navel. And God— it's perfect. Of course, it's perfect. I remember what it felt like inside me.

His eyes darken as he sees the way I look at him. He cups my jaw and tilts my face to his again, kissing me slow and deep. Then he leads me into the shower, one hand resting on my lower back. The water is hot, cascading over our shoulders, steam curling between our bodies.

Ford reaches for the shampoo, lathering it between his palms, then gently begins to wash my hair. His fingers stroke my scalp in circles, massaging. After he rinses it out, he kisses the top of my head. "Turn around."

I do.

His hand trails down my spine, resting low on my hip before slipping between my thighs from behind.

I gasp, my hands braced against the tile wall as his fingers slide along the slick center of me, his hard cock bobbing against my back.

"Can I touch you?" He asks, the question stealing air from my lungs.

"Please."

His hand moves slowly down my stomach, attentively, like he's relearning the shape of me. Heat rushes to my skin, my pulse fluttering in places I'd forgotten could ache like this. All I can do is stand here and let him touch me like he's remembering every part of me that he used to know by heart.

His hand doesn't stop. It trails lower as my body arches toward his hand, my thighs parting, and when his fingers slide between them, I swear my knees wobble.

"Still so fucking soft," he mutters as his fingers slide through my folds, slow and deliberate, until he pushes one finger inside. My breath catches as my body clenches around the sudden fullness.

"Still so wet," he murmurs, voice thick.

He slides two fingers into me next, curling them just right as his palm presses against that spot that makes my whole body jolt forward. "Ford—"

"I've got you," he breathes against my ear. "I've been dreaming about this. About touching you like this again. Making you fall apart for me."

I arch back into him, the pressure building fast and wild.

His fingers move in that slow, deliberate rhythm that only he knows. That only he ever got right. My body tightens, legs shaking.

"That's it," he murmurs, one arm wrapped around my waist now, holding me up, guiding me through the release. "Come for me, baby."

And I do. My body unravels under the heat and steam, remembering the way he knows exactly how to hold me together as I fall apart. Wrecked. And when it's over, he presses his lips to the back of my neck and whispers my name like it means something again.

I'm still catching my breath—my hands pressed to the tile, his arm around my waist, holding me like he's afraid I'll disappear. My muscles are loose, my heart racing. I've never felt so undone and so safe at the same time.

I turn in his arms slowly, water running down my back, and press my hand to his chest. His heart pounds beneath it.

"My turn to touch you," I whisper, glancing down, already reaching, but his hand catches mine gently.

"Not today," he murmurs, voice low, rough with restraint. "This was about you."

"But—"

He cuts me off with a kiss, soft and lingering. "You gave me what I wanted," he says against my lips. "I just wanted to take care of you. I wanted to see you again."

His words make my chest ache because I know what he means, and I know what I'm still hiding.

I nod slowly, resting my forehead against his.

We stay like that for another moment—bare skin, warm water, nothing between us but the truths we haven't said yet. He turns off the shower and reaches for a towel, wrapping it around me before grabbing one for himself. Back in the room, I sit on the edge of the bed, pulling the comforter into my lap.

Ford leans against the dresser across from me, towel slung low on his hips, water glistening on his chest. His eyes stay on me, like he's trying to memorize this version of me before it slips away again.

"I didn't think it would feel like this," I say softly, not quite looking at him.

"Like what?"

"Like I never left," I admit. "Like you're still..." I trail off, biting my bottom lip.

He walks toward me slowly and crouches in front of me, close enough that I can feel the heat radiating off his skin. "I never stopped being yours," he says quietly. "Even when you were gone."

The words gut me because I want to say them back. I want to say, *me too*, but I'm still hiding so much. Instead, I reach for him, my fingers brushing his cheek. "Thank you for last night."

He doesn't move. He just nods once and says, "Anytime, June."

And I swear he means it.

TWENTY-FOUR

F ord

I've been apart from Landyn for less than 24 hours and already miss her. I pull into the lot behind Cove, memories from the weekend we just spent together still cycling through my mind. It was incredible. A turning point.

We didn't talk about what it meant. Didn't define it. Didn't wake up with some earth-shattering revelation. But being with her again after so many years—really *with* her—it was something I hadn't let myself believe could ever happen again.

The last day in Whistler was quieter. There were panels, a few final meetings, but the space between us felt different. Easier. She didn't flinch when our hands brushed. Didn't look away when she caught me watching her across a room. We grabbed takeout after the conference had wrapped up and ate it sitting cross-legged on her bed, laughing about the bad hotel wine and the even worse room service eggs from the morning before. She let me tuck her into my side, her head on my chest like she belonged there. And when I kissed her, it wasn't rushed or frantic—it was slow. Certain.

I wanted more. I always do when it comes to her.

But it was enough.

We passed the two-hour drive home the next morning learning each other all over again. All-time favorite songs. All-time worst haircuts. Bad dates. Great concerts. Pet peeves. The little, seemingly unimportant things that you come to realize are actually pretty important after all. But when I pulled up in front of her place, Landyn thanked me for the weekend like it was a meeting I'd scheduled and then she got out and walked inside without looking back.

Inside Cove, the building is quiet. It's still too early for most of the team. With the exception of Noah, that is, who tends to beat even me to the office. I drop my things off in my office and then head toward the upper floor to find him camped out in the finance area in front of a stack of papers, red pen in hand. His calm, cool perspective is exactly what I need right now.

"You know there's software that does that for you now," I say as I lean against the doorframe.

Noah glances up. "Yeah. I don't trust it."

I step inside. "You don't trust most things."

"And yet I still pick up your calls," he says, still focused on his work.

I drop into the chair across from his desk. He watches me for a second, then caps the pen and sets the report aside. "You look like hell."

"Thanks. You're the second person to tell me that this week."

He leans back, folding his arms over his chest. "You want to talk about it?"

I rub a hand over my face, not sure where to begin. "The weekend with Landyn was... a lot."

He nods like he figured as much.

"It felt easy," I add. "Being with her again, it felt like nothing had changed."

"But something did," he says.

I stare past him, jaw tightening. "Yeah, it did. She did. Or maybe I did. Or maybe there's something she's not saying and I'm just finally noticing."

Noah studies me quietly, then says, "You trust her?"

I pause. "I want to."

"That's not the same thing."

I meet his eyes, realizing that what he said is right.

I leave Noah's office carrying more weight than I came in with. His words echo in the back of my mind as I head down the hallway, past the glass-walled conference room and the open workstations. The hum of Cove waking up for the day surrounds me: coffee brewing, keyboards tapping, someone laughing down the hall.

When I see her, my pace doesn't slow. I make a path directly to her. She's sitting there like it's just another Monday morning, like she didn't spend the weekend in my bed, in my arms, under my hands. When I reach her, she looks up like she's surprised to see me.

"Can I see you in my office?" I ask, but it comes out sounding more like a demand.

Becca and Marco, who until a second ago were in their own world chatting at the table across from us, suddenly go silent.

Landyn nods. "Sure. Just give me a minute."

I don't wait. I don't need to. She'll come. I turn and walk back down the hall, chest tight, pulse loud in my ears. She knocks once and steps into my office without waiting for a reply, then she closes the door and leans against it with arms crossed and her guard up.

"You need to stop looking at me like that," she says. "People are going to start talking."

I let my eyes settle on her, taking in her crisp white blouse and fitted, knee-length black skirt, the ankle boots that show off her toned legs, and the way her hair is neatly pulled back from her face. "Let them," I say with a smirk.

Her eyes narrow. "Ford—"

"I miss you," I say, because it's the truth, and I'm tired of trying to hide it.

She blinks, caught off guard. "You saw me less than 24 hours ago."

"Doesn't matter." I keep my voice steady, low. "Still true."

I cross the room so I'm standing in front of her. My hands move to her jaw, needing to touch her. The way she instinctively leans into it, I know she needs the contact too. She doesn't say anything, but I see the hesitation in her eyes as she calculates the risk of being together like this in my office. I lean forward and kiss her anyways, making it clear that I'm done pretending that we're just colleagues, acquaintances, two people who knew each other once upon a time. The kiss is slow and chaste and when I slowly pull away, I say, "Have lunch with me."

Her brow lifts. "Today?"

"Yes. I need to go to Vietnam tomorrow. I'll be gone the rest of the week. I'll order lunch, we can eat in my office. I know what you like."

She hesitates and for a second, I worry she might say no. But then she nods. "Okay."

"Good."

I watch her leave, then sink back into my chair, heart pounding. I'm relieved she agreed to have lunch with me, but one meal isn't enough. One weekend wasn't enough. I'm not sure anything ever will be. But it's a start, and I'll take whatever she's willing to give me.

The next three hours pass so slowly it's painful. I have a to-do list a mile long to get ready for this unexpected trip to Asia, but I manage to accomplish exactly none of it. Instead, I sit at my desk and re-hash the weekend we just spent together. It was impressive watching Landyn work. Jesse had said she was damn good at what she does, and he was right. And then afterwards, the nights I spent with her wrapped in my arms. The things she shared with me, and the things I know she's still keeping hidden.

Finally, after I've checked my watch approximately 42 times, it's noon, and there's a soft knock on my office door. Right on time.

"Food's already here," I say as she steps inside, closing the door gently behind her. "Hope you're still a fan of Chinese takeout."

She arches a brow as she crosses the room. "Depends. Did you get spring rolls?"

I hold out a take-out box. "Two orders. I don't share anymore."

She smirks, but it fades as soon as her fingers brush mine when she takes the container. That one small touch has me instantly remembering her bare legs tangled in the hotel bed sheets.

I watch her settle into the chair across from me, folding one leg under her like she belongs here. She opens the lid, glancing at me through her lashes. "I'm not eating in here if this turns into a thing," she says.

I lean back in my chair, my gaze steady. "What kind of thing?"

"The kind where you look at me like that." Her voice is teasing, but there's a warning in it.

"I can't help it."

"You could try."

I shake my head once. "Not when you're sitting across from me in that blouse looking as good as you do."

Her lips part just slightly. Her tongue darts out to wet her bottom lip and just like that, the space between us is too small. I take a bite of a roll—anything to distract my racing heart. Anything to stop myself from reaching out to her.

"You don't make it easy," I say quietly.

She leans forward, elbows on the desk now. "Make what easy?"

"You don't make it easy for me to be careful. Here, in this office, alone with you."

Her breath hitches, but she tries hard to hide it. I watch as she allows the silence to stretch on, then I tell her, "I want more of this."

She doesn't answer, but when she finally looks at me, it's not caution I see in her eyes, it's longing. I hold her gaze, seeing the heat in it, and I don't care anymore that we're in my office. I don't care that she's trying to keep this under control.

I rise from my chair slowly and walk around the desk, stopping to stand in front of her.

"I want more of this, Landyn," I repeat. "I want more of you."

Her throat works as she swallows. "Ford…"

I reach down and gently push her chair away from the desk, just enough so that I can step between her legs. I take the container from her hand and set it on my desk. She doesn't stop me. Her hands stay in her lap, but her eyes flick to my mouth like she's already tasting me. I run my knuckles slowly along her jaw. "Relax, baby."

She whispers, "Close the blinds."

I do, and when I turn back, I see she's standing now, pressed against the edge of my desk, her eyes dark.

I step into her space again and cup the side of her face. My thumb grazes her bottom lip, and she leans into the touch like she's already halfway gone. "I haven't stopped thinking about you," I murmur. "Not since the second I dropped you back off at the cottage."

She grabs my shirt and that's all I need. I kiss her—deep and sure, eliminating any space between us. She gasps against my mouth, and I swallow the sound as my hands slide down her back, anchoring her to me.

Her fingers fist in my shirt, pulling me closer, grinding against me as I press her back into the desk. I'm worked up—more turned on than I've ever been in my life. There's a wildfire burning just beneath my skin, searing through every inch of me. My palms are burning. My cheeks feel flushed. And my cock? So hard it's practically aching, demanding something, anything, to ease the pressure.

I reach into the front of my pants, adjusting my cock, and yeah, I can feel it. I'm already wet at the tip, proof of just how far gone I am. A shudder of arousal rips through me. Not small, not subtle. It's a full body, bone-deep shiver that grabs me by the shoulders and rattles me hard. I don't fight it because I wouldn't know how.

"You do something to me," I breathe against her lips. "Every damn time."

Her mouth finds mine again—hotter now, more desperate—and when I lift her onto the edge of the desk, she wraps her legs around my waist like she remembers exactly how good we are like this. My hand slips beneath her blouse, tracing the soft skin at her waist, then the edge of her bra. She moans into my mouth, hips rolling forward, and I nearly lose my mind.

"You want me to stop?" I whisper against her neck.

"No," she breathes. "God, no."

I tug her blouse up, exposing her bra, the swell of her chest flushed and rising fast with every breath. "I'm not going to fuck you on my desk," I murmur, dragging my mouth down her throat. "The first time I fuck you will be in my bed where I can take my time with you. But I want you to remember this every time you walk in here."

She lets out a shaky, wrecked laugh. "Mission accomplished."

I slide my hand under her skirt between her thighs and feel how soaked she is for me.

"Damn, June."

She gasps as my fingers slide her underwear to the side, insert one, then two fingers, fuck her just right. Her head tips back, hands clinging to my shoulders as I work her slowly, methodically, just enough to make her tremble. Just enough to make her fall apart.

Right here.

Right now.

Mine.

She's panting against my mouth now, her hands fisted in my shirt, her body tense and trembling under my touch. I'm coming apart at the seams. My balls are drawn up tight, and the head of my cock is pressed uncomfortably against my zipper. It's overload and not nearly enough all at once. The wrong kind of friction. The wrong kind of relief.

My fingers keep moving—quick, relentless strokes that I drag over every aching nerve, pushing deeper, curling just right, until she's trembling and gasping my name like it's the only word she knows. I feel it when she starts to lose it.

"Come on, Lan," I whisper against her throat. "Let go for me."

Her hips jerk forward, her breath catches, and then she's gasping my name like it's the only thing holding her together. She comes in my arms, quiet and desperate, her body arching off the desk. I keep my hand there, holding her through it, watching every second of her unraveling and fuck, she's beautiful like this.

Every part of me turns molten with lust as I watch her fall over the edge. Her head is arched back, her legs widened. Her eyes are closed, and she's riding my fingers.

I come without warning—without even realizing it's possible to come like this. From this. In my fucking pants. The pleasure is sharp, brutal, blinding—like a lightning strike that fractures me in half and leaves nothing but sensation behind.

It tears through me, raw and unstoppable, flooding out in

hot, pulsing waves that short-circuit everything else. My mind blanks, my body jerks, and I'm lost to it.

By the time Landyn comes down from her own high, I'm still trying to remember how to breathe. She slumps forward, forehead resting on my shoulder, her breathing still uneven.

She pulls back just enough to look at me, cheeks flushed, pupils still blown wide and yeah, there's something behind her eyes. Not regret, not quite. But something heavy. I smooth a hand over her hair. "You okay?"

She nods. "Yeah. Just...I didn't expect that...here."

"Me neither," I say. "But I'm not sorry."

She smiles, a little nervous, maybe, but genuine, and straightens her clothes. I help her down from the desk, keeping one hand on her hip until she's steady. She walks to the door, then pauses with her hand on the knob.

"It's hard to say no to you, Ford Winters."

I grin. "Exactly as I planned."

She laughs. "Safe travels. I'll see you when you get back."

And then she slips out of my office, leaving behind the faintest scent of her perfume and a mess in my pants I need to clean up.

TWENTY-FIVE

Landyn

The second I walk through the front door to the cottage after work, it all catches up to me.

The urgency.

His hands.

The way I fell apart in his arms with my back pressed to his desk in his office.

I still can't believe it—how reckless it was, how bold, how utterly unlike me. In the moment it felt intoxicating, dangerous in the best way, like we were playing with fire just to feel the burn. I'd forgotten what it felt like to be wanted like that. Touched like that. And not just by anyone...by him.

I kick off my shoes in the hallway and try to shake the look he gave me when I came undone, like I belonged to him. Like I always had.

God. I press a hand to my chest. I'm in trouble. And the worst part? I don't even care right now.

From the kitchen, I hear Poppy's laughter. My mom's, too. They're sitting at the table, my mom helping her trace letters with a purple glitter pen, the kind that always leaks. There's a half-eaten bowl of mac and cheese on the table beside them, and a crayon drawing of the dog Poppy's been begging for with the word "please" printed in wobbly letters underneath it stuck to the fridge.

"Hey," my mom says without looking up. "You're later than usual."

I fake a smile and hang my purse on the hook. "Got stuck in a meeting."

"Mmm." I have the distinct sense that she doesn't believe me, but thankfully she doesn't push.

Poppy turns and beams at me. "Mommy, I drew your dream house!"

I crouch beside her, resting my hand on her tiny knee. "Oh yeah? Lemme see."

She holds it up proudly, and I recognize the crooked little cabin with a heart above the door. "That's perfect," I whisper, kissing her temple.

Later, after bedtime, when Poppy's snuggled into her sheets and my mom's gone home, the silence settles around me again. I stand in the doorway of her bedroom for a minute, just watching her sleep. She looks so much like him, and he has no idea.

I back out slowly, pulling her door until it's almost closed, and head down the hallway to my room. My phone is still in my bag. I fish it out to find one new message.

> Ford: Still thinking about you and lunch and
> the sounds you made when I touched you.

I bite my lip then I turn off the screen and crawl into bed, the ache in my chest drowning out everything else.

It's been six days since he left.

Six days of early-morning texts and late-night check-ins. Ford may be halfway across the country, but he's made damn sure I haven't gone a single day without feeling his presence.

> Ford: Hope your day was better than mine.

> Ford: Lunch meeting was brutal. The conference room from hell. I miss you.

> Ford: Thinking about you and what I'm going to do to you when I get back. I want to see you. Friday?

The texts shouldn't undo me the way they do. This version of him—the thoughtful one, the steady one, the one who won't let a day go by without reaching out—is the one I fell for years ago. It's also the one I've been lying to.

Every night this week, after I've kissed Poppy goodnight, after I've set my phone aside, I've lied in bed and tried to convince myself that maybe I can keep this going just a little while longer. Maybe the secret I've been carrying for all these years doesn't need to be dragged out into the light just yet. Maybe I can just enjoy this thing—whatever it is—between us and wait and see what it could grow into.

But as hard as I try, I can't delude myself into thinking any of it could work.

Not anymore.

Not when he's talking about date nights and weekend getaways and things that sound dangerously like a future.

Ford is back tomorrow, and I have to tell him. I have to look him in the eye, and finally say it out loud.

You have a daughter.

Her name is Poppy.

She's six years old.

She has your eyes.

The thought of it makes my stomach twist, but I'm done running. If Ford and I have any shot at a future together, it has to start with the truth.

I just worry that the truth could be the thing that breaks us.

HE LANDS TODAY.

I've checked the clock at least 20 times since I woke up this morning, and I've read the text he sent me a couple of days ago at least as many times.

> Ford: Friday night. Just us. Dinner. No desks, no takeout. I want to see you, June.

God. I stare at the message on my phone like it'll disappear if I look away.

I worked from home all morning and am curled up on the couch in sweats, coffee going cold on the table in front of me. Poppy's at school so the house is quiet. A little too quiet. I've tidied up, put in a load of laundry, paid some bills, and watered the small vegetable garden my mom and I planted in the yard a few weeks ago. There's nothing left to distract me from the conversation I know I can't avoid any longer.

I've rehearsed it at least a dozen times, but I still don't know how I'm going to get through it. I've imagined every possible version. One where Ford yells. One where he walks away. One where he says nothing at all. And then there's the worst one of all—where he looks at me like he doesn't know me, with hurt and betrayal in his eyes.

But there's also a version where he listens. Where he looks at her photo and doesn't just see the time I stole from him—he just sees her.

Us.

When his flight finally lands, my phone buzzes with a message that knocks the breath right out of me.

> Ford: Home. I want to see you. You free in a
> couple hours?

I close my eyes and press the phone to my chest, then I text him back with shaking hands.

> Me: I'll be ready at 6pm.

I stare at the message for a long moment, heart thudding so loud I can hear it in my ears.

I don't deserve him, not when I'm still keeping this secret from him. I know that I could lose him once he knows the truth, and I'm not ready for that. After a week apart, and after what happened between us in his office the last time we were together, my entire body hums with anticipation at the thought of finally seeing Ford again.

I can't survive the weight of this secret for much longer, but there is a part of me that wants just one more night. One night to feel what it's like to be his again.

My phone buzzes in my hand with his response.

> Ford: Not sure I can make it that long. Make it
> worth the wait, June.

My cheeks flush, and a slow smile tugs at my lips. God, this man.

TWENTY-SIX

F ord
I swear the hands on the clock are moving backward because no matter how long I wait, 6 p.m. refuses to come.

After a week of long-distance teasing, nonstop travel days, and Landyn's voice in my head every time I close my eyes, I need her. Not through a screen. Not in a text bubble. Not at the office. Just us, together, in a place where we don't have to pretend we're not halfway in love again.

The drive to her place is fast, the sky already dipping into shades of gold and copper by the time I turn down her street. I don't bother running through what I'm going to say or do, I've been thinking about her too much to plan it out.

All I know is, I want tonight to feel different. I want more.

I want to take her out on a date.

Hold her hand.

Take things further.

I park out front of the little cottage and step out into the cooling air, the scent of the ocean immediately hitting me. I take the stairs two at a time and knock on her door. She opens it a moment later, and just like that my whole body lights up.

She's wearing a soft blue dress that hits mid-thigh, her hair loose in soft waves around her face. I can't stop staring.

"Hey," I say, a little lower than I mean to.

She smiles—nervous, but real. "Hey."

"You look…" I drag my eyes over her again, slower this time. "Like I've never seen anything more beautiful."

That gets a quiet laugh. "That must mean you like my dress."

I nod, stepping forward. "I do. Very much. Can I kiss you?"

She blushes, her hand sliding up my chest as my hands move to her nape. "That would be nice."

I touch my lips to her, humming as I kiss her.

I smile against her lips. "We should go before we're late."

It feels warm, familiar. I don't know where this night is going but I already know I don't want it to end. Ten minutes later, we're walking towards the front doors of the restaurant. I picked Wave and Wharf because it has a low-key vibe that felt perfect for tonight—dim lights, ocean views, and just far enough away from Deep Cove's hot spots that we shouldn't run into anyone from the office. I don't want any interruptions.

I watch her slide into the booth across from me, dress hugging her legs, those soft waves brushing her collarbone.

She looks around the restaurant, one brow raised. "Wow. Tablecloths and everything."

"I'm trying to win you over," I say, shrugging out of my jacket. "I don't mess around."

"I remember that about you. Some things never change."

"Apparently." I lean forward. "So, is it working?"

Her lips curl. "That depends. What am I in for?"

"Dinner. Wine. Me." I pause. "Dessert's negotiable."

She lifts her glass of water, hiding her grin behind the rim. "You're definitely not subtle."

"Never claimed to be." I pick up my menu. "But I'm very effective."

She hums. "We'll see about that."

Our server arrives a few minutes later and we order right away. She takes our menus before leaving, and as Landyn hands hers over, her foot brushes mine underneath the table.

My eyes meet hers. "You playing footsie, Sinclair?"

She shrugs, all innocence. "Small table."

"Sure." I wink.

"Is that why you chose this place? For its close quarters? You always did do your research. Take a look if you want—I can barely cross my legs without my foot ending up in your lap."

I arch a brow. "I'm not opposed to that. And believe me, I've been looking at your legs since we got here."

She takes a slow sip of wine, which does nothing to hide the fact that her cheeks are suddenly flushed. "I thought you were always more of an eyes guy."

"I'm a *you* guy."

That gets her. She presses her lips together like she's trying not to smile, but it slips out anyway. And I swear to God, that smile? I'd burn this place down for it.

"You've gotten better at this."

"At what?" I ask, taking note of the way she's leaned toward me, the way her eyes are locked on mine.

"The flirting. The teasing. The..." she gestures at me with a little wave of her fingers, "all of this."

"I've had a lot of time, thinking about what I'd do if I ever saw you again."

She tilts her head, one finger slowly circling the rim of her wine glass. "And?"

"I guess you'll have to wait and see. I'm still deciding which part to act on first."

"Start with dessert," she says, smirking. "Then we'll talk."

Just then, the server arrives with our food, cutting the moment short. Landyn settles back into her seat like this isn't the most sexually charged meal I've had in my life. Her bare leg brushes mine under the table again, and I don't move. I want her to feel me. Want her to know I'm right here, watching her, thinking about how that mouth of hers looks around a fork.

She takes another delicate bite of her salmon, pausing when she catches me staring at her.

"What's that look for?" she asks suspiciously.

I shrug. "Didn't peg you for the refined type. You're cutting that fish like we're at a Michelin-starred restaurant. No offense to Wave and Warf."

She lifts her chin. "I have layers."

"You definitely do." I spear a bite of my steak, lean forward, and offer it across the table. "You need to try this."

Her eyes narrow playfully. "I thought you don't share?"

"Just say *ah*, June."

She rolls her eyes but opens her mouth. Slowly. Deliberately, and when she leans in and wraps her lips around the bite, I swear every muscle in my body locks up.

She hums as she chews, her eyes briefly closing. "Mmm. That's so good."

And just like that, my cock gets hard.

We go back to eating—well, she does. I mostly just sit here and try to pretend that I'm not three seconds from pulling her over the table and tasting that damn wine off her lips. She wipes the corner of her mouth with a napkin, eyes flashing. "You're quiet."

"Just working on my self-control."

She leans back, slow and confident. "And how's that going?"

I rest my forearm on the table, hand close to hers, not touching. "Ask me in an hour."

She bites her lip, and for once, she doesn't respond with a quick comeback. She just looks at me like she wants the same thing I do and it's not just dinner.

Dinner winds down, but the energy between us doesn't. She finishes her wine with one last sip, tipping her head to drain the last of the glass, and I'm mesmerized watching the smooth column of her neck. Her dress has ridden up just enough to show more of her thigh than is fair, and I've given up pretending I'm not looking.

The server arrives with our bill, and it's not a second too soon for me. I pay for the meal, then stand and offer my hand to Landyn. She hesitates for just a second but then slides her palm into mine.

"Dinner was delicious. Thank you."

"I'm glad you enjoyed it."

The noise from the restaurant spills out behind us as I push the door open. It's dark now, and the night is cool and quiet. The restaurant is tucked away from the regular tourist haunts, so the street is deserted as we walk back to my car. We don't talk. We don't need to. Her fingers are still laced through mine and her hip brushes against me. Then again. When we reach the passenger side, I open the door for her, but she doesn't get in right away. She just looks up at me with heat in her chocolate eyes as the air between us grows thicker.

"Where are we going?" she asks, voice soft.

I step closer, entering her space without touching her.

"My place," I say simply. "Unless you want to end the night here."

She doesn't answer right away, but she doesn't need to when I notice the way her eyes drop to my mouth and stay there for a moment. Then she nods. "That sounds perfect."

She settles into the passenger seat of my Porsche like she belongs there, and I close the door, round the hood, and climb in beside her. Silence stretches out between us as I start the engine, it feels loaded, heavy with anticipation.

The car hums low as I shift into gear, hand brushing the gearstick just inches from her thigh. She doesn't move away. If anything, she shifts closer.

I glance at her, noticing the way she's twirling the ring on her index finger. "You nervous?"

She turns her head slowly, deliberately. "Are you?"

I reach for her hand, lacing her fingers between mine, resting them against her thigh. "No. I've been thinking about this for a long time."

A beat passes, then the corners of her lips tip up. She squeezes my hand in hers and I press the gas pedal a little harder. By the time I pull into the driveway, I'm gripping the wheel with one hand like it's the only thing keeping me in control. I throw the car in park, cut the engine, and turn to her.

"You sure?" I ask, even though I already know the answer.

Her lips part and she says the one word I've been waiting for. "Yes."

I slide out of the car and walk around to her door, opening it and offering her a hand to help her out. She takes it, and I swear when her hand slips back into mine, I feel it in every single part of me.

Pushing open the front door, I place a hand on the small of her back to guide her inside. Stella barrels into the room the second we're through the door, her nails clicking across the hardwood floor.

"Hi there, good girl." Landyn crouches automatically, her dress sliding up her thighs, and Stella leans all her weight into her like she belongs to her. Landyn grins happily, brushing her fingers along her head.

"I think she's your biggest fan," I tell her, watching as she rewards Stella's over-the-top display of affection with a belly rub. Eventually, once she's had her fill of attention, Stella gives a full-body shake, then trots to her bed in the kitchen, where she circles three times before flopping down with a dramatic sigh.

"She's got a tough life," I say, rolling my eyes, as Landyn stands and smoothes her hands over the hem of her dress. She laughs, and it's so sweet and genuine that I feel it in my core.

I cross the room to her. No more games. No more banter. Just the heat building in my chest and the way her breath stutters when I stop in front of her. She tilts her chin up, lips parted, and her eyes meet mine. "What?"

I don't answer. I just trace my knuckles down her cheek, then I lean in, close enough that I feel her breath on my mouth. "You drive me crazy," I murmur. "Goddammit, Lan. I want this. I want us. I want to give us a second chance."

The expression on her face is hard to read. It's hopeful, but there's hesitation there too.

"Do you want that?" I ask. "I mean, could you see us together again, without everything else in the way? Are you willing to try?"

My heart slams against my ribs and I wait, terrified at the possibility that she might not want me the same way I want her. My mind has been racing non-stop since she walked back into my life and right now, something has cracked inside of me. I'm done waiting. I need her.

"Ford...it's not that simple. We—"

"It *is* that simple. I'm not saying we can just go back to what we used to be. I know it's been a long time. But I still want you, Landyn. I never stopped."

"Me too," she finally admits. "But we're still us and we can't erase everything that has happened...I've hurt you. I know that."

"And we're lucky that we found each other again. We can't throw it away this time." I cup her jaw in my hands. "We can do it right this time. Get to know each other again without anyone in our way. We can go as slow as you want, Lan. It's always been you for me and I'm not willing to lose another seven years."

She lets out a soft laugh. "We don't know how to take things slow. That's never been our thing."

"Then let's not take it slow," I murmur.

She shakes her head and my heart twists. "Ford...there are things we need to talk about."

"There's nothing you could say that would change how I feel."

"You don't know that," she whispers. "We need to talk."

I lean forward, resting my forehead against hers. "Be with me tonight," I say. "No expectations. No past. Just us. You can say whatever you need to say in the morning."

Her brown eyes lock on mine, and then she nods.

So, I kiss her.

It's not soft or slow. I kiss her like I've been waiting years to do it. She gasps against my mouth, and I take full advantage, my tongue slipping past her lips, my hands sliding around her waist, pulling her into me, needing her to feel it. All of it.

She leans into me, her hips pressing to mine, and I know this is it. Tonight, I'm not letting her go.

There's nothing gentle or hesitant between us now—just need, and want, and the sound she makes when I back her into the wall beside the stairs. My hips roll into hers, searching for friction, and my hard cock against her clit has her lips falling open and a moan slipping from her lips.

"You're hard, Ford," she says against my mouth.

"I'm constantly hard when I'm around you, Lan. It's a problem," I growl before nipping at her bottom lip with my teeth.

She pulls at my shirt, fingers fumbling with the buttons. "Take it off."

I do, ripping it open, not bothering with finesse. Buttons scatter to the floor as I shrug it off, and her hands are on my chest like she's been starving for this.

"God," she breathes, dragging her nails down my ribs. Her bottom lip is trapped under her teeth as her eyes gaze down my body. "Ford..."

"Say it again," I growl, catching her mouth in another kiss

as my hands slide up her thighs and under her dress. "Say my name again." She whispers it as I grip her ass, lifting her easily off the floor. She locks her legs around my waist as I press her back into the wall, grinding against her. She moans, low and guttural, and I swear it goes straight to my already rock-hard cock.

"You've changed a lot in seven years. You're different but still the same," she says, drawing paths slowly over my muscles like she's seeing me for the first time. "I've missed this so much."

"You have no idea."

I carry her across the living room and drop her onto the couch, kneeling between her thighs. Her dress is hitched up to her hips, and when I drag it off her in one swift move, she lifts her arms, letting it go. Now she's in nothing but a pale blue lace bra and panties. Fuck me.

"You're unreal," I mutter, leaning down to kiss the curve of her stomach. "You know that?"

Her fingers slide into my hair as I kiss a trail lower. But I'm not giving her everything. Not yet. Instead, I rise again, pull her off the couch and into me.

She tugs at my belt, lips finding my neck. We're tangled. Desperate. "Bedroom."

I nod once, already walking her backward. In the hallway, she stops just long enough to pull my belt free with a wicked smile, then lets it drop to the floor.

"You're beautiful *and* you're a menace," I murmur, dragging my lips to my favorite freckle on her jaw and then down her neck.

She grins. "You love it."

She's right. Landyn might come off as soft and sweet, but behind closed doors, she's bold and curious. She's never been too shy to ask for what she wants. Take what she needs.

She's stunning. Smooth, olive skin. Toned and perfect in a

way that makes me ache to ruin her, to mark every inch as mine, to prove no one else could ever touch her the way I will. I pause to take her in. No one has ever been able to turn me on that way she does. When my heart slows to an almost normal pace, I lean in and kiss her, sweeping my tongue into her mouth.

I grab her ass, pick her up, and carry her to my bedroom. Once inside, I kick the door closed behind us, then she unwinds her legs from around my waist and slips down my body until her toes find the ground.

"Take your clothes off, Landyn. Nice and slow while I watch you."

She takes a few steps backward, closer to the bed, her brown eyes glued to mine the entire time. I watch her hands reach around to find the clasp of her bra, teasing me as the straps fall from her shoulders. When the lace drops to the floor, I lick my lips in anticipation. Landyn's tits are fucking perfect. I remember how her nipples would harden when I sucked on them, how she would moan, her head falling back when I nipped them with my teeth. I remember everything she likes. I'm hard as hell when her fingers slip under the lace around her hips, and she lowers her panties to the ground.

"Fucking perfect," I murmur. "I remember every inch of you, Lan."

"You really haven't forgotten?"

I reach for her, brushing the tips of my fingers over her hips. "There hasn't been a day since you left that I haven't pictured you in my mind."

She smiles against my mouth then she pulls back, her eyes filled with heat and something that feels a hell of a lot like trust.

I reach for the button on my jeans only for her to swat my hand away.

"Let me," she says dropping to her knees, tracing the line of hair leading from my belly button to my cock until her fingers reach the waistband of my pants. She flicks open the button then slowly unzips the fly. She pushes my pants and my briefs over my hips to the floor, leaving me bare when my cock springs free. Her eyes move over me slowly, like she's memorizing me again, and I swear I feel it in every nerve ending.

I cup her jaw. "Are you okay?"

She nods, just the slightest movement of her head, and a small smile tips her lips. "I think I forgot how big you are," she breathes, her voice trembling with awe as her gaze drags over my cock. "You just... took my breath away. It's my turn to make you feel good."

"Fuck, baby. You look so beautiful on your knees for me." I run my hand through her hair, my muscles coiled tight in anticipation waiting for her mouth. "I can only imagine how good you're going to look with my cock in your mouth."

"I've never stopped wanting you," she says, wrapping her hand around my shaft, and I groan, loud and guttural, as her mouth follows.

"Fuck," I hiss, my hand tangling in her hair as her lips close around the head of my cock, tongue swirling, teasing. "Goddamn, Landyn. You're gonna kill me."

She hums around me, and I swear I see stars. She's slow and deliberate, taking her time, teasing just the crown with her tongue, sucking me in inch by inch, looking up at me with eyes that make me want to wreck her.

"You have no idea what you're doing to me," I growl, straining to stay still, my legs already trembling.

She moans again, sending another jolt straight through me, swirling her tongue around the head. Then she teases me, licking slow paths up and down my shaft, cupping my balls, before she sucks me to the back of her throat.

"You're gonna make me come down your throat if you keep sucking me like that," I warn her.

She doesn't stop. She doesn't slow down. She continues to work me with her mouth while she jacks me off at the base with one hand and lightly dusts the skin of my balls with the other.

I try to focus on not coming but when she looks up at me, her mouth full of my cock, all I can do is hold her head in place and rock my hips into her mouth. I'm so damn close, I can feel the tip hit the back of her throat, but I want to be inside her too damn badly to come now.

I can't take much more. I pull her off gently, her lips glistening, cheeks flushed.

"Get up here," I say roughly, grabbing her and carrying her to the bed.

Her head falls back against the pillow while I crawl over her, burying my face into her neck. Her eyes close right before I kiss her—hot and deep, with years of ache poured into every stroke of my tongue against hers. She melts into me, hands gripping my shoulders, pulling me in like she needs me just as badly.

"You're perfect." I grind against her, my cock thick and heavy between us, rubbing against her wetness as I kiss her again, slow this time, knowing we have all night.

I take my time pressing kisses to her jaw, down her throat until I reach her two perfect tits. I pinch her nipples with my fingers before sucking both stiff peaks into my mouth. I grow painfully harder, if that's even possible, listening to every mewl and moan that leaves her mouth.

"I need you inside of me," she pants.

Fuck, those are words I never thought I'd hear from her again. But not yet. First, I need to make her come with my tongue.

I work my way down her stomach, slow and hungry, kissing

a trail over her skin as I go. Her thighs are already trembling just from the anticipation, her skin so fucking sensitive. I need to pause and grip the base of my dick to stop myself from coming at just thought of tasting her again. When I get my shit together, I hold her legs down, spreading her wide.

She moans when I settle between her legs and press my mouth to her center like I've been starving for it because I have. I groan against her as I taste her, one hand spreading her open, the other gripping her hip so she can't move, can't escape the way I devour her.

"Fuck, June," I rasp between licks. "You taste so fucking good."

Her fingers sink into my hair, back arching as I suck her clit into my mouth, then lick her long and slow before doing it all over again. I work her with my tongue and lips, teasing until she's writhing and breathless, whispering my name like a prayer. Her thighs tense around me, and I know she's close.

"Come for me, baby," I murmur, mouth pressed hot against her. "I need to feel you come on my tongue."

I bury my face between her thighs again, focusing on her clit because I know that's what she likes. I suck on the bundle of nerves while sinking two fingers inside her. When I curl my fingers, brushing her front wall, I feel her tighten around my knuckles, her entire body contracting as she comes.

She comes with a soft cry, her heels digging into my back as she falls apart under my mouth. I don't stop until I've wrung every last bit of pleasure from her, until she's trembling and twitching, gasping for air.

When I crawl up her body, her eyes are heavy-lidded, her lips kiss-bitten. "My God, Ford," she whispers, still breathless.

"I told you," I murmur, voice thick with heat. "I've been starving."

Her breath catches as I settle between her thighs again, this time with my cock teasing her entrance, slick and aching to be inside her. I hold still, watching her face, brushing her hair back from her cheek.

"I want you," I murmur, voice low and raw. "I've missed you."

Her hands slide up my back, nails grazing my skin. "Then take me, Ford."

TWENTY-SEVEN

L andyn
I'm in a post-orgasm daze, completely in a fog when he asks, "How do you want me to take you, Lan?"

I tell him I want it every way, and that we don't need to use protection.

"Are you sure?" he asks, his voice rough with restraint.

I nod, biting my bottom lip. "I'm on the pill," I whisper. "I want this. I want you bare."

That's all it takes. He kisses me again, hard and all-consuming. One hand slides down between us as he lines himself up, the thick head of his cock teasing my entrance. The stretch is slow and deliberate. Deep and devastating.

I gasp as he presses in, inch by inch, the sensation toeing that perfect line between too much and not enough. He's big—thick, heavy, and impossibly hard—and the way he fills me is both familiar and new. Like my body still remembers him. Like it's missed this.

My legs wrap around his waist instinctively, grounding myself as he sinks deeper.

"God, you feel—" I breathe, too overwhelmed to finish the sentence.

He groans against my throat, his mouth trailing fire along my skin. "So fucking tight. So warm. You take me so damn well, June."

The nickname nearly undoes me, the combination of him finally inside me and the sound of June on his lips sparks through my veins, like fire, lighting me up from the inside out.

He starts to move, slow and controlled, dragging every inch of himself out before thrusting back in. My head falls back against the pillow, my eyes closed, fingers clutching the sheets, the rhythm winding me up with every measured thrust. Each time he fills me, it's like he's carving something into me. Deeper than before. Deeper than I knew I could feel.

Ford Winters was always beautiful, but this older, more mature version of him—with the sharp angle of his jaw, the carved grid of his abs—takes it to a whole new level. He looks more rugged, more manly and sexier even than I had expected. And my expectations were sky-high.

I open my eyes, taking every inch of him in. When I finish my tour of his body, he's watching me, the full extent of what is happening written all over his face.

He's inside me.

Not just inside me, the root of his cock is flush with my pelvic bone.

I settle myself with a breath and place my hand where our bodies are joined. Both of our eyes flick down, caught in the sight of him buried inside me, and for a breathless moment we watch in stunned reverence as he draws back and sinks into me again.

"You always fit me like this," he murmurs. "Like you were made for me."

His words make me clench around him, make me arch into him with a soft, broken sound.

"Ford," I moan, breathless.

"I know," he says, voice strained. "I feel it too."

He pushes hair from my face, cups my jaw in his hands, his gray eyes seeping into mine saying without words what we're both feeling. This isn't just sex—it's so much more. This is really happening, and we are just so fucking lucky that we found each other again.

He runs his thumb over my bottom lip, my teeth nipping at the tip. "I've missed you so much."

My heart cracks wide open in my chest. Just a few months ago I never would have imagined *we* were a possibility. Ford leans down and presses a slow kiss to my lips before resting his forehead against mine.

"I can't lose you again," he murmurs, voice breaking against my lips.

He pulls out then pushes back in, slow and steady, his size filling me up like he's branding me from the inside out, every thrust a mark I'll never forget. We both groan at the same time, my legs tighten around him, my back arches, and I feel like I've come home.

"Fuck, you feel good, June."

He starts to move again. Long, deep thrusts that have me gasping, clutching at his thighs. His breath is hot against my neck as I beg him, "Harder."

He drives into me with more force, our bodies finding that rhythm they always had. The slap of skin, the breathless cries, the way he pulls my mouth to his between moans—I can't get enough.

"Goddamn, Landyn. You're mine. You always were."

He moans, clinging to me, while I meet every thrust like my body was made for him. I shudder from the blinding bliss when he finds that spot deep inside of me.

"Right there, baby?" he asks, voice gravel as he keeps thrusting into me.

"Yes, Ford. Don't stop."

He shifts, reaching under my thigh to hitch my leg higher, and the angle makes me cry out—sharper, louder. The pressure between us doubles, pleasure rolling through me like a slow, hot tide. It builds so fast I barely have time to catch it before I'm coming around him, my whole body shaking, breath caught, vision blurred.

He doesn't stop. He holds me through it, kissing my cheek, my shoulder, whispering praise as I fall apart beneath him. Then he flips us, so I'm straddling him, breath still ragged. I blink down at him, my body still trembling. His hands are firm on my hips, but gentle, waiting for me.

"You okay?" he asks, voice low and wrecked.

I nod, my mouth curving into a small smile. "More than okay."

"Then ride me," he says, dark eyes locked on mine. "I want to watch you come again."

The words send another tremor through me as I rise up on my knees and line up Ford's beautiful cock with my entrance. I tease him at first, gliding the head of him through my folds, coating him with me, tapping his crown against my clit. Then I slowly sink down, an inch at a time. I start to move, slowly at first, rolling my hips, testing the way it feels to be in control, to have him at my mercy. His hands slide up my thighs, along my waist, thumbs brushing just beneath my breasts as I lift and lower myself over him.

It's deep. Intimate. A kind of raw I didn't know I had left in me.

"Fuck, Landyn," he groans. "You're killing me. You feel so good. You're choking my dick, so greedy for me, baby. You're so fucking wet and tight."

I moan in response and my head falls back.

"Grab the headboard for me, baby. Be a good girl and hold on while I fuck you the way you deserve."

I lean forward, bracing my hands on the headboard as I grind down on him, harder now, needing more. His hands fall to my ass, guiding me, pushing me to take him deeper, rougher. His cock hits that perfect spot with each thrust, and I'm unravelling all over again, wrecked on the feel of him, lost in the high only he can give me.

When I come this time, it's with his name on my lips and his body beneath mine, every muscle taut as he loses control too. He spills inside me with a groan that's primal, guttural. His hands grip my hips like he's afraid I'll disappear, and I almost might because nothing's ever felt like this.

"You're ruining me."

"No," he rasps, pulling me into him, kissing the side of my throat. "I'm putting us back together."

We collapse together, tangled in sheets and sweat and everything we still are. After a long minute, Ford rolls me onto my back and curls me into his chest, his fingers tracing lazy lines over my heart. He runs a hand down my back, over the curve of my hip, anchoring me to him. He shifts, hooking his leg over mine, and his voice is quiet when he finally speaks. "We're still just as beautiful together."

I brush a kiss to his shoulder.

"I never forgot how to love you, June. I just...didn't think I'd ever get the chance again.

I don't say anything, worried that if I do, what comes out may shatter this perfect moment. So instead, I just breathe. I can feel the weight of it pressing between us—what I still haven't told him. I think he can feel it too, but he doesn't push, just whispers, "Was that okay?"

I nod, but I'm not sure it's very convincing.

"I meant what I said earlier," he murmurs. "We can take this slow, but I'm not going to pretend I don't want you. That I don't feel all of it, just like I used to."

I turn in his arms, eyes meeting his in the dim light. "I feel it too."

A beat of silence. "But?"

My lips part and I think maybe I'm going to tell him but I can't get the words out. Not now. "We need to talk," I say finally.

"We will. Tomorrow. Let's just live in this moment a little longer, yeah?"

I exhale. "Okay."

He tilts my chin gently so that I'm looking at him. "Let's not ruin anything. Let's just...lie here for now. No promises. No expectations."

I rest my head against his chest again, and I feel his whole body settle. Like I'm his. Like I'm still that safe place for him. And I realize something in the quiet, something I haven't let myself fully acknowledge until now.

I don't just want tonight.

I want everything.

TWENTY-EIGHT

L andyn
I wake to rain tapping softly against the windows. It takes me a second to remember where I am—the way the morning light slips through the curtains, the quiet rise and fall of his chest beneath my cheek. Ford's arm is wrapped tightly around me, his palm splayed low on my back like he's anchoring me in place.

For one long, blissful moment, I don't think about the truth I haven't told him. I just breathe and remember last night. God, we were reckless. God, he's still good at it.

The way his mouth moved down my body like he didn't care how long it took to make me come, only that he got to be the one to do it. His hands pinning me to the bed. His tongue stroking me until I was panting his name. I had forgotten what that kind of pleasure felt like. And when he finally pushed inside me, it was like my body had been waiting for that exact moment, that exact stretch, that exact man. It wasn't just the best sex I've had in years—it was the best sex I've had in my life. It was more than just chemistry, just desire. It was history.

It was what we used to be, what we still are, even if we don't know how to name it anymore.

But as incredible as it was, the secret I'm still carrying feels heavier than ever in the morning light.

"Hey," Ford murmurs, voice still thick with sleep, lips brushing the top of my head.

"Hi," I whisper back, but don't look up at him. I don't want to move. I'm not ready for this to end.

His hand slides up my spine, then down again, slower. "You sleep okay?"

I nod. "Yeah."

He shifts so I'm facing him, and for a second, I think, *this is it*. The moment I tell him. The moment everything changes.

I open my mouth—

And his phone rings.

He groans, dragging a hand down his face. "I'll ignore it," he says. But a few moments later, it rings again. He sighs and grabs it, squinting at the screen. "It's Noah."

I sit up, clutching the bedsheet to my chest as he swipes his phone screen to answer the call.

"Yeah?" A pause. Then his tone shifts, sharpening. "Wait, what? When?"

He glances at me. "I'll be there in 30."

The pit in my stomach forms fast as he hangs up and sits up fully, rubbing the back of his neck. "One of the factory reps flew in early. The walk-through that was supposed to happen tomorrow is now happening this morning. They need me there... now."

"Oh." I try not to sound as disappointed as I feel, but he seems to sense it anyways.

"I'm sorry, Lan," he says quickly. "This just got dumped on us. Believe me, I hate having to leave you after everything we just did."

"I get it," I say, even though my heart is thudding with

everything I didn't get to say. Everything still sitting in my throat.

He stands, pulling on his jeans and grabbing a Cove polo shirt from his closet. "Will you wait for me until I get back?"

I hesitate. "I should probably head home."

"Already?" he asks, sounding deflated.

I offer a small smile, hoping it reassures him. "I have a few things I need to do today."

He watches me for a long moment, eyes narrowed slightly, like he wants to press but he doesn't. "Okay. I'll call you later?"

I nod. "Yeah. Call me."

He closes the space between us, his fingers brushing my cheek, then tilting my chin just enough to press a soft kiss to my forehead. "Last night was perfect," he says, before kissing me slowly.

And then he's gone.

The house is quiet after Ford leaves, and for a while, I just sit on the edge of his bed, the sheets tangled around my waist, trying to remember how to breathe. Eventually, I gather my clothes from where we dropped them, get dressed and wander into the kitchen, the hardwood cool under my bare feet. Stella instantly greets me, and I crouch down to stroke the soft fur behind her ears.

I putter around the house for a few minutes under the pretense of tidying up—not because the place is messy (this is Ford, after all), but because I'm curious. The kitchen is spotless. No coffee cup left in the sink, no leftover toast crumbs scattered across the countertop. I move into the living room, noticing the large, polished wood bowl on the coffee table, the soft, heather-gray blanket folded neatly on the end of the couch.

Stella follows me as I walk down the hall, past the closed door to his office, past the framed photos of him alongside his brothers. I stop when I come to a picture of Ford standing beside a Cove van, caked in dirt with the biggest grin on his face.

A lump forms in my throat.

Suddenly I can see it all—how easy it would be to exist here. It's like watching a movie in my head, envisioning how this place would stretch and grow to become a home for us. A second coffee mug on the counter. Poppy's crayons in a drawer. Her sparkly, pink rain boots beside his rugged black ones in the closet.

I press my fingers to my lips and will the tears not to fall. This house feels like somewhere we could build a life together. If I could somehow find the courage to tell him what he deserves to know.

THE DOOR CREAKS OPEN AS I KNOCK LIGHTLY AND PUSH IT OPEN. "Hey, it's me," I call into the familiar entryway.

"In the kitchen," my mom answers.

I toe off my shoes and step inside my parents' modest home. Poppy's giggle comes from somewhere down the hall, likely her makeshift playroom. I find my mom sitting at the kitchen table in a robe, her hair still damp from a shower, an untouched cup of tea in front of her. She looks pale, tired.

"Are you okay?" I ask instantly, setting my purse down and crouching beside her chair.

She waves me off. "It's nothing. Just been feeling off a little this morning."

"You should've called me. I would have come earlier to pick up Poppy so you could get some rest."

She shrugs like it's nothing, but the tightness in her eyes tells me she's not being entirely truthful.

"What do you need? I can stay," I offer. "Or take you to the clinic."

"No, no," she says, gently squeezing my hand. "Go home, sweetheart. Take care of your girl. I'll rest. If I start to feel worse, I promise I'll call."

I nod but worry curls in my stomach. I stand up just as Poppy barrels into the kitchen, arms stretched high. "Mommy!"

I scoop her up, burying my face in her curls. "I missed you, Poppyseed," I say into her hair. "Are you ready to go?"

"Can we stop for a donut?"

I laugh. "Yeah, baby. We can get a donut."

I gather our things and kiss my mom's forehead on the way out, still not able to unravel the knot of worry that formed as soon as I saw her. There have been a couple of times since I've been back that she's seemed confused, her hair is thinning, and she has been getting increasingly sluggish, which is not like her at all. She tries to brush it off, but it's obvious now that something is wrong. My mom is always on the go, always vibrant and full of energy. My dad admitted to me not long ago that he's worried she's developing early onset dementia. Today she seemed small, almost frail.

After buckling Poppy in, I slide into the driver's seat and take a deep breath. I focus on the sound of my daughter humming in the back seat, reminding myself that I need to keep things normal for her, especially when it feels like everything else is shifting.

We hit the bakery for donuts, where she stares wide-eyed at the display case for ages, finally settling on a chocolate one with rainbow sprinkles. She talks nonstop about her sleepover, about the movie she watched with my dad, about how she thinks she might want to be a "kayak scientist" when she grows up. I nod and laugh and ask questions, but in the back of my mind, my mom is still there.

And so is Ford.

The memory of last night is still warm on my skin. The way he looked at me, touched me, kissed me like I was still his. The way I let him, and how the guilt had hit me as soon as I opened my eyes this morning.

It's all tangled together now. Ford. Poppy. My mom. This heavy truth I'm carrying. It all feels like a bomb waiting to explode, ticking louder by the day.

By the time we get home, Poppy's yawning between bites of her donut, so I scoop her up and carry her inside. She's getting too big for this, but I don't care. I need the closeness. The comfort.

Later, when she's curled up on the couch watching cartoons, I sit at the kitchen table with my phone in my hand, staring at the screen. I should call Ford, but there's something else I need to do first. I open my contacts, searching for the name of my mom's doctor.

"Hi, this is Landyn Sinclair, Carolyn's daughter. I'm wondering if she has any upcoming appointments. If not, I'd like to bring her in."

I'M CURLED UP IN BED, THE ROOM DARK EXCEPT FOR THE FAINT glow coming from my phone.

> Ford: Can't stop thinking about you in my bed last night. I barely made it through that meeting today.

A slow smile pulls at my lips.

> Me: That very important meeting that required your full attention?

Ford: I paid attention. Sort of. Not really. You
distracted the hell out of me. All I could see
was you riding me with your hands on my
headboard.

Heat floods my cheeks as I bite my lip, memories flooding
my mind. I shouldn't encourage him. But God, I want to.

Ford: I miss you, and my bed is way too
cold now.

I exhale, sinking deeper under the covers.

Me: I'm sure you will survive. So how did the
meeting go?

Ford: Not as good as I hoped. They want to
see me again tomorrow. I'll be tied up dealing
with this for the next couple days, still trying to
clean up the mess we're in.

My stomach twists slightly. Work. Reality. Everything
waiting to catch up to us.

Me: I'm sorry. You okay?

Ford: Getting there. I just hate that I won't
see you.

Me: I understand. You'll be busy saving Cove.

Ford: Still gonna think about you. Every night.
Every time I close my eyes. I'll make it up to
you, June. Promise. I miss you.

I stare at that nickname like it might break me. Then I write the only thing I can.

Me: I miss you too.

I set the phone down on the nightstand and sink deeper into my pillows, pressing the heels of my hands into my eyes to try to hold back the tears that threaten to fall. But it doesn't work. I pull the quilt up over my chin, hoping to muffle the sounds of my sobbing.

Poppy is asleep down the hall, tucked safely in her bed, surrounded by her favorite stuffed animals. She is sweet and funny and curious. She has the most infectious laugh, and loves being outside. She's perfect. And he has no idea. Ford has missed seven years of milestones that he will never be able to get back—first words, first steps, birthday candles, scraped knees, dance recitals, all the big and little moments that make up a life.

It's my fault that he doesn't know her. And it's my fault that I'm falling for him all over again without telling him the one thing that could change everything.

I close my eyes and try to sleep, but all I see is the way he looked at me last night—like I'm something he's been waiting for.

But the truth is, he doesn't know everything about me. And the parts I've kept from him may end up being more than he can forgive.

TWENTY-NINE

F ord

The meeting room at the new Cove site smells like fresh drywall and stale coffee. Jesse, Noah, Wes and I are huddled around the table, poring through the mock-ups for the sustainability campaign while the faint sound of the ongoing construction outside echoes around us. It should feel like progress. Like momentum. But all I feel is stress.

"We need more than a PR spin," I say, tugging at the back of my neck. "If we're going to rebuild trust, we need to show them what's changed, not just tell them."

Noah nods. "Factory tours, transparency reports. Let them see it for themselves."

"Maybe we pair the new campaign launch with a video series," Wes chimes in. "Real employees, behind-the-scenes footage."

It's a solid idea. Usually, this is where I would step up to flesh out the details, make sure we've thought of every possible obstacle and angle but all I can think about is her.

I glance at my phone on the table. Still nothing.

I texted Landyn hours ago. It was just a quick message

between meetings. *How's your day looking? Can't stop thinking about last night.* There's been no reply. The rational side of my brain knows she's probably busy at work but there's something tugging at me, telling me that maybe there is something wrong. I send off another quick text.

Me: Everything okay?

Telling myself not to panic, I return my focus to the meeting. I nod at the right moments, contribute when needed, but when I turn my phone over again 30 minutes later to find that there's still no response, something inside me knots.

I know Landyn, she always answers her messages. The hairs on the back of my neck are on end. I realize I'm getting desperate now, but I'm beyond caring how it looks. I tap out another message.

Me: Landyn?

The hum of unease grows in my chest. I know she has her own life, and there are plenty of perfectly reasonable explanations for why she hasn't replied. But something feels off, and I've never been good at waiting when it comes to her.

We work through lunch, so by the time five o'clock hits, we're all starving. We agree to take a quick break, and I use the time to go outside and get some fresh air, hopefully get my head on straight. But it doesn't help. Instead, the knot in my stomach tightens into something sharper. Something closer to fear.

I pull out my phone and stare at the thread. Three messages. No replies. No read receipts.

Me: Landyn, just checking in. Can you let me
know you're okay?

I hesitate for half a second before tapping her name and pressing the call button. It rings once, twice, then goes to voicemail.

"Hey, it's Landyn. Leave a message—"

I hang up. That sinking feeling in my gut kicks hard. This silence doesn't feel like her. I send one more message, my thumb flying across the screen.

> Me: Please text me when you see this. I'm
> starting to worry.

Behind me, I hear the creak of a door and turn to see all three of my brothers standing on the landing, staring at me.

"What?" I ask, regretting how irritable it sounds.

"Alright," Wes says, coming to stand next to me. "You've looked at your phone more than the budget projections. Who are you texting?"

I scrub a hand over my jaw. "Landyn. She's not answering."

Jesse looks up from his phone. "Is that strange?"

"She always answers." I frown. "Pretty much right away. But it's been all day."

"What's up with you two these days?" Noah asks. "Is it serious?

I exhale slowly, the weight of it pressing against my ribs. "Yeah. I think it is."

That gets a reaction. Jesse whistles low. Wes raises an eyebrow.

"You think it is?" Jesse asks, grinning. "Big words, Winters."

"It's been serious for me for a while."

My brothers go quiet for a beat.

"You worried about her?" Wes asks, voice more serious now.

"I don't know what's going on, and I hate it," I admit. "I don't know if she's okay, or if something happened, or—"

"Okay, let's try not to freak out," Wes says. "Try the office. Maybe she's been in meetings all day."

I nod, swiping my phone to life and calling the Cove reception line. Chloe at reception answers on the second ring with her usual chipper greeting. "Cove! This is Chloe!"

"It's Ford. Did Landyn come in today?"

There's a beat of hesitation. "No. She called in this morning. Said it was a family emergency."

My stomach drops. "Did she tell you what's going on?"

"No, I'm sorry. She didn't elaborate. Would you like me to look up her phone number for you so you can ask her yourself?"

"No, it's fine, Chloe. Can you put Becca on?"

"Sure thing."

After a few minutes, Becca is on the line. "Hi Ford...this is Becca."

I lower my voice, tone firm but not unkind. "I know you and Landyn are friends, I know you talk. I'm not asking as your boss. I just...I'm worried. I've been trying to reach her all day. Do you know where she is?"

The beat of silence on the other end of the phone tells me she knows something. "Becca, please."

"I—Ford, I don't think I should..."

"Please."

There's a sigh. Then a soft voice. "She's at the hospital... with her mom."

Everything stills. "What's wrong?"

"I don't know exactly. She just said her mom fainted this morning in her kitchen and she needed to take her in. That's all she told me, I swear."

"Everything okay?" Noah asks after I end the call.

"Not really...I mean, it sounds like Landyn's fine, but her mom's in the hospital. Landyn's there with her now. The two of them are very close, so she's probably pretty worried."

Noah claps a hand to my shoulder. "Then go find her, man. It might help her to see a friendly face. We'll handle things here."

I hesitate for a split second. Landyn would have told me if she wanted me there. Maybe she needs space. But the image of her pacing the hospital waiting room all alone pushes any doubt from my mind. I can't just sit here, not when she might need me. I'm out the door without even saying goodbye. I run across the parking lot, jump into my truck, and start the engine before I have a chance to talk myself out of it.

I throw the truck into gear and head straight for the highway. I don't know what I'll be walking into when I get to the hospital, but I know I'm not going to let her go through it alone.

After a 45-minute drive, which should have taken over an hour, I'm pulling into the hospital parking lot. As soon as I walk through the sliding glass doors of the ER, the sterile scent of antiseptic hits me in the face. My boots echo on the tile floor as I make a beeline for the front desk.

"Hi. I'm looking for a patient—Carolyn Sinclair. Can you tell me what room she's in?"

The nurse behind the counter gives me a quick once-over. "Are you family?"

"No. But I—" I scrub a hand through my hair. "I just need to know if she's okay. Please."

"I'm sorry, sir. I can't release any information unless you are immediate family."

Of course. Red tape. I grit my teeth and take a step back, trying to reel in my frustration. I'm about to pull out my phone again and try Landyn one more time when I spot a familiar face near the exit of the ER.

He's older now—grayer at the temples and a little broader —but I'd recognize Landyn's dad anywhere. And he's not alone.

He's holding the hand of a little girl with long, dark-blonde curls. She's clutching a juice box, her eyes darting around the hospital, curious and wide. Something tugs low in my gut.

Landyn's dad looks up and meets my gaze. He slows, clearly recognizing me. There's a beat—just one—before he angles toward me, his hand still firmly holding the little girl's.

"Ford," he says as he approaches.

I nod. "Hey, Mr. Sinclair."

"It's been a long time," he says, glancing down at the little girl, then back up at me. "Didn't expect to see you here."

"I heard about Carolyn. I—I couldn't get a hold of Landyn. I was worried."

His mouth presses into a line. He studies me for a moment, eyes narrowing like he's weighing something.

"She's inside. With her mom."

I nod. It seems like he's about to say more, but instead he clears his throat, looks away. There is an odd energy between us, like I'm not quite getting the whole picture and he's not quite willing to fill it in for me.

I glance down again at the little girl as the silence stretches on. She looks up at me, eyes big and startlingly familiar. Something stirs in my chest. A question I don't voice.

"I'll let Landyn know you're here," Mr. Sinclair says finally. "She will probably want to see you." He gives my shoulder a firm pat and then turns and heads toward the ER doors, the little girl skipping beside him.

And I'm left standing there, heart thudding, wondering why I suddenly feel like the ground just shifted beneath me.

THIRTY

Landyn

The steady beep of the monitor beside my mom's head is strangely soothing now. It's been hours, but the panic I walked into this hospital with has dulled to a manageable level. She's stable and awake. Chatting and giving me a hard time already.

"You should have seen the nurse trying to decipher your handwriting on the intake forms," she says with a teasing smile, her voice hoarse. "I thought she was going to prescribe you a penmanship class."

I roll my eyes, adjusting the blanket around her legs. "I was worried about you, Mom. I was writing in a hurry."

Well, next time maybe Poppy can fill out the forms," she says with a wink.

"Don't talk about next time," I say, tears pricking at my eyes for what feels like the hundredth time today. My mom in a hospital bed is something I can't get used to. No matter how good her spirits are. No matter how many tests they said they are going to run. I wish they could tell us what is wrong with her. I wish she didn't have to be here at all.

A soft knock sounds at the door, and my dad steps in holding Poppy's hand.

"That was fast," I say, turning to face them. "I thought you two were going to get a snack."

My dad immediately sets Poppy in the chair at the end of the bed and hands her the iPad I luckily thought to bring with me as I rushed out the door. He helps her with her head-phones, then catches my eye and exhales. "We didn't make it to the cafeteria," he says quietly. "Ran into someone on the way."

I furrow my brow. "Who?"

He shifts slightly. "Ford."

My heart jerks in my chest. "Ford is here?"

"He came looking for you. Said he'd been trying to get in touch."

I glance toward Poppy instinctively, nerves spiralling through me. My dad's voice softens. "He didn't ask any ques-tions," he reassures me. "But he did look worried, sweetheart."

I nod slowly, swallowing past the tight lump in my throat.

"He's still in the waiting area," Dad adds. "I told him you'd probably want to see him."

Before I can respond, my mom speaks, her voice quiet but firm. "You need to tell him, Lan."

My gaze swings back to Poppy, and for a beat, I feel like I can't breathe. My mom places her hand on mine. "You can't keep this from him forever. And the longer you wait, the harder it's going to be."

I close my eyes. "I don't know how to tell him after all this time."

"I know you're scared," she says gently. "But you didn't build this lie because you were cruel. You thought it was the right thing to do. But he deserves the truth…" she pauses and nods at P. "And so does she."

I blink fast, trying to keep the tears from spilling.

"He's a good man, Landyn," she finishes. "And he still loves you."

My chest tightens. We haven't said those three words, but I know Ford loves me. I have felt it in every conversation, in every moment we've spent together. The fact that he left work and all of his obligations to show up here for me today shows how much he cares. He doesn't do things unless he means them. That undoes me a little.

I draw in a deep breath, stand, and kiss my mom on the head. "Can you guys stay with her for a bit?"

My dad nods immediately. "Of course."

Poppy giggles over something on her iPad as I reach out and push the curls back from her face, my hand lingering there for just a second before I turn and leave the room.

I spot him before he sees me.

Ford is sitting in a rigid plastic chair in the waiting room, one hand wrapped around a paper coffee cup. His other hand is raking through his hair, that familiar gesture that always meant he was thinking too hard.

The sight of him hits me like a wave.

He looks tired. Anxious. His brows are drawn tight, his eyes fixed on the floor like he's willing it to give him answers. He doesn't belong here—he's all power and control, and hospitals are made of worry and waiting. But still, he came.

I walk toward him slowly, like I'm approaching something fragile.

He lifts his head.

His eyes meet mine and the way they soften—just slightly —is enough to make my throat close. He's on his feet in an instant.

"Landyn."

I smile. "Hey."

He steps closer, then stops himself. "Are you okay?"

I nod. "My mom's stable. They're running tests. It's...it's been a long day."

His shoulders deflate just a little. "I called. Texted."

"I'm sorry. I was in such a rush when my dad called me this morning that I forgot my phone at home."

"You don't have to apologize." His voice drops an octave, warm and steady. "I just—I didn't know where you were. And when Becca said there was a family emergency—"

"I didn't mean to scare you."

He swallows hard, eyes dragging over me like he's checking for visible damage. "You did."

For a long second, we just stand there. The two of us in the middle of this too-bright waiting room, surrounded by ugly chairs and cheap vending machines. Somehow, he still looks like home.

I break the silence. "You came all this way."

His gaze holds mine. "Of course I did."

I nod again, feeling that knot in my chest twist a little tighter. "Do you wanna sit?" I ask, because I can't take the way he's looking at me—like he's reading every lie I've ever told him, trying to rearrange them into the truth.

I nod toward a quieter corner with two padded chairs with a crooked side table between them. Ford follows, silent, as we sit.

He puts his coffee cup on the table and waits. And because I've kept enough from him, I give him something real.

"She hasn't been feeling great for a while," I say, staring at the floor. "I guess it started around a year ago with fatigue. Then stomach aches. She was dizzy all the time. Her appetite dropped. Some days she couldn't even make it to lunch without needing to take a nap."

"Did she see a doctor about it?"

"She brushed it off for too long," I tell him. "Said it was just stress. Or maybe hormones. Then she fainted one afternoon and hit her head on the corner of the counter."

"Jesus."

"That's when I decided to come back to Deep Cove. I needed to be closer to home. I found the cottage to rent and landed the interview with Cove."

Ford leans forward, elbows on his knees. "So that's why you came back."

I nod slowly. "Yeah."

He looks at me for a moment, his gaze steady, like he's trying to figure me out.

"You could've told me," he says after a long pause.

"I'm not great at talking about it," I whisper. "We're still not sure what's wrong. They've been running tests. She's my mom. If anything ever happened to her—"

Ford reaches for my hand, lacing my fingers with his. "Whatever I can do—anything—you know I will do it. I will find her the best doctors. The best team."

"Ford—"

"You're not in this alone. Let me be there for you, June."

My eyes blur with tears that I try my best to contain and his hand squeezes mine just a little harder. We sit this way for one, two, maybe three heartbeats before he shifts in his seat and faces me. "When I got here, your dad was walking out of the ER with a little girl."

My stomach drops.

His voice is quiet now. Careful. "Who is she, Landyn?"

I try to look away, but he doesn't let me, his eyes pinned to mine.

"Lan, is she yours?" His voice is barely above a whisper. "Do you have a daughter?"

I can't run from it anymore.

I take a deep breath, my heart rattling against my ribcage. "Yes."

THIRTY-ONE

F ord

Yes.

A single word that hits like a fist to the chest.

I don't move. I can't.

Everything inside me has gone still. It feels like the ground my feet are firmly planted on has cracked wide open and I'm standing at the chasm of a truth I didn't see coming.

Landyn has a daughter.

I turn away from her, my eyes landing on the small TV mounted in the corner of the waiting room. It's playing muted local news coverage. A fluorescent light flickers overhead. I try to ground myself in something, but it's useless. Inside, everything is spinning out of control.

"Ford," Landyn says, leaning closer to me. "Please. Say something."

"What should I say?" I ask her, my voice hoarse. "You have a kid. You're a mother. And in all this time, you didn't tell me."

She flinches like I slapped her. "I wanted to, Ford, I really did."

"How old is she?" I ask, already knowing, already counting the years backward in my head.

"She's six," Landyn whispers.

"Six?" I repeat, the number catching like gravel in my throat.

Landyn nods.

I stand slowly. I don't know what I'm doing, where I'm going. I just know I need to not be here anymore. My brain is suddenly running circles—doing the math, stitching moments together, breaking them back apart.

Jesus Christ.

I push a hand through my hair and step away from her. My pulse is thudding hard in my ears. There are too many people here. Too many eyes. Not enough oxygen.

"I need air," I mutter.

I don't wait for her to respond. I just walk away, pushing through the double doors and out into the parking lot. I pace the pavement, feeling like I'm coming out of my skin. The air is cold. Sharp. But it doesn't touch the heat roaring in my chest.

I feel her behind me. She doesn't say anything, doesn't come any closer to me. I turn to find her watching me, her arms wrapped around her stomach.

"Jesus Christ." I shake my head, heart pounding. "She's mine, isn't she?"

Silence.

"Answer me, Landyn," I shout. "She's mine, isn't she?"

Then a whisper. "Yes."

I exhale like I've been punched. My hands drop to my sides, and I look at her again. Really look. And everything is different now. She's not just the woman I used to love, the one I never stopped wanting. She's the mother of my child.

My daughter. I have a six-year-old daughter.

I step back, needing distance from her, needing space to breathe... but she moves toward me.

"I didn't know how to tell you," she says, the words coming quickly now. "And once I saw you again, it just—it got harder. I—Ford, I was scared. I didn't want to ruin it all before we had a chance to fix what we lost."

My jaw clenches. "You had six years to tell me, Landyn."

Tears shine in her eyes, but she doesn't look away. "I was 23 years old. I was terrified. I found out and I wanted to tell you, but I didn't know how. And then I kept telling myself I'd do it when the timing was right, but the right time never came. And every year that passed, the truth got heavier and harder to say."

I swallow hard, torn between anger and heartbreak and a thousand unanswered questions. "Does she know?"

"No," she whispers. "She knows I loved someone once. That he was important to me. But she doesn't know who you are."

I squeeze my eyes shut and let the weight of it all settle into my bones. A daughter. I missed first steps. First words. First everything. I can still see her in my mind, walking out of the ER with Landyn's dad. That little girl with her hair. With my gray eyes. The way she looked up at him, her small hand wrapped in his.

"You kept her from me," I say. The words feel foreign in my mouth. Like they belong to someone else. "For *six years*, Landyn."

Her eyes are shiny now. "I know—"

"No. Don't say you know." I shake my head, my voice sharper now. "Because if you knew, you never would've done it. You never would've looked at my face all these weeks, kissed me, slept with me, while hiding my daughter from me."

"I wasn't trying to hurt you—" she says, tears spilling down her cheeks.

"But you did. You have fucking wrecked me."

"I was scared. I didn't know how to tell you. I didn't even know if I should. And then when I came back to town, everything got complicated—"

I let out a humorless laugh. "You think this is complicated? No, Landyn. Complicated is figuring out how to co-parent. This is really pretty simple. This is betrayal."

She flinches. And it guts me. But it's the truth.

I take another step back, needing space from her and from all of it. From everything I've missed out on. From everything this means. From the fact that she didn't trust me enough to tell me the truth.

"I missed everything," I say, my voice breaking at the edges. "Things I can never get back. Her first laugh. Her first word. Her first fucking birthday. You've been there for every moment. I wasn't even a name in her life."

"I'm so sorry," she whispers, tears streaming.

"Yeah," I say hoarsely. "Me too."

Silence drapes over us like a weighted blanket. She's crying, and even now part of me wants to move toward her, but I can't. Not with my whole world cracking in two.

"I want to meet her," I say finally, anchoring myself with the one thing I know for sure. "I have to meet her. I won't let you keep her from me. Do you understand me?"

Landyn lifts her eyes to mine. There's so much pain in her gaze I almost look away. "You will," she says. "If you still want to after all this—"

"Don't," I cut her off. "Don't put that on me."

She blinks.

"I lost six years," I say. "I'm not losing another moment."

Every second that ticks by feels like another second that's been stolen away from the little girl I didn't even know existed until five minutes ago.

My daughter.

I freeze suddenly, heartache rooting itself deeper inside of me. "What's her name?" I ask, my voice barely audible.

Landyn hesitates, like even this will undo me. "Poppy," she finally whispers.

My knees nearly give out. Poppy... after my mom.

I stare at her. I can't even blink. "Poppy," I repeat, like the word itself is a punch to the gut.

Landyn nods. Her chin trembles. "Even when you weren't beside me, I couldn't bring myself to cut you out of her story. I gave her your mom's name as a piece of you she'd always carry."

I run both hands over my face, dragging them through my hair before bracing them on my hips. "Jesus Christ, Landyn."

I walk away from her. I can't stand still. I can't breathe.

"What am I supposed to say to that?" I say, turning back. My voice breaks. "You still kept her from me. You lied."

"I didn't lie—"

"Don't," I cut in, sharper than I mean to. "Don't stand there and try to soften it. You kept my kid from me."

"I was scared."

"You've said that," I snap. "But being scared isn't a good enough reason. Because this? This is the kind of thing that shatters people."

Her face crumples.

"I would've shown up," I say, swallowing hard. "I would've been at the hospital. I would've held her first. Stayed up with her at night. I would've been there. For all of it. I would have been her dad."

Tears spill from her eyes, and I want to catch them. I want to yell. I want to disappear.

I lean against a random car, trying not to slide down it. My voice drops to a whisper. "I missed her whole life."

Landyn crosses her arms over her chest like she's holding herself together. "I was young and terrified, and I thought I was doing what was right. You were building a company, and I had no idea if you'd want her or if you'd resent me—"

"So you decided for both of us?" My voice is hoarse, wrecked. "You didn't even give me a chance to try."

She's crying now. Sobbing quiet tears. Controlled. She always was composed. Even in chaos.

"I'm sorry," she whispers. "I've been sorry for years."

Silence opens between us, vast and unbridgeable. A pain in my chest makes it hard to breathe. I press a fist to my ribs. "You named her. Raised her. Loved her. And I never got to touch a single second of it."

"I know," she chokes out.

I look at her, eyes burning. "You didn't just keep her from me. You kept me from her."

She starts to step forward, but I back away, shaking my head.

"I need...I need time, Landyn. I need to wrap my head around this without losing my goddamn mind."

"I understand."

I look at her. The woman I've never stopped loving. And right now, I don't know what the hell to do with her. For the first time, I feel like I don't understand her at all.

There is only one thing I know for certain.

"I want to meet her," I say again.

Landyn nods, voice trembling. "You will."

Then I walk away because if I don't, I'll break.

The drive home is a blur. I don't remember backing out of the hospital parking lot. Don't remember the highway turns or the lights I must've sat through. I just remember the sound of Landyn's voice in my head when she told me we have a daughter.

I pull into the driveway and park the truck in the same spot I always do. The house looks the same. Stella greets me as soon as I open the front door, running circles around my feet. Everything is the same as it always is, but at the same time, something in me knows that nothing will ever be the same again.

I flick on a light. Toss my keys on the counter. Toe off my boots. I'm halfway to the kitchen before I stop, suddenly breathless. I make it to the counter, bracing both my hands on it like I might lose my footing.

She didn't tell me.

She knew where I was. She could have picked up the phone. Hell, she could have sent me an email. For six years, she watched our daughter grow up without me. The thought of it guts me, but the worst part is knowing that every time we were together over these past few weeks—every smile, every touch, every kiss, every late-night text goodnight—she didn't say a word. She was keeping this huge fucking secret the whole time. And I knew something was off. I knew she was holding something back. But not this. Never this.

I grab a glass from the cabinet and shakily pour a few inches of whiskey into it, no ice.

Her name is Poppy.

That little girl in the hospital with wide eyes and blonde hair like her mom's. She's mine. I didn't need Landyn to say it. Somehow, I could see it. In the shape of her chin. The color of her eyes. She's my daughter. And she doesn't even know me. My gut twists so hard it feels like something rips open inside me.

I sink into the couch, whiskey in one hand, phone in the other. I stare at the screen. I want to call her. Demand answers. I want to scream. Fall apart. But I don't move. I just sit in the dark, glass clenched tight, staring out the window into nothing.

Because I don't know who I am right now—ex, betrayed lover, man still in love, father—and I'm scared as hell I'm all of them.

THIRTY-TWO

Landyn

The front door clicks shut behind us and I lean against it for a moment, relieved to be home. I set my purse on the entryway bench and glance down at Poppy. She's holding onto my pinky, her face drawn in a way that makes her look older than six. She's too quiet, too still. She was brave at the hospital, my dad and I did our best to keep her occupied, but I know today has left her with worries.

I smooth a hand over her hair and bend down slightly. "It's late, baby. Why don't you go get your pajamas on and brush your teeth, and I'll come tuck you in, okay?"

She nods tiredly, and disappears down the hallway, bare feet padding softly over the hardwood. As soon as she's out of sight, I let my eyes fall shut as the weight of the day crashes into me.

Mom is still at the hospital. She's stable and they're running more tests, but for now, there's still so much we don't know.

And then there's Ford. The look on his face in the hospital parking lot when he said, *"I missed her whole life."* I can't get it out of my head. It shattered me.

I press a hand to my chest, wishing I could stop the erratic beating of my heart. I want to fall apart. I want to scream. I want to curl up and cry. But I can't. Not yet. Not while Poppy is still up.

"Mommy?" her voice calls from down the hallway.

I swipe at the corner of my eye quickly and force a smile into my voice. "I'm here, baby. You ready for your story?"

I find her standing at the foot of her bed, looking half-asleep already. We go through the usual bedtime routine—pulling back her covers, turning on the little cloud-shaped nightlight beside her bed, picking out her favorite book about a purple dragon who breathes out sparkles instead of fire.

She's asleep by the third page, her cheek resting on my shoulder and one hand clutching mine. I stay that way for a little while longer, finding comfort in the stillness, in her sweet little face. When I finally get up and slip out of her room, it all comes crashing in again.

He was so angry. He looked at me like I was the enemy, like I'd done something unforgivable—and I know I have. Every accusation he hurled at me was true. I tried to explain, but there's nothing I could say that would make this better or lessen his pain.

Before he left the hospital, he said he wanted to meet her, and I immediately agreed. Of course. He deserves that. They both do.

I sink into the couch, tucking my knees up and wrapping my arms around them. My life feels like it's spinning out of control—my mom, this secret, the man I've loved for so long. The father of my daughter.

When I made this decision seven years ago, I thought I was protecting us all. But maybe all I did was take away their chance to love each other from the beginning.

THE SUN IS JUST STARTING TO BREAK THROUGH THE LOW-HANGING clouds as I pull out of the school parking lot, the weight from yesterday still pressing heavily on my chest.

Dropping Poppy off at before-school care felt like peeling off a part of myself. She was quiet again this morning, still trying to process what happened at the hospital. What she saw. What she felt. And I didn't have the heart, or the strength, to unpack it all with her. Not yet.

I take the familiar turn down toward Cove, sipping lukewarm coffee. When I walk into the office, Becca and Marco are already sitting at the worktable, whispering like they do when something is off. I haven't even put down my bag before Becca's eyes land on me.

"There she is," she says softly, giving me a once-over. "How's your mom?"

I manage a smile that feels stretched too thin. "Stable. They're running more tests today. My dad stayed with her overnight and I'm heading back there after work."

Becca nods, stepping closer. "We've been thinking about you. If you need anything..."

"You look tired," Marco cuts in, brow creased.

"That's because I am," I answer with a weak laugh.

"You should have taken the day off. Ford would have understood." Becca says, pulling me into a hug. "But seriously, anything at all—rides for Poppy, meals, even someone to run interference here—we've got you."

"Don't try to be a hero," Marco admonishes. "You've had a lot dumped on you this week. You can't do everything."

I shrug. "I don't really have a choice."

Becca's gaze softens. "You do, actually. You don't have to do everything on your own. You've got people now. We're your friends, Landyn."

I blink at that—friends. It's been a long time since anyone other than my mom felt like a sure thing. I lost contact with most of my friends soon after leaving Deep Cove. And once Poppy arrived, I was a single mom, working in every spare moment I could find. I didn't have time to make new friends.

"Thank you. That means a lot," I tell them, meaning it.

Becca leans in a little, dropping her voice. "Something's weird around here today. The vibes are off."

I arch a brow. "Weird? How so?"

"Ford didn't come in. No one's seen him. And even stranger...nobody seems to know where he is."

My chest clenches, but I keep my expression neutral. "Work has really ramped up at the new site, maybe he's dealing with things out there," I offer.

Becca gives me a look like, *sure, girl*, but she doesn't push. Before I can say anything else, Jesse's voice calls from behind me. "Landyn, you got a sec?"

I turn to find him standing in the break room doorway, hands stuffed into the pockets of his Cove zip-up. His usual easy charm is dimmed today, softer around the edges.

"Sure," I nod, following him inside. The break room is empty, quiet. Jesse leans against the counter and for a long moment, he just watches me. It makes me wonder how much he knows.

"How's your mom, really?" he asks gently.

"She's okay, but worried. We all are. They don't know what it is yet." I hesitate. "Thanks for asking."

He nods, then exhales slowly. "I hope it's okay that I know. Ford couldn't hide it."

My stomach turns. "He told you?"

"Not exactly. But when he couldn't get a hold of you yesterday, he... panicked. I've never seen him like that." Jesse crosses his arms. "He tried to keep it together at the site, but we all saw it."

I look down at the floor. "I didn't mean for any of this to get messy."

"Life's messy," Jesse says. "But you should know he sent me a message this morning."

My heart stops. "What kind of message?"

He offers a small smile. "An order, more like. I was instructed to tell you to take the rest of the week off. Be with your mom. No debate."

I blink. "Seriously?"

"Seriously," he says. "And between us? I think he'd be there himself if something wasn't tearing him up."

I nod, throat tight. So, Ford didn't tell his brother. "It's complicated, Jesse."

He steps closer, voice soft. "Whatever's going on between you two... he's still that guy. The one who'd do anything for you."

I don't say anything, because I'm not so sure that's true anymore. Not after the way he looked at me outside that hospital.

Jesse pushes off the counter. "I meant it when I said take the week. Ford will have my head if you aren't at the hospital with your mom."

I clear my throat. "Okay. Thanks. Really."

He gives me a quick, reassuring smile. "Go be with your mom. You only get one."

As I walk out of the break room, I can feel the weight of everything that's waiting for me. The grief I've been holding at bay, the guilt I can't shake, the fallout I'm still bracing for, and somewhere beneath all of that...the aching hope that maybe, just maybe, Ford can find a way to forgive me.

I gather my things from my desk and slip my phone into my

bag, grateful to Ford for knowing that I need to be with my mom. Right now, my mind is anywhere but Cove.

Becca catches my eye as I pass her desk. She doesn't say anything, but there's concern written all over her face. She doesn't know the whole story, but she knows enough. Enough to see the exhaustion in my eyes, the cracks I'm doing a poor job of hiding.

Outside, I wince against the bright glare of the sun. The air has a crisp bite, and I pull my sweater around myself as I head to my car, wishing I had put on something warmer this morning. Or maybe I'm just cold from the inside out.

The moment I close the car door, the silence swallows me whole. No voices. No questions. Just me and the ache I can't shake.

I drive on autopilot, familiar streets blurring past the window. I should be thinking about my mom and what the doctors might say, about the way my dad hovered around her yesterday like she might disappear if he blinked.

Instead, my thoughts drift—again—to Ford.

I haven't heard from him since he left me standing in the parking lot. The questions in his eyes, the pain—it wrecked me. And now, nothing. No calls. No texts. Just silence so loud it feels like punishment. A punishment I know I deserve.

I pull into the hospital lot, white-knuckling the steering wheel for a beat before I finally let go. My legs are heavy when I step out of the car, anxiety building with each step toward the hospital doors.

I need to focus on my mom, and on what today might bring. But in the back of my mind, I can't stop thinking about *him*.

Because if Ford can't find a way to come back from this, I'm not sure I'll be able to either.

THIRTY-THREE

Ford

I don't remember pouring the second drink. Or the third.

The bottle sits half-empty near the edge of the counter, watching me spiral. Judging me. I know I shouldn't have drank this much, but I couldn't stand to be stone cold sober with my thoughts.

The house is quiet, the kind of silence that settles deep in your bones and sits there. Stella's asleep near the door, tired of begging to go for a walk. The lights are off. I haven't eaten. I've barely slept. I just keep thinking about the look on her face when she said it. *Yes.*

Yes, she's your child. Yes, you're a father. Yes, I've been lying to you.

One word, and everything shifted. Every moment, every memory.

I lean forward, elbows on the kitchen island, pressing my palms against my forehead like maybe I can push away the headache that's brewing. I feel like shit, but my heart is still beating, like it doesn't understand it's been broken.

The glass in my hand shakes slightly under the pressure of my grip. I set it on the table, shoving it away before I throw it against the wall. Why didn't she tell me? Why didn't she tell me when she found out she was pregnant? Why wasn't it the first thing she said to me when she came back to town? Why did she keep it a secret when we started getting closer? After we slept together? I thought we were getting somewhere, that maybe we could get past all the obstacles and the years that separated us. That what we had still meant something.

I slam the rest of the whiskey and wince as it burns down my throat.

My phone lights up on the counter. Jesse again. I've ignored every call since I left the site. I've never not showed up to work before. He's probably wondering what the hell is going on. I don't have the energy to talk to him. None of it fucking matters right now.

A sharp knock at the door pulls me from my thoughts. I stay where I am, even when the knocking turns into banging. Eventually, I hear a key in the lock, followed by the sound of the door opening.

"Ford, we're coming in."

Jesse, of course. He walks into the kitchen like he owns the place, Wes and Noah trailing behind him.

"Christ, it's like a cave in here," Jesse says, flicking the light switch. They all freeze when they see me—shirt untucked, eyes bloodshot, bottle near empty.

Noah whistles low. "Shit. You look like hell."

"I feel worse," I mutter.

Wes grabs a glass from the cupboard then takes the bottle without asking and pours himself a splash. He doesn't say anything, just leans back against the counter.

Noah watches me carefully. "What's going on?"

I grab the edge of the sink, steadying myself before I answer him. "She has a kid."

Three sets of eyes land on me.

"Landyn," I clarify. "She has a six-year-old little girl."

Jesse nods. "Okay…"

They still don't get it.

"The kid is mine."

Noah is the first to react. His brows lift, stunned. "You're sure?"

"She's six." My voice cracks. "We broke up seven years ago. And I saw her at the hospital. I didn't need anyone to tell me. I knew."

Wes lets out a long breath and then silence settles heavy over the room.

"She didn't tell you?" Jesse asks finally.

"No. I found out." I rake a hand through my hair. "I saw her. And it hit me like a freight train. And when I asked Landyn point blank, she confirmed it."

Jesse sinks onto a stool at the island. "And you haven't talked to her since?"

I shake my head. "I left. I was afraid if I stayed, I'd say something I couldn't take back. I had to get out of there."

Noah crosses the room and claps a hand on my shoulder. "You've got every right to be angry, but you need to talk to her, man."

"I don't know if I can," I admit. "I don't know what to say. What kind of person does this? Keeps a child a secret?"

"A scared one," Wes says quietly. "I'm not defending her, Ford. But maybe she thought she was doing the right thing at the time."

I walk into the living room and drop into the chair beside the fireplace, my body heavy and useless. Jesse, Wes, and Noah follow.

"I wanted a life with her," I whisper. "Part of me still does."

The truth of it wrecks me. All these years. All that love. And now I don't even know if I'll ever trust her again.

Noah sits on the coffee table, his eyes locked on mine. "It's messed up, man. The way you're feeling right now? You deserve to feel that way. But, I know how much she matters to you. That's a lot to walk away from."

I look at him and ask the question that's been running through my head all day. "How the hell am I supposed to forgive Landyn for keeping her from me?"

The silence that follows is thick. Noah is the first to speak, his voice steady, always calm when the rest of us are spiralling. "You don't have to forgive her tonight. You let yourself be mad. Be hurt. Feel it all."

Jesse nods. "And then you ask her why. I've known Landyn a long time, and she's not cruel."

"There has to be a reason," Wes says. "And you should know what it is."

I shake my head, "She had *years*, Wes. Seven fucking years."

"I know," he says. "And you're not just going to get over that. But giving up on what you still want might only make it hurt more."

I don't answer but I know exactly what he means. I know what I want, and I feel like an idiot for still wanting it. I want Landyn. I want Poppy. I want every beautiful, messy, complicated thing about it. But there's a wall between us now, and I'm not sure how the hell to cross it.

Quietly, Jesse adds, "She should've told you. You have every right to be angry over it, but I've never seen you act the way you do when you're around her. I haven't seen you that happy in a really long time. Don't let pride keep you from something you've wanted for years."

I close my eyes, rub the heels of my hands against them, and swallow the truth I'm not ready to admit out loud. *I still love her.* God help me, I do.

An hour later, I'm alone again. Jesse offered to spend the

night in a guest room, but I made him leave with the others, promising them I'd get some sleep. But I can't, not yet.

I should go to bed. Instead, I pour another shot and sit at the kitchen table with a thousand memories running through my mind. I remember the exact moment I realized she was really gone all those years ago. It wasn't when I woke up to an empty bed. It wasn't even when I saw her toothbrush was missing from my bathroom. It wasn't until a few days later, when I opened the fridge and saw the stupid oat milk she always insisted on buying sitting unopened on the shelf.

That's when it hit me. She wasn't coming back.

And the thing is...I didn't see it coming. Not even a hint. The night before, she kissed me goodnight like she always did. Tucked her cold feet between my legs under the blanket and whispered that she loved me.

And the next afternoon she was just gone. There was no fight. No big, dramatic exit. No closure.

I waited weeks before I told anyone. I kept making excuses for her, checking my phone like a lunatic, thinking maybe she just needed space. Maybe something had happened. The alternative—that she just left me like we hadn't built something, like I hadn't loved her with everything I had—just didn't make sense. I even called her parents when she hadn't responded to any of my messages, worried that maybe she was in trouble. Her mom had told me that Landyn was okay, but that she'd had to leave town. She needed time, she'd said, sympathy in her voice. And that was it.

And the worst part? I never did get a reason. She took all of it—the love, the plans, the future we talked about—and disappeared. And I was left here with nothing but unanswered questions. Even now, years later, I have no idea what was going through her mind.

I stand abruptly, the scrape of my chair loud against the wood floor. My drink is still half full on the table, but I can't sit still. I pace, heart pounding, fists clenched. "How the hell was I supposed to move on from her," I mutter aloud, "when I never got the truth?"

I stop in the middle of the room, breathing hard, staring out into the dark like it might offer answers, but all I see is my own reflection in the window.

Haunted. Lost. Wrecked. Just like I felt back then. Only now, I'm not just broken over Landyn walking away. I'm broken over the little girl who never got to know me.

The child I didn't even know to miss.

I WAS UP A HALF DOZEN TIMES LAST NIGHT, THINKING I HEARD something outside. Each time, I jolted awake and rushed through my house to the living room. I wrenched the glass door open, but there was nothing there. Just the rhythmic sound of the ocean hitting the shore somewhere below.

I'm so tired. I can't sleep. I haven't been able to set foot in the office. Haven't been able to look at my phone without wondering if she's going to call. It's pathetic. I know it is. I need to get a grip.

Landyn Sinclair is the only person who has ever had the power to unravel me like this. I run a multimillion-dollar company. My time is spent thinking about supply chains and product launches, about keeping hundreds of employees paid, about keeping a roof over my brothers' heads. I go to sleep every night knowing that I've taken care of my family. That's what matters. That's what I think about.

I don't need to fucking think about Landyn anymore.

It's done. Whatever there was between us, it's over. Seven years is a long damn time to keep dragging a memory around. The girl I once knew is nothing but a ghost. I can't keep letting her live rent-free in my head, can't keep picturing her every time I close my eyes.

It's time to move on. Time to stop acting like some lovesick kid who doesn't know when to quit.

Time to walk away from Landyn.

But not from Poppy.

That little girl is mine, and I'm not going anywhere when it comes to her. We're going to have to figure something out, whether Landyn likes it or not because I want to know my daughter. And I will.

I lace up my running shoes like it's any other morning. Time to get my head back on straight. Time to get back into a routine, burn off some of the restless energy, remind my body what normal feels like. I've always been fit since I was a teenager in highchool. Unless I am sick, I never miss a workout.

I head out and run downhill toward the town. The air's crisp, the pavement familiar under my feet. I keep my pace steady, lungs working, legs pumping. I tell myself I'm focusing on my breathing, on the rhythm of my strides, on nothing else.

I end up taking the long loop. The one that cuts past the waterfront, snakes up through the quiet streets, and—by pure coincidence, I tell myself—runs right by Landyn's house.

It means nothing. Just a route. Just a stretch of road I haven't taken in a while.

When I come up on her place, I slow my pace just enough to take it in. There's no sign of Landyn or Poppy. I wonder if everything is okay with her mom. Maybe they're at the hospital. Maybe I should make sure Carolyn is okay. Like it or not, Landyn and I share a daughter, so I should probably know what's going on with her family.

I keep moving, eyes forward, checking my watch for pace.

It's nothing. Just part of the run.

I punch in the hospital's phone number and hit call without thinking too hard about it. This is not about Landyn, I tell myself. All I'm going to do is check on her mother's health. If something affects Poppy, it affects me now too. There's nothing more to it than that. I just about manage to convince myself.

"Good afternoon, Deep Cove General," a woman answers.

"I'm calling to check on a patient," I say, shifting the phone to my other ear. "Carolyn Sinclair."

"Are you family?"

"Yes." The word comes out smoothly. "Son-in-law," I add, because it seems like it will open more doors than it closes.

She tells me she's just going to need a minute. There's a pause, the faint sound of typing on the other end, a cough somewhere in the background. I stare at the far wall, jaw tight, until she speaks again.

"She's stable. Resting comfortably."

I nod, even though she can't see me. "Good. That's good."

I'm hunched over the kitchen table, laptop open, Stella at my feet, trying to push through the low, dull ache in my gut. It's been there all damn day. Must've been something I ate, though I can't remember the last time food slowed me down. I get now why people complain about stomach aches. It's no way to spend a day.

I click through a few tabs on my screen, half-paying attention, until a headline catches my eye. It's about Cove.

I open the article. It's good—better than good. Positive press. A feature about the new Sierra line, the company's commitment to sustainability, the turnaround we've managed to pull off. Words like innovative, responsible, admired.

All the long nights. All the damage control. Landyn's work. Jesse's too. It's all here in black and white.

I snap the laptop shut, stand, and walk to the fridge. I pull out a bottle of water, twist the cap off, then rummage in my cupboard for Pepto-Bismol.

Four hours later and it hasn't done a damn thing.

THIRTY-FOUR

L andyn

She's napping, finally. I'm curled up in the chair by the window, watching my mom's chest slowly rise and fall as she sleeps in the hospital bed. The journal Ford gave me is balanced on my knees, pen hovering over the page as I try to write down my thoughts. But the words don't come easily. They haven't since I saw the wrecked look on his face.

Still, I start.

Sometimes I wonder what it would've been like if I'd stayed. If I'd told him. If we'd figured it out together instead of me figuring it out alone, terrified, sitting in a bathroom with a plastic stick with two pink lines and no plan. Would he have stepped up? Would he have run? Would I have still lost him anyways? I used to believe I was doing the right thing. That not telling him protected everyone—especially her. But now? Now I'm not so sure.

I stop, breathe, then keep going.

I wish I could go back. Not to change what happened, but to let myself trust him with the truth. I told myself I was protecting him. That knowing about Poppy would change his life in a way he didn't want. That it would tie him to something he hadn't chosen. That I was saving both of us. But I think the truth is simpler than that... I was afraid.

I press the pen harder than I should, dotting the page with ink. My hand trembles as I write the next line.

And now that he knows, I keep wondering if we've reached the end or if this is just the beginning.

My mom stirs in her bed, murmuring something unintelligible, and I glance over to find her eyes fluttering open. I close the journal gently, smoothing my hand over the cover.

"Hey," I say softly, standing and crossing the small room to her.

She offers a tired smile. "Hey, sweetheart."

I help her sit up a little, adjusting the pillows behind her as she reaches for the small tray beside her. The hospital food is... well, it's hospital food, but she eats slowly. She smiles at me, like she's trying to convince me she's fine, but I can see it. The dark circles under her eyes. The faint tremor in her hand as she lifts the fork. The effort it takes just to stay upright.

"I'm fine, Landyn," she says gently, not even looking up.

"You always say that, even when you aren't fine," I reply, sitting on the edge of the bed.

"And you always say you're okay when I know you're breaking."

I blink hard, looking down at my hands.

"You don't seem like yourself. What's going on?"

I sigh. "A lot has happened this week."

Her hand covers mine, cool and fragile. "He came."

"Yeah," I whisper. "He came."

She nods, understanding. "That man's heart has always been yours, Landyn. Even when you pretended otherwise."

Before I can respond, a gentle knock sounds at the door, and the handle turns. It's the doctor, clipboard in hand, a nurse shadowing him. He smiles warmly, but it's tight. Measured. My stomach twists.

"Hi Carolyn," he says, glancing toward my mom. "How are we feeling today?"

"I've had better days," she replies with a small laugh.

The doctor smiles warmly, then looks at me. "Hi Landyn, is your father around?"

I nod, my hands folding tightly in front of me. "He just stepped out for a walk. Should be back soon."

"Okay," he says. "We do have the test results."

My heart stops. My breath lodges in my throat. My mom reaches for my hand without looking away from the doctor.

He glances at the nurse, then back at us. "Would you like me to wait until your husband returns?"

"No," she says firmly, her voice surprisingly steady. "We've waited long enough."

But all I can think is…I'm not ready.

And in the silence that stretches out between us, the weight of every worst-case scenario presses down on my shoulders.

THE WIND LIFTS THE EDGES OF MY COAT AS I WAIT ON THE sidewalk outside Poppy's school, the sky low and gray. It's the kind of day where the world feels quieter than usual. My phone is in my hands, not because I'm expecting him to call, but because in a strange sort of way I'm willing him to.

He hasn't.

I haven't heard from Ford since we talked at the hospital. Not a text. Not a phone call. Nothing. It's not like I'm surprised. Four days ago, I dropped a bomb on him. A 6-year-old secret I never should've kept.

And now I have to live in the silence that follows.

I shift on my feet, trying to focus on something else. Anything else. My mom. The diagnosis that finally came. Myxedema coma.

The words still echo in my head. The doctor had said she was lucky. A lot of people don't catch it in time. Thankfully my dad brought her to the hospital when he did.

And now she's stable. She's still tired but feeling better. Every day, she's a little more like the woman I've known my entire life. The doctor told us her thyroid had stopped working almost entirely, slowing her body until it nearly stopped altogether. That's why she was always cold, why her hands trembled, why her hair thinned and her eyes dulled. She was disappearing right in front of us, and the guilt of knowing this wraps around me like a vice. My mother was so good at brushing off her symptoms that it took me almost a year before I moved back home to be closer to my parents. Thankfully, she's going to be okay.

"Mom!"

Poppy runs toward me, her purple backpack bouncing, a wild curl coming loose from her braid. She crashes into my legs, arms wrapping tightly around my waist.

"Hi, baby," I say, sinking down to kiss her head. She smells like finger paint and cinnamon and for a second, I let myself close my eyes and breathe her in.

She peers up at me as we walk toward the car, her hand curled tightly around mine. "Can we stop for a donut on the way home?" she asks, her voice hopeful.

"Only if you tell me what you painted today," I say, opening the back door for her.

"A jellyfish," she grins, climbing into her booster seat. "With glitter."

"Of course it had glitter." I buckle her in, brushing a curl off her cheek. "You'd add glitter to your cereal if you could."

She giggles as I close the door and round the car. I slide into the driver's seat and she's still talking, midway through a story now about someone crying underneath the parachute in the gym.

"But Mama, I like being under the parachute because I pretend I'm living in a rainbow," she tells me. "But it's okay, because I helped her to feel better."

"You're such a good friend, Poppyseed," I say, smiling at her in the rearview mirror. I'm about to shift the car into gear when my phone buzzes from the console next to me. I pick it up and a single message lights up the screen.

Ford: We need to talk. I want to see her.

My breath catches. I double check the message, like maybe I misread it. But it's there. He texted.

My fingers hover over the screen for a moment before I start to type.

Me: Of course. Anytime. Just say when.

I hit send before I can overthink it, then set the phone down. My hands wrap around the steering wheel, and I glance at Poppy, humming softly to herself, staring out the window, lost in a world of glitter jellyfish and rainbow houses.

By the time we pull into High Tide Donuts a few minutes later, there's another text from Ford.

Ford: We need to talk first about how we do this.11 a.m. at the Cedar Bluff Trail lookout tomorrow.

F ord

Cedar Bluff comes into view. Our old spot, the one with the best view of the coastline below. From up here, the ocean looks endless. Today it's calm and glassy, a vast pool of blue that disappears into the horizon.

She's already here, sitting on a flat rock, knees pulled up to her chest. Her long hair is tied back in a ponytail, her face is bare, and she's still the most beautiful woman I've ever seen. A long time ago, she told me this place made her feel like she could breathe. Now she looks like she is suffocating.

The sight of her twists something inside me and a familiar tension threads into my shoulders. I hate that part of me still aches for her while another part is still filled with anger and betrayal.

She must hear me as I approach, because she suddenly turns and looks over her shoulder. "Hi," she says, her voice sounding small and hesitant.

I don't answer right away. Instead, I drop onto the rock beside her, keeping a safe distance. We sit like this in silence, the sun warming our backs, the air clean and still. Seagulls float far below, their cries faint against the breeze.

"How's your mom?" I ask eventually, realizing one of us needs to break the silence if we're going to get anywhere.

Her arms tighten a little around her legs. "She's going to be okay, thanks. It's manageable...just going to take time."

I nod, relieved. I stare at her profile, her gaze still locked on the ocean, and the words slip out before I can stop them. "Why didn't you tell me?"

Her head turns. Our eyes lock. "I'm so sorry, Ford." She swallows hard. "I did what I thought was right at the time."

"What does that even mean?"

"You're mad, I know, and I don't blame you. I should have told you—"

"But you didn't," I interrupt, voice raised. "Tell me the real reason, Lan. Tell me why you didn't tell me you were pregnant with our child. Tell me why you just disappeared."

She stands suddenly, the tension between us breaking wide open as she puts space between our bodies. I stand too. "I left because I knew what would happen. You would've given every-thing up for me. For us. You would've thrown away everything you were building—Cove, the life you dreamed of. I knew how important that was to you, to build something that was more than what you came from. I didn't want to get in the way of all of that."

"It wasn't your decision to make," I argue.

"Maybe you're right, but I knew that you didn't want kids. You didn't want a family."

My eyes widen. "I didn't want kids—?"

"It's the truth," she says, her voice louder now, the tears filling her eyes even as she tries to fight them back. "You didn't want kids. You made it clear."

I stare at her, confused. My brain is a storm, trying to

rewind the years. "What the hell are you talking about, Landyn?"

She lets out a broken sigh. "You had all these plans. The 5-year plan. The 10-year vision. You were so laser-focused on it, and I was barely even part of it anymore, let alone a baby. I asked you about kids. I told you that I wanted to be a mom one day, that it was important to me. You said maybe, one day, but that you weren't really sure you even wanted to be a dad. And I understood, even if it broke my heart a little. I know you had a hard time growing up, that your dad wasn't good to you. I know how much that impacted you."

I feel like the air's been punched out of me. She turns back toward the water, wiping at her face with the sleeve of her hoodie.

"You thought I wouldn't have wanted her?" My voice is hoarse. "That I would've walked away?"

"No. I thought you would've stayed," she says without looking at me. "And that it would've killed you inside to give up the life you were building. You would've done it out of obligation. Not love."

"I wouldn't have felt trapped, if that's what you're trying to insinuate," I say fiercely, my voice rough with emotion. "I would've been a dad to our little girl, Landyn. I would've stepped up. I would've shifted my whole goddamn life plan if that's what it meant to be with you. To raise our daughter together."

Her breath hitches, but she doesn't look away this time. "And that's exactly what I was afraid of."

I stare at her. "What does that mean?"

She's crying again now, tears slipping quietly down her cheeks. "You would've dropped everything, Ford. You would've walked away from Cove, from all the things you were building for you and your brothers. I knew that meant *everything* to you. Don't you see? I couldn't let that happen."

I shake my head, trying to catch up with the storm of her logic. "You think I would've regretted choosing you? Choosing her?"

"I think," she whispers, "you would've buried that regret and lived with it quietly because that's who you are. You take care of the people you love. You never let anyone down even if it means letting yourself down."

I pace a few steps away, heart pounding so hard it drowns out the crashing waves in the distance. "So, you just made the choice for me?"

"I made a mistake, I know that now, but, you were trying to build a better life—not just for you, but for your brothers. You carried so much on your shoulders. And I knew what you'd do the second I told you."

"You thought I'd walk away from it all."

"I knew you would."

I turn back to her, my voice cracking. "And I would've, Landyn. In a heartbeat. None of that mattered if it didn't include you."

Her lips tremble, and she shakes her head. "I couldn't let you sacrifice that. I couldn't watch you walk away from it all when I knew how much it would change your life."

There's silence again. Heavier now. Raw. I close my eyes and press my fingers to my temples, trying to breathe through the ache spreading in my chest. "You didn't trust me to choose you. That's what kills me."

She looks like she's about to shatter. "I didn't trust myself to let you."

I don't know how to make sense of all of it. Of the love still in her eyes. Of the years that we lost. Of the little girl I didn't know existed. Of everything we could've been. "I missed six goddamn years, Landyn," I bite out, the words tasting like blood. "She doesn't even know who I am."

She flinches, her arms tightening around herself. "I know."

I step closer, my hands fisting at my sides. "I don't know how I move past this."

Her eyes flash, brimming with tears. "I took everything. I know that. I know, Ford."

"You robbed me—of her, of being a dad. Of knowing her laugh, her favorite color, the things she's afraid of." My voice cracks, low and guttural. "You made that choice for me because you thought I couldn't handle it."

"I—," she says, her voice just as raw. "I knew you'd give up everything you'd worked for. Because you loved me. And I loved you too much to let you do that."

Her words slice me open. I look away, the truth hitting me like a freight train. She's right. I would've walked away from Cove. From every damn thing I'd worked so hard to build, everything I'd bled for with my brothers. I would've thrown it all into the fire to be with her. To raise our daughter.

Because she always mattered more to me than anything else.

I look back at her and she's already watching me, her face crumpled with pain.

"It was the hardest thing I've ever had to do," she says quietly. "Walking away from you. Carrying her. Raising her without you. There hasn't been a single day in seven years where I didn't miss you. Where I didn't want you. I was miserable without you, Ford."

We stare at each other, hearts exposed, and in that moment, I don't know if I want to pull her into my arms or fall apart at her feet.

"Jesus, Landyn." I rake a hand through my hair. "You had my heart since we were 20. You really thought I wouldn't have wanted to be there for you? For her?"

"You had my heart, too." Her face is blotchy and wet with tears. "But I couldn't risk making you hate me. I couldn't trap you. I couldn't ruin you."

"I was in love with you." Silence drops like a bomb between us. "I still am," I say finally, my voice breaking. "Even though I'm mad as hell at you."

Her eyes squeeze shut.

"I don't know if I can ever forgive you," I admit, my chest splitting open. "But I don't think I know how to stop loving you either."

"I didn't date," she says suddenly, swiping the tears from her cheeks. "I moved away and focused on Poppy. I didn't want anyone else. I couldn't even think about it."

Her words wind around my ribs like a vice. I blink at her, stunned. "You didn't...?"

She shakes her head. "How could I when I never wanted anyone but you? I still don't."

For a second, all the anger, the heartbreak—it twists into something else. Something deeper. Something that makes me want to drop to my knees and beg for the years we lost. I move toward her before I can stop myself. "You think I would've been ruined by her? By you?" I murmur. "I would've been made by you."

She breathes in sharply, tears clinging to her lashes.

"You built Cove," she whispers. "You did it. It's incredible. I didn't want to be the reason you walked away from making that happen."

Taking a deep breath, I pull myself back together. "Don't you see? You were always the reason I wanted more."

Landyn looks away first. The silence between us is softer now, but still heavy with everything we've said and everything still to come.

I let out a breath. "So where do we go from here?"

She hesitates, sniffles. "You mean...with Poppy?"

I nod. "One step at a time. I don't need answers about us right now. But I want to know her. I need to know her."

She smiles for the first time, her eyes lighting up. "She's

amazing, Ford. Smart. So curious. She loves animals and books and...she's got your eyes."

That knocks the breath from me more than anything else has today. "Does she...does she ask about her dad?"

"Not in the way you're thinking," she says quietly. "She knows families look different. But...yeah. Sometimes."

I rub the back of my neck, grounding myself. "I want to meet her. However you think is best. We can take it slow. You don't have to drop everything and throw me into your lives."

Landyn lets out a laugh. "Good. Because she's got a lot of questions when she meets new people. She might interrogate you."

"I can handle a 6-year-old," I tell her. "Maybe we start with something low-key. Ice cream, or the beach. Somewhere she's comfortable."

"She'd love that," Landyn says, finally meeting my gaze again. "How about Saturday? They have story time at the library. It's one of her favorite things."

"Saturday," I repeat, nodding. "It's a date."

Her brows lift.

"I mean...with her," I add quickly. "Not—not that kind of date."

She smiles, but it's faint. Unsure. Still, it's a start and right now, that's all I'm ready for.

THIRTY-SIX

Landyn

Poppy is buckled into the backseat, chatting to herself as she flips through a dog-eared book she's probably read 20 times. I can barely hear her over the sound of my own heart pounding.

I check the clock on the dash. We're early. Too early. But sitting around the house felt impossible, so instead we're here, parked outside the Deep Cove Public Library, waiting for the minutes to tick by.

"Mom?" Poppy leans forward as far as her seatbelt will let her. "Can we go inside now?"

I grip the steering wheel and force a calm smile. "Yes, baby. I'm sorry. Let's go in and find a new book to bring home before story time starts."

She squints at me like she can tell I'm not myself today, but then shrugs. "Okay. Can I get one with dragons this time?"

"You can get two," I say, unbuckling her. "Let's go."

The library is quiet and bright, with high windows that flood the space with natural light. Poppy immediately makes a beeline for the kids' section, and I trail after her, heart in my throat. Ford texted me this morning. "I'll be there. I don't know what to say yet, but I'll be there."

I knew he wouldn't miss it. Now I just have to believe that it will all be okay. That the truth won't ruin her—this sweet, sensitive girl with a heart the size of the ocean. It's always just been the two of us and now I'm about to change everything she's ever known.

"Do you want to sit over there?" I ask, nodding toward a reading nook at the back of the room next to a wall of windows.

"Sure." She tucks a picture book under her arm and skips ahead, settling cross-legged in a beanbag chair. I lower myself into the seat across from her, my back to the entrance so I don't spend the next five minutes watching the door like a crazy person.

But I feel it when he walks in. My body knows his presence before I set eyes on him. I hear the quiet sound of his boots on the polished floor as he approaches us, and then—

"Hi," he says, voice low.

Poppy looks up first. Her head tilts. She stares at him like she's trying to place him.

I turn slowly. Ford's standing a few feet away, hands shoved in his jean pockets. Uncertainty is written all over his face but he's still so breathtakingly handsome. His eyes flick to me, then back to Poppy.

"Hi," I say, voice catching.

Poppy glances between us. "Do you know my mom?"

Ford crouches down slowly, coming to eye-level with her. "I do," he says. "I've known her a long time."

She studies him, then looks at me. "Is this the friend you said we were meeting?"

My stomach twists. I nod. "Yeah, baby. This is Ford."

Ford's throat moves like he's trying to swallow the lump in it. "Hi, Poppy."

She stares at him for another long beat. Then, with perfect, innocent ease, she offers her hand. "Nice to meet you, Ford."

He smiles, just slightly—but it softens everything about him. He shakes her hand like it's the most important thing he's done all day. "Nice to meet you too."

And just like that, the world shifts beneath us.

Poppy gestures to the chair beside her. "Do you want to read a book with us? It's about a girl who finds a baby dragon in the forest."

Ford lowers his six-foot-one body carefully into the seat, and I watch the way his knees fold awkwardly to fit in the kid-sized chair. It's sweet and a little comical. "I'd love to hear about it," he says.

Poppy beams and starts flipping through the pages. "Okay, so this is Ember, she's the dragon, and she's scared of people, but the girl brings her strawberries and sings to her every day until she's not scared anymore."

Ford leans in closer, elbows resting on his knees, eyes on Poppy like no one else exists in the world. "Sounds like a smart girl."

"She is," Poppy says, nodding. "And Ember lets her ride on her back, and they fly over the mountains. That's as far as I got, I haven't finished it yet."

"Wow," Ford says, his smile tugging wider. "You're really good at telling stories."

She preens under the compliment, glancing at me. "Mom says I'm a storyteller just like her."

Ford's eyes lift to mine. "She's not wrong."

There's a tenderness in his voice I didn't expect, and I have to look away before the weight of it makes my chest cave in. Poppy leans over and hands the book to Ford. "You read it now."

He takes it from her gently, glancing over the cover. I can tell he's nervous by the bob of his Adam's apple and the faint stutter in his voice. He begins anyways. "Alright, let's see what Ember's up to."

For the next 10 minutes, I sit there in silence and watch the two of them. Ford's voice is soft and careful, with just enough playfulness to hold Poppy's attention. She laughs at the silly parts. She rests her chin in her hands, taking in every detail. And Ford watches her like he's trying to memorize every blink, every giggle, every smile.

Something cracks open in me as I take it all in. A glimpse of what could have been. What still might be. I don't know what I was expecting, but it wasn't my broody Ford being so open and natural with a 6-year-old.

When they finish the book, Poppy sighs dramatically. "I wish Ember was real."

"Me too," Ford says, handing it back. "I think you'd be a good dragon friend."

Poppy grins at that. "Do you like dragons, Ford?"

"I do," he says. "Especially purple ones."

She giggles and then, out of nowhere, she says, "You have the same eyes as me. They're gray."

Ford freezes.

My breath catches.

He doesn't say anything at first. But then very softly, he says, "Yeah. I guess I do."

Poppy doesn't think anything of it. She's already moved on, busy sorting through the pile of books in the basket beside her. Ford is still staring at her like she just cracked the earth in two.

The librarian announces the start of story time and Poppy takes off running across the room with her usual gusto. She plops down right at the front of the rainbow rug, legs criss-crossed, her little chin tipped up, eyes already wide with anticipation.

"She doesn't even look back," Ford murmurs beside me.

"She never does," I say, smiling. "She loves books more than almost anything. Her imagination is always running wild."

We both watch as she waves at another little girl, whispers something, then giggles behind her hand. I know Poppy by heart—every mannerism, every expression, but right now I'm seeing her through Ford's eyes, and it overwhelms me.

"She's magnetic," Ford whispers. "She's at the center of everything."

I glance at him, heart clenching. "She's always been like that. Even as a baby. Curious. Fierce. So full of life I could barely keep up."

He smiles, a real one this time. "She has your mouth."

"And your eyebrows," I whisper, letting myself look at him. "And your exact way of narrowing her eyes when she's thinking too hard."

His breath catches, and we both just sit and watch her, not speaking for a moment.

"Tell me more about her?" he asks, turning to look at me.

"She has this way of making everything sound like a story," I tell him, smiling. "The weather. Her dreams. What she had for lunch. She talks like everything matters."

"She's...beautiful," Ford says quietly.

I nod, swallowing past the lump in my throat. "She's my whole heart."

Ford doesn't speak, but I feel the shift in him, like something inside is slowly rearranging itself, making room.

"I want her to know me," he says finally.

"She will," I say. "It will just take time."

He nods again, slower this time. "You two...she looks so much like you, Lan."

"I see so much of you, too. Every day. It hasn't been easy to wake up every morning and see your eyes, the shape of your face, your mannerisms."

He pulls both hands down his face, shaking his head. I

know he must be thinking of all the time he's lost, of every minute I kept from him. If I had made a different choice years ago, he wouldn't have to ask me to tell him about his own daughter. He wouldn't be a stranger to her.

Poppy turns on the rug to grin at us. I wave, and Ford lifts his hand too—a beat late, like he's still trying to absorb it all.

"She's going to change your life," I say softly.

His gaze is still fixed on her, warm and reverent. "I think she already has."

Then his gray eyes shift to meet mine and he's the only person in the room. Everything else fades away until it's just him and me, tangled in a silence that says everything we're too afraid to voice out loud. The space between us feels impossibly charged—full of unsaid things, full of years we can't get back. I blink hard, forcing the tears back, and then the librarian closes the book with a soft snap and a dozen little voices erupt with excitement as story time ends. The moment shatters like glass.

Poppy's head whips around, eyes locking on mine, and she lights up like a sunrise. She races back, weaving through toddlers and strollers and parents, until she skids to a stop at my side. "I'm hungry," she says, clutching her stomach like it's been days since she last ate rather than an hour or so ago.

I smile, brushing her hair back behind one ear. "Good thing we've got your favorite at home: grilled cheese."

She grins. "With the special cheese?"

"Three kinds. Just for you."

She nods like that's the only acceptable number, then looks at Ford, her eyes narrowing in thought. "You should come too," she announces.

Ford's eyebrows lift, just slightly. "To try the famous grilled cheese?"

Poppy shrugs. "It's really good."

Ford looks at me. Not pushing, just waiting. His expression is tentative. Hopeful.

I nod. "You're welcome to join us. If you're not busy…"

"I'm not busy," he says softly.

Poppy's already skipping toward the exit, blissfully unaware of the magnitude of this moment. Ford and I fall in step behind her, close but not touching.

"Are you sure, Lan?" he asks suddenly, and I can hear the raw vulnerability in his voice.

"I'm sure."

We follow her out of the library and into the golden afternoon with something hopeful growing between us. I don't know what comes next but today feels like a shift. A beginning.

THIRTY-SEVEN

Ford

Poppy is standing on her step stool at the kitchen counter, carefully placing slices of cheese on buttered bread with surgical precision. When she's satisfied that she has each one just right, she carefully passes the plate of sandwiches to her mom at the stove.

"These look great, Poppyseed," Landyn coos as a sandwich sizzles in the hot frying pan and the smell of toasted bread fills the room.

I can't stop watching them both.

Landyn moves around the kitchen barefoot, her hair in a messy knot, a spatula in one hand. She laughs at something Poppy just said, the sound warm and soft and so damn easy. She flips the sandwich in the pan, then reaches over to gently tug a curl that's fallen out of Poppy's braid.

It's all so natural, so effortless. It looks like the two of them have done this together a hundred times—they probably have. I don't have many memories of moments like this from my own childhood, but I get the sense that Poppy's little life has been filled with them.

And Landyn—she's glowing. My eyes stay glued to her, to the way her T-shirt reveals a sliver of smooth skin just above her jeans, the way she tucks a strand of hair behind her ear. They're just small things, they should be nothing at all. But it hits me dead center.

She glances up, catches me watching, and grins. It's a slow, wicked curve of her lips that settles deep in my chest and spreads.

And yeah. It's a lot.

I lean back against the counter, suddenly too warm and too aware of everything about her—the way she moves, the way she laughs, the way that stupid grilled cheese is getting more of her attention than I am. Then she bites her bottom lip, eyes still on mine, and it feels like she's taken me by the collar, pulled me in close, and whispered, *watch closely, Ford.*

I am. God help me, I am. I haven't forgotten what Landyn took from me, but I also haven't forgotten everything we've been to each other. And underneath the hurt and the anger, there is a part of me that can't stop imagining everything we still could be.

The lighting in her kitchen is warm, golden. It glows off her skin, catching in the curve of her neck, the sweep of her jaw. I don't think she knows how beautiful she looks right now—how impossible it is to look away.

She leans closer to Poppy, who has moved her step stool close to the stove and is taking her turn flipping the sandwiches. Landyn offers guidance in a gentle, steady voice. "Now press it down, just a little. Hear that sizzle? That's the good stuff."

Poppy grins, proud of herself, and Landyn smiles back at her. I can tell that she's memorizing every inch of this moment, every single detail like she's locking it into place.

Then she looks at me and something in her eyes hits me square in the chest. She takes a deep breath then shakes her head just once, like she's brushing off whatever just passed between us. But it lingers. Heavy. Electric.

I tighten my grip on the edge of the counter, jaw clenched, pulse doing stupid things.

Jesus, I'm so in love with her it physically hurts.

I loved Landyn when we were together all those years ago. I've probably loved her ever since then. But this is something deeper. Now she's a mother to my daughter. Our daughter.

"You're supervising, right?" she says, glancing down at Poppy.

Poppy nods solemnly. "I am. Next time Ford should cook too. Chef Ford has to earn his apron."

Next time. I laugh, resting a hand on the doorframe. "Is that so?"

"We watch a lot of cooking shows," Landyn admits with a sheepish grin. "But I agree, Poppy. I think we can put Ford in charge of the grilled cheese next time."

There's a crack in her voice as she finishes the sentence, and that warmth in my chest? That flicker of hope? It surges again, stronger now.

I look at Poppy. Her tiny fingers are tapping a rhythm on the counter, her braid falling over one shoulder. She's humming to herself, like this is just another regular afternoon. And for her, it probably is, but for me, it's everything. I can't believe how much I already feel for her.

I'm in awe at the kind, smart, funny little girl she is, and I can see that her mom is the reason for that.

Landyn slides the last of the sandwiches onto a plate and turns off the stove. "Lunch is served," she says with a smile, moving to set the plates on the small kitchen table.

I take the empty chair beside them, picking up a piece of the sandwich from the pink plate with cartoon characters I don't recognize. And for a second, I imagine this is my life, that

I'm not here as Landyn's friend but as Poppy's daddy. I want that more than I've ever wanted anything.

Poppy takes a big bite and hums her approval. "This is so good. You should open a restaurant, Mommy."

Landyn laughs softly. "Chef Poppy, you did most of the work."

Poppy peers over at me, toast crumbs on her cheek. "You have to try it, Ford."

She watches, wide-eyed with anticipation as I take a bite.

"Do you like it?" she asks as soon as I've finished chewing.

"I love it," I say, wiping my hands on a napkin. "It's the best grilled cheese I've ever had."

Poppy's whole face lights up, and with that out of the way, she moves on to telling me everything. That grilled cheese is actually her second favorite sandwich, her first favorite being turkey and cheddar, but only if the bread is not squishy; that her best friend at school is Maisie, who apparently eats paste; that if she could have any pet in the world, she would pick a dog, preferably a black one with bright white spots on it.

I can't keep up, but I hang on every word. Landyn watches us from across the table quietly, but I can feel her heart beating as clearly as if it were my own.

When lunch is over, Poppy wipes her hands on a towel and slides off her chair. "Can I go outside?" she asks.

"Shoes first," Landyn says automatically, but Poppy is already halfway to the back door. I gather the plates from the table as Landyn wipes down the countertops.

"She's something," I say, loading the plates into the dishwasher.

Landyn nods. "She is." I look out the kitchen window to the yard, where Poppy is twirling around with her hand held high, a rainbow ribbon trailing along behind her. "She does that when she's happy," Landyn says quietly, coming to stand beside me. "Spins in circles like that. Says it makes her feel like a princess."

"I missed so much," I murmur, not meaning to say it out loud.

Landyn's shoulders go tight. "I know," she whispers.

"I'm not saying it to make you feel worse."

The hurt is still there, still heavy, but I can't hold onto it when I see Poppy drop to the grass to pick a bouquet of dandelions. "I want to be part of this," I say to her, drying my hands on a towel. "Of her life. Whatever it takes."

Landyn's voice is soft. "I know you do."

I glance at her, jaw tight. "But you should know...I'm still angry."

She meets my eyes. "I know that too."

We fall quiet again, watching the little girl who ties us together, spinning and laughing with no clue of the weight of the moment hanging between us. Right now, the three of us are together, and we're doing our best to make the most of the second chance we've been given.

Landyn and I finish the dishes slowly, neither of us in a hurry to see the moment end. Finally, she dries her hands on a dish towel and glances at me over her shoulder.

"We don't have any plans the rest of the day," she says carefully. "If you want to stay awhile..."

My chest tightens, but I nod. "Yeah. I'd like that."

She smiles—small, hesitant—but it still knocks the wind out of me. We walk outside into the warm afternoon air, the sun is slanting just enough to cast golden shadows across the patchy lawn. Poppy's sitting cross-legged in the grass now, collecting tiny rocks like they're treasure. The backyard is small but inviting. There's a herb garden near the fence, two plastic Adirondack chairs, and a set of fairy lights strung haphazardly above the deck railing. I make a mental note of the fact that there's no swing set. Later. I'll get her one later.

Landyn settles onto one of the faded chairs, tucking her feet underneath her. I take the one beside her.

"She plays out here a lot?" I ask.

"Every day that the sun's out. Sometimes even when it's not."

"What was she like, Landyn...as a baby?" I ask quietly.

Her face softens and she smiles. "She was serious. Alert from the start. Didn't cry a lot. Always watching... like she was studying the world before she decided what to think of it."

"That tracks," I murmur, looking back at Poppy. "She's smart."

"Too smart," Landyn agrees. "She picked up on everything. Emotions, energy. When she was a toddler, when I had a hard day, she'd just curl up beside me and hum. Like she was trying to soothe me before she could even talk."

There's a lump in my throat I can't quite swallow. I missed all of it.

Landyn shifts beside me, her voice gentle. "She has this one stuffed animal she never let go of—a bunny named Cinnamon."

"Cinnamon?" I chuckle.

"She named it when she was three. She still has him. He lives on her bed."

I nod, committing all of it to memory. "She's..." I exhale. "She's kind of perfect, Lan."

Landyn doesn't answer right away. Just stares down at her hands in her lap. "She really is."

Before I can say more, Poppy is suddenly standing right beside me. "Hey! Ford!"

I blink, turning toward her. "Yeah?"

"Do you know how to kick a soccer ball?"

I grin. "I've been known to kick a ball or two."

She disappears around the side of the house and returns

with a slightly deflated pink soccer ball. She drops it between us like a challenge.

"You sure you're ready for this?" I ask, standing up.

Poppy puts her hands on her hips. "Ready. Show me what you got."

Landyn laughs behind me as I follow Poppy into the yard.

We start slowly—just passing it back and forth, her little foot darting out with precision. She's got good instincts. Light on her toes. Before long, I'm jogging after her as she chases the ball down.

I can feel Landyn watching from the deck, and when I glance up, she has a look on her face that just about undoes me. Happy. Proud. A little bit broken.

I'd give anything to go back in time, but I can't. All I can do is be here now. So, I chase the ball again, and when I finally steal it from Poppy and she falls to the grass in giggles, I think —maybe this is what healing looks like.

We kick the ball around for a little while longer, the warm afternoon sun beating down on us. Poppy is about to take a shot when she stops suddenly, eyes wide with excitement.

"I'm gonna go inside and get you something really cool," she announces, already turning toward the house. "Don't leave, okay?"

"I won't," I promise, watching her dash toward the back door, her braid swinging behind her.

I walk back up the slope toward the deck, where Landyn sits with her knees pulled up, sipping a glass of iced tea. Her eyes track Poppy's little figure until the door closes behind her, and then they shift to me. I sit beside her, a comfortable hush settling into the space between us.

"I meant to ask, is she doing okay?" I ask gently, nodding toward the house. "I mean, with everything going on with your mom?"

Landyn exhales. "Yeah. She doesn't know the full extent of

it, just that she's not feeling well. We're...trying to keep things light for her."

"And how is your mom?" I ask.

She hesitates. "If all goes well, she's being discharged tomorrow. We caught it in time, but it's going to be a long road. It's a relief to know that with the right medication and time, she'll feel like herself again. My dad's stepping up a lot, and I'll be juggling some of it too."

"Tell me what you need, Landyn," I say, my voice firm. "Anything. I want to help."

She looks over at me, something soft and unreadable in her eyes. "Thank you. That means more than you know."

"I mean it," I say.

She nods slowly, then sips her tea. "I'll be back at work Monday. My dad will be with my mom, and I've got everything else lined up."

I lean back, resting my elbows on the arms of the chair, looking up at the stretch of clear blue sky. The ache in my chest is still there—everything I lost, everything I missed out on—but it's softer now. I've got something to hold onto.

Today was a good day. Pretty close to perfect. For the first time in a long time, I feel like something in me might actually be healing.

And then the back door swings open, and Poppy runs out clutching a tiny pink photo album, yelling, "Ford! I found it! It's my baby pictures!"

Landyn laughs beside me, and I turn just in time to catch our daughter launching herself into my lap.

Yeah. Things are going to be okay.

THIRTY-EIGHT

Ford

It's Monday. Landyn's back at the office, and so am I, and for the first time in what feels like forever, things are going pretty smoothly. I can feel it in the way my shoulders seem to have dropped half an inch, in the muscles that have slowly unclenched. The media storm surrounding Cove has died down for the time being—thanks in part to Landyn and the team's had work and in part to the fact that the CEO of another local company just got caught embezzling funds. New day, new scandal. I'm not complaining. The weight that's been pressing on my chest for months feels a little lighter. For now.

As for Landyn and me—things between us aren't perfect. Not even close. There's still plenty of anger and regret there, but there's also something new. Something exciting.

Poppy.

I think about her all the time. It's only been a few days, but already the thought of a world without her in it feels impossible to imagine. Her tiny voice, her infectious giggle, her nonstop stream of questions and stories. When she ran toward me with a photo album like she couldn't wait to share a piece of her life with me I thought my heart would explode right there on the spot. I didn't know I could love someone I barely know this much, but here we are. The anger I felt when Landyn first told me about her—when the truth detonated everything I thought I knew—has dulled. It's not gone, not completely, but it's mellowed, settled. The ache has turned into something else entirely. When I think about Poppy now, it's not rage that floods my veins, it's this wild, all-consuming protective instinct. All I need is for everything in her little world to be okay. And all I want to do is get to know her better.

This morning, Landyn popped into my office to ask if she could leave a bit early to pick Poppy up from school. With Carolyn still recovering and no after-school care set up yet, she has a lot on her plate. When I asked if I could come too, she looked surprised but then she said yes.

So now it's 2:45, and I'm grabbing my keys from my desk and trying without success to keep my nervous energy under control.

Noah peeks his head into my office, Jesse not far behind him. "You heading out?"

"Yeah," I say. "I'm going with Lan to pick up Poppy."

He grins, that rare kind of genuine smile that cuts through our usual sibling gibes and sarcasm. "You're a dad now, huh?"

Something flickers in my chest. I nod.

"Don't let her hustle you for snacks," Jesse warns. "Kids are pros at that."

"Noted."

He leans on the doorframe, already mid-smirk. "So, how's it feel? Knowing you made a whole person?"

"Feels...big," I answer honestly. "Like I'm still catching up."

They're both curious and they've earned the right to be, but they've been careful not to push too hard, trying to give Landyn and me space to work through it. I'm grateful for that, but they've also made it known that they can't wait to meet their niece.

I check the time again. 2:50.

I grab my sunglasses and head for the parking lot, where I said I'd meet Landyn. I've been to hundreds of meetings in my life. Sat through investor pitches, boardroom brawls, interviews, presentations, crisis talks, but nothing has my heart racing like the thought of hopefully seeing Poppy's face light up when she sees me waiting outside her school.

Landyn sees me as soon as I reach the parking lot, lifting a hand in a small wave.

"You made it," she says as I approach.

"Wouldn't miss it," I tell her, voice steady even though I'm a mess on the inside. "You want me to drive?"

She eyes me for a beat, like she's deciding whether or not it's a good idea to be in a car with me. Eventually she nods. "Sure, but I need to grab Poppy's car seat."

"I can get it," I tell her, feeling a need to be helpful, to be involved. I second guess myself when she opens the back door to her small car, and I can't figure out how to get the seat out of it.

Landyn watches me with an amused smile tugging at her lips. "You okay?"

I shake my head. "I built an entire company, but I think this may be more complicated. Any tips?"

She explains that the booster seat has hooks that attach to metal bars stuffed between the seats. After some trial and error and Landyn telling me what to do, I finally get it free. I set it up in the back seat of my truck, triple checking every attachment.

"I think it's good," she tells me as I give it one more solid shake.

"Just trying not to screw this up. This feels like a test," I mutter.

"It kind of is."

We drive the eight minutes to Poppy's school and park just outside the schoolyard gate. Kids are already pouring out of the building, backpacks bouncing, voices loud and excited. As I scan the crowd trying to find Poppy, something close to panic blooms in my chest.

"She's always one of the last ones out," Landyn says, perhaps sensing my unease. "The kid can talk, as you probably noticed the other day. Her teacher has the patience of a saint."

My hands are jammed into my pockets. I'm trying to play it cool, but the nerves are back, worse than any boardroom pitch I've ever had to make.

Until I see her.

Poppy's wild curls are in twin braids, and she's scanning the crowd with wide, searching eyes.

Landyn's smile is wide the second she sees her and then Poppy is a streak of motion, her backpack bouncing wildly as she barrels through the schoolyard.

"Mom!"

Her little feet barely touch the ground before she's in Landyn's arms, leaping up, clinging like a monkey, arms and legs wrapping around her mom with practiced ease. Landyn catches her effortlessly, like she's done it a thousand times, and her eyes close as she cradles Poppy to her chest. Her hands spread wide, one at her back, the other cupping the base of her daughter's head like a lifeline. "Missed you," she says, low and fierce. "Missed you so much."

I stand there, completely still, afraid that if I move, I'll shatter the moment. It's raw and intimate and—hell—beautiful. Poppy pulls back just enough to look at her mom, then turns her head and spots me. "Ford!" she beams, wiggling in Landyn's arms. "Put me down, Mom! I need to say hi to Ford!"

Landyn laughs before setting her down gently on the pavement. Poppy doesn't waste a second. She jumps in front of me, and I drop to one knee to meet her. I don't know what I expected, but when her little arms wrap around my neck, it brings me to my knees in every sense.

"Ford," Poppy says after she's let go of me. "Are you coming to the studio with us?"

I blink. "The studio?"

"That's where I dance," Poppy explains.

I look at Landyn, not sure what to say. "Yeah, you should come," she says, smiling. "She has ballet today. One of her favorite classes."

I look between the two of them. Poppy's beaming, her hands still clutching my forearm like she's afraid I might say no. I'm completely unprepared for how desperately I want to say yes.

"Yeah," I hear myself say. "I'd love to."

Poppy cheers. "Can we get there early, Mom? I think Mia is going to be there early today."

"Sure," Landyn agrees. "Ford's going to drive us in his truck," she says, nodding towards my F-150. I open the back door and Poppy scrambles inside.

"I like your truck, Ford," she tells me as I buckle her in, checking the booster seat yet again to make sure it's secure.

"I'm glad to hear it," I tell her. "Do you want to drive?"

She shakes her head, giggling. "I'm only six!"

"Oh, that's right," I tease her. "I guess I'll drive then."

I shut the door, turning to face Landyn.

"She really wants me to come?" I ask quietly as we fall into step together.

She smiles, and there's something soft underlying it— something careful. "You made an impression, Ford."

I round the front of the truck and slide into the driver's seat, surprised by the lump that's formed in my throat.

The whole drive to the studio, Poppy talks non-stop from the back seat about her teacher, the sparkly bodysuit she gets to wear at her recital, the way she can do an arabesque now, "but not the hard kind, just the beginner one." She says she can't wait to show us.

Us.

When we get to the dance studio, Landyn takes Poppy to the bathroom to get her changed while I hover near the chairs by the front desk, trying not to feel out of place.

"This way," Landyn calls to me as they step out of the washroom, Poppy in her pink leotard and tights, her pale pink ballet shoes dangling from her hand.

Poppy takes off, and we follow her down the hall to the viewing window where Landyn and I stand quietly side by side. Soft music filters into the hallway, classical and light, and all the girls in the class start to move. It's chaos, really, with kids flailing a beat too late or skipping steps entirely. But one little dancer stands out.

Poppy.

She moves with purpose, her arms lift to exactly where they should be, her toes pointed, her posture poised. She's perfectly on rhythm, a tiny storm of grace and focus amid the spinning mess of pink tulle.

"Landyn," I murmur, leaning in. "Is she a prodigy?"

Landyn stifles a laugh and elbows me lightly. "Keep your voice down, dance dad."

"I'm serious," I whisper. "Look at her. She's...she's doing everything exactly right. She's leaps and bounds better than any of the other kids. She dances circles around them."

My eyes are glued to her, so full of concentration and quiet confidence. She moves through the routine like it's second nature to her, like this is where she's meant to be.

Landyn smiles. "She's always been like that. Determined. She works her little butt off. I think she gets that from you," she adds quietly, not looking at me.

"Landyn," I say, my voice low as I tear my gaze away from

the window and look at her. "My brothers want to meet her eventually."

She nods, turning her head to meet my gaze. "I figured they would."

"I haven't told them much. Just that she's ours." I pause. "They'll love her."

"I'm sure she'll love them too." She swallows. There's a beat of silence. "Do they hate me?"

Her voice is barely above a whisper, and it hits something tender inside me. I shake my head slowly. "No. They're...protective. But they don't hate you, Landyn."

She lets out a breath, but I can see the worry still flickering in her eyes. "I wouldn't blame them if they did."

"They watched me fall apart when you left," I start. "So, they're looking out for me. But they'll come around...for Poppy's sake."

The tension crackles between us like a wire pulled too tight. I should say something to ease it, but I don't. I'm not ready yet. There's a part of me that is still so mad.

Eventually, Landyn's shoulder brushes mine. "You know what she said to me yesterday?"

I turn to her. "What?"

"She said, 'I think Ford is one of my favorite people. Like you and Grandma and Grandpa." She gives me a small smile. "Then she asked if that was okay."

My throat tightens. "She said that?"

Landyn nods. "She likes you. A lot."

I look back through the glass, where Poppy is twirling near the front of the room.

"Yeah," I murmur. "The feeling's mutual."

"Can Ford come over for dinner?" Poppy asks from the back seat as we pull out of the dance studio parking lot. "Please, Mom? We can have grilled cheese again, and he can see my fort! I made it even better this morning."

Landyn turns in her seat to look at her. "We're going to visit Grandma, remember? She's still at the hospital."

Poppy lets out a groan and flops her head against the car seat. "But I went to the hospital yesterday."

"And we're going again today," Landyn says gently. "Grandma loves to see you."

"But I miss Ford," she says, dramatically putting a hand on her heart like she's starring in her own little play.

Landyn presses her lips together to hide a smile. "I can stay with her, if that helps," I offer, voice low so only Landyn can hear me. "You can spend some time with your mom."

Landyn looks over at me with surprise in her eyes. "You would be okay with that?"

"I wouldn't offer if I wasn't."

She nods a little, like she's thinking it over. "Hey, P," she says, turning to look back at Poppy. "Would you like to hang out with Ford for a little while tonight while I go visit Grandma?"

Poppy sits up straighter, eyes going huge. "YES! Yes, yes, yes! Can we have grilled cheese, Ford? And maybe... you can teach me how to whistle better?"

Landyn and I stare at each other with grins on our faces.

"I think that sounds like a pretty perfect evening," I say, glancing at Landyn. "I happen to be very good at whistling."

Poppy claps in her seat, practically vibrating with excitement. Landyn looks at me and something unspoken passes between us. Relief, maybe, or gratitude.

And for a moment, everything else—every trace of anger and guilt, every complicated thought and unanswered question—melts away.

THIRTY-NINE

Landyn

It's been a week since Ford spent his first afternoon alone with Poppy, and somehow, everything feels...normal. Easy, even. I can't quite wrap my head around the fact that he's part of our life—not just mine, but Poppy's too. Not that long ago, that felt impossible.

Poppy's in the kitchen with me, standing on a stool beside the island and stirring a bowl of pasta sauce. She's humming under her breath, hair tied up in a messy bun. She's thrilled because Ford's coming over for dinner. Again.

I was surprised at how readily I agreed to leave them on their own together. They haven't known each other for long, and I'm not used to being without her. But Ford didn't hesitate when he made the offer, and Poppy was over the moon about it. I still felt the pull of guilt when I left the house, but I didn't have any second thoughts about it.

When I returned home a couple of hours later, there was an even bigger fort in the living room and the two of them were curled up underneath it under a canopy of fairy lights. Poppy was nestled into the crook of his arm, her head on his chest, one of his big hands resting gently on her back. She was sound asleep, and he was watching her like she was the most precious thing he'd ever been entrusted with.

And something inside me cracked open.

He kissed the top of her head without waking her before climbing out of the fort and left the house with a look in his eyes I couldn't shake. Poppy talked about him nonstop for the next two days.

As for the grilled cheese sandwiches, apparently, Ford's were just as good as mine. Poppy had been very clear about that.

The rest of the week flew by. Work has been busy. Poppy's schedule has been packed. My mom's getting better—still not quite herself, but home from the hospital and feeling better every day. And Ford has been there through it all.

He helped me find a great after-school care program for Poppy and insisted I leave the office early until it started. He texted me a link to a YouTube video about black and white spotted puppies with the message, "For Poppy?" He came with me to pick her up from school and take her to dance class, where he stood watching her like she was a world class balle-rina—which he insists she very well could be one day.

We haven't talked about us, about what we're doing or where we're going. Right now, we're just focused on the two of them getting to know each other. That's all that matters.

"Do you think he'll like it?" Poppy asks, holding up the bowl of sauce proudly, a little smear of tomato sauce on her cheek.

I smile, reaching over to wipe it away with my thumb. "He's going to love it, Poppyseed." And in my chest, something aches—soft and hopeful.

There's a knock at the door just as I'm draining the pasta and Poppy immediately darts toward it, yelling, "I'll get it!"

I laugh under my breath. "Check who it is first!" I call after her, but I already know.

She swings the door open. "Ford! You're here!"

"Wouldn't dream of missing this," he says, smiling as he steps inside, holding a paper bag in one hand. "I brought dessert. I was told donuts were non-negotiable."

Poppy gasps and all but grabs the bag from him, already peeking inside. "You got the good kind!"

He winks. "Only the best for my girl."

My girl. Something inside me flutters at the sound of it, but it's quickly replaced by a deep jab of guilt because Poppy still doesn't know who Ford really is.

"I have to set the table now," she says, suddenly remembering her job. She skips back into the kitchen, her bare feet padding against the hardwood floor. I linger in the doorway for a second, drying my hands on a dishtowel as I watch her carefully place plates down—three of them. She lines up the silverware with concentration, tongue poking out the side of her mouth as always.

Three place settings.

It hits me harder than I expect.

Ford moves to stand beside me, and I know he notices it too. The way his arm brushes mine doesn't feel like an accident.

"She set the table for three," I whisper, voice thick. "It's just a small thing but..."

"It's not small," he says. "It's a big deal."

We eat at the little table by the window with the fading sun painting the sky in watercolors. Poppy talks a mile a minute, telling Ford all about her teacher and how she's learning to do the splits and how someone at school brought a tarantula for show and tell and how she is never going near that person again.

Ford listens like she's reciting poetry.

After dinner, we each have one of the donuts Ford brought.

He pretends to steal Poppy's last bite just to make her squeal, and when she gets chocolate on her chin, he wipes it off with a napkin like it's second nature. And somewhere between the laughter and the easy rhythm of conversation, the ache in my chest eases.

This? This feels like something real.

Like something we could keep.

After dinner, Poppy insists on showing Ford her latest drawings and he looks at each one very seriously, holding them up like they belong in a gallery.

She beams, soaking up every second. I would be happy if this night could stretch on forever, but when I glance at the clock, I clear my throat gently. "Alright, my love. Time to wash up and get ready for bed."

"Do I have to?" she whines with a pout, curling herself into Ford's side.

"You do," I say, trying not to smile. "But if you hustle, I'll read you two chapters tonight."

She groans but drags herself toward the bathroom. At the doorway, she turns and asks, "Ford, are you staying for bedtime?"

My eyes flick to his, unsure how he'll answer. But he just gives her a smile and says gently, "Not tonight, monkey. But I'll see you really soon."

"Promise?"

He places a hand over his heart. "Promise."

She nods, satisfied, and disappears down the hallway. I let out a slow breath, moving toward the kitchen, but Ford stops me with a touch to my wrist. "You want me to hang out until she's asleep?

He says it softly, without any pressure. I shake my head. "She'll be out in five minutes flat. Girl ran on full energy today. She's going to crash."

He nods but doesn't make a move to leave. I hesitate for a moment, trying to read the look lingering in his eyes.

"Mom! Ready!" Poppy calls out from down the hall, breaking the moment between us. I pull myself away and join her in her bedroom, where I tuck her in and read until her breathing evens out.

When I come back out, Ford is still here, standing at the window, looking out at the darkened yard. The dishes are done. The lights are low. And suddenly, it's quiet.

Just us.

"You didn't have to clean up," I say softly as I walk into the room.

"I wanted to," he says, turning to face me.

I cross my arms, suddenly feeling uncertain. The weight of everything we haven't said yet feels like it's humming between us, unavoidable.

"We need to talk." We say it at the same time.

He wipes his hands on a towel, tosses it onto the counter, and walks toward me with a look I've come to recognize— serious and determined, but softer now, like he's treading carefully.

"I don't want to wait," he says. "We need to tell her. Soon."

I nod, but my throat tightens.

He steps closer, drops his voice. "She's smart, Landyn. She's going to figure out we're keeping something from her, and the longer we wait, the more it might feel like a lie. Like we were hiding it from her."

"I know," I whisper, eyes stinging. "I know."

"I'm not saying we blurt it out tomorrow, but I can't keep pretending I'm just some guy she likes hanging out with. She's my daughter. I want her to know that. I want her to hear it from us, not piece it together on her own."

I swallow hard and sink into one of the kitchen chairs. He

looks at me for a moment before pulling out the chair beside me and sitting down.

"I know you're right," I say. "I do." He waits, watching me closely. I press my palms to the table, trying to keep myself grounded. "I'm just scared, Ford," I admit, my voice cracking as I swipe tears from my eyes. "I've already messed this up for her. What if telling her now only makes it worse? She's... she's everything to me. And I kept you from her. That's on me. I know that I did this to you both."

I'm so afraid. Fuck, it kills me that I've put Ford in this position. And Poppy, is she going to hate me? I don't think I could take it if she looked at me with betrayal in her eyes. A sob escapes me, and I cave in like I've been punched in the gut.

Ford grabs me, hauling me into his lap and crushing me to him. I pull back to look at him, surprised. He's been so careful to keep distance between us ever since the night I told him about Poppy. The concern on his face only makes me cry more. I shift, creating space, knowing that I'm undeserving of his kindness and care. But he tightens his grip on me, his hand moving to cradle the back of my neck, and I finally let myself sink into him, my head resting against his shoulder.

"Lan, this isn't about blame, or secrets. Not now," he says, voice low and rough. "That used to be the thing keeping me up at night. But now... it's just her. It's Poppy."

He runs his hand over the length of my spine, over and over, while my tears stain his gray shirt. He just keeps holding me, his heartbeat slow and steady, until I've cried the last tear. When I do, he tilts my face up and when our eyes meet, I see that he's not angry. He's not the man I lied to. He's not the 20-year-old whose kisses made me dizzy, or the broody CEO who makes my heart beat double time. He's just Ford. Steady, strong, in control. And right now, he's quietly supporting me while my whole body trembles from the weight of what needs to be done.

"You know what's killing me now? Thinking that when we tell her, it might hurt her. That *I* might hurt her. That she'll look at me and feel confused or betrayed or think I wasn't there because I didn't care enough to show up And I can't—" his voice catches. "It kills me, Lan. I can't be the reason she feels like that."

I nod, understanding exactly what he means. How he feels.

We stay like that for a long time, his arms wrapped around me, my head on his shoulder. We're both quiet now, but somehow, it feels like we've said enough. Or maybe just enough for now. We heard each other. Really heard each other. And that alone settles something inside me.

Eventually, Ford shifts me gently off his lap and stands to leave. I walk him to the door, watching as he descends the front steps slowly, pausing at the bottom to glance back at me. I lift a hand in a soft wave. He gives me one in return.

I should let it be. Let him go. Let the moment end.

But I can't.

When he reaches his car, he looks back again—and that's when it hits me. It doesn't feel right, watching him walk away. It rattles something loose inside me.

Panic blooms fast and hot in my chest. What if he didn't hear the things I didn't say? The ones I couldn't bring myself to voice?

I don't think. I just move. Down the porch steps and across the walkway, my feet barely touching the ground. When I reach him, I throw myself into his chest with enough force to make him stumble back a step, a soft *oof* escaping his lips as his arms instinctively come up around me.

I cling to him, wrapping myself around him like I might never get another chance. I bury my face in the warm, familiar spot where his neck meets his shoulder, breathing him in like oxygen.

"Thank you," I whisper, my voice already thick. "For not

shutting me out when you have every reason to. For being patient and kind to me. For showing up for her—" my voices catches. "For loving her."

He's still, then one arm slides up the back of my neck and I feel the scratch of his jaw against my temple.

"Loving her is the easy part of all of this."

I let go of him and stand here in the dark, hugging my arms around my stomach as I watch him drive away.

FORTY

F ord

The trail cuts through the forest like a ribbon, flanked by towering Douglas firs and clusters of cedar trees that still smell like rain even though it hasn't fallen in days. The sunlight filters through the dense canopy in narrow shafts, catching on the morning mist that still clings to the undergrowth. It's cool here, even in June.

Jesse, Noah, and I have been running for a while, up past the ridge above Deep Cove where the town feels miles away. This is where I come to think. Or not think. Where I go when my chest is too tight, and my brain won't shut up. The trails are just hard enough to make your body burn and your lungs stretch wide, perfect for when your mind's racing and you need something physical to chase the noise out.

Jesse finally breaks the silence, his breathing steady but strained. "So... how's she doing?"

He means Poppy. They've all known her name since the night I came home from the hospital and nearly put my fist through the wall.

"She's good," I say, dodging a root and keeping my stride.

"Better than good. She's... incredible. She's got this laugh that makes your chest ache. And she looks just like me, it's fucking wild. She has so much of Lan in her too."

"She sounds great," Noah says.

"Yeah. She's amazing."

We stop to catch our breath when we hit the lookout point, a break in the trees where the land drops off and the ocean stretches out to the horizon. I stretch my arms over my head, watching the wind ripple across the bay.

Noah speaks up. "So, you guys gonna tell her soon?"

"Yeah. This week." I swallow hard. "Landyn and I are telling her together. It's the right thing to do. But, man..." I pause, shaking my head. "I'm scared shitless."

"You think she's gonna take it hard?" Noah asks.

"I don't know. I just know I don't want to be the reason she's upset. I can't...I can't stand the idea of being the person who breaks her heart. It feels like we've been making good progress, and I don't want to do anything to jeopardize that."

There's silence again, then Jesse says, "And what about Landyn?"

"What about her?"

"You two figuring things out?"

I let out a long breath. "That's messier. I'm still mad. I lost six years I'll never get back and she's the reason why."

"But you also still love her," Jesse says. It's not a question.

"Of course I do," I admit, almost angry at how true the statement is. "I always have. Even when she left. Even now, when I don't know how to look at her without feeling like I'm breaking open."

Noah nods. "Love can't undo the betrayal. But it might be the thing that helps you heal from it."

I glance at both of them. They are the only two people, aside from Wes, in the world who know what it took to crawl out of the life we were given. And even now, after everything

I've built, as I stand on the edge of everything I thought I wanted, all I know is this:

Poppy changed everything.

I want to be a man she can look up to, even if I'm still figuring out how to forgive the woman who made me a father.

"I get why she did it," I say again, quieter this time. "That's the hardest part. She was scared that I wouldn't want the baby. That she'd ruin my life. She thought she was doing the right thing. But none of that makes it any easier."

I kick a rock off the trail, watching it tumble down the slope.

"And in some ways, she wasn't wrong," I admit, pain lacing every word. "I would've dropped everything. I would've thrown away my shot at Cove, at getting all of us out of that shitty life and giving us something better. I would've done it for her. For our kid." My voice breaks at the end, and I have to stop for a second, rubbing a hand across my forehead. "That's what kills me. She knew I loved her enough to burn the whole goddamn plan to the ground, and she couldn't live with being the reason I did that."

Jesse and Noah don't say anything, letting the silence breathe.

"It's just... heartbreaking. She raised our daughter on her own. She built this whole life without me. And now that I'm finally here, part of me wants to scream at her for taking it away, and the other part just wants to hold on to what I've got."

"Do you think you can you move past it?" Jesse asks.

I look out at the ocean, my jaw tight. "I don't know," I say honestly. "I want to. God, I want to. Every time I look at Poppy, I think... this is it. This is what matters. But then I look at Landyn and I still feel the bruise. I still hear the silence of those seven years. And I don't know how to stop feeling it."

Noah claps a hand on my shoulder. "Give it time, man. If you're both still in it, you'll get there."

I nod, but the ache in my chest doesn't leave me.

Because I already know I'm still in it. I never left.

I'VE SPENT THE PAST THREE DAYS RUNNING OVER THE WORDS IN MY head, playing out every possible reaction she might have, hoping for the best but mentally preparing myself for the worst.

The three of us are sitting on the porch at the cottage. Poppy's bike—pink, of course, with glittery streamers—is tipped over on the driveway. I spent the past 30 minutes jogging alongside her, helping her learn to ride without training wheels. She's determined like her mom. And like me. She fell once, skinning her knee. She cried for about 10 seconds before hopping back on, gritting her teeth like it was personal. I think I've said "I'm so proud of you" at least a hundred times today. I'll say it a hundred more. Now she's curled beside me on the porch swing, between me and Landyn. The air smells like cut grass and summer and the porch light is starting to glow against the deepening evening sky.

It would be a perfect night, if it weren't for the weight of what needs to be said bearing down on us. I look at Landyn, catching her eye over Poppy's head We haven't touched since she flew down the driveway and into my arms the other night. A quiet tension lives between us, like we're both waiting to exhale.

Poppy swings her feet, her cheeks pink, her curls wild and sweaty under her helmet. "Did you see that last one?" she asks, beaming. "I almost went all the way down the driveway."

"You crushed it," I say, bumping her shoulder lightly with mine. "Total pro."

She grins up at me, all confidence and sunshine. Landyn shifts in her seat. The moment is here. She sets the mug down gently on the porch rail. "Hey, Poppy? Can we talk to you for a second?"

"Okay," she says, still smiling, though she tilts her head, sensing something in our tone. I reach over, unbuckling her helmet strap, more to buy time than anything else. My heart is pounding.

Landyn brushes a curl from our daughter's face. "You know how special you are, right? How loved?"

Poppy nods, suddenly quieter.

"There's something really important we want to tell you," I say, my voice thick. "Something that might surprise you."

She blinks up at me, her eyes round and curious. "Okay."

"I love you so much," Landyn says again, brushing her hand down Poppy's back. "You know that, right?"

Poppy nods. "Yeah."

"And sometimes," I add, swallowing the nerves building in my throat, "grown-ups have to tell you things that are a little... big. Things that might be confusing at first, but they come from a really good place."

Poppy's brows pinch together. "Like what?"

Landyn's eyes meet mine. They're wet. Brimming. She nods once.

I take a deep breath. "Like the truth," I say. "The kind of truth that changes everything. That makes things even better."

Poppy sits up a little straighter and looks between us, suddenly unsure.

"There's something I've been wanting to tell you." I shift to face her, trying to keep my voice soft. "Something really important."

She blinks up at me and all I can see is how innocent and trusting she is. I rub my hands on my jeans and try again. "You know how we've been hanging out lots lately? Bike rides, grilled cheese, dance class?"

She nods slowly, like she's not sure where I'm going with this.

"Well...there's a reason I keep showing up. A reason I want to be around you so much." I look at Landyn again, and she squeezes Poppy's hand gently.

I inhale. "The truth is...I didn't just come into your life because I think you're cool—though you are. I'm here because..." I pause, my voice catching. "Because you're mine," I finally say. "I'm your dad, Poppy."

She freezes.

"I didn't know that until a little while ago," I say gently, quickly, needing her to understand. "If I had known—God, Poppy—I would've been here every single day since the moment you were born."

Her mouth opens slightly, but no sound comes out.

"I'm so sorry I missed so much," I whisper. "But I'm here now. If you'll let me be."

Poppy doesn't say anything at first. She just...stares. At me. And then at Landyn. Then back at me again. Her little chin wobbles and her lips part like she wants to say something but isn't sure how. Her fingers curl in the fabric of Landyn's skirt. My heart pounds so hard I'm sure they can hear it. Finally, her voice comes soft and trembling. "But...why didn't you know?"

Landyn closes her eyes. "That's my fault, sweet girl."

"It's not about fault," I say gently. "Sometimes grown-ups make really hard choices. Your mom...she did what she thought was best at the time. But if I'd known you existed? I would've been here the whole time. I promise."

Her bottom lip trembles, and tears slip down her cheeks. "You're really my dad?"

I nod. "Yeah. I am."

She swipes at her eyes, messy and overwhelmed, and it wrecks me. I'm on my knees in front of her before I realize I've moved. My hands hover in the space between us. I want to hold her so bad it physically hurts, but I wait.

"I know this is a lot," I tell her. "And it's okay if you feel weird or mad or sad, or even happy. Whatever you feel, it's okay. I'm just...really, really happy I finally get to know you."

She sniffles. "You taught me how to ride my bike."

I blink. "Yeah."

"You made me grilled cheese."

A small laugh chokes out of me. "I did."

She studies me for another long second. Then, slowly—so slowly—it happens. She leans forward and wraps her arms around my neck. I freeze for a second, not quite letting myself believe it's real. Then I pull her in tight, burying my face in her shoulder, and I don't even try to stop the tears.

"I love you already," she whispers, barely audible. "Even if I just found out."

I can't speak. I just hold her tighter. Landyn's hand is on my back, rubbing gentle circles, and all I can do is press my lips to the side of our daughter's head and breathe her in.

This is it.

This is everything.

FORTY-ONE

F ord

It's been three weeks.

Twenty-one days of waking up with the sound of Poppy's giggles echoing in my head and going to sleep making plans of things I want to teach her, places I want to show her; of crayon drawings pinned to the board in my office and tiny pink socks showing up in my laundry; of brushing popcorn out of the couch cushions after movie nights and realizing I couldn't care less about the mess. I'd sit through a dozen animated princess films and clean up a thousand kernels just to see her curled up on the couch between Landyn and me.

Poppy's been spending more time at my place. She's taken over the guest room and turned it into a shrine of glitter and picture books, a second home for her stuffed bunny, Cinnamon. I haven't moved a thing.

Landyn and I... if you didn't know any better, you'd think we're just like any other family. Sunday mornings at the farmer's market. An afternoon at a berry farm where Poppy's face and fingers got stained deep red and Landyn laughed so hard she cried. P's dance recital where I showed up with flowers and left with a lump in my throat because she looked like sunlight twirling across the stage.

And yet, not once have I kissed Landyn

Not once have I let my fingers linger too long when they brush hers in the kitchen, even though I want to. Not once have I closed the distance between us when she looks at me like maybe, just maybe, she wants me to.

We haven't slept under the same roof or shared coffee in the morning. We haven't crossed any lines. Not because I don't want to. Hell, it's all I want. What it would be like to kiss her in the quiet of her kitchen while Poppy sleeps upstairs. To touch her like I used to. Like I've never stopped wanting to. But this thing between us—this delicate, fragile thing we're rebuilding —it has to become solid. It has to be steady. For Poppy. For Landyn. For me.

Still, every day the betrayal hurts a little less and every day, I fall a little harder.

It's in the way she looks at me when I walk through the door. The way she still laughs at my dry humor, even when it's been a long day and she's tired. The way she leans toward me without realizing she's doing it, like her body remembers what we were before everything broke.

The pain is still there. But so is something else—something warmer, deeper, steadier. And somewhere in the middle of it all, it seems like we are finding our rhythm.

From the backseat comes the sound of Poppy humming some made-up tune she's been singing since we pulled out of Landyn's driveway 10 minutes ago. She's swinging her legs, clutching a hand-drawn card she made for her grandma, and asking every 30 seconds if we're almost there. Landyn's mom is thankfully feeling a lot better since being on her new medication. When Lan asked me if I wanted to join them on their visit today, I hesitated, not wanting to crowd in on their family time. But when she insisted it was her mom's idea, I accepted the invitation. It has been years since I've spent time with Carolyn Sinclair, a woman who was always nothing but kind to me, even when I had next to nothing.

"We're still two blocks away," I tell her for the second time, glancing at her in the rearview mirror.

"That's what you said last time!" Poppy says, folding her arms across her chest.

"That's because last time was only one minute ago," I tease her. "Don't worry, we'll be there really soon."

Beside me, Landyn's turned slightly toward the backseat, one hand resting on the console between us, the other brushing a piece of lint off her jeans. She's been quieter than usual, but not in a bad way. Just thoughtful. Watching. Absorbing this new version of her life that I've only recently been let into.

Poppy lets out a squeal as soon as I pull into the driveway and starts unbuckling her seatbelt before we've even come to a full stop.

"Hold up, little monkey," I say, laughing. "We need to park first."

Landyn reaches into the back to help her with the buckle. "You excited to see Grandma and Grandpa?"

"Yes! I have so much to tell them. And Grandma said last time that I could braid her hair if she's feeling okay!"

Landyn's hand brushes against mine as she turns back to the front seat. She looks at me and I can see the hesitation in her eyes. As we get to the front door, Poppy barrels ahead, knocking fast and loud. Carolyn opens it just a few moments later, and the way her face lights up when she sees us—all three of us—sparks a familiar sensation in me. It's hard to pin this feeling down. Loss, maybe. An ache for something I never had. Landyn has never once had to doubt her parents' love for her. It's written all over her mom's face, even now. That's something I didn't get to experience when I was growing up, but I'm so grateful that Poppy has it in her life.

"Look at this crew," she says warmly, stepping aside to let us in. "I must be pretty special to have all of you on my doorstep."

"You are," Landyn says, kissing her cheek gently.

"You are!" Poppy echoes, wrapping her arms around Carolyn's waist.

"Ford," she says, smiling as she runs a hand down Poppy's soft curls. "I'm so happy you came."

"Of course," I say. "It's good to see you."

"It's really good to see you too."

Poppy holds up the card she's been clutching ever since we left the cottage. "I made you something!"

Carolyn clutches her granddaughter to her chest, pressing a kiss to the top of her head. "I've been looking forward to seeing you all day."

We step into the cozy sunlit living room. Nothing's changed —same light-beige floral curtains, same mahogany side table, even the same hummingbird coaster I remember from years ago. It smells like chamomile and lemons, and I can already feel my shoulders relaxing.

Carolyn takes a seat and pats the cushion beside her for Poppy. Landyn's dad, John, joins us in the living room, sinking into the La-Z-Boy chair that's always been reserved for him. "Ford, good to see you, again," he says with a warm smile.

"Come, tell me everything." Carolyn says as Landyn and I take our seats on the old sofa. We end up a little too close, but neither of us moves. Poppy doesn't miss a beat, launching into a barrage of stories about her week, complete with wild hand gestures. Carolyn hangs on her every word like the world depends on it as John disappears into the kitchen. He returns with a couple of beers and sets a pitcher of lemonade and a few glasses on the coffee table.

"I've been thinking," Carolyn says when Poppy finally

comes up for air a few minutes later. "I'd really love to spend the afternoon with Poppy. I think Grandpa would like that too. Just the three of us. If you two don't mind."

Landyn's brows lift in surprise. "Mom, I don't think that's a good idea—"

"I'm feeling good today, and your dad is here too," her mom says, and this time I see the conviction in her eyes and maybe a twinkle of mischief. "And I have been missing my time with her. Besides, I'm sure you two haven't had a moment alone in weeks."

Landyn looks at me, and something unspoken passes between us. I nod, keeping my voice quiet. "If you're sure, Carolyn. We could grab a coffee. Take a walk."

She waves us off. "Go. We'll be fine."

Poppy is already dragging out a deck of cards from the drawer. "Grandma's gonna teach me Go Fish! Wanna play too, Grandpa?"

"You're in good hands, then," I say, smiling at my daughter and her grandparents.

Landyn's fingers brush mine as we stand. She gives her mom a hug and kisses the top of Poppy's head. I do the same.

"Ready?" I ask as we step onto the porch.

Landyn nods. "I think so."

"There's a great place around the corner," she says as we pull out of Landyn's parents' driveway. "They make this cake that is so decadent. It's basically just a slab of pure chocolate."

"Sounds good to me."

Five minutes later, we pull up to a tucked-away café with a bright fuchsia-pink door. We debate over the incredible desserts on display at the counter but in the end order a slice of chocolate cake to share and two espresso macchiatos.

"This place is great," I say after we've found an empty table at the back of the café. "It's been while since I've had a good piece of chocolate cake. Me and my brothers...we all used to ask for it for our birthdays. Our mom made us one from scratch a couple of times when we were little. It was gone in a day. Sometimes in a few hours."

Landyn smiles, and it hits me square in the chest. "You never told me that before," she says with colour in her cheeks. "I like knowing that about your past."

There's a pit in my belly as memories of my mom come rushing back to me. Love. Longing. Heartache. They all twist together, heavy and restless inside me. I smile as I bite into a forkful of the rich dessert. "Okay, you're right. This is amazing. I'd take chocolate cake over steak any day."

She laughs and for a second, it feels like nothing's changed. She tucks a piece of hair behind her ear then dips her fork into the cake and lifts it to her mouth, the movement slow and deliberate, like she's savoring every part of it.

Her lips part slightly, just enough to show the soft pink of her tongue and the flash of white teeth. Then—fuck me—she closes them around the bite like it's the first real pleasure she's had in weeks. I watch her lick a crumb from her finger and I swear time bends.

My cock stirs.

"Mmm,' she hums as she chews. It's not even a sexual sound, but my body doesn't know the damn difference. There's icing on the corner of her mouth. I want to lean in and lick it off.

Jesus.

I grip my coffee cup a little tighter, take a sip, and remind myself that now is not the time to fantasize about making out with Landyn. Still, I can't stop watching her. The curve of her mouth. The way she moves, graceful and totally unaware of the slow, sexy death she's dealing me from across the table.

She looks over and catches me staring, so I clear my throat, reach for another forkful of the cake, and do my best to chew like a normal human being. Not like someone who just had a full-body reaction to a goddamn dessert.

"How are your brothers, really? Jesse and I have talked, but we haven't *really* talked," she says. "He seems just like I remember him, though."

I lean back in my chair, rubbing my palm across my jaw as I think about how to answer. "Jesse is Jesse. Still single. Loves being in the spotlight, hates anything that smells like commitment."

She nods like that tracks. "What about Wes?"

"Quit flying commercial," I say. "He liked it, but the schedule got to him. Now he's doing private charters, he says it gives him more freedom."

"That sounds like Wes," she says with a smile. "Always wanting to do his own thing."

"And Noah's still skiing every chance he gets. Spends half his life up at his place in Whistler." I shake my head, smiling faintly. "I don't know what he does up there all on his own, honestly. He says it clears his head. I think he just likes the altitude."

Landyn laughs softly, and the sound settles something in me. We fall into silence again, the conversation lagging, but it doesn't feel awkward now. I look at her across the table, and for a second, I let myself remember what it used to be like between us. Back when I didn't know what she'd kept from me, when just sitting with her like this felt like everything I'd ever need.

She breaks the silence first. "You're lucky."

My brow pulls together. "How come?"

She looks at me with tenderness in her eyes. "Your brothers. You've always had each other."

I nod, swallowing against the sudden thickness in my throat. "Yeah," I say. "We didn't have much growing up. But we had that. Each other."

I don't say anything else. I don't need to. She's one of the few people who knows what our life was like back then. She understands where I came from.

Her fingers twitch against the table like she wants to reach for me but isn't sure she's allowed to. There's a flicker of something in her expression, concern that runs so deep it casts shadows.

And fuck, I feel it. Everywhere.

"Ford, do you think you can ever forgive me?"

Her eyes are wide, vulnerable in a way that guts me. Like she's bracing herself for the answer she knows is coming but asked anyway because she has to. Because we can't move forward without it.

We've tiptoed around this question for a long time now. I should've seen it coming, but it still knocks the air out of me when she says it out loud. She's not asking to be let off the hook. She wants to know if there is still space in me that belongs to her, or if that door has been closed forever.

It's not like I haven't thought about it—sometimes it's felt like it's all I can think about. I've just never been able to settle on an answer. I know what she thinks I'll say—that what she did is too big to forgive, that I can't even if I wanted to. But looking at her now, that doesn't feel like the truth.

I take a deep inhale, let it burn all the way down. "I think…" I start, voice rough, "I already am."

Her breath catches. I lean in, resting my arms on the table, like maybe that'll help to keep me steady, help me hold this line I've been walking between everything I lost and everything I still want. "I've been mad, Lan. Hurt. All of it. I still am, sometimes," I admit. "But every time I look at you, at Poppy…that part gets quieter. And I know I don't want to live in that pain anymore."

She looks at me, unblinking, and I can see the tears pooling.

"I don't want to carry it if it means I miss what's in front of me now." I pause, let the words settle in the space between us.

"I'm trying," I tell her. "I think that's what forgiveness starts with."

She doesn't speak right away, she just stares at me like maybe she doesn't trust the softness in my voice, or maybe she doesn't trust that she's allowed to hope. Then she says, so quietly I almost miss it, "I don't deserve that."

"You don't get to decide that," I say, and my voice is rougher than I mean it to be.

And then, just as the words settle between us, she looks at me—really looks—and asks, "What's happening with us, Ford?"

She doesn't ask it casually. She asks it like it matters. My heart kicks hard behind my ribs because I've been asking myself the same thing every night for the past few weeks.

"I don't have it all figured out yet," I tell her honestly. "But I know I don't want this to be temporary. I want to work on this. On us. I want to try." A breath escapes her like she's been holding it in for a long time. "And I want to be her dad, Lan. Not just a few nights a week. I want to figure out what it looks like to be a family." I pause, then add, "With both of you."

Her bottom lip trembles, just barely, and she drops her gaze to the last bite of cake sitting on the table between us. "I want that too" she whispers, one hand stretched around her cup, her other resting in her lap, palm facing up and open.

I drop my hand under the table without even thinking. I find her knee first, warm under my palm. I let my fingers trail upward, slow and uncertain, until they find the curve of her thigh. My hand settles there, like I need to touch her to keep from unraveling.

I've been hard on her. I've kept her at arm's length. I've let my silence speak louder than my words, let it build a wall between us instead of working to tear one down. But I'm done holding back. I don't want to stay on opposite sides of this anymore. I don't want her walking out of this café and wondering what I'm thinking. I don't want to keep pretending like I'm okay with the distance I've put between us.

I want more. I want all of it. So, I let go.

And so does she. Her hand reaches for mine under the table, like she's been waiting a long time for a signal to do it. At first, she brushes her pinkie finger against mine. The touch is so soft, that I wonder if I imagined it, but then she does it again. It sends a slow ripple up my arm, flooding my chest with heat. She traces circles over my knuckles and runs the tips of her fingers over my wrist until her fingers thread through mine. We stay like that, our hands tangled underneath the table, and everything after that softens. The air grows thicker. Sweeter. It feels like opening a window after a storm. Whatever dam I've been holding up inside me gives way and something beautiful rushes in to take its place.

She smiles. I smile back because I'm sitting in a crowded coffee shop with the girl who's been in my head since the day she left seven years ago. I'm smiling because I can touch her again, and no one here knows what that means.

"Can we get out of here?" she says, echoing the words that are on the tip of my tongue.

Our eyes meet. No explanation needed.

We're already gone.

FORTY-TWO

F ord

The anticipation is so intense it almost doesn't feel real.

It's electric, buzzing under my skin, in my chest, in every shallow breath I take. My grip on the steering wheel is too tight, knuckles white, but I don't loosen it. I don't want to. Everything around me feels sharper. Louder. The hum of tires on hot pavement, the distant wail of a siren, the late afternoon city clatter—all of it lands harder than it should, like my body can't filter any of it out.

The air outside is warm, just shy of hot. It seeps through the cracked window and grazes the side of my neck like a ghost. My skin reacts instantly in goosebumps, a shiver that feels less like a response and more like a need, deep inside me, wound tight and ready to snap.

I feel everything.

She's beside me.

Our hands are still clasped together, resting on her lap. There's energy rolling off us in waves. I can feel it, the same way I feel my pulse—undeniable, alive, real. Hard. I haven't been this hard for this long since I was a goddamn teenager. I'm not in control. Not entirely, but God, I feel awake. Every inch of me. And the knowledge of what we're about to do—what we're not saying out loud, but both know—takes root in me.

I put the car in park in my driveway and kill the engine, my pulse hammering beneath my skin.

Landyn is turned away from me, looking out the window toward the house. Her profile is lit up by the streetlamp out front and fuck me, she's beautiful.

That perfect nose of hers—the soft slope of it that I've stared at more times than I can count. And all I can think about is pressing my mouth to the bridge of it. Just because I can. Just because I need to. Then there's her mouth. *Jesus.* That full bottom lip—soft, flushed, the kind that practically begs to be pulled into mine. I want to bite it. Not hard. Just enough to feel it stretch between my teeth. Just enough to make her gasp.

Be cool, I tell myself as she undoes her seatbelt and reaches for the door handle like we're not sitting in the middle of a four-alarm fire. Spoiler: I ignore my own advice completely. Something low and raw rumbles in my throat—part want, part warning, part I'm not going to make it inside, I need her that badly. Now.

I'm on her in the next second, before she can even step out of the car. My hand is in her hair, mouth crashing into hers like I've been starved and she's the only thing that's ever fed me. It's not careful. It's not slow. It's weeks, of silence, regret, and desire all colliding into a single kiss that knocks the wind out of both of us.

She moans against my mouth, and I grip the back of her neck tighter, pulling her closer, devouring every sound, every breath.

This isn't a kiss, it's a reckoning.

The second her tongue slides against mine, I'm moving— reaching, grabbing, pulling her across the center console like

I've been waiting my whole damn life to do it. I drag her into my lap, one arm around her hips, the other pushing my seat back in a hard, jarring motion that gives me just enough space to get her where I need her—on top of me, flush and hot and trembling.

My cock grinds up against her center through her clothes, and it's not enough. Not even close. But it's something. And fuck, it feels like everything.

"Is this mine?" I ask clearly and slowly to avoid any confusion.

Landyn nods a yes as if she's forgotten how to speak. She's trembling, until I part her lips with my tongue and kiss her until I feel drunk.

"Is this body mine, Landyn? I need an answer."

A broken, desperate sound slips from her throat when I pinch her nipple between my fingers. I keep the pressure light, measured, even though I know it's driving her crazy. She's aching for more, but I need to hear her say it first.

Yours. The word leaves her mouth, slipping past her lips softly, like it barely has the strength to form at all.

I grip her hips tightly and rock her against me, grazing my cock against the thin cotton of her dress, over and over, rougher each time. The friction is pure torture—sweet and maddening. She gasps, hands braced on my shoulders as I bury my face in her neck. Her scent. Her skin. Her fucking presence, it hits me like a drug, and I take it like I need it to breathe.

"And this, June?" I say, gripping and rolling her ass in my palms, claiming every curve before dragging a finger down between her thighs. When it grazes her centre, her ass lifts off my lap in a sharp, needy buck. "What about this?"

"Yours, Yes, yours, Ford," she groans.

Yes, fucking, yes. She's mine again.

Now I'm going to fuck her like I know she likes it.

She tilts her head, exposing her throat like she's giving me permission to lose control. So, I do. I press my mouth to her neck, kiss and suck until she moans. A raw, desperate sound that lights me on fire. "I need you to fuck me. Now, Ford!"

I stop and take her face in both hands. "I'm going to fuck you, June. I promise you that. I'm going to fuck you hard and fast like I know we both need… then I'll fuck you slow and steady when I get you inside."

She grinds her pelvis over my cock, and I groan, hands already working at her clothes. Her dress. My pants. All of it. Barriers I suddenly can't stand. Buttons. Zippers. Seams. All of it's in my way.

She's already helping, fingers tugging, unfastening, yanking at the belt that's never felt so unnecessary. My hands are shaking as I fumble with her dress, not even bothering to be gentle as I work the powder-blue material over her head.

She lifts her arms, gasping as I pull. I rip my pants and my boxer briefs down to my knees. And then my cock is free. Hard. Ready. Pink and throbbing and barely holding on.

Mine.

June.

I take a minute to really look at us and I see her smooth olive skin bared for me, white lace bralette and matching panties that I want to shred from her body. She's in nothing but sheer underwear, stretched across my lap like a vision I couldn't have dreamed up if I tried.

It's obscene.

It's beautiful.

There's a raw, aching power in the way she looks right now —half-wild, flushed, breath shaky. My cock is hard and pulsing, trapped between us, leaking against the softness of her belly, begging for relief. But I don't move. Not yet because I've never felt like this before. Yeah, I want to bury myself so deep inside her that she forgets her own name. I want to fuck her until we're both wrecked and shaking and completely undone. But more than that? I want to feel her. Every inch of her. I want to kiss her slowly. Stroke my hands over every part of her body until she melts into me. I want to love her in a way that erases the space between us, until there's no more her and no more me. Just us. One breath. One heartbeat. Everything. I've never wanted anything more in my goddamn life.

I hook my fingers under the thin band of her underwear and drag it to the side.

The second I see her—wet, swollen, slick just for me—something snaps. I lose whatever fragile grip I had on control. My mouth is on her before I can think, lips crashing into her skin—her chest, her collarbone, her shoulder, her throat. I kiss like I'm starved, like I've got minutes to taste her and a lifetime's worth of hunger to burn through.

My tongue follows, frantic and hot, lapping over her. When that isn't enough—and it's not, it's never enough—I use my teeth.

I graze the tender slope of her neck, biting just enough to make her gasp. Her head falls back, exposing more, and I take it, pressing wet, open-mouthed kisses to the curve of her jaw, her shoulder, the dip above her breast. My hands can't stay still. One grips her ass, squeezing, dragging her tighter against the thick length of my cock still pinned between us, the other slides between her thighs, fingers slick with her arousal the second they find her center.

I groan—fuck—and slip one finger inside her. Then another. She's soaked and tight and pulsing around me, and the sound she makes when I curl them nearly makes me come on the spot. Her moan is high and panicked, desperate, as she reaches between us, fumbling, fingers wrapping around the base of me like she can't stand to be one more second without me inside her.

Neither can I.

She braces her hands on my shoulders, fingers splayed wide and rises up onto her knees in an offering.

Slow. Sure. God, so beautiful.

Her thighs part around me, and I go still.

Utterly still.

I don't breathe. I don't blink. Because this—*this*—feels like more than just sex. It's not just her body settling over mine. It's a before and an after. A line in the sand we'll never be able to cross back over. Everything narrows to this moment. Her. Me. The heat between us. The weight of everything we lost, everything we've found, and everything we've yet to discover. I could live forever right here in the space before everything changes. Before she sinks down and takes me inside her. Before I lose myself completely.

It's not just want—it's the start of something new, and all I can do is sit here, jaw tight, chest aching, as she spreads herself open for me... like a prayer. Like a promise. Like she knows this isn't just about getting off.

It's about everything.

And fuck, I'm ready.

I grab the base of my cock, thick and leaking, and line myself up with her slick, swollen entrance. She looks down, watching me do it, eyes glazed over like she's lost somewhere between want and desperation. So am I. The second the head slips past her folds—hot, wet, perfect—I groan.

"Fuck," I grit, and it comes out as a breath more than a word.

Then Landyn sinks down with no hesitation, no tease. She takes me and everything inside me shatters. It's slick skin and unbearable heat, her pussy gripping me like it was made for this, for me. Tight and hot and beautiful. So fucking beautiful. I can't even think straight.

She moves fast, riding me hard, frantic, grinding with short, perfect thrusts that steal the breath from my lungs. I grab her hips and fuck up into her, fast and brutal, my thighs slapping against her ass as she takes every inch. My insides quake, my nerves are on fire, and every time she moans, I feel it in my spine—a live wire of electricity snapping through me.

She clenches around me, and I curse again, forehead pressing to hers, sweat slicking our skin. Every thrust is a memory I burn into my bones. Every cry, every tremble, every desperate grind of her hips, I feel it all.

It's hot. Heavy. It builds low in my gut, in my balls, thick and unstoppable, and I know I'm not going to last. Not when she feels like this. Not when she sounds like that. Not when she's finally mine.

Her rhythm falters. I feel the sudden clench before I hear it, the broken gasp that shatters against my mouth. Then she's coming. Hard. Her whole body tightens around me, pussy fluttering like it's trying to pull me deeper, wring me dry. Her nails dig into my shoulders as she rides it out, and I fuck into her like I'm losing my mind.

"Yeah, that's it, baby," I growl, voice raw. "Come for me. Just like that. Fuck, Landyn—you feel so good, I almost can't take it."

She cries out—sharp, desperate—and I don't stop. I can't stop. Not when my balls are drawn up so tight it hurts. Not when I'm right there, teetering on the edge of my last ounce of control.

"I'm right there," I breathe. My bones are weightless, it feels like I'm floating and about to burst at the same time. "I'm going to come, Lan. I'm going to fill you up, baby, so deep you feel me for days."

She whimpers, *yes* with her and reaching behind her to cup my balls, and that's all it takes. The need flips, fast and violent, and suddenly it's mine. I'm not giving anymore. I'm taking.

I grip her hips hard, plant my feet against the floorboard, and fuck up into her with everything I have left.

It's ecstasy.

Euphoria.

And then I'm gone. Heat explodes behind my eyes, white-hot and blinding. I slam deep and stay there, cock throbbing as I spill into her. Pleasure rips through my cock and balls, hips jerking with each pulse. I shoot. I come hard. Pulse after pulse ripping through me, spilling everything I have into her.

My body locks up, shuddering, breath caught in my throat as I keep driving into her, every last spurt wrung from me with sharp, helpless groans.

It's not just release. It's flight. Like I'm finally taking off after being grounded for years. Only this time, I'm not crashing. I'm not spiralling. I'm in control, soaring, weightless, riding something so good, so fucking pure, I don't know if I'll ever touch the ground again.

FORTY-THREE

L andyn
   So...

That was an orgasm.

I sit here for a moment, dazed and blinking, still straddling Ford's lap, still full of him, still very much wrecked in the best, most unholy way possible.

Huh. Apparently, I have a thing for car sex, because holy shit—nothing I've ever felt even belongs in the same category as what just happened in this car.

I feel lit up and weightless. Liquid bones. Heart racing. Muscles quivering.

Ford's hand rests on my thigh, warm and grounding, but his breathing's still ragged—harsh, uneven gasps. He doesn't speak.

"Ford?" I say softly, brushing my knuckles over his forehead. "Are you okay?"

No answer.

My chest tightens, worry creeping up my spine like a cold draft. "Ford," I repeat, more firmly this time. "Is everything okay?"

He finally lifts his head, eyes meeting mine. "I'm good," he rasps. "I'm so good. I'm happy."

Something about the way he says it makes my stomach twist in a sharp, sweet way. "I'm just... happy, Landyn," he repeats. "Happier than I've been in a long fucking time. And I want to take care of you."

Before I can respond—before I can even figure out what to say—his lips are on mine in a slow, lingering kiss. "That was me getting everything I've ever wanted. Everything I've ever wished for over the past seven years, June." Then he's helping me off his lap, his hands gentle, guiding.

He finds my dress crumpled in the footwell and eases it back over my head, pulling the soft fabric down my arms, smoothing it into place with a reverence that makes me ache. He reaches for his pants, tugging them up his hips. His breath is still ragged, but it's quieter now. There's no hesitation as he opens the door and takes my hand and then we're walking into his house through, the front hall, and up the stairs.

My body's still humming, my legs still shaky. I follow him, barefoot and wordless, something tight curling around my heart. He leads me into his bedroom and then through a second door that opens into a moody-toned ensuite. I watch, silently, as he walks to the tub.

"I'm going to run us a bath." He turns on the tap. Adjusts the water. Dips his hand under the stream.

I don't know what I expected but it sure as hell wasn't this. Not Ford Winters running me a bath. Not this quiet, stripped-down version of him. I just watch, heart thudding. I watch him move around the bathroom like this is normal. Like he didn't' just wreck me in the front seat of his car.

Ford disappears into the bedroom and comes back with a cluster of pillar candles. He sets them around the room—on the edge of the tub, the vanity, the back of the toilet—then strikes a match. One by one, they flicker to life. The scent of vanilla blooms almost instantly, sweet and warm.

Steam rises from the tub in curling ribbons, softening everything. It's nearly full when he turns off the tap and looks at me. His voice is low. "Here, June, I've got you."

It's not a question. I blink, pulse ticking high again. He steps toward me, hands moving to the hem of my dress. He lifts it slowly, peeling it up and over my head like he's unwrapping something fragile. He pulls it free and lets it fall to the floor. My bralette and underwear go next.

I don't have time to feel shy or exposed before he steps back and starts removing his shirt, his shorts, his boxers. They're all left on the floor exposing every hard line of him.

His chest is all thick muscle, broad and tapered, arms veined and flexing with every small movement. His abs catch the candlelight like a sculpture, cut deep and solid. And then there's his cock, already thickening again.

My thighs clench without permission before I dip a toe into the water. Hot, but not scalding. I slide in slowly, easing under the surface inch by inch until the water cradles me, rising just beneath my collarbones. I exhale, my entire body unwinding into it, tension melting away only to be replaced by a similar sensation, this one tightening low in my belly because I can feel him watching me. Like a hunter waiting to pounce.

I slide lower, dipping under the surface until the tips of my shoulders are submerged and my skin is tingling. Ford gets in after me and I rise up so he can climb in behind me. Water sloshes over the edge and hits the tile with a soft slap as he sinks lower.

We settle. His chest presses to my back, his thighs bracket mine. Neither of us speaks. Neither of us moves except for Ford's big, steady hand that dips into the water, cupping it and pouring it over my shoulders, my arms, the parts of me not fully submerged. Over and over. Patient. Careful. The only sound is our breathing and the trickle of water.

We stay like that forever, or maybe just long enough for me to wonder how I ever survived without this. When he does speak, his voice is low, quiet and careful in a way that makes my heart ache. "Do you want more kids?"

My fingers drift along the surface of the water, tracing nothing. "Only with you."

He stills behind me. I feel it in his breath, in the way his chest halts for half a second.

"You mean that?" he asks, his voice rough with emotion.

I nod. "Yeah. I do." Because I can't imagine starting over with anyone else. Because the idea of building something—everything—with him doesn't scare me the way it used to.

"What about you? Would you want another?"

He wraps his arms around me, pulling me tighter against his chest. His mouth brushes the edge of my shoulder. "You already gave me the best thing I've ever had," he says. "If I got the chance to do it again—with you—I'd say yes in a heartbeat."

"We're not broken anymore," I whisper.

"No," he agrees, his mouth soft against my skin. "We're just getting started."

And in the stillness of the bath, wrapped in candlelight and the arms of the only man who's ever truly had me...I believe him.

His lips brush the side of my head, a quiet kiss against my damp hair, and I lean into it. The water is starting to cool, but his arms stay warm around me, his chest a steady, solid wall at my back.

When his hands slide over my stomach, I know it's not just comfort he's giving me. His palms move slowly, purposefully, skimming my ribs before drifting up, cupping one breast beneath the water. My breath catches, but I don't pull away.

Ford's mouth finds the curve of my shoulder, his teeth grazing it before his lips soothe the spot. "Come to bed," he murmurs against my skin.

We rise together, water cascading from our bodies, pooling on the tile. He wraps me in a towel before I can reach for one, his thumb sweeping along my jaw, his eyes searching mine like he's asking a question without words.

In his bedroom, the sheets are cool against my skin as he eases me back onto the bed. He kneels at the foot, and my breath stutters when his hands grip my knees, urging them apart.

"Ford…"

He slides his palms up my thighs, spreading me wider, lowering himself until the heat of his breath ghosts over me. The first stroke of his tongue through my folds is slow, deliberate, like he's reacquainting himself with every inch of me.

I arch into him, a soft sound catching in my throat. His hands lock around my hips, holding me still as his tongue moves in lazy, devastating patterns, flicking over my clit before drawing it between his lips.

"God—" My head falls back, fingers clutching the sheets. He doesn't let up, alternating between deep, languid licks and quick, precise flicks that have my thighs trembling. Every time I try to grind against him for more, his grip tightens, forcing me to take what he gives, exactly how he gives it. When he finally slips a finger inside me, curling just right, the pleasure spikes so sharply I nearly cry out. He adds a second, his tongue never leaving me, coaxing me higher, closer, until the tension inside me snaps.

I shatter against him, the release hot and blinding, my body shaking as his name spills from my lips in a high-pitched cry. He doesn't pull away until I've ridden out every wave, until I'm limp against the mattress.

Ford crawls up over me, his mouth finding mine, letting me

taste myself on his tongue. His hard cock is trapped between us, the weight of him pressing against my stomach. We kiss and kiss until I'm desperate to feel him inside me. Until I reach between us wrapping my fingers around the base of him, hot and heavy in my hand. The weigh of him makes my pulse tick. I guide him to where I need him, the blunt head of his cock sliding against me in a way that makes my whole-body shiver. The first push steals my breath, and when he slides into me slowly, like he wants to feel every second of it, every inch, my legs curl around him, pulling him deeper. His forehead rests against mine, our breaths mingling, the sound of skin on skin filling the room.

This isn't frantic like the car. It's slower, heavier. It's about claiming and keeping. His thumb strokes along my jaw, his eyes holding mine like he's afraid to look away.

Then his hips start to move, slowly at first, then deeper, harder, until the rhythm sinks into my bones. My toes curl when he's buried to the hilt, and a strangled sound slips from me every time he pulls almost all the way out.

Every thrust feels intentional and deliberate, like he's crafting something out of me. His thick, solid length drags against every tender place inside me, hitting the one spot that makes my vision blur. He does it again and again, until I can't remember a time when he wasn't filling me like this until the only truth I know is that I'll shatter if I don't come soon. My hand starts to drift down between my legs, desperate for the friction I need, but he catches my wrist, pushing it back to the mattress. "I've got you, baby," he says, his voice absolute, his pupils blown wide, near black in the dim light.

His hand comes between us, his fingers finding my clit, rubbing in slow, perfect circles that make me quiver. The moment he surges forward, the air leaves my lungs in a sharp, helpless sound. My body begins to unravel, and my muscles turn molten, every nerve lit up.

The heat swells so fast it steals my breath. There's no time to brace, no space between the wave building and the moment it crashes. My body tightens, my thighs trembling around him, and then I'm falling apart—quaking, clenching, coming so hard it feels like pleasure and pain blurring into one sensation.

Seconds later, Ford's rhythm falters, his breath hitching against my mouth. Then he's driving into me with a desperate edge, a guttural sound ripping from his throat. For a few perfect seconds, the deep, primal roar of him spilling into me drowns out the broken sounds of my own release.

For a moment, neither of us move. When I look at him, there's something different in his gaze that makes my throat tighten. My vision blurs as fresh tears slip down my face.

"I'm not sad," I tell him softly.

Ford lifts a hand, and brushes my hair back from my face, cradling my cheek in his palm.

He examines me for several long seconds, then he whispers, "I know."

His thumbs brush under my eyes, catching the tears before they can fall any farther. The gesture is gentle, almost reverent, and it makes my chest ache in a way that has nothing to do with the sex we just had.

He eases us to our sides keeping his cock still inside of me, guiding me with him until my back is flush to his chest. I feel weightless, dazed, like the air around us has thickened.

Carefully reaching down, he tugs the blankets up from the foot of the bed, wrapping them around me until I'm swallowed in the heat of him, his scent, the steady rise and fall of his breathing, and the deep weight of his cock still buried inside of me.

He tucks my head under his jaw, and I blink against the warmth of his neck.

"We've got a little while longer," he murmurs. "Just let me hold you."

So, I do.

THREE DAYS LATER, I'M HALFWAY THROUGH ANSWERING EMAILS when Becca slides into the empty chair beside my desk, holding her coffee like it's a glass of wine and we're about to gossip at happy hour. A slow, knowing smile tugs at her lips as she leans in slightly.

"Laaaandyn," she whispers, drawing it out for dramatic effect. "Okay. Spill it. What's happening?"

I blink. "What do you mean?"

Becca raises a brow. "You're glowing. What's up?"

"I'm not glowing."

"She's glowing," Marco calls from the next desk over without even looking up.

"I hate you both," I mutter, trying not to smile as I type out a reply to a vendor.

Becca leans in even closer, her voice conspiratorial. "You sleeping with the boss or something?"

That does it. My face breaks wide open, a smile curling at the corners of my mouth. I don't even try to hide it. My cheeks flush...and Becca's jaw drops.

"Oh my God," she hisses. "You are!"

Marco spins in his chair so fast that it squeaks. "No. Shut up. No."

I press my lips together, trying to look innocent. And apparently failing.

Becca points at me, eyes wide. "You totally are!"

I shrug, still smiling.

Marco throws a folder at my desk. "You sneaky little secret keeper. You've been sitting here drinking oat milk lattes and acting normal while you are clearly getting wrecked after hours."

Becca chokes on her coffee. "Marco!"

"What? Look at her face! That's not a well-rested smile. That's a well-sexed smile."

I laugh, burying my face in my hands. Becca grins like she just solved a mystery. "Well, damn. Good for you."

Marco raises his coffee cup in a mock toast. "May your meetings be short, and your make-outs be long."

"You two are impossible," I say, but my smile doesn't falter. Because they're right. And I've never felt more okay about being found out.

"Go with the dark roast," a voice says behind me. "Vanilla's a trap."

I turn, smiling before I even see him. "Hey Jesse."

He grins, leaning against the doorframe with a half-eaten protein bar in one hand and a backwards ball cap on his head. In the office. It's a look only he could pull off.

"You hiding in here?" he asks.

"Are you?"

He shrugs. "Maybe. Noah is on a spreadsheet warpath. Something about variance margins and quarterly goals, and I don't have the emotional bandwidth for that kind of energy before noon."

I laugh and turn back to the machine, taking his advice and picking the dark roast. Jesse moves into the room, opens the fridge, pokes around like he might find buried treasure in there.

"So..." he starts, casually. Too casually. "Ford mentioned this weekend."

I glance over my shoulder. "Yeah?"

He straightens and closes the fridge door. "Barbecue at his place with your tiny human."

There's a soft catch in my chest. "Poppy," I say.

He nods, voice quieter. "Poppy." He says her name like he's remembering his mom.

"I'm excited," he says, flashing a crooked smile. "Been waiting a long time to meet her."

"I know," I say. It's quiet for a beat before he leans against the counter beside me, arms crossed, voice still light.

"You know, when Ford told us, I didn't say much. Mostly because I was stunned and wanted to murder someone, but also because I figured it wasn't my story to react to."

I grip the edge of the counter, meeting his eyes.

"But I've been thinking about it. And I just want you to know...I get it."

I blink, surprised. "You do?"

He nods. "Look, I'm not built for deep. I'm going to be the fun uncle. But I know Ford and I know what this means to him. I see what you're doing to make this right."

My chest pulls tight. "Jesse..."

"You don't have to explain," he says, looking at me. "You don't even have to say anything."

I don't realize my eyes are glossy until I blink too fast, and a tear escapes. He grins—a little lopsided. "Also, if she doesn't like me, I'll be the one who's crying in the corner. Just giving you fair warning."

"She's going to love you," I say, meaning it. "You're ridiculous. She's going to think you're the greatest thing ever."

"Perfect," he says. "That's the energy I'm bringing. Uncle of the year. She'll be like, Wes and Noah who? I'm going to buy her love with a Hello Kitty scooter and probably a pink leather jacket."

I laugh. "You'll spoil her."

"That's the whole point."

He gives me a wink and a gentle nudge with his elbow before pushing off the counter and for the door, leaving my heart feeling full and just the tiniest bit fragile in the very best way.

Four hours later, a message pings on my screen, and I sit up straighter before I even register who it's from.

Ford Winters.

My heart skips—actually *skips*—like I'm 20 again and he's texting me to meet him, which is ridiculous. Embarrassing actually. One message from him should not make me feel this way, yet here I am, staring at my screen and smiling like an idiot.

Ford: I miss you.

Ford: I want to take you home.

My stomach does that ridiculous swoop again. *Home.* It doesn't matter that we live in different houses, wherever Ford is will always be my home.

I shut down my computer, grab my bag, and tell Becca I'm heading out, ignoring the smug little smirk she throws my way. Then I make my way to his office. He's standing near the window, sleeves rolled, hair tousled, the late afternoon light painting him in gold. God, he's beautiful. Masculine. Steady. Mine.

"Hey," I say softly.

He turns and smiles, eyes immediately warming. "Let's get out of here."

I nod.

"Your place or mine?" he asks, already grabbing his jacket.

"Mine," I say. "We'll pick up Poppy on the way. I thought we could work on bike riding again?"

His smile deepens. "You mean she'll work on it, and I'll pretend not to have a heart attack when she veers into the bushes."

"She only veered once."

"She hit a tree."

"A tiny tree."

He grins and opens the door for me. We're halfway down the hall when he pauses and pats his pockets. "Shit," he mutters. "I forgot my keys."

"I'll grab them," I offer, already turning.

He calls after me. "Top drawer."

I head back into his office, the door clicking closed behind me. I move around his desk, and pull open the top drawer, expecting to find his keys. What I find instead makes me freeze.

There, tucked in the corner like something private, sacred, is the old black leather bracelet I gave him when we were in college. It's worn, the edges fraying. The little silver clasp I added is tarnished but still intact.

He kept it. All this time.

A lump rises in my throat as I pick it up. My fingers tremble slightly as I run them along the edge, memories hitting me in waves. He wore this every day the summer we fell in love.

I turn as the door opens behind me. He sees what's in my hand and stops. Neither of us speaks right away.

"You kept it," I whisper.

He nods once. "I couldn't throw it away."

My throat tightens.

"It was the only thing I had left of you. Of us."

I walk toward him slowly, bracelet still in hand. When I reach him, I take his wrist gently in mine and slide it on.

It still fits.

Of course it does.

He watches me, eyes unreadable but soft.

"I used to think it was just a silly, cheap bracelet," I say, fingers brushing over the worn leather. "But maybe it was more than that."

He lifts his hand, places it over mine. "It was everything," he says quietly.

We stand there for a second, hearts thudding, that bracelet between us like the past and the present finally lining up.

And then he presses a kiss to my forehead, simple and soft. "Let's go pick up our girl."

FORTY-FOUR

Landyn
Ford's brothers showed up with six kinds of chips, two coolers of beer, and enough nervous energy to make me feel like I was hosting a job interview instead of a backyard barbecue.

Poppy didn't notice. She took one look at Jesse, who greeted her with a bracelet making kit and a Hello Kitty stuffie, and immediately decided he was her favorite.

"No offense," she whispered to me later, "but Uncle Jesse is the coolest person I've ever met."

Wes was quieter. Gentle. He helped her scoop potato salad onto her plate and cut her hamburger into two equal halves without being asked. And when she accidentally knocked over her juice, he was the first to clean it up, telling her, "Don't even worry about it, kiddo. Happens to the best of us."

Noah taught her a secret handshake. It had six steps and ended with a fist bump and a wink. She practiced it all evening like it was the most important thing she'd ever learned.

Ford didn't say much. He manned the grill, opened beers,

kept one eye on her the whole time like he didn't want to miss a single moment.

And me?

I just watched with my heart in my throat. Watched the way she slid into their lives like she'd always been part of them. No awkwardness. No hesitation. Just a little girl, meeting the rest of her family.

There was a moment, later on after she'd curled up between Jesse and Noah on the deck steps, licking the last of a popsicle from her fingers and giggling at something I couldn't hear, when Ford came up behind me and wrapped his arms around my waist.

"She's going to be so loved," he whispered into my hair and something in my chest cracked open.

It's been a week since that night, but the feeling hasn't left me. If anything, it's only grown.

Ford told me to come over tonight, which has become a pretty regular occurrence. I have a key now, which still blows my mind a little.

He told me he and Poppy were going to cook dinner for me after their date day today. These daddy-daughter dates have become the thing that Poppy most looks forward to. Just the two of them. Ford picks her up in the morning and the two of them spend the whole day together doing something fun. I think today was going to be mini-golf and milkshakes.

They've been glued together lately with bike rides, soccer in the park, and Saturday morning pancakes with chocolate chips and way too much syrup. He's showing up for her, and she's soaking it up like sunlight.

I pull up to his house just after five, expecting to find them in the kitchen, Poppy waiting eagerly to tell me all about who got the most holes in one.

But the second I step inside, I stop.

There are daisies everywhere.

Not a few. Not a vase or two. Hundreds of them. Everywhere.

White and yellow blossoms line the front entry table, the staircase, the kitchen island. There's a trail of petals scattered along the hardwood floor, leading upstairs towards his bedroom.

I blink, stunned, hand still on the doorknob. Ford knows I love daisies. I've mentioned it more than once. But this...this is something else.

I follow the petals up the stairs and down the hall, through the warm quiet of his house until I find him sitting on his bed, leaning against the headboard.

He smiles when he sees me. Just the sight of him makes my knees wobble. He's in jeans and a plain black T-shirt, barefoot, relaxed in a way that makes him look unfairly gorgeous.

"Where's Poppy?" I ask, still dazed, making my way to him.

"Movie night with Jesse and Wes. She's thrilled. I think Jesse promised her Twizzlers and popcorn for dinner."

I laugh softly, stepping towards the bed to join him. "You tricked me."

"I did," he says, unapologetically. "I wanted a night with just you. We have three hours before they bring her back."

I glance back toward the door. "Did you buy out an entire florist's inventory to make this happen?"

He shrugs one shoulder, a little sheepish. "You said daisies made you feel like magic once. I wanted to give you some magic."

My heart stutters. "It's the most beautiful thing I've ever seen."

He sits up, gently taking my hands in his. Nervously, I go up on my knees, kiss his mouth. His hands slide to either side of my face and stay there. He doesn't move. He just keeps holding me, his breath slow and steady, as if he's waiting for something. Waiting for me.

It takes a moment for the quaking inside of me to quiet, for my hands to stop clutching at the front of his shirt like I'll fall if I let go. When I finally go still, he tips my chin up with a single finger until I have no choice but to meet his eyes. I don't know what he sees in mine, but what I see in his steals the air from my lungs.

Not just the college kid who used to kiss me until my head spun. Not just the impossible man who can rile me up with a single look across a room. It's something more. It's the man I see in command at Cove. The one who makes impossible things happen because he's decided that they should. It's the same unshakable presence I've seen in him since the day we met, only sharper now, honed with years of life and loss. It's the man who used to charge through the world like a wrecking ball and somehow grew into someone who knows exactly when to hold back, exactly when to push.

And right now, he's using every ounce of that strength to hold me up while my insides tremble and my heart pounds so hard I can hear it. There's something in his eyes that pins me where I am, something fierce and certain.

And before he even opens his mouth, I feel it. I know.

"I've been waiting to say something to you," he says. "And I didn't want to say it in the middle of chaos. Not when we were still catching our breath."

His eyes search mine, steady and warm.

"I love you, Landyn." The words are quiet, but clear. Undeniable. "I've never been more sure of anything in my life."

I don't realize I'm crying until he lifts one hand and brushes his thumb across my cheek.

"Want to know why I'm so sure?" he asks.

I nod once and everything about him softens. His eyes. His posture. The grip he has on me shifts—less holding me in place, more holding me steady. Even his voice changes, low and careful, like he's handing something fragile.

"It's because I've been in love before," he says. The words land heavy in my chest, and I feel my body instinctively tense in response. He catches it but keeps going.

"Only once. And it was with you. So, I know what it feels like, Landyn. I know the way it pulls at me, the way it changes everything. I know it because I've been here before. And right now? I feel the same thing. Only now it's stronger. Deeper. Like it's carved out a home in me."

He leans in, pressing a kiss to my mouth so soft and certain it robs me of every coherent thought.

"I know I love you," he murmurs against my lips. "I know it, like really know it. I love you, Landyn. I love you. I love you. I love you."

He exhales, and I feel it more than I hear it. He's stripped bare in front of me, heart wide open. "And it's the same as when I first fell in love with you, but it's different too," he says, kissing me again, deeper now. "Because this time..." his mouth brushes mine once more. "This time is the last time I will ever fall in love. It's you and me, June. From now until the end. Because I will never—ever—feel like this about anyone else."

My heart beats and aches, beats and aches, and I can't get a single word past the knot in my throat. Instead I just launch myself at him. Arms around his neck, holding onto him like I might never let go. I'm crying, tears streaking hot down my cheeks.

"Ford," I breathe, my voice breaking. The air in the room stops moving. For all I know, the planets stops turning. I slide my fingers up into his hair, messy and falling over his forehead, and push it back so I can see him. His face. His mouth. The strong cut of his cheekbones. And those eyes. God, those eyes. Everything good I've ever known is in them. And holy hell... how did I ever think I could stay away from this man? I must have been out of my mind. I never stood a chance. Not then. Not now. Not ever.

I look into those deep, stormy-gray eyes and watch them shift. I take a breath that feels like the first real one I've taken in years. And then

I dive in, no safety net, no looking back.

"I love you too, Ford," I say, my voice steady now. "I've loved you all my life."

EPILOGUE

3 MONTHS LATER

F ord

The swing set creaks in rhythm with Poppy's laughter, bright and breathless as I push her higher, her sneakers kicking toward the crisp autumn sky. The air smells like woodsmoke and fallen leaves, cool enough that I can see my breath when I laugh with her. It's that time of the year when the sun's dropping low by dinner time, slipping through branches touched with amber and gold, casting the backyard in that fiery autumn haze that makes everything glow.

I look around, still surprised at how quickly Poppy has transformed everything in my life. What used to be just a patch of grass, a fence, and a deck I never used has been taken over by chalk drawings smeared across the patio stones, daisies blooming along the fence line, and a pink soccer net in the middle of the lawn. It's lived-in. It's ours.

I glance toward the deck where Landyn is curled into one of the Adirondack chairs, white socks pulled up to her calves and a plaid blanket draped across her lap. A steaming mug rests on the table beside her, the scent of coffee carried on the cool breeze. She's smiling—that soft, easy smile that still hits me square in the chest. I've had her back in my life for months now, and it still knocks me out cold.

I slow the swing, letting Poppy drag her toes along the grass to stop herself. She hops off and bolts across the yard with a squeal, not toward me, but toward the wiggling black-and-white puppy tumbling over its own paws to greet her.

"Pancake!" she calls, laughter spilling out of her as she drops to her knees. The pup's ears flop as he bounds into her arms, tail wagging furiously. She scoops him up, his spotted fur pressed to her cheek, and he rewards her with an eager lick that makes her giggle even louder.

Poppy adores Stella, trails her everywhere like a shadow, but the older dog has always been mine. This puppy is hers. Landyn thought it was spoiling her, that six years old was too young for the responsibility of a pet, but Poppy's my girl. If she wanted a black-and-white spotted puppy, she was going to have one.

So, here's Pancake—ears too big for his head, clumsy paws tripping across the grass—already learning to curl up in Poppy's lap like he was made for her. Stella pretends she's above it all, huffing when the puppy steals her toys or tumbles over her bed, but she's softening. They're working out their differences.

And when Poppy buries her giggles in Pancake's fur, cheeks pink from the chill and joy, I know I'd do it a hundred times over just to see her like this.

"Okay, you two. Fun is over. I need hands in the kitchen."

My brothers and Landyn's parents are coming over tonight. These dinners have become a regular thing; every Sunday, without fail, the house fills up with noise and food and way too many opinions. That's Landyn's doing. She wants Poppy growing up surrounded by family, with the kind of traditions she still remembers, the kind I never had.

"You heard Mom. Let's get Pancake into his bed."

"Right this minute?" Poppy asks, clutching her dog to her chest and looking up at me with pleading eyes. "But, Dad, Pancake wants to play."

The word still hits me as hard as it did the first time she said it—Dad. The night after she and Landyn moved in with me it slipped it out so naturally, I almost missed it. We were brushing our teeth side by side, her little face smeared with toothpaste, and when she asked me for a towel, it wasn't Ford, it was Dad. Just like she'd been saving it, waiting until she was sure it fit.

Now, I crouch down and smooth her hair away from her face. "Pancake can wait, kiddo. Your mom needs us."

She nods, a little begrudgingly, and hands me the pup before slipping her hand into mine. Stella trots ahead, nails clicking on the deck. We follow Landyn inside, the three of us trailing her like gravity's got a hold on us, like we belong nowhere else but right here.

Half an hour later, Landyn's mom and dad are perched at the kitchen island, a spread of appetizers in front of them, while the smell of roasted garlic and herbs fills the air. Her mom's laughing around a bite of bruschetta, cheeks rosy and bright, healthier than I've seen her in a long time. She looks like herself again, steady and strong.

The front door swings open and Noah walks in with a bouquet of flowers, Wes behind him carrying a bottle of wine. Not long after, Jesse appears, late as usual, scrolling on his phone and muttering something under his breath about "Financing breathing down my neck."

I catch the way his mouth tilts, noticing it's not his usual carefree, cocky smirk. He looks a little rattled, like someone just tossed him a challenge.

"You good?" I ask, one eyebrow raised, handing him a glass of wine.

He takes the glass from my hand with a smirk, which only makes me more suspicious.

Noah's already got him pegged. "What's with the face?"

Jesse waves his phone at me like it's incriminating evidence. "You brought someone in to 'assist' me on the marketing launch." He actually does air quotes. "Apparently I need supervision?"

I grin. "And?"

"And," he says, dragging it out, "this woman is intolerable. Bossy. Been there for a couple of days and already thinks she knows my job better than I do."

Noah laughs. "So... she's better at your job and it's pissing you off."

"That's not what I said," Jesse snaps, though his sheepish grin betrays him. "She's a firecracker with a clipboard. And she's always in my space. She sits and makes notes—actual handwritten notes—about my campaigns. Like we're in the '90s."

"Sounds like you've met your match," Noah says.

"She's not my match. She's a temporary headache," Jesse insists, then mutters under his breath, "A beautiful, infuriating headache."

I raise my eyebrows. I'm pretty sure the look on his face is the exact look I had when Landyn walked back into my life. Speaking of...she steps into the entry way, dress swaying around her legs, hair catching in the light. My girl. My fiancée.

A few weeks ago, I asked Landyn to marry me.

I knew I didn't want to take her somewhere fancy. That's not us. I wanted it here, in the place I want us to build our life. I roped Poppy in, and she had plenty of ideas as to how I should do it. She wanted hundreds of fairy lights, so we strung them in the trees and wrapped them around the deck posts until the whole backyard looked like something out of a dream. She picked daisies from the market, more than we could carry, and insisted we put them everywhere. They lined the deck, we scattered them across the table, petals leading a path from the kitchen door to the yard.

She even made a little sign, which we propped beside the swing set: "Will You Marry Us?"

I can still see Landyn's face when she walked into the yard that night. Her hands flew to her mouth, eyes shining with tears before she even saw the ring. I told her the truth—that I couldn't imagine another day of my life without her in it, without the two of them in it. Then I dropped to one knee while Poppy giggled beside me, holding the velvet box.

She said yes before I could even get the words out.

Now we have a wedding on the horizon. New Year's Eve. Landyn wanted a night that felt like fresh starts and second chances, and I wanted to give her the kind of celebration she deserved. There'll be fairy lights strung in the trees again, champagne flowing, and Poppy tossing white petals down the aisle before her mom walks to meet me. I can already picture the countdown to midnight, and the kiss that seals forever.

Tonight's dinner is loud in the best way, with my brothers trading jabs across the table, Landyn's dad asking for the bruschetta recipe for the third time, her mom laughing so hard she's wiping tears from her cheeks. Poppy sits between Wes and Noah, chattering away, sneaking Stella scraps under the table while Pancake crashes at her feet. It's chaos, pure and simple, the kind I never knew I wanted. The kind I'll spend the rest of my life protecting.

When the dessert's done and the last glass of wine is poured, hugs are passed around like they're mandatory. One by one, family spills out into the cool night, voices carrying across the porch until the house finally softens into quiet again.

Upstairs, our bedroom is dim, lit only by the lamp on Landyn's nightstand. She's already curled beneath the quilt, hair spilling across the pillow. She tilts her head when I close the door behind me, and the look in her eyes damn near buckles me.

"Successful night," she murmurs, voice soft from wine and warmth.

I strip off my shirt so I'm in only my boxer briefs and climb in beside her, pulling her against me. "Every night's a successful night with you here."

She laughs, the sound muffled against my chest. "You're getting sappy."

"Maybe," I admit, brushing a kiss against her hair. "But it's true. This—" I sweep a hand toward the door, to the memory of her parents and my brothers around the dinner table, the dogs sprawled out on the rug, our daughter fast asleep down the hall, "this is everything. I didn't think I'd ever have it. Then you came back, and you gave it to me."

Her hand finds mine under the covers. She lifts her head, eyes shining in the low light, and I see every promise I've ever wanted reflected back at me.

"I love you, Ford," she whispers.

I press my forehead to hers, letting the words sink in, letting them fill the spaces I thought would always be empty. "I love you too. Always have, always will. I've been yours since the day I met you."

She kisses me slowly, deeply, and when we finally pull apart, I realize the truth I've been chasing my whole damn life: She is my purpose. Landyn and Poppy. They are the reason for every breath I take.

This is it. The life I didn't think I'd ever have. The family I didn't know I needed. The woman who's always been it for me.

This is home. This is everything.

There are a hundred reasons we shouldn't have worked. A thousand ways it could've gone wrong.

But in the end?

There was only one deal-breaker.

A life without her.
And that's a deal I'll never take.

The End

STILL SWOONING OVER FORD AND LANDYN? Good. If you're curious how Ford and sweet Poppy pulled off the most romantic proposal, I've got a free bonus scene just for you. All you have to do is click this bonus scene link and it's yours.

READY FOR JESSE? Jesse Winters, Deep Cove's favorite flirt, is up next and he's about to meet the one woman who won't play by his rules—and he's never wanted to break them more. PREORDER RULE BREAKER now so you don't miss a second in Deep Cove.

ALSO BY LILY MILLER

HAVEN HARBOR SERIES

One Good Move

Play For Keeps

Never Say Never

Wish You Would

BENNETT FAMILY SERIES

Always Been You

Had To Be You

Heart Set On You

Crazy Over You

ACKNOWLEDGMENTS

Writing Deal Breaker felt like stepping into my millionaire era, and honestly, I never want to leave. I spent the springtime with Ford—my favorite MMC I've ever written—at a time when I was craving something a little darker, a little edgier. He was a dream to bring to life: broody, loyal, and everything I could ever want in a romance hero. Add in the tender, messy, beautiful moments between Landyn, Ford, and Poppy, and... well, those scenes melted me every single time. Thank you, readers, for letting me share them with you. You're the reason I get to live in these love stories, and I hope you see a little piece of your own heart in theirs.

Now for the people who made this book sparkle:

To Carolyn De Melo, my brilliant editor—thank you for taking all my chaos and turning it into something polished and powerful. You pushed me in the best ways and helped Ford and Landyn shine brighter than I ever imagined.

To Emily Wittig, cover queen extraordinaire—thank you for designing not one but TWO covers I'm obsessed with. The illustrated, the model, both absolute perfection. You get me.

To Sarah Martin Photo Artistry, who gave me the exact photo I didn't even know I was dreaming of—you brought Ford and Landyn to life in such a swoony, breathtaking way. I'm still not over it. Big love to Corey and Emily, my cover models and real-life couple, for nailing the shot.

To my husband and my two girls, E and M—thank you for being my forever cheerleaders. You're the reason I keep chasing these dreams, and you're also the reason I remember to step away from my laptop sometimes.

To my PA, Stephanie—thank you for keeping me sane, organized, and (mostly) on time. You juggle all the behind-the-scenes pieces so beautifully, and I'm endlessly grateful to have you on my team.

To my signing PA's, Anita and Mel—thank you for assisting me at signings, hopping on planes for me and working long days. I'd be lost without you.

To Will Sanderson—thank you for your invaluable help in navigating Carolyn's diagnosis and for providing the medical insight I needed to bring authenticity to this story. Your guidance and generosity with your knowledge made all the difference, and I'm so grateful.

To Carmen—thank you for schooling me on the business side of things and for patiently answering my very dramatic "what if this happened?" questions. Your expertise (and sense of humour) made this part of the book way more fun than it had any right to be!

To Mandy Durnil—thank you for helping me in all the ways you did as I wrote, edited and dreamt up Ford and Landyn's story. You are such a wonderful friend.

To my readers—you guys are the magic. Truly. Every message, review, preorder, or late-night DM fuels me more than you'll ever know. You're the reason I get to keep writing happily-ever-afters, and I love you for it.

To my author besties—Emily Silver, Julia Connors, and Erin Hawkins—thank you for being my daily sounding boards, hype squad, and partners in crime. I love doing this author life with you. I'd be lost (and probably boring) without our constant chats. A special ILY to Becka Mack for being my friend, for supporting me in countless ways and for my new favourite way to spend my time—zoom calls and wine!

Finally, to YOU, holding this book right now: thank you for

giving Deal Breaker a place in your heart. Ford, Landyn, and Poppy were a dream to write and sharing them with you makes it all the more special. Here's to my millionaire era, and to you for being the very best part of it.

I love you all,

Lily xx

AFTERWORD

Thank you for reading! If you loved the story, I'd be so grateful if you left an honest review—it helps more that you know. Your time and thoughts mean the world.

Want to stay connected? Join Lily's newsletter to get the latest updates, special sales, audiobook news, and first looks at new releases.

Lily Miller Newsletter

ABOUT THE AUTHOR

Lily Miller lives in Vancouver, BC with her husband—her real-life book boyfriend—and their two daughters. When she's not writing love stories full of heat, heart, and happily-ever-afters, you can usually find her in the kitchen cooking, sailing the Pacific Ocean, or with country music playing in the background.

A lifelong romantic, Lily has been hooked on happy endings since she was a kid, and now she channels that passion into writing small-town, contemporary spicy romance that celebrates love in all its messy, swoony, unforgettable forms.

* 9 7 8 1 7 3 8 2 8 9 9 8 1 *